BENT
ROAD

LORI ROY

A PLUME BOOK

PLUME
Published by the Penguin Group
Penguin Group (USA) Inc., 375 Hudson Street, New York, New York 10014, U.S.A.
Penguin Group (Canada), 90 Eglinton Avenue East, Suite 700, Toronto, Ontario, Canada M4P 2Y3 (a division
of Pearson Penguin Canada Inc.); Penguin Books Ltd., 80 Strand, London WC2R 0RL, England; Penguin
Ireland, 25 St. Stephen's Green, Dublin 2, Ireland (a division of Penguin Books Ltd.); Penguin Group
(Australia), 250 Camberwell Road, Camberwell, Victoria 3124, Australia (a division of Pearson Australia
Group Pty. Ltd.); Penguin Books India Pvt. Ltd., 11 Community Centre, Panchsheel Park,
New Delhi – 110 017, India; Penguin Group (NZ), 67 Apollo Drive, Rosedale, Auckland 0632, New Zealand
(a division of Pearson New Zealand Ltd.); Penguin Books (South Africa) (Pty.) Ltd., 24 Sturdee Avenue,
Rosebank, Johannesburg 2196, South Africa

Penguin Books Ltd., Registered Offices: 80 Strand, London WC2R 0RL, England

Published by Plume, a member of Penguin Group (USA) Inc. Previously published in a Dutton edition.

First Plume Printing, March 2012

1   3   5   7   9   10   8   6   4   2

 REGISTERED TRADEMARK—MARCA REGISTRADA

The Library of Congress has catalogued the Dutton edition as follows:
Roy, Lori.
Bent Road/Lori Roy.
p.   cm.
ISBN 978-0-525-95183-4 (hc.)
ISBN 978-0-452-29759-3 (pbk.)
1. Country life—Kansas—Fiction. 2. Farm life—Kansas—Fiction.
3. Rural families—Fiction. 4. Girls—Crimes against—Fiction. I. Title.
PS3618.O89265B46   2011
813'.6—dc22   2010037239

Printed in the United States of America
Original hardcover design by Alissa Amell

To Bill, Andrew, and Savanna

BENT

ROAD

Chapter 1

Celia squeezes the steering wheel and squints into the darkness. Her tires bounce across the dirt road and kick up gravel that rains down like hail. Sweat gathers where the flat underbelly of her chin meets her neck. She leans forward but can't see Arthur's truck. There is a shuffling in the backseat. If they were still living in Detroit, maybe driving to St. Alban's for Sunday mass, she would check on Evie and Daniel. But not now. For three days she has driven, slept one night in a motel, all five of the family in one room, another in her own car, and now that the trip is nearly over, Arthur is gone.

"Are we there yet, Mama?" Evie says, her small voice drifting out of the backseat.

Celia presses on the brake. The car rattles beneath her hands. She tightens her grip, clenches her teeth, holds her arms firm.

"No, baby," she whispers. "Soon."

"Can you see Daddy and Elaine?" Evie says.

"Not now, honey. Try to sleep. I'll wake you kids when we get to Grandma's."

Outside Celia's window, quiet fields glow under the moonlight and roll off into the darkness. She knows to call them fields, not pastures. She knows the wheat will have been harvested by now and the fields left bare. On their last night in Detroit, Arthur had lain next to her in bed and whispered about their new life in Kansas. "Fields are best laid flat," he had said, tracing a line down Celia's neck. "Wheat will rot in a low spot, scatter if it's too high." Then he pulled the satin ribbon tied in a delicate bow at her neckline. "Pastures, those are for grazing. Most any land will do for a good pasture."

Celia shivers, not sure if it's because of the memory of his warm breath on the tip of her earlobe or the words that, like her new life, are finally seeping in. In Kansas, Arthur will be the son; she, just the wife.

As the car climbs another hill, the front tires slip and spin in the dry dirt. The back end rides low, packed full of her mother's antique linens and bone china, the things she wouldn't let Arthur strap to his truck. She blinks, tries to look beyond the yellow cone that her headlights spray across the road. She's sure she will see Arthur parked up ahead, waiting for her to catch up. The clouds shift and the night grows brighter. It's a good sign.

From the backseat, Evie fluffs her favorite pillow, the one that Celia's mother embroidered with lavender lilacs. Celia inhales her mother's perfume and blinks away the thought of her grave and Father's, both left untouched now that Celia is gone. Taking another deep breath, she lets her hands and arms relax. Her knuckles burn as she loosens her grip. She rolls her head from side to side. Driving uphill is easier.

Broken glass, sparkling green and brown shards scattered across Willingham Avenue on a Sunday morning in the spring of 1965, had been the first sign of the move to come. "This is trouble," Arthur said, dumping the glass into a trash barrel with a tip of his metal dustpan. "Just kids," Celia said. But soon after the glass, the phone calls began. Negro boys, whose words tilted a different way, calling for Elaine. They used ma'am and sir, but still Arthur said he knew a Negro's voice. A colored man had no place in the life of one of Arthur Scott's daughters. Of this, he was damned sure, and after twenty years away, those phone calls must have scared Arthur more than the thought of moving back to Kansas.

Not once, in all their time together, has Arthur taken Celia back to his hometown, never even considered a visit. Here, on Bent Road, he lost his oldest sister, Eve, when he was a teenager. She died, killed in a fashion that Arthur has never been willing to share. He'll look at Evie sometimes, their youngest daughter, usually when the morning light catches her blue eyes or when her hair is freshly washed and combed, and he'll smile and say she is the spitting image of his sister. Nothing more, rarely even uses her name—Eve. But now, the closer he gets to home, the faster he drives, as if he is suddenly regretting all those years away.

Under the full moon, Daniel leans forward, hanging his arms over the front seat. Dad's truck is definitely gone. Ever since sunset, Mama has clenched the steering wheel with both hands, leaned forward with a straight back and struggled to keep Dad's taillights in sight. But the road ahead has been dark for the last several minutes.

At the top of the hill, Daniel lifts his hind end off his seat and stretches to get the best view. That could be a set of taillights disappearing over the next rise. Mama must see them, too, because she presses on the gas. Once they've crested the hill, the wind grabs the station wagon, rocking it from side to side. Daniel lays a hand on Mama's shoulder. Since he's not old enough to drive, it's the best he can do. Before they left Detroit, Dad said he hoped Kansas would make a man of Daniel since Detroit damn sure didn't. A hand on Mama's shoulder is part of being a man.

"Mama, look there," he whispers, sitting back so that he can see out the window on the other side of Evie. For a moment, he sounds like Dad, but then his voice breaks and he is a boy again.

"Is it your father?" Mama leans right and then left, straining to see what lies ahead.

"No," Daniel says. "Out in the field. Something is out there."

Mama locks her elbows. "I can't look right now. What is it?"

"I see it," Evie says. "Two of them. Three maybe. What are they?"

"There," Daniels says. "Coming toward us. They're getting closer."

Outside the passenger side window, two shadows race toward the car—round, clumsy shadows that bounce and skip over the rolling field. Behind them comes a third. The shadows grow, jumping higher as they near the road. The wind picks up the third and tosses it ahead of the second. They're several times the size of watermelons and gaining speed as they draw closer.

"What do you see, Daniel?" Mama asks.

"Don't know, Mama. I don't know."

Nearing another shallow valley, Mama eases up on the brakes.

There they are again. As the car begins another climb, the front end riding higher than the back, the shadows return, running along the side of the road, gaining on the car as the hill slows it down. The shadows skip into the moonlight and turn into round bunches of bristle, rolling, tumbling.

"Tumbleweeds," Evie shouts, rolling down her window. "They're tumbleweeds." The wind rushes into the car, drowning out the last of her voice.

"Daniel, do you see your father?" Mama tries to shout but there's not much left of her voice. It barely carries over the noise of the wind. She leans forward, like she's willing the car up the hill, willing Dad's truck to reappear. "Close that window," she says.

The rush of air slows as Evie cranks her window shut. On her small, chubby hands, tiny dimples pucker over each knuckle. Outside the car, the tumbleweeds are trailing them, gaining on them. It's almost as if they're hunting them. Up ahead, near the top of the hill, the road curves.

"Daniel, look. Can you see him?"

"No, Mama. No."

A tight swirl of dust, rising like smoke in the yellow light, marks the road ahead. Mama drives into the cloud that is probably dirt kicked up by Dad's truck. The road bends hard to the right and disappears beyond the top of the hill. Mama jams her palms against the steering wheel, leans into the door. The wind slams into the long, broad side of the station wagon.

"Hold tight," she shouts.

Daniel thinks it's another tumbleweed at first, coming at them from the other side. A large dark shadow darting across the road in front of the car. But those are arms, heavy and thick, and a rounded back. Two legs take long, clumsy steps.

"Mama," Daniel shouts. "Look out."

Mama yanks on the steering wheel, pulling it hard to the right. The car slides toward the dark ditch and stops, throwing Daniel and Evie forward. Outside the front window, the running shadow stumbles, rolls down into the ditch, disappears. The round weeds spin and bounce toward them, tumble over one another and fall into a bristly pile, snagged up by a barbed-wire fence strung between limestone posts.

Slowly unwrapping her fingers from the steering wheel, Mama shifts the car into park. Beneath them, the engine still rattles. Headlights throw cloudy light into the field. The dust settles. Mama exhales one loud breath. Leaning over Evie, Daniel presses his hands to the side window. The road drops off into a deep ditch and rises up again into the bare field that stretches out before them. At the bottom of the dark valley they have just driven out of, a pond reflects the full moon. The shadow is gone.

Evie shoves Daniel aside and takes his place at the window. "Mama, look at all the tumbleweeds," she says. "Look how many. They're all stuck together."

"Did we hit him?" Daniel says. "Did we hit that man?"

Evie looks back at him. "There's no man, silly," she says, starting to roll down her window so she can stick her head out. "Those are tumbleweeds."

"No, don't." Daniel slaps her hand away. "Didn't you see him?"

This isn't at all what Evie thought Kansas would look like. Mama said it would be flat and covered with yellow wheat. She tosses her arms over the front seat and stands on the floorboard for a better look. At the top of the hill, a fence follows the gentle curve of the road like a giant lazy tail draped across the field. The tumbleweeds, hundreds of them, thousands maybe, snagged up by the barbed wire, look like a monster's arching spine.

"It's not a man. It's a monster," she says, pointing straight ahead. "See? That's its back and tail." Maybe this is why Daddy never wanted to visit Kansas.

"Mama," Daniel says. "You saw him, too, didn't you?"

"You two sit," Mama says. She exhales, wipes a hand over her face and down the front of her dress, not even bothering with a handkerchief. Mama never did that in Detroit. She would have told Evie it was bad manners. "I didn't hit anything, Daniel. Just took the curve too fast. Everything is fine now. I'm sorry I frightened you, but you shouldn't shout out like that. Not when I'm driving."

"But I think we did hit him. The man in the road. I saw him fall."

Evie shakes her head. "No, it's tumbleweeds."

Resting on the steering wheel, Mama stares out the front window. "I'm sure it was just a deer or a coyote maybe," she says and with her elbow pushes down the lock and motions with her head for Evie to do the same. She turns and smiles. "We'll ask your father. Whatever it was, it's gone now."

"Yeah, Daniel," Evie says. "There's no man. Just tumbleweeds." She throws her arms over the front seat again and rests her chin there. "Look, Mama."

Near the bottom of the hill, Daddy's truck sits where the road turns into a long drive. It is weighted down by all of their furniture, wrapped with a tarp and tied off with Daddy's sisal rope. The truck's cab lights up when the driver's side door opens. Daddy steps out, and waddling into the glow of the headlights is Grandma Reesa. Evie has never met Grandma Reesa. Neither has Daniel, because Daddy always said that come hell or high water, he'd never set foot in Kansas again. That was before the Negro boys called Elaine on the telephone.

Mama drops her head one last time and breathes in through her nose and out through her mouth. Keeping both hands on the steering wheel, she lets her head hang between her arms. She looks like she's saying a prayer.

"Guess we made it," Evie says.

This is the road, Bent Road, where Daddy grew up.

"Yes," Mama says. "Looks like we're home."

Chapter 2

Daniel opens his eyes and there, peeking through the bedroom door, is Mama. Smiling, she presses one finger to her lips, draws her hands together, holds them to her cheek and tilts her head as if to say, "Go back to sleep." The door closes and Mama whispers with Elaine on the other side. She is probably telling Elaine that things will be fine. Since the day Dad sat at the head of the dinner table and announced that the family was moving to Kansas, Elaine has pouted and Mama has told her things would be fine, just fine.

Waiting until Mama's voice fades down the hallway, Daniel sits up and shades his eyes with one hand. At the foot of the bed, a statue of the Virgin Mary, wearing a brown shawl over a simple blue gown, stands on a small end table. Her arms reach out, as if toward Daniel, but both hands are missing. The paint has chipped away from her wrists, uncovering the red clay she is molded from. The Virgin Mary is bleeding. On the table near her feet lie her missing hands.

"Hey," Evie says from her spot next to Daniel where she had been sleeping. "We're here, aren't we?" She first smiles at the Virgin Mary but frowns when she notices the missing hands. "This is Grandma Reesa's house."

"Guess so," Daniel says, pushing his hair from his eyes.

Evie pops to her knees and crawls to the head of the bed. "Come see," she says, leaning so the fan propped in the window doesn't hit her. "It's Kansas. All the way, as far as I can see." She starts jumping, the box springs creaking every time she lands.

"Hush already," Daniel says, not sure why he cares except that the bleeding statue makes him think Grandma Reesa likes a quiet house.

"There's cows, Danny," she says. "Four of them."

Daniel crawls across the bed until he can see out the second-story window. When he's kneeling next to Evie, who is standing, they're almost the same size. She lifts onto her tiptoes and smiles down on Daniel. He rolls his eyes at her but doesn't say anything. Evie's being small stopped seeming funny when she was six. Now, at nine years old, she is lucky to be mistaken for a kindergartner. Even though Mama says Evie will grow plenty tall in her own time, Daniel knows she is hoping that people will be smaller in Kansas, that she will be the right size.

Besides seeing four cows, Daniel gets his first glimpse of Kansas in the daylight. He cocks his head, trying to decide if the buildings outside are crooked or if Grandma Reesa's house tilts. He wonders what Mama will have to say about Grandma's crooked house. Before they left Detroit, Mama smiled every time Dad mentioned Kansas, but it wasn't the smile she gave when she was really happy. When she smiled about Kansas, Mama never showed her teeth and she always nodded her head along with the smile, probably thinking the nod would do the trick if the smile didn't.

Beyond the garage and shed, brown fields outlined by barbed-wire fences stretch to the horizon. Dad says most of the old fence posts are made from hedge tree branches and a few from limestone. He says there will be plenty of fence post driving in Daniel's future, plenty for sure. That'll make a man of him. Squinting out the window, Daniel counts the posts that carry the fence up and over the curve in Bent Road where the tumbleweeds were snagged up. The man he saw last night must have run through Grandma Reesa's pasture and hopped the fence at the hill's highest point. No sign of him now. Dad said it was probably a deer, but Daniel is sure it was a man—a large man in a big hurry. Dad promised to check the ditches to make sure the man wasn't lying there dead. Daniel drops his eyes back to Grandma's driveway where the four cows raise their heads and together walk toward the fence. He hears it before he sees it, a truck driving up Grandma Reesa's gravel drive.

"Hey," Evie says, popping off the bed, her bare feet skipping across the wooden floor. "Look at this."

"Yeah, what is it?" Daniel says, still watching through the window.

A red truck pulls around the side of the house and parks in front of the sagging garage.

"They're dresses," Evie says. "Look how many."

Across the room, Evie holds a blue dress up by its hanger, rotating it so she sees both sides. The dress flutters as the fan sweeps across the room, the tips of its hem dragging on the wooden floor.

Frowning, Evie pulls at the frayed ends of a piece of blue trim left unstitched at the collar.

"Stop that," Daniel says. "You're getting it dirty. Those are Grandma Reesa's."

Evie frowns at the bleeding Virgin Mary. "No they aren't. Grandma Reesa is too big for these dresses."

"Well, they belong to somebody."

"Whoever wore these was small like me," Evie says, holding up a second dress. "Not big like Grandma Reesa."

"Just put them back and close that door," Daniel says as a second truck that is towing a trailer pulls into the drive. "I think Uncle Ray and Aunt Ruth are here. We'd better get downstairs."

Letting the hug fade, Celia slowly pulls away, feeling that Ruth's slender arms might never let go. While Arthur is tall and broad enough to fill any doorway, his older sister is petite, almost breakable, and her skin is cool, as if she doesn't have the strength to warm herself on a hot August afternoon. On the other side of the car, Ruth's husband, Ray, shakes Arthur's hand. Reesa stands behind them, watching, nodding.

"Damn good to see you," Ray says, taking off his hat and slapping it against his thigh. Underneath, his dark hair is matted and sweat sparkles on his forehead. Even from several feet away, he smells of bourbon.

After shaking Arthur's hand, Ray replaces his hat and bends down to look through the truck's cab. His cloudy gray eye, the left one, which Celia only remembers when she sees him up close again, wanders off to the side while the eye that is clear and brown stares at Celia. He winks the bad eye.

"Well, if you damn sure aren't still the prettiest thing I ever seen," he says, scratching his two-day-old beard. "The good Lord's done well by you, Arthur."

Ray's good eye inches down Celia's body and settles at her waist. He had looked at her the same way on her wedding day, like her taking one man meant she would take any man.

Celia wrinkles her nose at his sour smell. "So good to see you, Ruth," she says, reaching for the pie that Ruth holds out to her.

"It's strawberry." Ruth straightens the pleats on her tan calico dress. "We had a late season this year. Thought they'd never ripen."

Celia cups the chilled pie plate. "You always did bake up the nicest desserts."

Celia says this even though her own wedding was the last and only time she saw Ruth. Almost twenty years ago. They were barely more than kids; Ruth a new bride herself. The years have worn heavy on her, stooped her shoulders, yellowed her skin, and peppered her brown hair with gray, though she still wears it in the same tightly knit bun that she did all those years ago.

"Arthur said you had an accident on your way in," Ruth says, still pressing her pleats. "You and the children are all right?"

Celia rubs her neck with one hand and rolls her head from side to side. "Shook us up a little. Frightened the children, but we're fine."

Once they finally settled into bed the night before, Arthur had said they probably saw a deer. Or maybe not. Never could tell. "But that spot at the top of Bent Road is a tricky one," he had said. "Better take it slow next time." Celia had rolled over, putting her back to him, and said that perhaps next time he would be inclined to slow himself down. When she woke this morning, she had a sore neck, an ache in her lower back and made Arthur promise to check the front of her car for damage. He found nothing but still couldn't say for sure what they had seen out there.

"Good God damn," Ray shouts to the driver of a second truck towing a trailer into the drive. "I don't pay you to drive like a fool, boy."

A young man steps out of the other truck. His light brown hair hangs below his collar and covers the tips of his ears. He wears a sleeveless chambray shirt, the frayed shirttail left untucked. Ruth tells Celia that his name is Jonathon Howard. He's a local boy who has come to help Ray, though he's not so much a boy anymore.

"You don't pay me at all, Ray," Jonathon says. "Quit all that fuss you're making." He nods at Celia and Arthur, tugs on the raw edge of his Silver Belly hat and walks toward his trailer.

At the back porch, the screened door squeals open and slams shut. Elaine walks across the drive, blotting her cheeks with a tissue. Though she is small like Celia—narrow shoulders, a slender waist, hips that flare ever so slightly beneath her skirt—she has Arthur's brown hair and eyes.

"Elaine," Celia says. "Come say hello to Aunt Ruth."

Tucking the tissue into her apron and smoothing back her hair that hangs in dark waves down her back, Elaine steps around the truck's open door and leans inside to hug Ruth. "So nice to meet you, Aunt Ruth," she says, and standing straight, she looks down the drive toward the young man with the frayed chambray shirt. As if trying to get a better view of him, she leans away from the truck and stumbles over Celia. "Sorry," she says.

"Quite all right." Celia smiles and glances between Elaine and the young man.

"Celia," Ray shouts through the truck's open cab. Seeing Elaine, he studies her for a moment, tips his hat and stands. "Get those kids out here. Good God damn, I brought this thing for them."

"Ray brought the children a cow," Ruth says. "You go on and see it. I'll check on lunch and send the children out."

Celia steps aside to let Ruth pass. Across the drive, Reesa and Arthur follow Ray toward the trailer. Celia watches Ray, fearing that he'll take another look at Elaine, but he doesn't. As the three pass a small shed, which sets across the drive, Arthur stops and studies it, perhaps considering how to best fix the sagging roof or straighten the crooked walls. Reesa stops alongside him, stepping into his shadow. A thick patch of cordgrass grows around the small building and nearly swallows it up. The two of them stand silently for a moment, and then Reesa pats him on the back and, with both hands, gently pulls him away and they continue toward the trailer.

Celia knew there would be secrets between Arthur and his mother, a history that they share and that Celia has had no part in. Surely, Reesa knows what kept Arthur away all these years, and as they pass by, neither of them looking at Celia, it is clear that the past is already flaring up.

*　　*　　*

When everyone is clustered around the new cow and Ray gives a loud shout of laughter, Ruth walks toward the back door. She smells them before she sees them—a patch of devil's claw growing between the garage and the back porch. The pink flowers, thriving in dry sandy soil, give off a nasty smell that is strong this year, stronger every year since Father died. He was dead and buried before Mother called to tell Arthur. "No need to trouble him so far away," she had said. "It's his own father," Ruth said. "Let him make peace with his own father."

Mother had turned away, the black cotton dress she wore to the church service only lightly creased. "A funeral is no place for making peace," she had said. "That time is dead and buried for both of them."

The flowers, whose feathery centers are sprinkled with red and purple freckles, have grown thicker this year and richer in color. The plant's broad, heart-shaped leaves give off the bitter smell and pods hang like okra from the hairy stems. Eventually, the woody husks will split open and curl like claws that will grab onto passing animals who will spread the seeds.

As a new bride, Ruth had picked the plump green pods, sliced them and sautéed them in buttery onions and garlic. They'll bring a strong woman twins, her mother's mother once said. Ruth cooked up these pods because, had Eve lived, she would have done the same. In the weeks and months following Eve's death, everything Ruth did was because Eve would have done the same. Ruth began to visit Ray every week since Eve no longer could. When his laundry piled up in the hamper, she washed it and hung it to dry on the line. She swept his floors, scrubbed his bathroom tile and left casseroles in his icebox. Because Ray was a young man who needed a wife and because it was the thing Eve would have done, Ruth married him and began to wish for a baby. But soon enough her marriage aged a few years, and Ray realized that Ruth would never be the woman he had intended to marry. She would never be Eve. So she stopped cooking the pods and never looked back when she passed a patch of devil's claw.

Inside the kitchen, Ruth puts the pie into the refrigerator and lifts the lid on the cast-iron skillet where several pieces of Mother's fried chicken sizzle and pop. A rich, salty smell fills the house. She turns down the flame, checks the timer on the sweet bread and slides a pot of chicken broth onto the stove. In the open window, the curtains hang motionless. Outside, everyone is still gathered around the cow that Ray bought cheap at the sale barn because no one wants an apple-assed cow. Patting the animal on its hind end and saying something that Ruth can't hear, Ray throws back his head and laughs. Ruth steps away from the window and turns when footsteps cross the living room and stop at the kitchen's threshold.

"Are you Aunt Ruth?"

Ruth dries her hands on a dish towel. "I am," she says. "And you are Eve?"

"Evie."

Evie has long, fuzzy braids and a heavy fringe of white bangs that fall across her forehead and catch in her eyelashes. Her skin is like pink satin.

"Evie," Ruth says, trying out the name. "And you're Daniel?"

Daniel is only a few months shy of Arthur's height, and eventually, after some good Kansas cooking, he'll be as broad, too. However, unlike his father, Daniel is blond with pale blue eyes that shine against his tanned skin.

"I'm so glad you've moved to Kansas." Ruth pats her face with the dish towel that smells of soap and bleach.

"We're happy to be here, ma'am," Daniel says, staring at his feet.

"Please, call me Aunt Ruth."

"Whose room is that upstairs?" Evie asks, tapping the floor with the toe of one black shoe. "The one we slept in?"

Ruth swallows before she can answer. "I'm not sure which room you were in, sweet pea." She slips, forgets that Evie is not her sister, calls her sweet pea. A sugary, delicate bloom like Eve.

Evie looks at her brother and then at the ground. "The one with the statue and the dresses."

"That's Eve's room," Ruth says. Her chin quivers. She clears her throat. "My sister, Eve."

"Eve," Evie says. "Like me."

Ruth smiles. "Yes, very much like you."

"She's small, too, isn't she? I can tell from the dresses. Small like me, and you, too. Not like Grandma Reesa."

Ruth laughs aloud. The first in so long. "She was perfect like you. The exact right size."

"I like her dresses," Evie says, standing where the living room meets the kitchen. "Will she come for dinner, too?"

"No, I'm afraid not."

The chicken broth has grown from a slow simmer to a rolling boil. From outside, Ray gives off another burst of laughter. Ruth steps aside and waves Evie and Daniel toward the kitchen window.

"Come," she says. "See what Uncle Ray has brought for you."

While Daniel hangs back, not seeming to care about the shouts and laughter coming from outside, Evie joins Ruth at the window and hoists herself up onto the counter for a better view.

"A cow," she says, her pink cheeks plumping up with a smile. "Uncle Ray has brought us a cow. And he's a cowboy, Dan." She slides off the counter and turns toward her brother. "He's wearing a hat and boots, too. He's a real cowboy."

Ruth brushes aside the fringe of bangs that fall across Evie's brow. "You two should go on out and get a closer look."

"Yes, ma'am," Daniel says, taking Evie's hand.

Evie stops before disappearing into the back hallway. "I'm glad we're here, Aunt Ruth," she says. "I'm going to like Kansas very much."

"And we're happy to have you."

The hinges on the back door whine as they open and close. Pressing the dish towel to her face, Ruth returns to the kitchen window and breathes in the lemon-scented soap until she knows she won't cry. She is a child again, nine years old, seeing her own sister, Eve. She was the oldest, perfect in almost every way. Evie is so like her, has her light blue eyes and shimmering blond hair. They could be twins, Eve and Evie, separated by many years but twins just the same.

Outside the kitchen window, Evie skips across the drive, kicking up small clouds of dust. Nearing the cow, she slows and walks to Ray's side. She raises one hand to her forehead, shielding her eyes from the sun, and looks up at him. Ray steps back and lifts the brim of his hat as if taking a closer look. All these years, Arthur has lived with this painful reminder. Now Ruth and Ray will do the same.

Chapter 3

Evie sits next to Daddy in the cab of his truck, her stomach stuffed full from her first Kansas meal. Daniel slouches in the seat next to her, a dish of Grandma's leftover fried chicken resting on his knees. After everyone finished eating lunch, Grandma asked them to take the food to the Buchers because Mrs. Bucher just had a new baby. Uncle Ray said the Buchers are one lucky family because their baby was born a blue baby and nearly died. Evie asked Daddy what a blue baby was, and he said the Bucher baby was pink as any other.

Cradling a loaf of sweet bread, Evie leans against Daddy so he'll shield her from the hot dry wind blowing through the truck. "Tell me about Aunt Eve," she says.

Keeping one hand on the steering wheel, Daddy wipes the other over his eyes and down his face. "She always wore her hair in braids when she was a girl. Same as you." Daddy looks down at Evie. "Looked a good damn bit like you."

Over lunch, Grandma Reesa said that in her house Evie is to be called Eve. Mama frowned and asked Daddy what he thought about that. Instead of giving Mama an answer, Daddy patted his stomach and said Grandma's fried chicken was the best in the Midwest. Mama frowned about that, too. But Evie won't mind being called Eve. It makes her believe that in Kansas she'll grow like a weed and one day soon, she'll be big enough to wear Aunt Eve's dresses.

Evie giggles to hear Daddy curse. "She doesn't live here anymore?"

Daddy shakes his head, stops and shakes it again. His white teeth shine against his dark skin. "No, Evie, not anymore."

Driving through the dust kicked up by Jonathon's truck, they near the tumbleweed-lined fence. Jonathon is towing their cow to the new house. Mama had thought Elaine should get to name the cow because she is the oldest, but Uncle Ray said he figured it was a job for the youngest in the family, so Evie picked Mama's middle name—Olivia. This made Uncle Ray smile. He tugged on one of Evie's braids and then winked his milky eye at Mama, patted the new cow on the rump and said that Olivia was a damn fine name. Mama frowned about that, too, but it was too late because Olivia was already Olivia.

Daddy slows at the top of the hill and the truck drifts toward the side of the road until it feels that the wheels might slip off into the ditch. Evie looks for the monster they saw the night before. Daniel leans forward, too, but he's probably looking for the man he thinks Mama hit. In the daylight, Evie doesn't see a monster, only a fence that Daddy says will cave in if someone doesn't pull off those weeds soon. She doesn't see a strange man, either. Once over the highest point, a truck driving the other direction appears. The other truck swerves toward the tumbleweed fence, slows and stops. Daddy stops, too.

A dark hand hangs out of the driver's side window of the other truck. "Damn good to see you, Arthur." A man wearing a round straw hat leans out his open window.

"Afternoon, Orville." Daddy nods and lifts one finger. "Good to be back."

The man glances in his rearview mirror. "Been a long damn time."

Daddy nods. "These here are two of my kids," he says, tipping his head in Evie and Daniel's direction.

Evie leans forward and waves at the man. Daniel lifts a hand.

"Pleasure," the man says. Mama would have said he had a strong nose. Thick creases fan out from the corners of his eyes and his skin is as dark as any Negro except he isn't a Negro.

Daddy and the man talk for a few minutes about the long drive from Detroit, the price of wheat and when the next good rain will fall. Then with another tip of his round straw hat, the man says, "Glad you remembered this stretch of road. Can be a good bit tricky. You all take care." And slapping the side of his truck, the man pulls away.

As Daddy eases onto road, Evie looks back toward the tumble-weed monster. In the other truck, a young girl stares out the rear window, one hand and her nose pressed to the glass. She must have been scrunched down in the seat because Evie didn't see her before.

She is about Evie's age and has long blond hair that hangs over her shoulders. The girl lifts her hand from the glass and waves. Evie waves back and watches until the truck disappears down Bent Road, and the girl is gone.

Daniel climbs out of the truck, glances at the Buchers' house and then at the group of boys near the barn—the Bucher brothers—and wishes he had a hat to pull on like Dad's. So far, not one person in Kansas has blond hair except Evie and Mama.

"Go on over and say hello," Dad says, taking the dish of chicken from Daniel. "You've been so worried about friends. Well, there's a whole mess of them."

Tugging at the tan pants Mama made him wear because he was meeting new people, Daniel walks toward five boys who are huddled together, digging a hole in the ground with their bare hands. The youngest is probably seven; the oldest, fifteen or sixteen. All are barefooted and dirty up to their ankles. One boy close to Daniel's age sits off by himself, leaning against the barn.

"Hey," the tallest brother says. "You one of the Scotts?"

Daniel nods. "Yeah. Daniel."

The boys drift together and stand with their arms crossed over their chests. They all have straight dark hair that hangs over their ears and wear jeans cut off at the knee instead of tan pants with a crease ironed into each leg.

"Moving into the old Murray place?" one of them says.

A smaller boy steps forward, tossing back his head to get the hair out of his eyes. "Yeah, it's the Murray place," he says before Daniel can answer. "Saw them hauling off Mrs. Murray's stuff."

"She died in that house, you know," another of the younger boys says. With his elbow, he nudges the brother next to him. "About six years ago. They found her dead, slumped over the radiator. Cooked up real good."

The oldest-looking boy shoves his brother. "Shut up. She was just old."

Daniel jams his hands in his pockets and steps into the shade so his hair won't sparkle. Behind him, the boy leaning against the barn pulls the fuzzy seeds off a giant foxtail, holds them between two fingers and blows them away.

"Sure she was old, but that ain't what killed her," the same younger boy says. "It was one of them crazy guys from Clark City. You know about Clark City, right?"

"Never heard of it," Daniel says as he digs a hole in the ground with the toe of his left shoe, wearing off the shine Mama made him buff on before they left the house.

"That's where they lock up crazy folks," the tallest boy says. He leans against a tree and gestures with his head off to the left. "It's a town about twenty miles southwest of here. Happens a few times a year. One of them gets out and heads this way. Should probably lock up your house. But mostly they're just looking for food. Mostly."

Behind Daniel, the screened door opens and slams shut with a bang. Evie steps onto the porch.

"One just escaped," one of the smaller boys says, nudging the same brother again. "Seen it in yesterday's paper. Say his name is Jack Mayer. Has a taste for boys. Don't know the difference between his wife and kid's hind end."

The tallest brother kicks a cloud of dust at the smaller boy. "No paper said nothing about hind ends."

"No," the boy says. "But it did say Jack Mayer couldn't be found because his skin is black as night. Said he's as good as invisible when the sun sets."

Walking up behind Daniel and standing next to him, Evie flips her braids over her shoulders, crosses her arms and stares up at the new boys. Back near the barn, the boy sitting by himself uses both hands to push off the ground and walks toward them.

"Anyone see that fellow around here?" Daniel asks. "Any of you see him?"

"Got one," shouts a different boy as he walks out of a shed a few yards beyond the barn. This one, who is five, maybe six years old, has a kitten cupped in his hands. He walks over to the hole that the boys were digging when Daniel first walked up.

"You got to watch this," one of the brothers says, ignoring Daniel's question.

The boy who was sitting near the barn has almost reached them. Up close, his head seems too large for his body, as if his neck can't quite hold it up, and both legs bow to the right. He has the same dark hair but his is cut high off his forehead.

"Come on," the crippled boy says. "These guys are stupid."

The youngest boy is still fussing with the hole and the kitten, patting down the dirt like he is planting a tomato. An older brother walks toward the hole with a weed whip.

Following the boy across the drive, Daniel tucks Evie under one arm and presses her face into his side, holding tight so she can't squirm away. The boy walks with an awkward rhythm—step, step, pause, step, step, pause—as if he has to think about each set of steps before he takes them. Reaching Dad's truck, the crippled boy throws open the passenger side door and Daniel shoves Evie inside.

Up on the porch, Dad walks out of the house, followed by a large man who must be Mr. Bucher, although he seems too big to have a son as small and broken as this boy. The two men shake hands and Dad walks down the steps, his hat tucked under his arm.

"Thanks," Daniel says to the boy and climbs in after Evie. "See you around?"

The boy nods and limps toward the house. "Lock your windows," he says. "Doors, too. Just in case."

From over near the barn, someone calls out, "Fore."

Ray must feel it, too, Ruth thinks as they pull away from Arthur's new house. Jonathon has taken Mother home and Arthur and his family are settled in their new house. They have full stomachs, freshly made beds, and fans are perched in every bedroom window. She worried that when Arthur came home, he would look at her like all of the others in town. She worried that he, like everyone else, had always wondered if Ruth married the man who killed her own sister. Ruth swallows, blinks away the feeling that she's betraying

Eve, thinking ill of the dead. But Arthur didn't look at her like the rest of them. He looked at her like they were young again, before anything bad happened. Before Eve died. He looked at her like he still loved her.

Rolling down her window, Ruth inhales the smell of cut feed and freshly plowed sod. Nearing the top of the hill that separates her and Ray's house from Arthur's new home, the landscape even seems prettier. The gently rolling hills, the dark fields, the brome-lined ditches. Ray must see it, too. He seemed happier today. He stopped with one glass of whiskey at Mother's. His eyes never drooped. His speech never slurred. At Arthur's new house, just half a mile from Ruth and Ray's home, Ray had worked hard, unpacking and piecing together the bed frames, hauling boxes in from the truck, unwrapping dishes and silverware. And as they began the short ride home, he drove with his hat pushed high on his head and one arm draped around Ruth's shoulders. He had seemed content with Ruth, as happy as he had been in their earliest days together. Never as happy as he had been with Eve. But almost happy.

Once they are over the top of the hill, Ruth sees their house down below. As new and different as the landscape looks and the air smells, their house is the same. By the time they reach the bottom of the hill, the happiness is gone. It's a subtle change, like a shifting shadow. Arthur is home again and he still loves Ruth, but no one else is coming with him. He is a reminder of happier times but also of all that has been lost. And Evie, too. Ruth had wondered if Ray would notice the resemblance. When Evie first walked out of Mother's house, skipping across the gravel drive, cheeks flushed with heat, braids swinging behind, bangs brushing her forehead, Ray had blinked and cleared his throat into a closed fist as he looked down on her. Then the memory was gone, or Ruth thought it was. Now, as she and Ray sit in front of their house, the truck idling beneath them, she realizes they have not come home to the same place they have lived for twenty years. They have come home to a worse place, a lonelier place, and Ruth is more afraid of Ray than ever.

Chapter 4

Walking down St. Anthony's stone steps for the first time, Celia pins her pillbox hat to her head with one white-gloved hand. In Detroit, all of the ladies wore gloves to church. Here, the women have bare hands and dirty nails. Midway down the stairs that widen as they near street level, Celia stops, the other parishioners filtering around her, and plucks a few cockleburs from the hem of her blue cotton skirt. She frowns at the brown oval smudges that stain each fingertip of her white Sunday gloves. Perhaps the reason none of the women wear them. Having lost Arthur in the crowd that filed out of the church following the end of service, she lets the flow of the other churchgoers lead her. All around, people talk in whispers even though church is over.

"Didn't you hear?" one woman asks another.

"Such terrible news," says a third. "Simply terrible."

Tugging off her stained gloves one finger at a time, Celia scans the crowd until she finds Ruth standing near the bottom of the stairs where everyone seems to be gathering. Her perfectly formed oval face wrapped in a blue and yellow print scarf is tilted up, smiling.

While fending off houseflies with her church bulletin, Celia had spent her first Kansas sermon looking from one hometown parishioner to the next, noticing, as they shifted about on the pews and swatted at flies, that they all had the same overgrown ears and fleshy noses. There were a few, probably in-laws like herself, and the priest, Father Flannery, who hadn't inherited the trait. And as she studied them, she felt them studying her. Her navy blue skirt was too proper with its sharp pleats and tailored waistband. The other women wore skirts that ballooned over their large hips. They wore floral scarves, not gossamer trimmed hats. Theirs were white cotton blouses, wrinkled and nearly gray. Hers was a silk print, hand washed and dried flat on a towel. By the end of the service, Celia even looked at Arthur, crossing and uncrossing her legs so she could turn unnoticed to study the size and shape of his ears and nose, but he looked like an outsider, and Ruth, too, with her delicate brow and graceful neck. Reesa, however, could have birthed the entire congregation.

"Good morning," Ruth says, clasping her hands together and stepping back when Celia reaches the bottom stair. Her eyelashes cast a feathery shadow on her cheeks and the silver and gray in her hair shimmers in the sunlight. "Lovely service."

"Yes," Celia says. "A little warm though," and she shields her eyes. No sign of Arthur, though she does spot Reesa standing with the three women who were whispering about the terrible news. She is shaking her head as the women talk. Feeling that she has spent the better part of her short time in Kansas swatting bugs, swallowing dust and searching for Arthur, Celia drops her hand and stops looking.

Ruth smiles with closed lips. "There he is," she says, pointing up at Arthur, who is standing at the top of the stairs among a group of men wearing short-sleeve dress shirts and thick black belts.

Celia nods and gives a small wave when Arthur motions in her direction as if to point out his wife to his old friends. Elaine stands nearby at Jonathon's side, both of them talking with the other young men who must, like Jonathon, work in the oil fields. Weeks of moaning and complaining and already Elaine is at home. Ray, who is also standing with Jonathon, seems to return Celia's wave, which was meant for Elaine, but because of the way his left eye drifts off to the side, she's not quite sure where he's looking. She frowns anyway and after the group of men, all of whom have large ears and noses, turns away, she asks, "Is this where everyone meets?"

"Yes," Ruth says. "The sheriff will talk from up there." She motions toward the church's double doors at the top of the stone staircase. "Except if it's wintertime. Then we all gather in the church basement."

"Does he come every Sunday?"

"No. Only when he has business, news to tell."

Celia pulls the gold pins from her pillbox hat, drops them into her change pouch and tucks the hat under one arm. "News of what?"

Ruth lowers her head and glances over her shoulder in a way that Celia has come to recognize as common.

"A girl," she says. "A local girl's gone missing."

Behind them, a car pulls up to the curb and parks. The congregation quiets as a small, narrow-shouldered man steps out of a black and white police car. He wears a dark blue uniform and a beige tie that has pulled loose at the knot and hangs crooked around his open collar. Passing them by, he tips his hat, seemingly at Ruth, and shakes a few hands as he makes his way to the top of the stairs, where he waits silently, hands on hips. The churchgoers gathering on the sidewalk push Celia and Ruth to the back.

"Some of you folks will already be knowing this," the sheriff says, clearing his throat into a closed fist. The six-pointed silver star pinned to his shirt sparkles in the sunlight. "But I'll tell you all now. Little Julianne Robison has turned up missing." He pauses again. "Her folks called us in last evening. Now, chances are the child has just wandered off. Lost her way in the fields or maybe down by the river. Out playing is all she was doing."

Shielding her eyes with one hand and holding her hair with the other, Celia steps away from the crowd so she can see Daniel and Evie. They both stand where last she saw them—in the steeple's shadow this side of the whitewashed fence that wraps around the church's small cemetery. Evie is bent down near the fence, picking the downy-like seeds from a dandelion. Daniel, standing with both hands shoved in his front pockets, watches the sheriff.

"I'll need for any of you kids to talk with me if you've seen our Julianne of late," the sheriff says. "Some of us men have already been out looking but I'd like the rest of you gentlemen to join us in a search. We'll start our looking in town and work our way out. Orville and Mary say the girl's prone to going off alone. A hungry stomach'll probably bring her home, but the more of you can help, the quicker we'll all get home to Sunday supper."

*   *   *

Taking a step backward because the shade from the steeple keeps falling away from him, Daniel sees the crippled boy leaning on the bumper of a truck parked across the street, rubbing his thighs with the palm of each hand. Waiting until the boy glances his way, Daniel gives a wave. The boy waves back, pushes himself off the bumper and walks across the street. Step, step, pause. Step, step, pause, until he reaches the tip of the shade where Daniel stands.

"Hey," the boy says, crossing his arms and leaning against the white wooden fence that separates them from the cemetery.

"Hey."

"Name's Ian."

"I'm Daniel. This is Evie."

Evie blows a tuft of dandelion feathers at Ian.

"What do you think?" Ian asks, nodding at the sheriff still standing near the church doors.

"Didn't know her."

"She's younger." He dips his head toward Evie. "More about her age."

"Sounds like she'll be home by dinner," Daniel says, watching all the Bucher brothers meet up at the truck Ian had been leaning against. Like the red ants in Mama's kitchen, they keep coming, one after another.

"Like hell," Ian says, shuffling closer. "I know what happened. I know exactly what happened." He pauses and looks around like he's afraid someone might hear. "After Jack Mayer escaped from Clark City, he snatched her right up. That's what happened."

Daniel crosses his arms over his chest. "Think I might have seen that Jack Mayer," he says. "The night we got here. Pretty sure I saw him."

"At your place?" Ian says, shifting his weight from his short leg to his long one. "You catch him stealing food?"

Daniel shakes his head. "Back that way. On the drive in. Saw him running across the road. Car might have hit him. Can't be sure. He must have been black as midnight because I could barely see him. Just like you said."

"It was a tumbleweed," Evie says, peeling apart a dandelion stem and draping the thin pieces across her bare knee.

Daniel nudges her with his foot. "Wasn't a tumbleweed."

"Over on Bent Road?" Ian asks. "Where the road takes a hard turn? That where you saw him?"

Daniel nods.

"Could have happened. That's the only spot that still has water this time of year. Everything else has dried up. That's where a fellow'd have to head." Ian looks up at Daniel and smiles. "Yeah, could have happened just that way."

"Sure, I guess."

All night, Daniel had lain awake, imagining the whites of Jack Mayer's eyes shining outside his bedroom window, which he had locked and checked twice. Probably chains hung from both wrists and he did all his traveling at night because his coal-black skin hid him in the darkness. Jack Mayer is a big man, that's for sure. Even in the dark, at the top of Bent Road, Daniel could judge the man's size. Hearing a rattle inside Ian's chest, Daniel takes a step backward.

"Yep, snatched her up," Ian says. "Probably right out of her own front yard. 'Course, that means you didn't hit him with your car. Would have been dead if you did. Couldn't swipe Julianne Robison if he was dead."

Evie brushes the rounded, fuzzy tip of another dandelion against her cheek and looks up at Ian, her pinched eyebrows making a crease above her nose.

"Maybe," Daniel says, glancing down at Evie. "Or maybe she just wandered off."

"Nobody wanders off for a whole night." Ian gives a wave to the group of brothers across the street. "Hey," he says. "I got to go. We're going searching for her. Me and my brothers. Be out all day." He takes a few steps, his left foot swinging out because it's too long. Then he stops and looks back at Daniel. "You know," he says, "your house is the first place those crazies come across when they escape. After the old Brewster place, that is. Just be sure you make a lot of noise when you get home. Bang around for a while. It'll scare them off if they're inside."

"Sure thing," Daniel says, crossing his arms over his chest and thinking he'll let Dad go inside first. "We'll do."

After the sheriff finishes his announcement, the crowd breaks up and Celia drifts back toward Ruth, all the while keeping Evie and Daniel in sight. From the top of the church steps, the sheriff points and gestures to the group of men who have gathered with him, his black pistol slapping against his thigh. Every so often, he pats the gun and scans the crowd as if one of these fine Christians is hiding Julianne Robison in an attic or under a porch. After all of the men have gone their separate ways, apparently following the direction of the sheriff, Arthur walks down the stairs toward Celia. With arms crossed and feet spread wide, the sheriff watches Arthur take the stairs two at a time and hand Celia his car keys and tie. The sheriff is listening and nodding to the men standing around him but he is watching Arthur.

"Why don't you and the kids go on home?" Arthur says. "I'll be along later. And take Ruth. No sense Mother driving her."

When Arthur leans in to kiss Celia's cheek, she grabs his upper arm and draws him to her. "Arthur, I don't like this," she says, still watching the sheriff. "I'd rather have you home." She glances at Evie and Daniel and whispers, "This will scare the children."

"Nothing to worry about," Arthur says, laying one hand over Celia's. "We'll have her home in no time." He kisses Celia's cheek, peels open her fingers and gives her a wave as he walks away.

Still standing at the top of the stairs, the sheriff watches Arthur until he climbs into Jonathon's truck. This seems to put him at ease because he lets both arms drop and walks toward his patrol car. As he passes by, he tips his hat in Celia's direction. She exhales, only then realizing that she had been holding her breath.

"Guess it's just us," she says and waves at Daniel and Evie, motioning for them to come along.

"Poor Mary must be sick with worry," Ruth says.

"How did you know?" Celia glances at Ruth across the top of the car. She pauses while the children run toward them. Daniel outpaces Evie, who struggles to keep up in black leather shoes that are too big and slip off her heels with every stride. A few car lengths ahead, where he stands at his truck waiting to follow the sheriff and the other men, Ray watches Evie, too. He removes his hat, wipes his forehead with a kerchief and when Evie finally reaches the car, her face red and her upper lip damp with perspiration, he slips into his truck. Once Daniel and Evie have crawled into the backseat, and while Elaine is too far away to hear, Celia says, "You already knew about the little girl, didn't you?"

Ruth makes a small motion as if she is going to look over her shoulder but stops herself. "A person hears things."

"Do you think it was that man everyone is on the lookout for?" Celia asks. "The one Daniel thinks we saw the other night?"

Ruth shakes her head. "Those fellows from Clark City are harmless. Never caused any trouble before."

At the end of the block, where the street changes from concrete to dirt, Ray's truck kicks up dust and then disappears. Celia opens her door and Elaine slips into the backseat alongside Evie and Daniel.

"They share a pew with us," Ruth says once both women are inside the car. She unrolls her window after Celia starts the engine. "Orville and Mary Robison sit on the other end of our pew. Them with only one child. Me and Ray without any. We fit fine."

Heading south out of town, Celia holds the steering wheel with two hands, her shoulders and forearms still sore from driving so much a few days earlier. "Do you know them well?" she says.

"As well as anyone, I suppose. And no better than most. We were friends, closer friends, when we were young. A long time ago."

"We saw that girl, Mama," Evie says, leaning forward and draping her arms over the front seat. "We saw her on the way to Ian's house." She turns toward Daniel. "In the truck. You remember?"

Daniel shrugs.

"Is that right, Daniel?" Celia asks, keeping her eyes on the road. "Did you see her?"

"Don't know. I wasn't looking."

"I saw her. I know I did," Evie says. "Will I go missing, too?"

"No, Evie," Celia says, not turning around because she's afraid of losing her grip on the steering wheel. "Julianne will be home by dinner. The sheriff said so. No one is going missing. No one."

Ruth smiles at Celia's children sitting shoulder to shoulder across the backseat and rests her smile the longest on Evie so she'll believe what her mama told her—that bad things don't happen to nice girls. Except Ruth knows that's not true. Sheriff Bigler must know it, too. He was full of hope up on those steps, shielding his eyes and looking at the Robisons' house three doors down from the church as if Julianne might walk right up the sidewalk at any moment. But early this morning when he knocked on Ruth's back door, he wasn't so hopeful. Standing on her porch, his hat in hand, he must have known that if a hungry stomach was all it took to bring Julianne Robison home, she would have already eaten Mary Robison's Saturday night roast and potatoes and been tucked in good and tight. Instead, at 7:00 on Sunday morning when the sheriff came knocking, Julianne Robison had been missing for well over twelve hours and a hungry stomach hadn't done a thing to help her.

"It's Floyd," he had said when Ruth pulled open the curtain on the back door. "Floyd Bigler. Sorry for the early hour."

Ruth tugged at her terrycloth belt and smoothed back her hair. "Ray's sleeping," she said, steaming the windowpane as she talked through the glass. Dark clouds in the east dampened the rising sun so Ruth flipped on the porch light. Floyd stepped back, the glare making him squint and bow his head.

"Yes, ma'am, I know it's early. A quick word is all. Just a few questions."

Over the backdrop of a percolating coffeepot, with Floyd sitting at her kitchen table, Ruth learned that Julianne Robison hadn't come home to supper the day before. Mary Robison had walked the neighborhood searching for her, calling out the way mothers do when the kids wander too far. She was mad as a grizzly when she first called Floyd, but after he drove the town for two hours and darkness settled in, she wasn't so mad. Just plain scared. A group of fellows from town were already looking for her, had been all night, and Floyd had been to see most folks living in the outlying areas, asking them to search their barns, abandoned wells, cellars, any place a young girl might get herself stuck. He'd been checking in with all the folks. Good old-fashioned questions. Maybe someone had seen the girl out walking one of the back roads or catching a ride. Ruth told him that she and Ray had spent Saturday helping her brother and his family settle in. Arthur was gone a good many years but he's back now. Thank goodness. They all met at Mother's, ate a heavy lunch and unloaded the truck at the new house. Ruth baked a straw-berry pie—not so nice with brown sugar on top—and they unpacked boxes until late afternoon. Didn't see a thing out of the ordinary. Not a thing.

"I'm real sorry to hear this," Ruth said, hoping that Floyd would forget about his cup of coffee. "Real sorry indeed."

When Floyd took another sip, Ruth pressed both hands into the pockets of her robe. In her right one were the two stones she had pulled from Ray's pants pocket that morning. Both stones were smooth and together fit in the palm of her hand. Waiting for what Floyd would say next, Ruth rolled the stones between her fingers and rubbed her thumb over their smooth edges. Outside, the breeze that kicked up with the early-morning clouds had died out and the air was still. Maybe it wouldn't rain after all.

"I'll keep a good eye out. Any more questions? Is that all?"

"I suspect it is. For now, I'd say yes. Please ask Ray to have a look around the place. You, too, if you have a mind to."

Watching behind Floyd, waiting for the bedroom door to open, Ruth wiped her top lip with a dish towel. She has known Julianne Robison since she was a bundle wrapped in a pink fleece blanket. "There's still time for you," Mary had said as she handed Julianne to Ruth on the first Sunday the Robisons brought their new baby to church. Mary Robison was Ruth's age, even a few years older, and Orville Robison was a good bit older than Ray. Still, the Robisons had been blessed with a little girl. Now, the sweet baby that had smelled of talc and vanilla was gone.

"Will you come again?" Ruth said. "Ask any more questions?"

Floyd twisted his lips up the same way he did when they were kids figuring multiplication facts in Mrs. Franklin's class. "Might be more. Can't tell. I'll come along if there are."

Ruth leaned against the kitchen counter, shifting a little to the right so she could see the knob on the bedroom door. "I'm real sorry," she said. "Mary must be beside herself from worry. You tell her I'll bring her a casserole. A real nice one."

Taking his hat from the table and tucking it under his arm, Floyd stood and pushed in his chair. "Sorry to bother you so early, Ruth. I'll see myself out."

Ruth tightened her robe. "No bother."

"One more quick question." Floyd slapped his beige hat against his left thigh a few times. "You say you were busy at your brother's all afternoon."

Ruth nodded, swallowed and continued to watch the bedroom door.

"And you folks came home around five o'clock?"

Again, Ruth nodded.

"Didn't stay for supper?"

"Arthur's family had such a long day and Mother made a late lunch. Didn't bother with eating again. Left them alone to a quiet evening."

"So, you and Ray were home here all night?"

Behind Floyd, the bedroom door opened.

Floyd turned. "Morning, Ray," he said. "Hope I didn't wake you."

Ray ran one hand through his dark hair, pushing it off his face. "First thing home, ate some of Ruth's meat loaf," he said. Both eyes, even the gray overcast one, settled directly on Floyd. "Leftover pie for dessert."

"She does make a fine pie," Floyd said and at the same time studied Ruth as if waiting for her to confirm Ray's story.

Ruth cleared her throat and nodded again. "Pie wasn't so nice. Strawberries were tart."

Lowering her eyes to avoid Floyd's stare, Ruth tried to remember the last time she had seen little Julianne. Church, probably. Most likely, last Sunday. Julianne, with silky blond hair that hung to her waist, always wore a pink dress to services. She'd wear it until she outgrew it or until the weather turned too cold.

"Guess you heard, then," Floyd said because it seemed that Ray had listened to their conversation. "You know the girl? Know what she looks like?"

"Sure do," Ray said, nodding once.

"Good enough." Floyd pulled on his hat. "If you don't mind, give things a good going over. I suspect someone'll show up with her at church this morning. Probably found her out wandering, gave her a bed to sleep in and a warm breakfast. But in case that doesn't happen, Father's going to cut the service short and I'll be gathering up some more fellows. Continue the search. Suppose you can give a hand if it comes to that?"

"Will do," Ray had said. "Won't leave a stone unturned."

Ruth smiles one last time at Evie, who is chewing on her lower lip as if she is still worried about disappearing like Julianne, and then lifting her face into the hot, dry wind that blows through her open car window, Ruth tightens the knot on her scarf so it won't slip from under her chin. It's been a long time since she's bothered with one, but she doesn't want Arthur and Celia to see her bruises. All through church, she wore the scarf. Most of the other ladies slip theirs off once inside and tie them on again as services end. Ruth's scarf, however, draped over her head and tied under her chin, covers the red spot on her lower jaw where Ray struck her with the back of his hand when Floyd left the house that morning. Without the hangover that Ruth could smell on Ray even after his shower, he might have ignored Floyd's visit. But wherever Ray had been the night before, which was not at home eating strawberry pie, he had drunk plenty.

"I think you're right, Celia," Ruth says, smiling back at Evie again. "Julianne will be home by supper."

But two months later, Julianne Robison is still not home.

Chapter 5

Standing at her own kitchen sink, Celia pushes aside the yellow gingham curtains and white sheers and takes in her first icy breath since moving to Kansas two months earlier. Outside the window, the waxy leaves of a silver maple filter quiet rain. The leaves flutter in the gentle breeze, their silvery white undersides sparkling beneath the gray sky. Even on the hottest August days, the tree had cast a cool, heavy shadow over the kitchen but the sprinkling of golden leaves among the green reminds Celia that soon the tree will be bare. Leaning on the counter, rinsing a colander of white beans that have soaked through the night, Celia misses her Detroit kitchen window. She misses the sound of Al Templeton pull starting his lawn mower, Sarah Jenkins beating her kitchen rugs with a broom handle, the garbage truck hissing in the back alley.

Feeling heavy footsteps coming toward her, Celia lifts her head. She straightens, wrings out her washcloth and hangs it over the faucet. The footsteps slow and stop directly behind her. She closes her eyes. Arthur leans against her, wrapping his arms around her waist.

"Good morning," he whispers.

His coarse voice, the voice she normally only hears when he lies on the pillow next to her, makes her smile.

"Coffee?" he asks. His breath is warm on her left ear.

Celia draws one hand across his rough cheek and nods toward the pot that is still steaming. "You need a shave," she says, her smile fading when she looks back outside and sees the golden leaves.

Arthur pushes aside her loose hair and rubs his rough chin and jaw against her neck. "No razors on Saturday."

In Detroit, Arthur ran a lathe, carving metal into ball bearings and shafts that were shipped to the automotive factories where they ended up in alternators and generators. The red and blue patch that Celia sewed on the front of each work shirt read MACHINIST. Spinning metal for ten hours a day made Arthur's forearms strong and hard and he came home most nights smelling of motor oil and rubbing the back of his neck. Now, in Kansas, thanks to Gene Bucher, he drives a backhoe and a grader for the county and he comes home at night rubbing his lower back, sometimes hurting so badly from the vibration of the heavy equipment that his legs flare out at the knee and he walks with a rounded back. Grading the dry roads that ride like a washboard gives him the worst ache, and on those nights, Celia rubs Evie's old baby oil between her palms to warm it and kneads it into his back and shoulders.

"Will you work today? What with the rain." Celia stretches and relaxes into Arthur's hold. He seems bigger here in Kansas and thicker through the chest.

"Later," Arthur whispers. "I'll drive around, check the outlying roads." He leans closer, moving his hands over her stomach. "Better not take the car out until the ground drains. Don't want to gut the driveway." Pressing against her, he gathers two handfuls of her skirt and gently pulls until the hem lifts up over her knees. "The kids still sleeping?"

Celia tries to reach for a mug in the cupboard overhead, but Arthur keeps his hold on her.

"All except Elaine. She's gone off fishing with Jonathon."

Arthur rubs his jaw against her cheek.

"Ruth's coming today," Celia says, nodding toward the white beans she has rinsed and set aside. "She'll be helping me with those ham and beans you were wanting."

In Detroit, Celia had shopped daily at Ambrozy's Deli where Mr. Ambrozy made the best kielbasa in the city. He added beef and veal to the finest cuts of pork and cooked it up with garlic and a touch of marjoram, his secret ingredient. Every Friday, she made Hunter's Stew with Mr. Ambrozy's kielbasa and sweet sauerkraut, and Arthur always liked her cooking just fine. But on the first morning in September, he had said that a good old-fashioned plate of ham and beans sure would be nice. Not knowing how to prepare such a thing, Celia had asked for Ruth's help.

Arthur mumbles something about Ruth always running late. Then he drops Celia's skirt and presses against the entire length of her body.

"Now stop that," she says, smiling and trying to turn into his embrace, but he places his hands on the counter, trapping her so she can't move. "Ruth will have food for the Robisons, too. Will probably want you to run it over straightaway."

"What is that?" Arthur says, his tone suddenly clear and strong. His voice comes from over the top of Celia's head instead of near her left ear. "What the hell is that?"

Studying the three sets of muddy footprints on her kitchen floor, Ruth takes a bottle of ammonia from under the sink and sets it on the counter so she won't forget to clean them when the men leave. Next, she checks the timer she set for her banana bread. It'll be ready in seven minutes and she hopes the men will be gone by then.

"Sorry to barge in like this," Floyd says, pushing the creamer across the table to the other two men.

Ruth pours three cups of coffee.

"Mostly these two fellows are going to ask the same questions I have."

One of the men, the larger of the two and the one who doesn't bother to take off his hat, pulls out a small pad of paper. He taps a pencil on the edge of the kitchen table and tips his head to one side, giving Ruth a sideways glance. "Won't take long, ma'am," he says.

The other man, who is no bigger than Floyd, nods down at the floor. "Sorry about this mess." Then he pours cream in his coffee and after checking the sole of each shoe, he glances up at Ruth and smiles with closed lips.

"More questions?" Ruth asks, standing at the kitchen sink

where she can watch out the window for Ray's truck. Floyd must have waited until Ray left for the day because not five minutes after he pulled away, Floyd drove up with these two men in his car.

"These fellows are from Wichita. Work for the Kansas Bureau of Investigation. They've been down here helping us search for Julianne seeing as how we haven't gotten so far."

"That's good," Ruth says. "That's very good."

"Where's your husband off to this morning?" the larger man says. He knows Ray is gone without asking.

"Smells mighty good," the smaller man says, nodding at the stove where two loaves of banana bread are baking.

"The Stockland Café," Ruth says, answering the larger man's question. "Always has breakfast there on Saturday mornings. And then to the farm."

Their own land is too small to make a living from, so Ray has leased the Hathaway place since Mr. Hathaway died fifteen years earlier. It's a twelve-mile drive toward town and usually, almost always, keeps Ray away until dusk.

The larger man studies his pad of paper. "That's the Hathaway place you're talking about?"

"Yes," Ruth says, glancing out the window before letting her eyes settle on the center of the kitchen table. "Goes there every day."

The larger man asks most of the questions. They are the same ones Floyd asked on his three other trips to the house. A few days after Floyd's first visit, he came back with a black notebook and a ballpoint pen and said he hadn't taken notes the first time, would

Ruth and Ray mind going over the questions again. He said that most folks in town were getting the same visit. The third time he came, he asked how many acres Ray figured he had between the two farms and did he know of any place that might put a young girl in trouble. A fellow who lived over near Stockton found a soft spot on his land that must have been an old shaft or a dug-out foundation. Nothing in there but the fellow never would have found it if he hadn't looked. Floyd offered to help Ray check over his land and the Hathaways' since Mrs. Hathaway couldn't be expected to do it. "Can look plenty good on my own," Ray had said, so Floyd tipped his hat and didn't come back again until today.

"Sure I can't clean up for you, ma'am?" the smaller man says, waving a hand toward the muddy footprints.

He's the kinder of the two and seems to believe Ruth when she tells her story about strawberry pie and a quiet evening at home. The larger man doesn't believe so easily. He shakes his head when he scribbles in his book like he knows what he's writing isn't true. Floyd has surely told them about the past, about how Ray only married Ruth because Eve died. The men from Wichita, especially the larger one, look at Ruth like most of the people in town do, like anything bad she has to bear is her own doing so she shouldn't complain.

The whole town, Floyd included, has always thought that Ray was the one who killed Eve because no other killer was ever found. Father told everyone a crazy man did it. Broke in the house, took his daughter, slaughtered her on a dirt floor. But the town never believed it. They have always figured that Ruth married the man who killed her sister. But Ray didn't kill Eve. He loved her and no good will come from digging up the past. No good will come from speaking ill of the dead.

But these men sitting in Ruth's kitchen don't know how much Ray loved Eve. All three of them suspect Ray did something to little Julianne Robison because, even though she was just a child, she looked so much like Eve. Blond hair, blue eyes, pink satin skin. And Ray is a troublemaker, always has been because he drinks too much and Floyd is constantly throwing him out of Williamson's bar.

Despite the twenty-five years that separate the lives of Julianne and Eve, Floyd and these two men think their looking alike means something, and Ruth will let them keep thinking that because then they will keep a close eye on Ray. If these men believe the past has something to do with what happened to Julianne Robison and that Julianne's disappearance will turn out to be Palco's first murder in twenty-five years, they won't believe Ruth's lie and they'll keep digging. If Ray is the one who took Julianne Robison, they'll figure it out as long as they keep looking. Because Ruth's too afraid to tell Floyd the truth about that Saturday night, this is the best she can do.

With Arthur still trapping her against the counter, Celia looks through the maple's branches, makes a small humming sound and says, "I don't see anything."

Arthur stands straight, his sudden movement causing Celia to stumble.

"The paddock," he says. "The God damned paddock is empty."

Celia looks again, this time leaning over the sink. The gate near the barn hangs open.

"I've told that boy to mind the latch," Arthur says as he grabs his hat from the top of the refrigerator. "Dan. Get out here."

"Arthur, please," Celia says, following him toward the porch.

Ever since Julianne Robison went missing and stayed missing, Celia feels a rush of fear every time she or Arthur gets angry with the children. It's the fear that anger will be the thing they are left with should one of them go missing, too. It's silly, she knows, but even eight weeks later, even as the town seems to be forgetting, even as the search has ended for Julianne Robison, the fear is a reflex.

"Maybe she's gone around the back of the barn," Celia says. "You don't know she got out. Please don't overreact."

"Well, that's not the point, is it?"

While Celia tries to rein in her anger and frustration since Julianne disappeared, Arthur has unleashed his. His temper explodes without warning as if he thinks Julianne must have been careless, irresponsible, and that these two things led to her disappearance. He won't have the same happen to his children.

"Dan," Arthur shouts again. "Get out here."

Pulling on a shirt, Daniel stumbles from his room. "What?" he says, blinking and forcing his eyes open. "What is it?"

"You latch Olivia's gate last night?" Arthur says, pulling on his second boot.

"Sir?"

"The gate. You latch it?"

"Yes, sir."

Giving his boot a final tug, Arthur stands straight. "You sure about that?"

"I'll check, sir."

"He'll check," Celia says, reaching for Arthur's hand. "Let him check."

Arthur yanks away. "I'll give you your answer, son. You didn't latch it. Now get your shoes on and see to it that cow hasn't gotten out."

Daniel walks into his room, his shoulders rounded, his arms hanging at his sides, while Arthur stands in the threshold leading onto the back porch. He crosses his arms, leans against the doorjamb and stares at Celia.

"Don't be too hard on him," she says. "He's still learning."

Standing straight so that his shoulders fill the doorway, Arthur says, "He's had plenty of time for learning."

"Please be patient. It's only been a couple months."

Arthur yanks on his hat. "Two months is long enough. That boy doesn't give one damn thought to what he's doing around here, and it's high time that changes."

At the end of the driveway, Ruth stands behind the cover of an evergreen. Cradling the two loaves of banana bread and a chicken and broccoli casserole, she leans forward, checking right and left and right again. Floyd and the men from Wichita left without finishing their coffee, and if Ruth hurries, she can get to Arthur's house before anyone worries. From inside the tree, she straightens and listens. It is definitely a truck she hears, driving east to west. She takes two steps back, knowing just where to stand so that the tree's branches will wrap around her, hide her.

Yes, it's a truck, not a car. The wide tires, the heavy cab, the tailgate. She listens, holding her breath as she waits for the change in pitch of a truck slowing to turn. A tailgate rattles, metal slapping against metal. Just like Ray's. Large tires kick up muddy gravel, almost close enough to spray it across Ruth's face if she weren't hidden inside the tree. She slowly exhales, listening but not hearing the change in pitch. The truck drives by, never slowing to turn. It's blue with a white cab. Out-of-state tags. Nebraska. Not Ray.

Stepping out of the tree, a branch pulls the hood from Ruth's head. The banana bread that she stirred up the night before and baked while Floyd and the men from Wichita drank their coffee is warm in her arms. Outside the evergreen, the rain has slowed to a mist and the road to Arthur's house is empty except for the deep scars carved into it by the blue and white truck. Balancing the casserole dish and bread loaves on one hip, Ruth pulls the braid that hangs down her back from under her coat and lets it fall between her shoulder blades.

She goes to Arthur's now every Saturday morning, each time taking food for Orville and Mary Robison. Most weekends she only manages a small batch of cookies or half dozen sweet rolls. Never too much. Ray might notice. She leaves the food with Celia, who always promises to take it straight to the Robisons and then they drink coffee and sometimes eat cookies or maybe a sweet roll if Ruth made extra. After a few weeks of these trips, Ruth has started to put on a little weight, filling out like she was when she was younger. Her hip bones are cushioned now and her shoulders softened. Even her hair is stronger and thicker since Arthur's family moved home. This past week, as they sipped coffee in Celia's kitchen, Celia had brushed Ruth's hair, carefully so as not to tear the ends, and wove it into a thick braid that she tied off with one of Evie's pink hair bands. "The apple cider vinegar is working," Celia said as she brushed out Ruth's hair. Thinking Ray might notice her new braid, Ruth had practiced and was ready to show him how she could braid her own hair, but she had no explanation for the pink band. Standing on the edge of the road, she smiles and tosses her head from side to side, the braid swinging softly across her back.

Arthur's home is a half mile away. At the top of the hill that separates their two houses, Ruth slows. This is where she stops every Saturday morning and scans the tightly knit rows of winter wheat sprouts that etch the fields, hoping for a glimpse of Julianne Robison. Tattered yellow ribbons tied to a dozen fence posts along the road by the high school kids in the early days following Julianne's disappearance remind Ruth how long the child has been gone. Too long. But still Ruth watches for her from the top of the hill.

There are other reminders besides the yellow ribbons. The flyers with Julianne's black and white picture, wrinkled and faded, that still cling to the telephone poles along Main Street. The car wash that the Boy Scouts held a month ago. They gave the money to Mary and Orville. Mary said she would tuck it away for a rainy day. The abandoned well that James Williamson reported last Sunday. Floyd Bigler and a half dozen of the town's men gathered around the hole while their women gathered at the church just in case. But the men found nothing and backfilled the hole with crushed rock and cement.

Careful to avoid the soft ruts carved by the truck that drove past, Ruth walks to the edge of the road and fingers one of the yellow ribbons. On her next trip to Arthur's house, she'll bring along some yellow fabric scraps and tie them over the tattered plastic ribbons. She scans both sides of the road, counting the ribbons so she'll know how many to cut. And then she hears it. Yelling, shouting. It sounds like Arthur. She walks to the center of the road and from there she sees them.

Arthur is running down the hill, away from Ruth. He is waving and shouting at Daniel, who is running along the other side of the road, trailed by Evie. Between them, Olivia the cow weaves left and right, first toward Arthur and then toward Daniel. Near the bottom of the hill, where gravity seems to get the better of him, Arthur tries to slow down but slips in the mud instead. He stumbles, arms shooting up into the air, both feet flying out from under him, and lands on his hind end. Daniel stops, coming up a few steps short of his father, and leans over, resting both hands on his knees. This gives Evie time to catch up. Arthur holds up one hand as if to quiet them and pushes himself off the ground. He shakes the dirt from his boots and stands straight, his muddy hands hanging at his sides.

As the commotion settles down, Olivia stops a few feet in front of them. She drops her head and nuzzles something on the ground. Everyone seems to be resting until Arthur suddenly breaks into a sprint, slipping and stumbling for several strides before finding his footing. Olivia startles, jerks her head, throws her hind legs into the air, kicking up mud and gravel, and begins to run. Daniel and Evie duck, both holding their hands over their faces and run after their father. Ruth hugs her bread and laughs. She laughs, without making any sound. She laughs until tears pool in the corner of each eye. She laughs until she hears another truck.

Up ahead, Jonathon drives around the curve in the road. Daniel stops running, leans forward and props himself up by bracing his hands on his knees. Jonathon parks his truck at an angle, blocking the road. Through the windshield, Daniel sees Elaine sitting in the center of the front seat, nearly in Jonathon's lap. Since the afternoon Jonathon loaded Olivia in his trailer and followed Uncle Ray to Grandma Reesa's, he has been at their house almost every day. He comes straight from work and stays for dinner, always talking about the house he is building from scraps and spare parts. He's been around so much that he has become Dad's extra set of hands. Before they moved from Detroit, Dad said that the farm would turn Daniel into a man, that it would roughen up his hands and put hair on his chest. Instead, Dad found Jonathon, who is already a man, and Daniel is still Mama's extra set of hands.

Elaine is smiling as Jonathon slowly and quietly opens his door and slides out of the truck. She follows, both of them stifling their laughter so they don't startle Olivia, who has stopped in the center of the road. The truck has confused her or maybe she is plain tired out.

"Give you a hand, Arthur?" Jonathon says, tugging on his gray hat.

"We've got her from this side," Dad says and motions Daniel to close the gap between them and the cow.

"I'd say this old gal has had about enough." Jonathon bends to look into Olivia's face. He takes two steps forward, reaches out with one hand and grabs her neck strap. "Yep, good and tired."

"How many times is that, Dan?" Elaine says, standing next to Jonathon and hooking a finger onto one of his belt loops. "Three?"

"Why'd you get so made up to go fishing?" Daniel says as Dad walks over to take the lead from Jonathon.

"Get over here, Dan," Dad says, giving Elaine a second look. She is wearing a lavender dress and her brown hair hangs in soft waves the way it does when she sleeps in rag curlers. "You two catch anything?"

"Daddy, don't be silly," Elaine says. "Who fishes in the rain?"

"Daddy fishes in the rain all the time," Evie says, smiling up at Jonathon. He tugs one of her braids.

"Caught a lot of fine fish in the rain," Dad says, holding onto Olivia and studying Elaine. Olivia snorts and tosses her head. Dad jerks her lead. "Hold up there, girl."

Daniel thinks maybe Dad will forget to ground him since Elaine is too dressed up for fishing.

"We went to my mother's for breakfast, sir," Jonathon says, patting Olivia's jowl. "She enjoys the company."

"Good enough," Dad says. "Daniel, get this animal home."

"Yes, sir," Daniel says, wrapping both hands around the leather lead.

"Are you coming to Grandma's for lunch tomorrow?" Evie asks Jonathon. She twirls a braid around her finger, the same braid Jonathon tugged. "She makes fried chicken. Daddy says it's the best ever."

"Imagine so, squirt," Jonathon says, giving Evie a pat on the head and turning on one heel to leave.

"Don't forget to latch the gate, Dan," Elaine says, laughing and still hanging onto Jonathon's belt loop as they walk back to the truck.

While Dad directs Jonathon so his truck won't get stuck in one of the muddy ditches, Evie waves goodbye and Daniel pulls Olivia until her head turns toward home. Thinking he'll check for mail because Mama says his old friends are sure to write any day now, Daniel stops at the mailbox, tugs open the small door and looks inside. Empty. Not a single letter since they moved. Already, every Detroit friend has forgotten him. He shakes his head, gives Olivia's lead another yank to get her moving and looks up. There, at the top of the hill, he sees them.

"Hey, Dad," he says, squinting up the road. "Isn't that Aunt Ruth up there?"

At the top of the hill that separates Aunt Ruth and Uncle Ray's house from their house, Uncle Ray has parked his truck and is standing next to the passenger side door, which is open. At first, Daniel thinks Uncle Ray has come to help catch Olivia, too—that Dad has called out the whole county to run her down. But then he sees Aunt Ruth standing at the side of the road. Her shoulders are hunched forward as if she is carrying something and she looks no bigger than Evie from so far away. Uncle Ray motions for Aunt Ruth to get into the truck but instead she stares down the road where Daniel stands with Olivia. Daniel looks over at his cow. Her chestnut coat is slick and shiny, her breath comes in short, heavy snorts. She hangs her head, then looks up at Daniel with her brown eyes and bats her thick, black lashes.

When Daniel looks back, Aunt Ruth is gone. The truck door is closed. And Uncle Ray is walking back to the driver's side. He pauses as he passes in front of the truck, waves down at Daniel and his family and slips inside the cab. Evie jumps up and down, waves her hands over her head. Dad watches as the truck rolls backward down the far side of the hill. He is looking for something, though Daniel isn't sure what.

Chapter 6

Breathing in the cool morning air that ruffles her kitchen curtains and still smells of rain, Ruth crosses her legs, Indian style as Evie would say, and rearranges her skirt so it lies around her on the floor like a halo. Pieces of broken glass scatter as she settles into position. On the stove, a small saucepan sets inside a larger one that is filled with two inches of boiling water—a homemade double boiler. A cheesecloth draped over both traps the heavy, rising steam. On the counter, where it will stay cool, waits a small brown bottle.

From her spot on the floor, Ruth glances at the clock sitting on the stove and dips a teaspoon into a box of baking soda, levels it by dragging it under the box top and drops it into a small glass dish. Using a tight whipping motion, she stirs it into the water already in the bowl and, thinking the paste isn't thick enough yet, she adds another scoop of soda. She taps her spoon on the side of the glass bowl. Still not thick enough. As she adds a third spoonful, a truck pulls around the side of the house and parks near the garage. A door slams followed by footsteps that climb the outside stairs. Ruth pulls her knees to her chest, cups the small bowl in one hand and stirs the baking soda paste with the other.

The screened door rattles in its frame.

"Ruth. Ruth. You in there?"

Ruth lets her legs fall down into a crisscross position again and uses the back of her spoon to mash the paste against the side of the bowl.

"Ruth, it's Arthur. You home? I saw you out there on the road. You and Ray. Olivia got out again. Did you see? Damn cow. Everything okay in there?"

The screen creaks as it opens. Arthur knocks on the wooden door loud enough that Ruth feels it through the floorboards. She closes her eyes, actually only her left eye, and holds her breath, bracing herself. But the vibration beneath her is not enough to stir up the pain. She'll feel it tomorrow.

"Thought you might have something to eat in there," Arthur says, shaking the locked doorknob. "Eggs are cold at my house. You in there?"

Ruth sets aside the glass bowl and, supporting herself with one hand, she stretches toward a silver frame that lies barely within reach. She hooks the frame with one finger, pulls it toward her and sits straight again. Because the glass is broken, she slips off the cardboard backing, removes the picture and sets it on the floor next to her. A spot of blood drips off the palm that braced her when she reached for the frame. The blood lands on the center of the picture just below Eve's right eye. First one drop and then another. Eve was fifteen when the picture was taken, maybe sixteen. A few years before she died. Ruth pulls a small shard of glass from her palm and presses her hand against her skirt to stop the bleeding.

"Ruth, hey, Ruth." Arthur knocks again. "Celia says to come on over for coffee. She's got those white beans ready to go. Thought you'd like a ride."

Heavy footsteps cross the porch, pause and walk back. The door rattles in its frame as Arthur tries it again.

"You in there?"

Once the bleeding has stopped, Ruth dips a corner of her skirt into the baking soda paste and begins to polish the silver frame. She starts at the top, scrubbing in tiny circles, a white haze marking her path. The frame had been a wedding present. She polishes it every month, sometimes with baking soda, sometimes with toothpaste. The tarnish is quick to gather in the scalloped edges. Cheap silver, Ray always says.

Having finished the top, Ruth adjusts her grip, folding her hand over the jagged edges of glass clinging to the frame. The pointed shards prick her fingers. She changes position, shifting her weight from side to side, her back beginning to ache where he kicked her. Something cuts into her hip. Another piece of glass, she thinks. All around her, glass lays shattered. Crescent-shaped pieces of wineglasses never used, cleared out of the china hutch with one swipe of Ray's right hand. The frame had been an accident. It bounced across the wooden floor and came to rest at Ray's feet. From inside the silver frame, Eve's shattered face, her eyes bright, smiled up at him from under the brim of her best Sunday hat.

He had stood for a moment, staring at the photo, his clenched fists at his side and without bothering to look at her, he called Ruth a whore, a God damned whore with no business sneaking off like she did. A God damned whore wearing a pink band in her hair who had no business feeding the folks who thought he stole their girl. He had seen those Wichita men down at Izzy's café. Thought he'd have himself a decent God damned breakfast for once but then he sees those men with Floyd. Those God damned Wichita men tipped their hats at him, told him what a pleasant wife he had and what good coffee Ruth brewed up for them. Whole damn town is talking about it now. Everyone talking about how much that girl looked like Eve, talking about it like it means something. Ruth couldn't lie when Ray asked if they'd been to talk to her but promised him that she only told those men the truth—that Ray'd been home all night, eating meat loaf and strawberry pie. The truth is all. Ray had stood for a long time, his good eye staring at Ruth before he kicked the silver frame across the floor into the kitchen. As Ruth crawled after it, glass crackling under her knees, he lifted the same boot and kicked her in the back and again in the left side of the head. When Ruth woke, he was gone.

A door slams and Arthur's truck fires up. Gravel crunches beneath his tires as he slowly backs up and starts down the driveway. The truck stops when it passes the front of the house, idles there for a moment, and the sound of the engine fades as he drives away.

Chapter 7

Celia stands at Reesa's stove, a place she finds herself now every Sunday after church services, with a teaspoon in hand and a checkered apron tied at her waist. Using her forearm to brush the hair from her eyes, she inhales the steam rising off a pot of simmering chicken broth, turns her head and coughs. The others sit behind her at the kitchen table. They are watching her, waiting for her, crossing and uncrossing their legs. The vinyl seat covers squeak as they shift positions. Someone drums his fingers on the table. Someone else sighs. Someone's stomach growls.

"Once it boils, you can start dropping dumplings," Reesa says. "Be sure that dough is plenty thick this time. Add more flour if it calls you to."

"And use small spoonfuls," Elaine says. "Jonathon and Dad like the small noodles. Right, Dad?"

Arthur doesn't answer. He knows better, Celia thinks, tapping her teaspoon on the side of the pot. The drumming fingers stop.

"Next time," Reesa says, "set the burner on high and we won't be holding up lunch until that broth boils. Lord a mercy. Father Flannery will be preaching next Sunday's mass before those noodles are done."

Celia digs a spoon into the thick batter and flashes a toothy grin at her mother-in-law whose large body spills over the chair. Scooping up a wad of dough the size of a chicken egg, she holds it over the pot, not really intending to drop it in, but wanting to enjoy the feeling of ruining Sunday lunch before dropping in a proper sized dumpling— one the size of a nickel. But as she holds the dough over the simmering broth, she hears a loud pop that startles her and the dumpling wad falls. Hot broth slashes her arms and face. She jumps back.

"Ray'll have to get that fixed one of these days," Arthur says at the sound of Ray's truck backfiring a second time. He stands, glances out the kitchen widow and walks toward the back door.

Jonathon scoots back from the table and pulls out Elaine's chair for her. "Let's give it a look," he says.

As the three of them walk from the kitchen, leaving Celia and Reesa alone, Celia turns her back on the stove, the chicken broth bubbling up behind her, and leans over the sink so she can see out the window. Ray hasn't moved from behind the steering wheel and the engine is choking and sputtering. In the passenger seat, Ruth sits with her head lowered. Celia crosses her arms and smiles, thinking she'll have to tease Arthur for all his worrying. All through church, he had fidgeted, shifting in his seat, crossing and uncrossing his legs as he watched the doors and scanned the pews. Ruth never misses a Sunday. Never, he whispered as the congregation began its first hymn. Perhaps she's under the weather or Ray overslept. Arthur only nodded and hung his arm over the back of the pew so he could watch the heavy wooden doors at the rear of the church.

"Mind that chicken doesn't burn," Reesa says, nodding toward the chicken frying in a cast-iron skillet and then she pushes back from the table, the legs of her chair grinding across the linoleum floor. "I'll go see to helping Ruth with her dessert. And get those dumplings going. We'll be all day waiting if you don't get started."

When Reesa has left the kitchen and Celia is alone, she looks back outside. Ruth's head is still lowered as if she's looking down at folded hands and Ray is beating on the steering wheel, seemingly because the truck's engine won't stop running. He is still ranting when Arthur walks up to the truck, followed by Elaine, Jonathon and Reesa. Celia steps back from the sink, pokes at the one giant dumpling that has floated to the top of the broth and, as the rolling bubbles grow into a heavy boil, she thinks she'll serve this one to Reesa. Reaching for the second burner, where the fried chicken sizzles and pops, Celia smiles as she turns up the heat.

Daniel, startled by a loud pop, ducks and presses against the wall, the wooden slats rough and wet against his back. Inside the small shed, it's dark and the air smells like Grandma Reesa's basement—moldy and stale. He tries to breathe through his mouth, thinking the air won't feel so heavy if he does.

For six weeks, Ian has asked Daniel to look inside the shed at Grandma Reesa's place. Ian's oldest brothers thought for sure Julianne Robison was rotting away inside, but Daniel said that was stupid because Grandma Reesa would have smelled her. Ian said to check anyway because his brothers were smart and a fellow could never be sure until he saw it with his own eyes.

Daniel readjusts his feet, careful not to break through one of the floorboards that creak every time he moves. Hearing another pop, he recognizes the sound as Uncle Ray's truck and, squinting with one eye, he looks through a small hole where part of a plank has rotted away. Dad walks out of the house, smiling, almost laughing. He turns to say something to Jonathon. Elaine laughs, latches onto Jonathon's side and dips her head into his shoulder. The back door swings open again and Grandma Reesa walks out, rocking from side to side with each step. Daniel thinks of Ian, how he walks with a staggered stride, too, but for a different reason. Tomorrow at school, Daniel will tell Ian that Julianne Robison is definitely not rotting in the shed.

As Grandma Reesa nears the truck where the others are standing and watching Uncle Ray curse the engine that won't stop rattling, she turns toward the shed and stops, her feet spread wide to support her weight, her hands on her hips. Daniel drops down and presses his head between his knees. He sits motionless, waiting, listening.

Every Sunday after church services, Daniel changes into his work clothes when they get to Grandma Reesa's so he can cut her lawn. Sometimes, Dad gives him other chores to do, too—clean the gutters, spray down the screens, tighten the banisters—but at least until the first hard frost, he mows every Sunday. And every week, as Dad pulls the reel mower from the garage, he says, "Don't bother around the shed. That's for later." But later has never come. "I could take a weed whip to it," Daniel said one Sunday, remembering Ian's brothers and the kitten in the hole. He was glad when Dad shook his head and said, "Not today, son." Since they moved to Kansas, Dad and Jonathon have used a truck and cables to straighten Grandma's garage and have hammered in new support beams on the porch. They have replaced her rotted windowpanes and reshingled her chimney but Dad hasn't lifted a single hammer or nail to fix the sagging shed that is no more than six feet by eight with a flat roof and lone door. Daniel asked Aunt Ruth once why Dad wouldn't let anyone near the shed. "Mind your father," she had said. "Some things are meant to rest in peace."

Afraid to look through the rotted plank again, Daniel hugs his knees to his chest and wraps himself into a tight ball. Large cobwebs hanging from the corners of the shed sparkle in the slivers of light that shine through the loosely woven wooden roof. Daniel muffles a cough by pressing his mouth to his forearm. Sitting in the dark and wondering if Grandma Reesa saw him, Daniel remembers the crazy men from Clark City and scans the empty shed for a set of eyes that might be watching him. It's definitely time to get out.

Lifting up on his knees so he can peek through the hole again, Daniel sees that Dad has stopped a few feet in front of Uncle Ray's truck. He isn't laughing anymore. He is staring straight ahead at Aunt Ruth, who has stepped out of the truck and is standing near the front bumper, her arms hanging at her sides. The hem of her blue calico dress flutters in the breeze. Dad stands with a straight back, his feet planted wide. His hat sits low on his forehead. After Dad is done staring at Aunt Ruth, he turns toward Uncle Ray.

*　　*　　*

Evie climbs onto the bed when she hears a loud pop outside. Holding up the hem of the blue silky dress that slips off her shoulders and bags at the neckline, she tiptoes across the white bedspread so she doesn't make the springs squeak. Daniel will be angry if he knows she's tried on the dresses. He'll probably tell Mama, and Daddy will take a switch to her hind end. That's what Grandma Reesa did when Daddy was a boy. On their second visit to Grandma Reesa's house, Daddy had taken Evie out back and showed her a weeping willow tree. It had long, lazy branches that hung to the ground. "That old tree sure gave up her share of switches," Daddy had said, rubbing his hind end and laughing.

Evie stops in the middle of the bed, one foot in front of the other, her hands spread wide for balance. Hearing no one in the hallway outside the bedroom, she takes another step toward the window. Another loud pop comes from down below, but this time she smiles because she knows it's only Uncle Ray's truck backfiring. The handkerchief hem of the dress brushes against her toes. She wiggles them, gathers up the skirt again and leans against the headboard where she can see outside.

After Daddy and the others have walked out the door toward Uncle Ray's truck, Evie goes back to imagining that she is Aunt Eve. She pushes away from the window, presses her shoulders back and lifts her chin so that she'll feel taller—as tall as Aunt Eve. No one ever told Aunt Eve she was too small to be a third grader or called her names. Aunt Eve always had friends to sit with in the cafeteria and never sat alone on the steps outside her classroom, watching the swings hang empty or beating the dust from Miss Olson's erasers. No one ever told Aunt Eve that she was going to disappear like Julianne Robison. Aunt Eve is beautiful and perfect and has the finest dresses. She was never, ever the smallest.

Wrapping her arms around her waist, Evie hugs the soft dress and smells Aunt Eve's perfume—sweet and light, like the bouquets of wildflowers that Aunt Ruth brings every Saturday morning. Evie closes her eyes and slowly twirls around, the bedsprings squeaking under foot. She spreads her arms wide, spinning faster and faster, lifting her knees to her chest so she won't trip on the hem and finally dropping down onto the center of the mattress with a loud crash.

She sits in the middle of the bed, not moving, not breathing, wondering if she has made the bed collapse. The headboard is still standing. She leans over the side. The bed is still standing, too. Then she hears the sound again. It's coming from outside. She crawls back to the window and lifts up high enough to see out. Daddy, now standing at the front of Uncle Ray's truck with Jonathon right behind him, is waving one hand toward Aunt Ruth and pointing at Uncle Ray with the other. As Jonathon reaches out for Daddy, Daddy bangs his fist on the truck's hood. The same crash that Evie heard. Daddy shakes off Jonathon and holds up one hand to stop Grandma Reesa, who has started walking toward him. Uncle Ray has backed up to the rear of his truck and is motioning at Daddy with both hands the same way he did when Olivia spooked as she walked out of the trailer. He's trying to calm Daddy, to make him settle down so he doesn't rear up. In four long steps, Daddy is standing face to face with Uncle Ray.

* * *

Shifting in her chair to hear more clearly through the open kitchen window, Celia smiles as Ray's truck finally quiets down. Next, one of the truck's doors opens, followed by heavy boots landing on the gravel drive. Another door opens.

"Help your Aunt Ruth." It's Reesa, probably calling out to Elaine. "She'll have a handful."

At the sound of her mother-in-law's voice, Celia presses her hands flat on the vinyl tablecloth, bracing herself, the smell of burnt chicken beginning to tug at her. Next to the chicken, which sizzles and pops, though quieter now because its juices have burned off, broth hisses as it splashes over the sides of Reesa's iron pot onto the hot stovetop and disappears in a puff of steam. Celia presses her feet on the white linoleum and repositions herself on the vinyl seat cover, rooting her body so she won't be tempted to stand. The God damned chicken can burn for all she cares.

Sundays were pleasant in Detroit. It was the day she wore white gloves and her favorite cocoa velour pillbox hat with the grosgrain ribbon trim. The children wore their finest clothes to church and never worried about dust ruining the shine on their patent leather shoes. Arthur always wore a tie. Sundays in Detroit were properly creased and always well kept until the riots started and everything began to smell like burnt rubber and the Negro boys started calling Elaine. Now Sundays are dusty, filthy, wrinkled and spent watching Arthur pat his belly as Reesa fries up a chicken. Celia shivers thinking of Reesa's offer that next week she'll teach Celia how to pick a good fryer from the brood and wring its neck with a few flicks of the wrist.

"Look up at me, Ruth," Arthur says from outside the window.

Something about Arthur's voice makes Celia stand. She slides her chair back and leans over the sink where she can see out the kitchen window. Ray and Ruth have both stepped out of the truck. Ray is standing on the far side, where only the top of his hat is visible, and Ruth is standing on the near side, her back to Celia, her arms dangling, her head lowered.

"This why you weren't at church this morning?" Arthur says, his voice louder.

Ruth doesn't move. Arthur takes two steps forward and Jonathon grabs his arm. Arthur yanks away, raises a fist in the air and slams it against the hood of Ray's truck.

Celia startles, her hand slipping off the edge of the sink.

"Tell me, Ruth."

Ruth lifts her face. Arthur closes his eyes and drops his head. A braid hangs down Ruth's back, tied off by a bright pink band. After teaching Ruth how to braid her own hair, Celia had promised to wash and trim it when she came on Saturday and she even bought honey for their biscuits. But Ruth never came.

The thick braid moves up and down, no more than an inch as Ruth nods her head yes.

Arthur slams his fist on the truck again and holds up his other hand to Reesa, who has started to walk toward him. He turns to Ray.

"You lay your hands on her face?"

Ray doesn't answer but instead backs toward the rear of the truck.

"Answer me. You lay a hand on her?"

"This is business between me and my wife, Arthur. No place for you."

Arthur shoves Jonathon away when he tries again to take Arthur's arm, and in four quick steps, he is standing face to face with Ray. Ray backs up a few more feet until they are clear of the truck and Celia can see them both. She pushes off the counter, ignoring the charred smell drifting up from Reesa's best cast-iron skillet and runs from the kitchen.

Evie hangs from the window ledge with both hands, her face pressed to the screen. Daddy grabs Uncle Ray's collar with one hand and hits him in the face with the other. Uncle Ray holds his fists up in front of his good eye, but Daddy pushes them away and hits him again. Uncle Ray tries to shove Daddy but Daddy won't let go. He holds on, shaking Uncle Ray like a rag doll and hitting him again and again. Evie pushes away from the window, stumbles over her handkerchief hem and something rips as she pulls the dress off her shoulders, steps out of it and throws it on the floor under the other dresses. She slams the closet door and as she runs out of the room, she hears Mama shout, "Stop, Arthur. Stop."

Daniel presses his face against the hole in the shed wall. Uncle Ray holds up both hands. His nose and mouth are red. Dad keeps hitting Uncle Ray even when his hat falls off, even when Uncle Ray's head quits bouncing back, even when Mama cries out for him to quit. Finally, Dad stops, holding his right fist over his shoulder, cocked and ready to hit Uncle Ray again.

"You ask Ruth," Uncle Ray says. "She'll tell you why I did it." Blood runs out of Uncle Ray's nose. "Out there sneaking around on me. All these months, taking food to those God damned Robisons. God damned people say I took their girl."

Dad lunges and hits Uncle Ray again, splattering blood across the gravel drive. Uncle Ray stumbles backward, tripping over his own feet and lands on his hind end. Dad stands still, watching and waiting while Uncle Ray props himself up on one elbow. Dad's shoulders lift and lower each time he takes a breath. Uncle Ray starts to stand but stops when Dad reaches into the truck bed and pulls out a whiskey bottle, grabs it by its thin neck and flings it at the shed. The bottle shatters. Someone screams, maybe Mama, maybe Elaine. Daniel falls backward, shuffling like a crab until he is pressed flat against the shed's far wall. Glass and warm bourbon splash up on the other side of the hole he had been looking through. The bits of glass sparkle in the cool sunlight for an instant before disappearing. The gravel driveway is silent.

Once the glass has settled, Celia turns to Arthur. He has not moved. Reesa reaches out to him but instead stops and walks inside. Ruth stands near the truck's front bumper, her head lowered, her arms hanging at her side.

"Ruth," Arthur says.

Ruth raises her head.

Celia gasps, covers her mouth again. Elaine and Jonathon lower their eyes.

"Oh, Ruth," Celia whispers.

"Go on with Celia," Arthur says, still staring at the shed, but Ruth doesn't move. "Now," he shouts.

Ruth's shoulders jerk.

"Go with Celia, now."

Celia wraps one arm around Elaine, both of them standing still, unable to move. Ray lies on the ground, blood smeared under his nose, down his chin, across his collar.

"Jonathon," Arthur says in a quieter voice.

Jonathon lifts his chin, pulls down his hat over his eyes and takes a step toward Arthur.

"Get them inside."

Jonathon nods, takes Ruth's forearm and, with his head lowered so that the brim of his hat hides his face, he guides her toward Celia and Elaine. Celia passes Elaine to Jonathon but shakes her head when he motions her to follow. She watches until the three have gone into the house and the screened door has slammed shut behind them.

"Gather yourself and leave," Arthur says to Ray. "Ruth isn't your concern anymore."

Ray pushes himself up, favoring his left side as if Arthur has broken a rib or two, picks up his hat, pulls it on so the front brim is cocked a little too high and limps toward his truck. "I don't see how you have any business between me and my wife."

"How many times, Ray?" Arthur says, picking up his hat and pulling it on. "How many times you lay a hand on her?"

Ray wipes the corner of his mouth, smearing the blood that drips down his chin. He spits red. A cut above his left brow drips blood into his bad eye.

Arthur throws open the truck door. "Not your wife anymore."

"Arthur," Celia says, grabbing his arm and pulling him toward the house and away from Ray. "Please, let him be on his way."

Arthur pulls away and without looking at Celia, says, "Get inside."

"You're a man, Arthur. Same as me," Ray says, though he is looking at Celia when he says it, not in her eyes, but lower. "You wouldn't have me telling you about your wife, would you? Wouldn't want me telling you when you could or couldn't have her."

"Well, I'm telling you now," Arthur says, taking one step to the left so he blocks Ray's view of Celia. "Ruth is no longer your concern."

With his forearm, Ray wipes the blood from under his nose and steps up to Arthur. The brims of their hats nearly touch.

"You wait until they come looking for you," Ray says, "thinking maybe you're the one took that girl. You ought to know, people think it's strange, you all moving back right when that girl goes missing. People think it's strange, all right."

Arthur nods. "Folks'll think what they think," he says and Ray slips inside the truck.

Evie stops on the last step, holds onto the banister and leans forward. The downstairs room is full of gray smoky air. Trying to see into the kitchen and beyond to the back porch, she listens for Daddy and Uncle Ray and wonders if they're still fighting. Mama shouted for them to stop but maybe Daddy and Uncle Ray won't listen to Mama. She blinks, clearing her tears. Not seeing anyone, she squeezes her nose closed with two fingers and steps down, touching the wooden floors with one toe. She holds that pose, trying not to breathe any of the smoky air and listens.

"Good Lord in heaven."

A crash follows Grandma Reesa's shout.

Evie presses her tiptoe foot flat on the floor and steps down with the other. Still pinching her nose, she walks through the living room and as she nears the front of the house, she covers her mouth and coughs. The gray smoke is thicker and swirls overhead. Waving it away, she steps into the kitchen. Grandma Reesa stands at the stove, her back to Evie, a silver potholder on one hand.

"Fine food charred to no good," Grandma Reesa says and, sliding the large iron skillet off the hot burner, she reaches into the sink, pulls out the cast-iron lid with the potholder, lifts it overhead and slams it back into the sink.

"What got burnt, Grandma?" Evie asks, her hands pressed to her ears in case Grandma throws anything else. She bites down on her lower lip when her chin wrinkles.

"Burned every last piece of chicken," Grandma Reesa says, holding the skillet up by its long thin handle. Black clumps of chicken stick to the bottom, even when she shakes it. "Help me, child. Get the bucket from the mudroom. We'll be scrubbing these walls for days."

Pulling a fan from under the sink, Grandma Reesa sets it in the kitchen window. "The mudroom, Eve. Get the bucket from the mudroom. My green bucket."

Evie runs into the large closet where everyone leaves their muddy boots on a rainy day, grabs the green bucket and hurries back to the kitchen. Grandma Reesa has begun pulling the white curtains off their rod. The fan drawing cool, outside air into the kitchen ruffles her gray hair and blows it across her blue eyes—the same color as Evie's, except older.

"Run the bathroom sink full of hot water and soak these," she says, brushing the hair from her eyes and handing the curtains to Evie. "Go on now. This mess will keep us busy all day if we let it."

"Daddy is fighting with Uncle Ray," Evie says, wrapping her arms around the bundle of curtains.

Grandma Reesa puts the green bucket in the sink and begins to fill it.

"I saw them," Evie says. "Outside. Fighting."

"Drop a bar of hand soap in the water." Grandma Reesa pulls a long-handled spoon from a drawer and points it at Evie. "No bleach. It will yellow the cotton."

"Daddy was hitting Uncle Ray in the face. Knocked him down and everything. I saw them from upstairs. I was in Aunt Eve's room, cleaning it for you. I dusted her dresser and fluffed her pillows. It'll be ready for her when she comes home."

Grandma Reesa stabs the spoon into a bowl. "Go on now," she says, yanking it out and jamming it back in. "This smoke will ruin my curtains. Go on now."

"Where's my daddy?" Evie feels her chin wrinkle again. She blinks as the air blown in by the fan parts her bangs. "He's hitting Uncle Ray."

"Run the water until it's good and hot. Get on with it."

"I saw them from Aunt Eve's room. I saw Daddy fighting." Evie stands in the middle of the kitchen, still hugging the curtains. "I wanted Aunt Eve's room to be nice for her. I wanted . . ."

Grandma Reesa lifts her white mixing bowl with both hands and slams it down on the counter. "Don't you speak to me about Eve, child. Don't you do it. Now get that hot water running. Get those curtains soaked."

Evie presses her face into the bundle of curtains. She lifts her eyes enough to see Grandma Reesa standing at the sink, her back to Evie, her right elbow jutting in and out as she scrubs the black skillet with a scouring pad. Evie nods her head, walks into the bathroom, breathing in the smell of the lemon-scented curtains, and closes the door behind her.

The devil's claws are waist high. Walking toward Mother's back porch, Jonathon guiding her by the elbow, Ruth brushes a hand over the pink, funnel-shaped blooms. The flowers are blurry through her one good eye. It still waters, as if she's been crying, but she never does. The tears will pool for a few more days. She licks her top lip, which is silky smooth where it has swelled to twice its normal size. Even though it hurts, she can't stop licking it. Sometime during the night, the shaking stopped. It always stops during the night. Ruth blinks her good eye and sees that some of the blossoms have died off, the tender petals shriveling and turn-ing brown. The rest will follow and Arthur will mow them down soon. They won't bloom again until spring. Before walking inside, Ruth touches one of the woody claws that has dropped its seeds, and she knows she's pregnant.

Chapter 8

At the top of the hill, their warm breath turning to a frosty cloud that settles in around them, Celia and Elaine stop and wait for Ruth and Evie to catch up. The wind is quiet today and the sun is bright, almost blinding through the cold, dry air. In the surrounding fields below, perfectly spaced rows of green seedlings curve and roll with the flow of the land—the first stages of winter wheat. Their own land isn't fit for wheat because it's too hilly. Arthur says that someday they'll have a few more cows and put the pasture to good use.

Celia knows this land well. She knows that the hollowed-out spot used to be a pond, that two fence posts need mending a quarter mile up the road and that there's a patch of quicksand over the first ridge to the south. She knows these things because all of them, the whole Scott family, walked these grounds many times searching for Julianne Robison. In the early weeks when she was first missing, they walked them almost every day, and then once a week and eventually in passing. Celia gasped the first time Arthur showed her the small patch of quicksand, thinking it had sucked poor Julianne to the bottom, but then Arthur stuck a stick in it and showed her it was only a few inches deep. As Evie and Ruth near the top of the hill, three olive, round-winged birds rise out of the thick bluestem growing along the road, glide across the red-tipped grass and settle in the ditch.

"Prairie chickens," Evie says, skipping up to Celia and pointing toward the spot where the birds disappeared.

Joining the others, Ruth nods but doesn't seem to have the breath to answer. She places one hand on her lower back and stretches.

"You feeling okay?" Celia says, motioning to the others to stop. "Did we go too far?"

Ruth shakes her head and signals that she needs a moment to rest. Before Ruth came to live with them, Celia took her walks along the dirt road, walking as far as County Road 54 before heading home. She needed fresh air, she would tell Arthur, and some time to herself. But what she really needed was a place to cry where no one would hear, a place where she could cry so hard that she choked and hiccupped and when she was done and her nose had stopped running, she would return home, saying her allergies were acting up or the wind and dust had reddened her eyes. She never told Arthur that she cried because she missed home and her parents, even though they were both dead. She never told him she missed walking Evie to school or visiting with the other ladies at Ambrozy's Deli. She never told him that she cried because in Kansas she is still afraid. She is afraid that he won't need her in the same way. She is afraid she'll never know how to be a mother in Kansas. And mostly, she is afraid of being alone. But now, she has Ruth. Thank goodness for

Ruth, but having her in the family also means they must walk the pastures instead of the road where Ray might happen along in his truck.

"Hey, look," Evie shouts, holding one mitten to her forehead to shade her eyes and pointing with the other toward the fields south of the house. "There's Daniel. And that's Ian with him."

"Where do you suppose they're going?" Celia asks, knowing that it's Daniel not because she can see his face but because Ian's limp gives them away.

"Out for a walk, I suppose," Elaine says as the two silhouettes disappear over a rise in the pasture.

"Well," Evie says, swiveling on one heel so she can march back down the hill. "I hope they're not up to no good."

Celia pats the small of Ruth's back and gestures for everyone to follow Evie toward home. "I'll tell you what," Celia says. "No good will be had if we don't all get warmed up soon."

At the bottom of the hill, Evie stops, points toward the road straight ahead where a black sedan appears out of the glare of the late-day sun and shouts, "Look. It's Father Flannery's car."

Celia stops midway down the hill and pulls her jacket closed. "We don't have to go back, Ruth," she says. The prairie chickens rise up again as the car passes, kicking up dust and gravel. "Arthur can see to him."

Elaine nods. "Yes, we could stay out a while longer."

"They'll be waiting," Ruth says, tugging on the edges of her stocking cap and continuing toward home. "Can't hide from this forever."

*   *   *

Daniel stares down at Ian and thinks that even flat on his stomach, Ian is crooked. Not as crooked as when he has to swing one leg over the bench seats in the school cafeteria, but crooked all the same. He is wearing his new black boots and even though his mother said they were only for church and school, Ian wears them all the time because they make things almost normal for him. One of the boots, the right one, has a two-inch heel while the other has a normal, flat heel. The thick heel is almost thick enough, but not quite and black boots don't do anything about a spine that looks like a stretched-out question mark. As Ian lifts up on his elbows, pressing his cheek to the stock of Daniel's new .22-caliber rifle, his shoulders sink under the weight of his head. Black boots don't do anything about Ian's oversized head, either. None of Daniel's Detroit friends had giant heads or lopsided legs. They were regular kids with regular-shaped bodies. Not knowing why but wanting to look somewhere else, anywhere else but at Ian, Daniel turns toward the road as a black sedan drives over the hill to the north.

"That Father Flannery?" Ian asks, lifting his head up out of his shoulders for a moment before letting it sink again.

"Yeah. How'd you know?"

"Everyone knows he's coming today." Ian rests his right cheek against the rifle.

Pulling his jacket closed, Daniel exhales and squats next to Ian.

"Not too close," Ian says so Daniel scoots a few feet away, flipping up his collar and wrapping his arms around his waist. "Go there, behind the grass where they won't see you."

Daniel waddles a few more feet to the left where he'll be hidden by a clump of brome grass. "Won't my folks hear the shots?" he asks, still able to see the roof of his house. "I mean, we're not so far away."

"No one thinks anything about a gunshot this time of year. Hush and let me get the first one. The rest are easier." Ian inhales and lifts his head again. "There," he whispers. "Did you see it?"

Daniel stretches enough to see beyond the grass into the pasture on the other side of the barbed-wire fence. "I don't know. Maybe."

"It'll be back. Sit tight."

"How does everyone know? About Father Flannery, I mean."

"Everyone knows everything." Ian props the gun in his right hand and breathes short puffs of warm air into his left fist. A clump of brown hair has fallen out of his hat and across his forehead. "Everyone knows everything about everybody," Ian says, tucking the clump of hair back under his stocking cap with his warmed-up left hand.

In Detroit, nobody knew anything about anybody. They were too busy worrying about the Negroes who wanted to work side by side with the white people. They were too busy worrying about the color of their neighborhood and kids who couldn't play outside anymore. Nobody had time to care about someone like Father Flannery or why he was visiting on a Saturday afternoon. People in Kansas have nothing but time. That's what Mama says whenever Grandma Reesa shows up without an invitation.

"Know what else they say?" Ian says, crawling forward a few inches on his hips and elbows. The boot with the thick heel drags behind.

Daniel shakes his head. "Got mud stuck in your shoes," he says, pointing at the tread on the bottom of Ian's boots. Ida Bucher will know he wore them in the field. She'll whip him because money doesn't grow on trees and neither do black boots with extra-thick heels. "You'll need a nail to dig that out."

"They say your Uncle Ray went crazy from drinking."

Daniel stands and looks back at his house. Though he can't see the driveway, he knows Father Flannery has parked his black car there. He will have gone inside and is probably sitting at the kitchen table. Mama will take his coat and serve him a piece of the apple pie that Aunt Ruth made after breakfast. Dad will drink a cup of coffee, cream and two sugars.

"He didn't even get his crop planted." Ian's head pops up, his legs go rigid and he fires.

Daniel stumbles backward, crushing a few feet of the new winter wheat and presses his hands over his ears. Beside him, Ian lifts up on his knees and watches his target. Wondering who or what may have heard them, Daniel scans the horizon.

"Got him," Ian says, flipping the safety and shifting the gun to the other side so he can pass it off to Daniel. "Now be real quiet. And get ready."

Keeping low to the ground where he'll stay out of sight, Daniel scoots toward Ian again and they switch places.

"Come on," Ian says, pulling back the bolt action. An empty casing pops out and flies over his left shoulder and after a new bullet has dropped into place, he pushes the rifle at Daniel. "Hurry up or you'll miss them."

"Who didn't plant his crop?"

"Your Uncle Ray," Ian says, flipping off the safety and pressing Daniel's right hand over the stock of the gun. "A lot of nice land going to waste. That's what Dad says. My brother says Ray got sick from all the drinking and the sheriff took him to Clark City. Says it's been coming for years. Says that's where people go to dry out."

"Dry out?" Daniel asks. Propping himself up on his elbows, he looks down the barrel of the gun and tries to balance it. The wooden stock is cold on his bare hands and against his cheek.

"Dry out. You know. Stop drinking. Your Uncle Ray is a drunk. Everyone says so. Says your Aunt Ruth is a married woman and belongs with her husband. Says he wouldn't be such a drunk if she'd go home."

With his lips pressed together, Daniel stares up at Ian.

"That's what they say. Not me. Hey, there's one."

Daniel flattens out so he can see under the barbed-wire fence. A hundred feet away, surrounded by unplowed ground covered with dry stubble, is the mound that had been Ian's target. One small head shaped like a giant walnut pops out of a hole in the center of the mound and then disappears. A few moments later, a prairie dog creeps out and lifts onto his hind legs. Its brown, furry body is plumper than the one Ian shot.

"Wait. Don't be too quick," Ian says.

"Who cares what they say about Aunt Ruth?" Daniel's breath warms the gun where it's pressed to his cheek. And then, remembering the words Dad used when he sent Uncle Ray away, Daniel says, "She's not my concern."

"Some people even say your Uncle Ray had something to do with taking Julianne Robison. Say that he is just that crazy. Even say he killed your Aunt Eve. But that was a long time ago."

"That's a lie," Daniel says, thinking that he'd know for sure if his own aunt was dead. "A God damned lie."

"I ain't saying it," Ian says. "'Course it's Jack Mayer who took Julianne. But you ought to know that since you're the only one who's seen him." Ian kneels behind the same clump of grass. "Watch what you're doing. Careful." Before the new boots, Ian didn't squat or sit on the ground much because getting up was too hard. It's easier now but he still groans on the way down. "Wait another second. We might see more."

The prairie dog that Ian shot lies at the base of the mound, which, according to Ian, means he grazed it. A direct hit would blow the animal a foot in the air. Ian said it was best when that happened. Best for who, Daniel thinks, as the prairie dog starts to chirp—slow steady chirps as it drops down onto all fours. His stubby tail flicks in sets of three.

"Ready." Ian waddles a few feet closer, close enough that Daniel smells his moldy clothes and new leather boots, but the prairie dog won't smell him because Ian made sure they were downwind.

"Whoever said that about Ray, you tell them I don't care," Daniel says, pressing his cheek against the gun until it digs into his cheekbone and his eyes water. "I don't give one good God damn."

Then he jabs his elbows into ground that is recently plowed and soft. Squinting through his right eye, he bites the inside of his cheek and tilts the barrel until the tip lines up in the sight.

"Don't talk. Take a deep breath, hold it, then fire."

The prairie dog crawls down the mound and begins to drag the injured one toward the hole.

"Not one good God damn bit," Daniel whispers.

"You got to be quick," Ian says, close enough that Daniel smells his breath. Slowly, Ian lifts his hands and covers both ears. "Now."

Daniel tightens his index finger, the trigger softening under the pressure. He inhales and squeezes his shoulder blades until his neck muscles ache and his lungs burn. The trigger collapses, and the gun fires. The prairie dog shoots up into the air and lands a few feet away. The chirping is gone.

"Got him," Ian shouts. He stumbles as he tries to stand, so stays put instead. "Now we have to wait. They'll be back. Be back for sure."

Peering through the rifle's sight, Daniel scans the field until he sees the dead prairie dog lying in the grass. Ian says prairie dogs are bad for the fields. He says they're rodents and that there will be lots more in the spring. Baby ones by June. They're the hardest to get. They don't come out like the others. Daniel drops the barrel of the rifle, flips the safety and pushes up on his knees.

"I'm not waiting around for another stupid prairie dog."

Being careful to step over the winter wheat, Daniel stands and walks toward home. Behind him, Ian stumbles with his old rhythm, the one he had before he got his new boots. God damn, Daniel hates that sound.

"Slow down," Ian calls out.

Holding the rifle at his side instead of over his shoulder, Daniel takes long steps toward home and doesn't look back.

Chapter 9

Trying to outrun the cold air that follows them onto the porch, Celia hustles everyone through the back door. Evie darts left, squeezes between Elaine and the doorframe and slips in front of Ruth.

"Sorry," she says, tripping over Ruth, and the two of them stumble into the kitchen.

"Evie." Celia grabs Evie's collar before she falls face-first on the kitchen floor. In a quieter voice, she says, "You be careful of Aunt Ruth. And mind yourself. We have company."

Celia pulls off her coat and tips her forehead toward Father Flannery, who sits at the head of the table. Arthur sits at the other end, and Reesa has taken a seat in between.

"So sorry to keep you waiting, Father," Celia says. "We lost track of time."

Evie steps up to Father Flannery, extends her hand the way she and Celia practiced in the living room the night before and says, "Hello, Father Flannery."

Father Flannery pushes back from the table, his knees falling open to make room for the belly that hangs between them. He takes the tips of Evie's fingers in both hands. "Fine day to see you, Miss Eve."

"I'm Evie in our house, Father. Eve is only for Grandma Reesa's house. And church."

Father Flannery studies Evie over the top of his glasses. The tip of his nose and chin are still red from the cold. He finally nods and drops Evie's hands. "Your hair is cut," he says to Ruth.

"Yes." Ruth touches the ends of her new shorter hair and smiles up at Elaine. When she looks back at the Father, he isn't smiling. Ruth drops her eyes to the floor.

"Elaine cut it, Father," Evie says. "She's going to color it, too. Red maybe."

Reesa, who has made herself at home in Celia's kitchen, having already brewed the coffee and set out the cream and sugar, shakes her head and squeezes her eyes shut. "Good gracious," she says.

Arthur scoots up to the table, the squeal of his chair legs silencing Evie and Reesa.

To break the sudden silence, Celia opens the refrigerator and says, "Has Reesa offered you pie, Father?"

Reesa frowns, causing deep creases to cave in at the top of her nose, and shakes her head at Celia. "Didn't seem the time for pie yet."

Father Flannery, still staring at Ruth, says, "Pie'd be real nice, Mrs. Scott. Real nice about now."

Arthur waves off Celia's offer of pie and focuses on Father Flannery. "Seems there must be something the church can do for Ruth," he says. "Something that can help her out of this mess."

"It's not that easy, Arthur. They've been married a good many years."

Arthur exhales and runs a hand through his hair, pushing it off his forehead.

"What about 'inadequacy of judgment'?" Celia says, leaning into the refrigerator and pushing aside a carton of eggs. No pie. She stands, hands on her hips, and looks around the kitchen. Everyone at the table is staring at her.

"One of my aunts on my mother's side married quite young," she whispers.

"That's good, Celia," Arthur says, motioning for her to hand him the coffee pot. "Does that work for us, Father?"

Celia unplugs the pot and passes it to Arthur. Without even tasting it, Celia knows the coffee is strong, too strong, because that's how Reesa makes it.

"That sounds like just what we need," Arthur says. "Inadequacy of judgment."

Father Flannery holds his mug out to Arthur and presses his glasses back onto the bridge of his nose. He sniffs as he does it, as if this will cement them into place. "That doesn't seem to apply, Arthur. Not after twenty years."

Reesa nods, closes her eyes and pats her forehead with a yellow handkerchief while pushing her mug across the table toward Celia to be refilled. Giving the pot a little shake to show that it's empty, Celia mouths the word "sorry" and steps to the counter to brew up some more.

"Sure it applies," Arthur says. "Inadequacy of judgment. We all had it."

He turns to Celia for help.

"They were very young when they married, right?" Celia says. "Young people don't always make good decisions." Then, dropping one spoonful of coffee into the percolator, shorting the batch by two scoops of grounds, she checks inside the stove. Still no pie.

"They were both adults," Father Flannery says, sipping his coffee. "Young, but adults. Both of sound mind. No undue force, I presume. How's that pie coming, Mrs. Scott?"

"Won't be but a moment, Father." Celia stands at the head of the table, her hands still on her hips. "I can't imagine what I've done with it."

Father Flannery leans back in his chair, his large stomach pushing against the edge of the table. "Did you try on top of the refrigerator? Some of the ladies like to keep their pies on top of the refrigerator."

"Father, there has to be something." Arthur rubs the heel of both hands into his eye sockets. "Undue force. There was undue force. You know what happened. We were all under undue force. That was a terrible time. For everyone."

Slipping behind Arthur, Celia grabs onto the top of the refrigerator and stands on her tiptoes. Nothing.

"I know. I know," Evie says, clapping her hands together. "The Clark City men took your pie."

"Please stop talking about Clark City," Celia says.

"But the kids at school say they escape all the time. Ian's brother says they catch rides on the backs of pickup trucks and jump off when they see the lights of the first house. Everyone knows that our house is the first house after the Brewster place. They take food. Like pie. They take food because they're hungry. Ian says a Clark City man cooked up old Mrs. Murray on the radiator, that radiator right over there in the corner. And Ian says a Clark City man stole Julianne Robison right out of her very own house."

"Good Lord in heaven," Reesa says. "Hush, child. No one took that pie. I put it on the front porch to cool."

Celia spins on her heel to face Reesa. "Reesa, why didn't you . . ." but Arthur gives her a look that tells her he's heard quite enough about the pie.

"So what about that undue force, Father?" Arthur says.

Father Flannery stands, staring at Ruth so hard that she can't lift her head. "I think we owe it to Ray to include him in these discussions. An annulment is no small matter."

"It damn sure isn't," Arthur says, also standing.

He is taller than Father Flannery by a good four inches but not nearly as round. Both men rest their fingertips on the edge of the table—Father Flannery on one end, Arthur on the other.

"Ray will not set foot in this house," Arthur says. "I'll make that perfectly clear."

"Understood," Father Flannery says. "We'll meet in the church, then. Or perhaps down at the café. When Ray returns, he'll have his thoughts heard." Father Flannery shakes his head as Elaine walks through the front door carrying the pie. "Thank you anyway, Mrs. Scott, but I'll need to be getting along."

"Twenty years this has been going on, Father. Where has the church been for twenty years?"

"And you, Arthur? Where have you been for twenty years?" The Father takes his coat from the back of the chair and drapes it over his arm.

Reesa pats her shiny, red cheeks with her handkerchief, the same one she carries into church every Sunday. Elaine sets the pie on the table and stands by Ruth, who is still staring at the floor. Celia crosses her arms and starts tapping her foot, but she stepped into her lavender slippers when they came back from their walk, so it doesn't make any noise.

"Thank you for the coffee, Mrs. Scott." The Father nods in Celia's direction. "Reesa," he says, giving Reesa the same nod.

"Father." From her spot near the stove, Ruth lifts her head, but not her eyes, and pulls her thin sweater closed as she wraps her arms around herself. "Maybe an annulment isn't called for."

"Ruth," Arthur says. "What are you saying? It damn sure is called for. That man beat you nearly senseless."

"Arthur," Celia says, holding up a hand, and then in a softer voice, "Ruth, you deserve some peace. I agree with Arthur. No matter what, that home is not safe for you."

Ruth touches the ends of her new hair. "I don't know if I can ever go back to him, Father." She turns toward Celia and Arthur.

"And I'm so grateful that you've taken me in. But I can't have an annulment."

Father Flannery crosses his arms and rests them on his large stomach. "A married woman goes back, Ruth. She doesn't live in her brother's house."

"Yes, Father. I'll stay married, but I don't know if I can go back."

"Ruth, honey," Celia says, running a hand over Ruth's new hair. "You don't have to do this."

"Damn sure don't," Arthur says.

Reesa crosses her arms and frowns because Arthur cursed again in front of Father Flannery.

"They're right, Ruth," Father Flannery says, sniffing and pushing his glasses into place. He stands for a moment, fixing his eyes on Ruth as if the Holy Spirit will sort out the problem if he gives it time and a little silence. "Is there something more I should know?"

"No, Father. Nothing."

Still staring at Ruth, Father Flannery pulls on his black overcoat, tugs his collar into position and puts on his hat. "Reesa," he says, keeping his eyes on Ruth. "Anything I should know about?"

Reesa stretches her chin into the air and pats the folds of her neck. With her eyes closed and her face tilted toward the ceiling, she says, "No, Father. Nothing at all."

"What about you, son?" Father Flannery says.

Inside the back door, Ian and Daniel stand, their cheeks red, their noses shiny because they've just come in from the cold.

"Do you think there's anything else I should know about?"

Daniel steps into the kitchen and looks around the room. "I'm not sure what you mean, Father. We were out"—he pauses—"walking."

"Yeah," Ian says, stepping up next to Daniel and rubbing his right hip with the heel of his palm. "Out walking." Ian seems to shrink every time Celia sees him.

"Very well, then." Father Flannery steps away from the table, pushes in his chair and tips his hat. "It seems we've no need to discuss this matter again." He turns toward Ruth. "I'd like to see you in church tomorrow."

"She hasn't been in church, Father," Arthur says, "because Ray beat her face to a pulp."

Father Flannery ignores Arthur. "Tomorrow, then. You're looking well, Ruth, quite well. Doesn't she look pretty with her new hair, Eve?"

"I'm Evie, Father."

Chapter 10

Leaning against the kitchen sink, her arms crossed, Celia taps her lavender slipper. Reesa struggles out of her chair and shuffles after Father Flannery. Facing Celia on the opposite side of the kitchen, Arthur stands, his arms also crossed. He lowers his head, staring at her from under the hood of his brow, and as his mother passes, he steps aside to make room without ever taking his eyes off Celia. Daniel and Ian have disappeared down the basement stairs, and Elaine, pressing a finger to her lips so Evie won't speak, leads Evie out of the kitchen toward her bedroom.

Celia and Arthur stand facing each other, not moving and not speaking. The floor creaks as the two girls pass, and when they have closed the bedroom door behind them, the house falls silent. Ruth slips into the small space between the side of the stove and wall, puts her hands in her apron pockets, and lowers her head. Outside, Father Flannery's engine starts up. Arthur straightens to his full height and unfolds his arms.

"Put a pot of water on to boil. The big pot," he says and follows his mother outside.

Celia, thinking Ruth is no bigger than Evie tucked between the wall and the stove, turns toward her and smiles. When they moved into the house, the stove sat square in the corner, but Reesa moved it because she said a person would want to get a mop in there. She said Mrs. Murray wasn't much of a housekeeper, God rest her soul, so it wasn't any wonder the stove was pushed to the wall.

"I'll speak to him," Celia says, wrapping her arms around her own waist. "You don't have to go back, Ruth. We want you here. With us. It will work out. It will."

Ruth nods. "I have to tell him. Waiting won't solve anything."

"No," Celia says, as gently as she can, as gently as if she were talking to a sick child. "Let me."

Ruth nods again. She starts to slip back into her corner until Celia pulls out a chair from the kitchen table and motions for her to sit. In the months since they moved to Kansas, Ruth's skin isn't as pale as it once was and she lifts her eyes when she talks to a person. Now, after sitting for a few minutes with Father Flannery, she is back again, to the frail woman, carrying a cold strawberry pie, who stepped so carefully out of the truck on the Scotts' first day in Kansas.

"Thank you," Ruth says. "I'll put on Arthur's water and start supper."

Celia smiles, and walking onto the back porch, she grabs her blue sweater from the row of hooks near the door. She breathes in dry, cool air and presses the sweater to her face, smelling her own perfume. It reminds her of Detroit because she doesn't bother with perfume here in Kansas. Taking a few more deep breaths, as if the cold air will fortify her, she pulls on the sweater, straightens the seam of each sleeve and steps outside.

The sun has moved low in the sky, hanging barely above the western horizon. Soon the chilly afternoon will be a cold evening. She would have said it smelled like snow had she still lived in Detroit, but she doesn't know if Kansas snow smells the same. Pulling her sweater closed, she walks down the three steps toward Arthur, who is standing just beyond the garage.

"What do you need the hot water for?" she calls out when she thinks she's close enough to be heard. Crossing in front of the garage where she can see around the far corner, she stops and drops her arms to her side. Arthur and Reesa stand at the edge of the light thrown from the back porch. "What are you doing?"

"Ma brought it for supper," Arthur says, without looking up.

"I have soup and sandwiches," Celia says. "Ruth is laying it out."

"Now we have chicken."

Standing next to Arthur, Reesa tugs on a rope tied off to a beam jutting out a few feet from the garage's roofline. On the other end of the rope, a chicken hangs, suspended by its wiry, yellow legs. The bird is nearly motionless, seemingly confused by its upside-down perspective. Arthur grabs its head and Reesa steps back.

"I need to talk to you, Arthur," Celia says, buttoning her sweater's bottom two buttons and squinting at the bird. "Reesa and I both need to talk to you."

Gripping the chicken's head in his left hand, Arthur raises his eyebrows at his mother. Reesa dabs the folds on her neck with the corner of the yellow and white checked apron tied around her waist.

"Whatever it is can wait," Arthur says. He lifts the knife in his right hand as if inspecting the sharpness of the blade and rotates it slowly. It would have sparkled if there had been any sunlight.

"No," Celia says, glancing at Reesa. "It really can't."

In one seamless motion, Arthur rolls the bird's head slightly to the left and pulls the knife across its neck. He doesn't cut so deeply that the head comes loose in his hand. Instead, it dangles as if hanging by a hinge. Blood shoots out, a bright red, perfectly shaped arch. Celia lets out a squeaking noise and stumbles backward. After the initial gush, the blood slows and begins to flow in a smooth steam that lands in a bucket that Arthur kicks a few times until it is in the right spot. Then, with the knife still in his hand, he says to Celia, "Okay, what is it?"

Celia watches the bird, both of them motionless. Steam rises up where Arthur made his cut.

"Well," Arthur says. "Tell me. We've only got a few minutes. That water ready?"

"No, I, well . . . Ruth is putting it on."

Reesa tugs at the knot tied around the bird's legs, testing that it's strong enough and then walks to the house. "We need the water for scalding, Celia."

It is the kindest tone she has ever used with her daughter-in-law.

"Ruth is pregnant," Celia says before Reesa can disappear into the house.

Arthur drops both hands to his sides and his chin to his chest. The porch light shines on the threesome, throwing a long thin shadow that falls at Celia's feet. Reesa stops at the bottom step leading to the back door. The bird, hanging upside down, its neck slit open, its blood slowing to a trickle, begins to beat its wings in the air. Celia jumps backward, Arthur doesn't move and Reesa dabs her neck again with her apron. The bird wildly flaps its wings one final time before hanging lifeless. Its heavy body sways on the end of the rope, but eventually, even that motion slows and stops. The only movement, tiny feathers, floating, spinning, drifting on the cold night air.

"What is it doing?" Celia asks, backing out of the yellow light.

"Dying," Arthur says. "What do you mean, pregnant?"

Celia glances at Reesa, who has taken her foot off the first step, and says, "Just that. She's pregnant."

"You knew?" Arthur asks Reesa.

She nods.

"How is she pregnant for God's sake? She's forty years old."

Celia takes two steps forward, back into the light, and cocks one hip to the side. "Forty is not so old."

"God damn it, Celia, this is not funny."

Reesa steps closer. "It's not meant to be funny, son. Ruth has carried three other babies over the years, but never more than a few months." She lowers her eyes and shakes her head. Her shoulders droop and roll forward, and her chin rests in the rolls of her neck. When she exhales, her breath shudders.

"Then why now?" Arthur asks. A dark shadow covers his lower jaw and his eyelids are heavy. He pulls off his leather gloves, and holding them in one hand, he shoves his knife in his back pocket and rubs his forehead.

"What do you mean, why now?" Celia says, holding up a hand to silence Reesa. "Why, it's not so hard to figure out. Look at her, after these months since we came back. She's happy. She's healthy. Thank God, she's healthy again. This baby has a chance."

"What chance does it have with a father like Ray?"

"Arthur," Reesa whispers.

Celia takes another few steps toward Arthur. "You will never call this baby an 'it' again. He or she will have everything. Love and a home and . . ."

Arthur leans forward, spitting his words in Celia's face. "What home? Our home? Christ, this is why she won't annul the marriage, isn't it? He'll be back, you know. You think this is how it'll be? Well, it won't. He'll be back and he'll want his wife and that baby."

"You don't know that. Maybe he'll stay in Damar."

Celia doesn't believe it even as she says it. She wishes the rumors were true. She wishes Floyd Bigler had shipped Ray off to Clark City where he'd rot and die behind those block walls. Instead, Arthur and William Ellis, Ray's other brother-in-law, threw Ray in the back of William's pickup truck. William, having had his fill of Ray's drinking over the years, agreed to keep him just long enough.

When Arthur came home stinking of vomit and whiskey, Celia asked him what "long enough" meant. Arthur shrugged as he stripped off his clothes. "Let's hope long enough is long enough," he had said.

"He'll be back, Celia," Arthur says. "That's for damn sure. You think any father is going to let his son grow up in another man's house?"

"We don't know it will be a boy."

Arthur throws his gloves on the ground. He looks like he wants to kick something, but the only thing close enough is the dead bird. He seems to think about it but kicks the ground instead.

"God damn it, Celia. Boy or girl, it doesn't matter. You think I'll be able to keep Ray away? I have to work, you know. I can't be here every God damned second. You think I'll be able to keep Ruth and her baby safe?"

Celia closes her eyes but does not back away. She can smell the aftershave Arthur splashed on for Father Flannery, his worn leather gloves, his wool jacket. He is more of a man now that they are living in Kansas. She would never say it to him, imply that he was less before, doesn't even like to think it. Waiting until Arthur has finished shouting and the night air has fallen silent again, Celia opens her eyes.

"Yes," she says, hoping Arthur will protect them all, hoping he is stronger here in Kansas because he has to be. "Yes, I do."

Ruth stands on the back porch. Father Flannery's cologne hangs in the air, rich and spicy. She breathes it in, the same smell as Sunday morning mass. Waiting for her face to heal, she hasn't been to St. Anthony's for almost a month. Celia and Arthur were afraid of the things people might say if they saw the swollen eyes, blackened and bruised cheek and jaw, split lip. They wanted to protect Ruth. In the early years of her marriage, Ruth had been afraid, too. The first time Ray put a fist to her, she hid her cuts and bruises with powder and scarves, but then she realized that people knew the beatings were inevitable, and shouldn't Ruth have known the same?

Through the screened door, she listens for Arthur and wishes he would come inside so they could deliver the food to the Robisons. Going there takes her close to church, a half block away, takes her close enough to feel like she's still being a good Christian. Now that Ruth is living with Arthur and his family, she rides along on the deliveries to the Robisons and walks the food to Mary's front door, even puts it in the refrigerator and cleans out the spoiled leftovers, mostly things Ruth brought the week before. She hopes Arthur will still take her, that he won't be too angry.

Mary never asks why Ruth suddenly started coming along, but she knows. Everyone knows. And every week, as Ruth jots baking instructions on the notepad near the telephone, Mary Robison tells Ruth to stop troubling herself, that all this lovely food won't bring Julianne home. Nothing, nothing, will bring Julianne home. Ruth always smiles as best she can and continues to bake the pies and mix up the casseroles, because once, when they were so much younger, she and Mary Robison were friends, and Eve, too. The three of them, when they were young, when they had long, shiny hair and bright, clear skin, before husbands and children, they were friends. Because this is true, and because maybe, even though she can't let the thought settle in long before blinking it away, Ray did something awful to Julianne Robison, Ruth still takes the food.

Ruth's first lie to Floyd was a reflex. Standing in her kitchen, Ray watching her, Floyd slapping his beige hat on his thigh, she nodded yes, that Ray had been home all night. She lied out of reflex, the same as a person raises her arms to her face to fend off a fist. She lied because she was afraid not to. A hundred nights, Ray had gone off without telling Ruth where he was going, and a hundred nights, no little girl went missing. But the night Julianne disappeared was different. Ray remembered that once he had been happy. He remembered Eve because she skipped out of Mother's back door and stood right before him, smiling up with blue eyes and tender, flushed cheeks. Only it wasn't Eve, it was Arthur's youngest, and as deeply as Ray must have remembered what it was like to be happy, the moment he walked back into his own home with Ruth, he must have remembered that it was all gone.

"Daniel," Ruth says, when a set of footsteps stop at the top of the basement stairs. She turns toward the house. "Is that you?"

"I'm sorry, Aunt Ruth." He is about to close the door but stops when he sees her. "I didn't see you out there."

Ruth points across the porch to the gun cabinet in the back hallway.

"I think you didn't quite get things put away as you'd like," she says. "I thought you might want to tend to it before your father does."

Daniel scoots a small stool to the cabinet. He can't quite reach the top where Arthur keeps the key to the lock.

"Thank you," Daniel says, as the cabinet hinges creak and the lock snaps into place. He stands in the dark doorway, the kitchen light shining behind him. "I think your water is boiling. Do you want me to shut it off?"

"No, thank you."

Outside, Arthur and Celia's voices fade.

"You know, Daniel," Ruth says. "Your father, when he was a boy, he was a good shot. I'll bet you are, too. In your blood, you know. Are you a good shot?"

Daniel shuffles his feet and clasps his hands behind his back. "Yes, ma'am," he says. "I guess I am."

"So I thought."

"Is everything okay, Aunt Ruth?" Daniel asks, setting the stool back in its spot on the porch. "Aren't you cold out here? Do you want a coat or something?"

Ruth smiles into the darkness to hear Daniel's voice sounding more like a man's than a boy's. These children, Daniel and Evie, are ghosts of her childhood. Daniel so like his father, a young Arthur, working his way toward manhood, hoping nothing will derail him. Evie, resembling Eve so strongly, sometimes too painful to look at.

"I'm fine," she says, nodding toward the cabinet. "You take care."

"Yes, ma'am."

Beyond the screened door, Mother stands at the bottom of the stairs, her back to Ruth. As large as she is, Mother looks small there at the bottom of the steps, her head lowered, her shoulders sagging. Past Mother, on the far side of the garage where the porch light barely reaches, Celia and Arthur have started arguing again. Arthur's voice is tired and desperate, as tired and desperate as Ruth has felt for twenty years, while Celia's words have hope, the same hope that Ruth knows is growing inside her. She felt this hope with all three of her babies, but knew, even from the beginning, that none of them would live. Ray had beaten them out of her. Not literally. He never even knew they had been there, nestled inside Ruth's womb. Sadness killed those babies.

The first pregnancy had surprised Ruth. The baby didn't come in the beginning months of marriage. Ray had needed her, almost loved her in those early days. Together, they had mourned Eve, leaving no room for anyone else, not even a baby. Soon after, Arthur left to follow the best jobs in the country all the way to Detroit, but really Father drove him away, and Mother said no one should judge what's between a man and his son. Best to let things rest in peace. Arthur's leaving was the end of something for Ruth and Ray, or maybe it was the beginning of living with the truth, and this was when Ruth felt the smallest inkling of her first baby. She didn't arrive with a vengeance, this baby that Ruth was certain was a girl, but with a blush of nausea, a hint of fatigue, the tiniest shift in perspective. And then she vanished, bled away in spots and smudges that Ruth bleached out in the bathroom sink while Ray slept in the next room. Then came the second and third. Something inside her, some glimmer of hope, sparked those babies that bled away like the first. Ruth knew that without hope, no more children would live or die, so she gave up on happiness and a future and that was the end of her babies—until now.

Chapter 11

Standing together in the small hallway between the kitchen and the back porch, Celia straightens Arthur's collar and centers his newly polished belt buckle.

"That should do it," she says, patting his chest with both hands.

"Do I have to go?"

Celia lifts up on her bare toes, kisses him once, but he pulls her back, and starts the kiss over. He smells like soap and the aftershave Celia insisted he splash on after she made him shave.

"Yes, you have to go," she says, wiping away the pink smudge on his upper lip and giving him one more quick kiss before ducking and slipping from between his arms.

"I shouldn't be leaving all of you alone." Arthur looks into the living room where Ruth and Evie are thumbing through a photo album, a table lamp throwing a warm circle of light on them. "Where's Daniel? He should be in here."

"He's outside," Celia says. "Watering Olivia like you told him to. We'll be fine, Arthur. Everything will be just fine."

In the week since Celia told Arthur that Ruth is pregnant, he has begun locking doors, something he didn't bother with once they left Detroit and the smell of burnt rubber behind. He comes home every day now over his lunch break, has fixed the locks on two windows, and has started barking at everyone in the house, except Ruth, about things like scooting in chairs and shutting off lights.

Celia takes his wool coat from the hook near the back door, and in a whisper that won't carry to the living room, she says, "You go have fun. It'll be nice that you and Jonathon spend some time together."

"I see the boy damn near every day."

"That may be, but you're going all the same. Enjoy. You always fare well in poker. We'll all be fine, just fine."

"You lock up after I leave?"

"Good enough," Celia says, kisses him one last time on the cheek and locks the door behind him.

Evie runs a hand over the patchwork quilt lying across her legs as Aunt Ruth points to a pink satin square.

"This was your Aunt Eve's first Sunday dress," she says. "And this piece is from your father's favorite pair of jeans. He wore them until his belly was bursting through the buttons."

Evie snuggles into Aunt Ruth, laughing at the thought of Daddy having such a big belly and searching for another quilt square that might belong to Aunt Eve. "What about this?" she asks, tracing a line around a lavender calico patch.

Aunt Ruth shakes her head. "That was mine. An apron from a doll I once had."

Next, Evie points to a green velvet square, and as Aunt Ruth nods and smiles, Evie leans forward and brushes one cheek against the soft fabric. It doesn't smell like Aunt Eve should smell, sweet like a flower, but instead like Grandma Reesa's basement.

"Eve's favorite Christmas dress," Aunt Ruth says. "She tried to wear it to school once. Mother caught her at the back door because the hem stuck out from under her overcoat. My goodness, Mother was angry." Aunt Ruth pulls a red leather photo album back onto her lap and flips through the early pages. "Here. Yes, here is a picture of that dress."

Evie wraps the quilt around her shoulders like a cape and presses closer to Aunt Ruth's side. "Do you think she looks like me?" Evie asks, staring down on a little girl standing on the steps of St. Anthony's, the same steps where Evie plays every Sunday morning while Daddy and Mama say their hellos.

Touching the little girl's picture, Aunt Ruth smiles through closed lips, nods but doesn't answer.

"Did Aunt Eve love the green dress as much as she loves the dresses in her closet?"

"Yes, I'm sure she did."

"Why does she have all of them?"

Aunt Ruth flips to the next page, and pointing out another picture of Aunt Eve, this one of a little girl sitting alone on Grandma Reesa's back porch, Aunt Ruth says, "They were to be for her wedding."

"Aunt Eve is getting married?" Evie pops up on her knees and pulls the quilt to her chin.

"Not now, sweet pea. A long time ago. She wanted each bridesmaid to have her own special dress."

"So she made all of them?"

"We all did. She and I and Mary Robison. Mrs. Robison was, is, a wonderful seamstress." Aunt Ruth flips to another page in the album. A picture pops loose as she lets the new page fall open. "Here we are," Aunt Ruth says, tucking the picture back into the white corner tabs. "All three of us. Your Aunt Eve wanted to work with Mary one day, to be as good a seamstress."

Evie leans forward and squints into the face of Mrs. Robison. The picture was taken long before she grew up and had Julianne, long before Julianne disappeared. The kids at school say that since Julianne is gone, maybe the Robisons will take Evie in trade. Maybe since Julianne was the same age as Evie and had the same white braids, the Robisons will make Evie move in with them. That very Tuesday at recess, Jonah Bucher said he was going to change Evie's name to Julianne. He said everyone liked Julianne better than Evie anyway. Every other kid said the same and they called Evie by her new name all through recess until Miss Olson made them stop or else she'd call every mother and father of every kid in school.

"What about you, Aunt Ruth? Did you want to sew, too?"

Aunt Ruth pokes both of her thumbs into the air. "I'm all thumbs. Never as handy as those two."

"Which dress were you going to wear?"

"I hadn't decided. Whichever Eve chose for me, I suppose. But she was young when we made those dresses. Only dreaming of a wedding. Someday."

"And did she get older and get married?"

Aunt Ruth closes the photo album, patting the top cover three times and resting her palm there. "Sometimes things don't work out like we plan." She smiles down at Evie.

"Well, I think they're the most beautiful dresses. Maybe I'll use them when I get married one day."

"That would make Eve very happy."

In the kitchen, Mama is making cooking noises—pots and pans rattle and the gas stove goes *click, click, click* as Mama turns on the back burner that doesn't work so well. Elaine is off with Jonathon's mama, learning how to make piecrusts. Evie wonders if Mama's feelings are hurt because Elaine would rather learn about pies from someone else's mama. Smelling pot roast and roasted new potatoes, Evie lays her head on Aunt Ruth's shoulder. The radiator kicks on, making her think of old Mrs. Murray, but only until she remembers that Mama said Mrs. Murray died in a hospital bed. Mama said no one was cooked up on that radiator or any other. Evie closes her eyes and lays her right hand on Aunt Ruth's stomach.

"Too soon," Aunt Ruth says. "In a few weeks, maybe."

Pressing her face into Aunt Ruth's arm where her nose and lips will warm, Evie knows the baby is too tiny to feel. Mama says it's like a bean now, like a lima bean, not a pinto bean. She says everyone has to take care of Aunt Ruth so her baby will have strong lungs and a healthy heart. Mama says when the baby comes, Aunt Ruth will move into Elaine's room and Elaine will move in with Evie, so Aunt Ruth and her baby can have a room all to themselves. Evie wants to ask Aunt Ruth if she will have a blue baby and will Daddy put it in the oven like they did Ian's baby sister. When Ian's dad first thought the baby was dead, he put her in the oven until the doctor could come. That's what Ian said. And then when they opened the door, she was kicking and breathing and all the way alive again. Instead of asking Aunt Ruth if her baby will be blue, Evie closes her eyes and imagines she is like the princess and the pea, except she will feel the lima bean in Aunt Ruth's stomach.

"Who was Aunt Eve going to marry?" Evie asks, thinking that she probably isn't a princess because she can't feel anything except the buttons on Aunt Ruth's dress.

Taking a deep breath, Aunt Ruth lifts her chin, and says, "A good man. She was supposed to marry a good man."

Daniel is glad Dad went out for the night. If he were home, he'd be yelling at Daniel about something. That's what Dad does most of the time now, yells at Daniel. Poking his potatoes and pushing them around the plate, he silently curses when one tumbles onto the red tablecloth Evie put out. Now he wonders if he'll have to confess to Father Flannery or does it not count if you only think the bad words without actually saying them. Waiting until Mama isn't paying attention, Daniel picks up the potato chunk and scoots his plate to cover the buttery stain. He glances up, wondering if anyone saw. Aunt Ruth winks and presses a finger to her lips.

Daniel tries to smile back, but every time he looks at Aunt Ruth since she caught him sneaking the rifle, he thinks she knows about the prairie dogs. He imagines that she saw him shoot that animal for no damn good reason, blow its head clean off. That's what Ian had said. He went back and found that prairie dog with its head blown all the way off and showed it to his brothers so they would stop calling Daniel a city kid. Ian said he lifted that dead prairie dog up by its tail and flung it as far as he could, and his brothers had said Daniel must be a pretty good shot to blow off the head but leave the rest. Biting his lower lip and stabbing a new potato with his fork, Daniel wishes he'd never shot that prairie dog because he can't ever take it back. But he did, and Aunt Ruth knows he has been taking the gun without permission.

"What was that?" Evie says, her mouth full of a buttered biscuit.

Daniel shakes his head at her. "Stop talking with food in your mouth."

Evie swallows, rocking her head forward to help the biscuit go down. "There's nothing in my mouth."

"There," Aunt Ruth says, staring past Daniel toward the kitchen window. "Is that what you heard?"

Mama pushes back from the table. "I didn't hear anything," she says, pressing out the pleats on the front of her dress. It's what she does when she's nervous, like when Dad went to meetings in Detroit about the Negro workers or the news showed pictures of burned-up cars and buildings. She hasn't done it much since they moved to Kansas where they haven't seen a single Negro or burned-up car. Also, Mama doesn't wear skirts with pleats much anymore.

Evie nods, wiping a crumb from her chin. "That. What is it?"

Daniel turns in his seat, careful not to scoot his chair or make any noise. Through the white sheers, the window is black. "It's the wind."

"That's not wind," Evie says too loudly.

Daniel frowns and quiets her with a finger to his lips.

Again, as loudly as before, Evie says, "That was not wind. That was a thud. There it is again."

"Yes," Mama says, still pressing her pleats. "I hear it."

"I think Daniel's right." Aunt Ruth tucks her napkin under the lip of her plate and stands. "Probably the wind. But to be on the safe side, I'll check."

"No, Aunt Ruth," Daniel says, standing with a jerk and catching his chair before it tumbles over. "I'll go. I should go."

"Both of you stay put," Mama says. "I'll have a look."

Evie jumps out of her seat and leaps toward Mama. "Let Daniel go," she says.

Mama wraps an arm around Evie and kisses the top of her head. All four turn when something bumps the side of the house just below the kitchen window. The white sheers tremble.

"Someone's outside the window," Evie says, her voice muffled because her face is pressed into Mama's side.

"Na," Daniel says, watching the curtains, waiting for another thud. "There's no one out there." But he's not sure now. The wind doesn't bump into the house or stumble around the side yard. He wishes his heart weren't beating so loudly because he can't hear over it. He hates his God damned beating heart when he can't hear over it, even tries to hold his breath to slow it down.

At the sound of another thud, Evie pulls away from Mama and points at the window. "It's a Clark City man," she says. "That's what it is." And then she whispers. "It's Jack Mayer. He's back and he's looking for food. Maybe he's even got Julianne with him."

"Shut up, Evie," Daniel says. "It's not a Clark City man. And it's not Jack Mayer. Shut up."

As the weather has turned colder, the pond near the curve in Bent Road has shrunk, dried up like every other pond around. Every time Daniel passes it, he looks for the tips of Jack Mayer's boots, thinking he might be lying at the bottom of that pond. Daniel has never seen him, and Ian says he won't because Jack Mayer has to be alive since he's the one who swiped Julianne Robison.

"Kids, please," Mama says. "Stop your bickering."

Aunt Ruth tucks Evie under her arm while Mama sidesteps toward the back door.

"I'm sure it's nothing," Mama says, but she's inching toward the porch like she definitely thinks it's something. "Evie, you stay here with Daniel and Ruth. I'll go . . ."

"No, Mama." Daniel walks around the table, tilts his head down and looks up at Mama from under his brow. "I'll give a look-see."

It's what Dad would have said.

Stepping onto the porch, Daniel pulls the door closed behind him and exhales a frosted cloud. He yanks on the knob again, listening for the click that tells him the door is latched good and tight, and once he hears it, he thinks he should feel more like a man. Instead, he slouches and pulls up the collar of Dad's flannel jacket because maybe whoever is stomping around their side yard will mistake Daniel for Dad. Mama says that by his next birthday, Daniel will be as tall as Dad. Keep eating Aunt Ruth's good cooking, she says, and you'll be as broad, too. He gives Aunt Ruth, Mama and Evie a thumbs-up sign through the window in the back door and walks across the screened-in porch. With the toes of his leather boots hanging over the first stair, he sees nothing or no one as far as the porch light reaches.

Ian had clipped out the latest story about Jack Mayer from page 3 of the *Hays Chronicle*, the shortest one yet, and one of many that didn't make page 1. After nearly four months, police now believe Jack Mayer has either left the Palco area or has died of exposure. Authorities at the Clark City State Hospital declined to comment on Jack Mayer's whereabouts, other than to say the hospital had successfully implemented new security measures. After Ian showed Daniel the article that he kept under his mattress along with a dozen others about Jack Mayer, he took Daniel out to the barn and showed him a wadded-up flannel blanket and empty tin can that were hidden behind three hay bales and an old wheelbarrow. Daniel kicked the can across the dirt floor. Ian stumbled after it, his right side lagging behind because he didn't have on his new boots, picked it up, and placed it back with the blanket because he thought the tin can and blanket were proof positive that Jack Mayer was alive and well and living in the Bucher barn. "No need to make a crazy man mad," Ian had said as he cleaned the brim of the can with his shirttail.

At the bottom of the stairs, Daniel tucks his bare hands under his arms, stomps his feet, and looking toward the barn, he wonders if Jack Mayer might just be hiding in there. Mama found the pie that Aunt Ruth baked for Father Flannery and nothing else has gone missing in the house except the last piece of Evie's birthday cake, which Daniel knows Dad ate but won't admit. Ian said their food disappeared all the time. He said Jack Mayer stole it right off their kitchen counter. He said Jack Mayer crawled through their windows every night and helped himself to corn muffins, sliced pork roast and ham and bean soup. Daniel asked Ian how he could be sure Jack Mayer was eating all that food with so many brothers living in the house. Ian had said that no man alive could eat like Jack Mayer because Jack Mayer is a mountain of a man.

Walking into the center of the gravel drive, Daniel turns in a slow circle. Mr. Murray's old rusted car is still parked behind the garage. Mama complains about it, says it's dangerous to have around with young children in the house, but Dad says the children aren't so young anymore and he'll get to it when he gets to it. Next to the garage, near the fence line, stands the chicken coop that Dad and Jonathon started to build. Halfway through, Mama said no chickens because she saw the mess they left at Grandma Reesa's and because she didn't want to have any more dead chickens hanging in her yard. Dad told Jonathon he could have the wood if he'd tear it down.

Beyond the three-sided chicken coup, and opposite the garage, the barn seems to lean more than it did when they moved in.

Wondering who or what is hiding out there, Daniel wishes he had grabbed his rifle. But what if it is Julianne? What if Jack Mayer stashed her in there? More than ever, Daniel wishes Mama would have slammed into Jack Mayer at the top of Bent Road. But Ian's right. Mama must not have hit him, at least not directly, because he swiped Julianne Robison and a dead man couldn't do that. If Mama would have hit Jack Mayer, Daniel wouldn't have to worry about accidentally shooting Julianne and blowing her head off like he did when he shot that prairie dog.

Twice, in the week since he killed that animal, Daniel has gone shooting with Ian. He can sneak the gun out and return it, tucked back in the gun cabinet, fingerprints wiped off the glass, lock snapped in place, before Dad gets home from work. Shooting tin cans and glass bottles instead of prairie dogs, Ian says Daniel is a good shot, a damn good shot. Ian says that if Daniel practices a lot, almost every day, he will be the best shot of any kid around. Daniel wants to run back to get that gun but it seems so far away now. He hears the sound again, a loud thud coming from the side of the house near the kitchen window.

Taking slow, quiet steps, Daniel slides one foot in a sideways direction and meets it with the other as he walks in an arch that will lead him around the side of the house. He looks behind and ahead, behind and ahead, and at the edge of the boundary laid down by the porch light, he stops and listens. In between wind gusts, he hears something crushing small patches of dry grass. There is a rustling sound, another thud, his own heartbeat. He leans to his right, peering around the side of the house without stepping outside the yellow light. He leans farther, bending forward and bracing himself with one hand on his knee. Something moves. A dark shadow. Daniel stumbles, stands straight and presses a hand over his heart.

He knows now that Sheriff Bigler didn't haul Uncle Ray off to Clark City but that he is living in Damar for as long as William Ellis will keep him, hopefully until he's dried out. When Daniel thought his uncle was locked up, he imagined Uncle Ray might escape like Jack Mayer and live off stolen leftovers. Before he knew Uncle Ray was living far away in Damar, Daniel would lie awake at night, listening for him. He would imagine opening his eyes and seeing Uncle Ray's face pressed against his window, his breath fogging the glass so Daniel couldn't quite see which way that bad eye was pointing. But Damar was a whole other town and Uncle Ray was with a whole other family. This is when Daniel began to imagine Jack Mayer's face pressed against his window. His breath would be cold and wouldn't fog the glass like Uncle Ray's. Then Christmas got closer, and Mama said the best store for wool fabric was in Damar, and since she needed a new dress for the holidays and Damar was only a few miles away, the whole family should go. Now, standing in the middle of the gravel drive, the thud ringing in his ears, Daniel doesn't know if he should be afraid of Uncle Ray, who isn't living so far away, or Jack Mayer.

His heart has begun to beat so loudly that Daniel isn't sure if he hears the next sound. If he had been sure, he wouldn't have looked around the corner again. Instead, he would have waited and listened or maybe run for the house, but his beating heart is like cotton in his ears, so he braces himself again and leans forward. Even though the maple that grows along the side of the house is bare, all of its leaves raked up and burned in the trash barrel, the moonlight shining through the empty branches is not enough to light up anything that might be hiding. The light from the kitchen throws shadows on the nearest branches but doesn't reach any farther. If the something is still there, hiding under the window, it isn't moving now, and Daniel can't tell it apart from the rest of the darkness. He takes a step forward, watching, listening, and the shadow shifts again.

Holding his breath, Daniel thinks he hears something. It sounds like metal clanking against metal, like a chain tangled up with itself. He crouches down, pressing both palms on the ground. The back door doesn't seem so far away now. He could run to it, reach it in a dozen steps, but he can't move. Yes, that is the sound of a tangled-up chain, broken handcuffs. He hears breathing—heavy, hot, long breaths—and footsteps crushing dry dead grass, footsteps kicking up gravel.

Hoping to see that Aunt Ruth and Mama are watching him through the screened door, he glances at the porch, but sees no one. Aunt Ruth's stomach is beginning to swell but she covers it with aprons and Elaine's skirts that she cinches up at the waist with safety pins. "You're in charge," Dad had said to Daniel before leaving. Mama had smiled and brushed the hair from his eyes. For a moment, Daniel imagines Julianne is sneaking around the side of the house. He could be the one to find her. He'd be a hero and kids would like him without even caring how good of a shot he is. Daniel drops his head again, knowing the breathing and chains and footsteps are closer even though his heartbeat has filled his ears.

He decides it can't be Julianne because she wouldn't be wrapped in chains. He inhales, raises his eyes first and next his chin. Still crouched, his palms pressed to the ground, he cries out and falls backward.

"God damn," he says. "Good God damn already."

Standing at the corner of the house, her head inside the yellow cone of light, Olivia the cow looks down on Daniel. She seems to nod at him, and then she drops her snout to nuzzle the cold, hard ground. Her lead dangles from the red leather neck strap, the buckle and bolt-snap rattling like loose chain. Dad will be angry if he sees someone forgot to take it off.

"Good God damn."

Chapter 12

Over and over in her head and a few times aloud, Celia says, "It's the wind. Nothing but the wind." But she isn't sure. In Detroit, she feared firebombs, tanks and the Negro boys who called Elaine, none of which banged up against the side of her house. Being so new to Kansas, she isn't sure what she should be afraid of, but whatever it is, it is walking through her yard. Shivering because she is wearing only a thin cotton dress and no stockings on her feet, she leans forward. On the other side of the screened door, across the driveway, Daniel sidesteps around the house. If he goes much farther, she'll lose him in the dark. Behind her, Ruth and Evie huddle together inside the back door that Celia made them lock. She cups her hands together and blows hot breath inside them to warm herself.

"Can you see him?" Evie calls from inside. Through the frosty pane of glass, her voice is muted. She has wrapped both arms around Ruth's waist and must be standing on her tiptoes to see out the window.

Celia reaches to open the screened door, but Evie cries out and presses her face into Ruth's side.

"Okay, okay," Celia says, letting go of the cold handle and leaning forward until she feels the imprint of the mesh screen against her right cheek. "There he is. I see him." Exhaling a deep breath and motioning for Ruth to open the back door, she says, "It's Olivia. Olivia got out again."

Ruth flips the deadbolt lock, and Evie skips across the cold wooden floor and lands at Celia's side. Celia wraps one arm around her and opens the screened door so they can both see. A cold breeze slaps them in the face.

"See?" Celia says. "He's walking her back. Looks like her lead is on. Did you put it on without remembering to take it off?"

Evie shakes her head. "I took it off. I'm sure I did," she says through chattering teeth. "I walked her a little. But I took it off."

Celia watches Daniel until he and Olivia have disappeared through the gate and into the barn. When she can no longer see them, she steps back and motions for Evie to join her on a nearby wooden bench. Ruth flips a switch that floods the porch with light, then steps inside for a moment and reappears with Celia's lavender house shoes, one in each hand. She waves the slippers, which makes Evie giggle, tiptoes across the porch and slips the fuzzy shoes on Evie's bare feet.

"We shouldn't really walk Olivia," Celia says, wrapping both arms around Evie. "Left to her own, she could get hung up on that lead." Evie nods as Celia tightens the pink ribbon tied at the end of her single braid. "Be careful to always lock up the gate and take care to do as you're told. You know Daddy would be upset about this."

"Will we tell him?" Evie says, twisting and frowning.

"I don't see the need. I'm sure Daniel will slip it off and lock things up good and tight."

Evie smiles, nods, and lowering her head, she says, "I guess it wasn't Julianne out there, huh?"

Celia lifts Evie's chin with her index finger. "No, honey. It wasn't Julianne. Did you really think it was?"

"Just hoped, is all."

Celia glances at Ruth across the top of Evie's head. "Yes, I guess we all did. How about we say an extra prayer tonight? Especially for Julianne."

"Yes," Evie says. "An extra prayer."

"Good enough, then." Celia winks at Ruth and together they help Evie untangle her slippers from the hem of her robe so she can stand.

Evie giggles over the size of Celia's lavender slippers on her own small feet. "Thanks," she says once she has straightened out her legs and planted both slippers on the ground.

Celia smiles, gives a few tugs on the belt around Evie's terry-cloth robe and, hearing footsteps on the stairs and the squeal of the screened door opening, she turns her smile toward Daniel.

"Ruth."

Ruth stands.

"Ray," she says.

In the beginning, in the very beginning, Ray felt badly for hitting Ruth. Over many morning cups of coffee, Ruth told Celia about the twenty years she had spent with Ray. When he would wake the day after, sober, he wouldn't remember the black eye he had given Ruth, the split lip, the bruised cheek. He would look at her, puzzled at first, and then apologize. "It's hard," he would say. "So damned hard." Ruth said she understood. She understood well enough to dab powder on those early bruises, withdraw from cake sales with an upset stomach when her lips were split open and swollen, cancel lunches with her mother and father because of one of her headaches when Ray had blackened her eyes. As the years passed, Ray began to wake, sometimes before he was fully sober, and say, "This is your doing as much as mine." Finally, just, "This is your doing."

"Why are you here, Ray?" Celia says, stepping in front of Evie and gently pulling Ruth backward a few steps.

Ray glances outside at the sound of Daniel's footsteps on the stairs, and then turns back, placing one hand on the doorframe, one foot on the threshold. "Thought it might be around dessert time. Thought about a piece of Ruth's pie."

"We're not having pie tonight." Celia takes another backward step toward the house, keeping Ruth and Evie behind her. Daniel walks halfway up the outside stairs but says nothing because Celia shakes her head—a tiny movement, but enough.

"A cup of coffee maybe," Ray says, moving aside, and with the sweep of one hand, he motions for Daniel to pass by.

Slipping between Ray and the doorframe, Daniel stops next to Celia. He takes a half step forward, trembling.

"Too late for coffee," Daniel says, his voice barely more than a whisper.

"What's that you say?" Ray fills the doorway but doesn't cross the threshold.

Under his brown hat, Ray's hair is clean and the skin on his face is smooth. Standing beneath the light of the single bulb hanging in the center of the porch, his hat shading his face, he looks like a younger Ray, like the one Celia saw on her wedding day. Besides being clean-shaven, his face is swollen. She knows it's the alcohol, years and years of it, that makes his cheeks and jowls puffy and the lid over his bad eye droop. He is hanging on, probably by nothing more than his fingertips. He is sober, barely.

"I didn't hear your truck," Ruth says.

"Truck's dead. Walked up here thinking Arthur could give me a jump." Ray takes off his hat, holds it at his side and tips a nod in Evie's direction. "Thought about that pie, too."

"Arthur's not here." Celia takes Daniel's arm. "Try again tomorrow."

"Dan can help, can't he?" Ray glances at Daniel. "Arthur letting you drive a truck these days?"

The tips of Ray's boots hang over the edge of the threshold, teetering there, not quite inside, not quite out.

"No, Ray."

Everyone turns toward Ruth. She is almost lost, wedged between Celia, Evie and Daniel. Celia glances down at Ruth's belly. She has wrapped both arms around her waist as if hugging herself for warmth.

"Daniel can't help," Ruth says. "You try tomorrow. When Arthur is here."

"Sure is a cold one tonight," Ray says, winking his droopy lid at Celia. His good eye travels from her face down to the white buttons on the front of her dress. It lingers there long enough to be too long, while his cloudy eye floats about. "I can wait maybe. Nothing wrong with waiting a spell. Arthur be home soon?"

Caught between two answers, Celia can't reply. It's something about the way he stares at her, taking his time, letting his eyes linger, maybe imagining something. Wondering if the others notice and feeling ashamed for it, she shuffles her bare feet and wraps her arms around her waist.

"Tomorrow," Celia finally says. "You'll see Arthur tomorrow and no sooner."

Daniel yanks off Dad's jacket, slings it toward an empty hook where one arm catches, leaving the jacket to hang lopsided, and stomps into the kitchen. Evie follows, still clutching Mama, while Aunt Ruth flips the deadbolt and waits in the window until Uncle Ray's footsteps go down the stairs. Then she hurries into the kitchen ahead of Daniel, Mama and Evie, and leaning over the sink, she stands on her tiptoes so she can see out the window.

"He's leaving," she says quietly, as if Uncle Ray might hear, and hoists herself onto the counter for a better view. "He's at the end of the drive now."

"Ruth," Mama says, dropping Evie in her seat at the kitchen table. "Please get down before you hurt yourself."

"He's gone for sure," Aunt Ruth says, holding her swollen belly as she slides off the counter. "I'm so sorry for the trouble. So sorry if he scared anyone."

"I wish it had been Julianne," Evie says, poking her cold potatoes with the tip of her butter knife. "I wish we would have found her."

Mama tilts her head, sighs and brushes the hair from Evie's forehead.

"I should have had my rifle," Daniel says.

Mama's head lifts straight up. "Daniel, no," she says, reaching out to him.

He steps back and doesn't take her hand.

"Don't say that. Don't you ever say that."

"A rifle would have stirred up a mess," Aunt Ruth says, moving to stand next to Mama. "A real mess."

"Would have made a mess of Uncle Ray."

"Daniel," Mama whispers. "That is never a good answer. Never. You did fine, just fine. Your father will be very proud of you."

Daniel leans a bit so he can see between Mama and Aunt Ruth. "You left that strap on Olivia," he says to Evie. "She's a cow, not a dog."

"Did not," Evie says, stabbing a potato and waving it at Daniel. "Did not. Did not. Did not. You left the gate open."

Daniel steps forward, wanting to grab Evie by the hair and fling her onto the porch, fling her all the way back to Detroit.

"It's done now, kids," Mama says, pressing a hand to Daniel's chest. And then in a quieter voice, as if she's afraid Uncle Ray might hear, she says, "Let's please not argue."

"Sorry, Mama," Evie says.

Mama smiles, but it isn't a real smile. It's the smile she gives when Grandma Reesa walks through the back door without calling first.

"Have a seat, Daniel," she says. "Our dinner has gone cold. I'll warm it up."

"I'm not hungry," he says.

As he walks across the kitchen, the floorboards creak under Daniel's feet. Near the back door, he sees the gun cabinet. It's locked up tight. His rifle is resting just where it should be. Next time, he'll be thinking. Next time, he won't forget. Mama calls out again, offering to warm up a few extra rolls for him. He waves her off, doesn't bother with an answer, and once inside his bedroom, he pulls the door closed behind him. Waiting for the click that will tell him it has latched, he walks to his bed, lies down, pulls his knees to his chest and closes his eyes. Next time, he'll be ready.

Chapter 13

Holding her hands behind her back and taking small sideways steps, Evie edges toward Grandma Reesa's living room. Everyone else is sitting at Grandma's kitchen table, talking about how upset they are that Uncle Ray came to the house last night wanting Aunt Ruth's pie and a jump for his truck. Three times, Mama has told Daddy what a fine job Daniel did watching over all the ladies of the house, but Daniel is still feeling bad about it because he pulls away when Mama tries to brush back his bangs. In between chopping up a chunk of meat, Grandma Reesa keeps filling everyone's coffee cup, and Mama frowns every time Grandma drops another sugar cube in Daddy's. Aunt Ruth sits with her hands folded in her lap, not saying much of anything. Occasionally, she lifts her hands from her lap, wraps them around her coffee mug and takes a sip.

"Maybe you should go along and play upstairs, Evie," Mama says.

Evie unclasps her hands, bites her lower lip and says, "Okay."

"Mind the stairs in those stocking feet," Grandma Reesa calls out.

At the sound of Grandma's voice, Evie stops running and breaks into a slide that sends her floating through Grandma's over-stuffed living room. She sweeps past the coffee table, knocking over a frame, rattling a few of Grandma's knickknacks, and stirring up the sour, moldy smell that always hangs over Grandma's house. At the bottom of the staircase, she grabs the small plastic tote that usually holds her favorite doll's dresses, the ones that Aunt Ruth sews for her. With a running start, she takes the stairs two at time, slides down the narrow hallway on the second floor and is breathing heavily when she pulls Aunt Eve's door closed behind her.

Celia waits until she hears Evie's footsteps overhead before asking her next question. "You know him best, Ruth. Was he sober?"

Daniel stands. "Barely," he says, stepping away from Celia and leaning against the refrigerator.

"What do you know about being barely sober?" Elaine asks. She is sitting across from Celia, and as she speaks, she gazes up at Jonathon, who is standing behind her. She looks like a woman about to be proposed to and Jonathon like a man about to do the asking.

"I know plenty," Daniel says. "I know I was there and you weren't."

Jonathon takes Elaine's hand, pats it and says, "I'd guess Daniel knows what he's talking about."

"He was sober," Ruth says, nodding at Daniel. "Just barely."

"Well, that's it then," Arthur says. "He's back."

Reesa, standing near her kitchen sink, reaches into an overhead cabinet, and as she takes down the saltshaker and seasons the cubed steak she has laid out on a cookie sheet, she leans back and whispers to Celia, "You should salt the meat before you grind it. Not after." And then, in a louder voice, "I think Ruth should move here. Farther away has to be better. Let the dust settle for a while." She sets aside the salt and, as she takes a bag of bread crumbs from the freezer, she says, "You do know how to make bread crumbs, don't you?"

Celia takes a deep breath and smiles. "Yes, Reesa. I do."

"Ruth isn't moving here," Arthur says.

Ruth exhales a little too loudly, which makes Celia chuckle. She presses her lips together when Arthur glances at her.

"I'll help out however I can, Arthur," Jonathon says.

"What was that for?" Elaine asks because she, like Celia, saw Daniel roll his eyes at Jonathon.

"Nothing," Daniel says, studying his dirty, chipped nails when Arthur looks up at him.

Reesa finishes scattering the bread crumbs over the cubed meat. "Do you want to watch, Celia?"

From her seat at the kitchen table, Celia says, "I can see fine from here. Thank you."

"Can we forget about the meat for a minute?" Arthur says.

"When you do this yourself," Reesa says, leaning toward Celia as if no one can hear, "you should freeze the meat first, after you've cubed it. Makes the grinding easier."

Celia flashes another smile and the meat grinder begins to whine.

"Are we done with the meat, everyone?"

Reesa, breathing heavily from the effort it takes to turn the hand crank, ignores the question.

"We're done," Celia says.

"This is bad," Arthur says. "He's awful close now, and pretty soon, you'll be big as a barn."

Celia exhales, nodding as Reesa tilts the bowl of ground meat so Celia can see what it's supposed to look like. "She won't be big as a barn," Celia says. "We can still hide that peanut for a few months."

Nearly knocking Daniel to the floor when he stands, Arthur pinches his brows at him as if Daniel is somehow always in the way. "And what then? A half a mile away, Celia. What then?"

"Why are you angry with me? I didn't invite the man back."

"I didn't say I was angry with you. I said . . ."

"Please," Ruth says, pushing back from the table with one hand and holding the other over her stomach. "Don't argue. Maybe Mother is right. Maybe I should live here. It is a good bit farther away."

"You plan on staying locked up here for good?" Arthur says. "Never going to church again? Never going to the store? That," he says, pointing at her stomach, "will be hard to hide in a very short time."

"That's uncalled for, Arthur," Celia says, starting to stand, but Ruth holds up a hand that stops her.

"I understand what you're saying, Arthur. Really, I do. But I'm not your problem to solve. Let me move here with Mother. It will be easier. I've done it before. Lived here for a time." She pauses. "Lived here until things quieted down. Besides, Ray was sober. Maybe he'll stay that way."

Daniel, one foot crossed lazily over the other, clears his throat. "Ian says some folks think Uncle Ray did something to Julianne. He says folks think Uncle Ray is that crazy."

"Ray didn't do anything to that girl," Arthur says, leaning against the wall. "Man's a damn fool and a drunk, but he didn't take that child. Folks are just trying to piece together the past."

"How do you know that, Arthur?" Celia says, feeling that she should believe her husband, have faith in him, know that he'll protect his family. But since the moment Ray stood on her porch, his one good eye staring at the buttons on her blouse, she doesn't feel any of those things anymore. She doesn't believe. She's heard the murmurs when she and Ruth walk through the deli in Palco, seen the sideways glances. More and more, people believe it. They believe Ray is the reason Julianne Robison has never come home.

"How can you be so sure?" she says. "We should be cautious, more mindful."

Outside, a truck rambles down Reesa's driveway, stops and idles near the garage.

"Think your ride is here, Dan," Jonathon says, stepping back from the table for a better view out the kitchen window. "Yep, it's Gene Bucher."

"Can I go, Mom?"

Celia nods, motioning for him not to forget his overnight bag.

"Your toothbrush is in the side pocket," she calls out as the screened door slams. "And mind your manners."

When the truck passes by on its way back to Bent Road, Arthur sits again, but this time, instead of pressing his back straight and sitting with one foot cocked over the opposite knee, he leans forward and rests his head in his hands.

"Ray didn't do anything to Julianne Robison." He looks up at Celia, holds her gaze. "He didn't do it." He stares at her until she lowers her eyes. "And please don't you start talking about leaving," he says, turning toward Ruth. "You know damn well I can't have you living in this house."

The meat crank stops.

"I'll stay," Ruth says. "But only if you promise to listen to Celia. Don't be so sure of what you don't really know."

"Fair enough," Arthur says. "And in the meantime, no one, I mean no one, breathes a word about this baby." He scans the table, fixing his eyes on each person for a moment before moving on to the next. "I need some time to figure this out."

Celia smiles until the meat grinder begins to squeal again.

Evie opens Aunt Eve's closet slowly so that it doesn't make any noise, lays her tote bag on the floor and walks across the room to make sure the bedroom door is latched. On the table near the closet, the Virgin Mary stands, holding out her new hands, the ones Daddy glued on after Evie told him that Aunt Eve would surely be upset if they didn't fix her statue. Daddy asked Grandma Reesa first. She looked sad about it, but nodded and handed Daddy a tube of glue from the kitchen junk drawer. Evie runs a finger over a tiny spot of glue that Daddy didn't wipe clean. It has dried into a hard, clear bubble. Pressing on the door twice, Evie tiptoes back to the closet, lowers to her knees and unhooks the buckles on her tote bag one at a time.

Evie tries to love all of Aunt Eve's dresses the same, thinks that if she has a favorite among them, it will hurt Aunt Eve's feelings but she can't help herself. She loves the blue one best. She loves the three soft ruffles and the silky sash. She loves the silver flowers embroidered on the lapel that feel cool when she runs a finger over them. Most of all, she loves it best because, as she slips the dress off its hanger and presses it to her face, she can smell Aunt Eve. After taking one deep breath to make sure the flowery sweet smell is still there, she holds the dress by the shoulders, folds one side toward the center and then the other. Next, she drapes the dress over her left forearm and again over her right, lays it in the bag and refastens the two buckles.

Chapter 14

Daniel exhales hot breath into his cupped hands. Even through the old green sleeping bag that Ian brought up from his basement, the wooden floor is cold. The Bucher house doesn't have a heater, only a parlor stove in the main room off the kitchen where Ian's two older brothers are sleeping. In Daniel's house, they have a radiator, the same radiator that cooked up Mrs. Murray. Mama says that never happened, but every time it clicks on, he thinks he can smell roasted skin.

Watching the Bucher brothers through the opened bedroom door, Daniel wonders if they are the lookouts for Jack Mayer. He pulls his knees to his chest and scoots farther down into the sleeping bag that smells like someone peed in it. Ian had said the cats did it, but Ian's brothers laughed like Ian was the one who did the peeing. Next to Daniel, Ian is sleeping, and by the dual snoring coming from the bed in the corner, so are the two brothers who share Ian's room. Daniel breathes through his mouth so he can't smell the sleeping bag and covers his ears so he won't hear Jack Mayer climb through the kitchen window to sneak off with Mrs. Bucher's leftover brisket and mashed potatoes.

By morning, the house is warmer. The Buchers may not have radiators in every room, but they have enough people in their family to warm up the place quickly. Daniel pulls on a gray sweatshirt and the wool socks Mama packed for him and follows Ian into the kitchen. It smells like his kitchen, except for the pee smell that is stuck to him. Coffee bubbles up, bacon pops on the stove and dish soap foams in a sink of hot water. Daniel presses down on his hair and straightens his sleeves.

"Good morning, sir," he says when Mr. Bucher nods in his direction.

Ian nudges Daniel and muffles a laugh. "Something quick for us, Ma," he says, walking on one flat foot and one tiptoe. Since he got his new boots, he walks that way whenever he doesn't have them on, probably so he can forget about being crooked.

"Yeah, Ma," one of the older brothers says. He scoops a handful of potato peels out of the sink and tosses them in an old coffee can. "Daniel's going to show us all what a great shot he is. Okay we use your .22, Pa?"

Mr. Bucher nods over his coffee cup.

One of the brothers, the biggest, and the only one wearing a hat, turns in his seat. Mrs. Bucher doesn't seem like the type of mother who would allow hats at the table. Except when the man turns, it isn't a Bucher brother.

"Morning there, Dan."

Uncle Ray raises his cup and tips his hat.

*   *   *

Celia pretends to sleep as Arthur slips out of bed. She knows they'll be late to church if they don't get a move on, because the sun is high enough in the sky to fill their bedroom with light. Once Arthur has left the room, Celia pulls the blankets to her chin and tucks them under her shoulders. The front door opens, closes, and opens again and Arthur stomps his heavy boots. He only uses the front door when he is gathering wood for the fireplace from along the side of the house. When the night temperatures dip so low, the radiator can't keep up, but Arthur will have a fine fire going in no time. Newspapers crackle as he twists them into kindling and, after a few minutes, the sweet, rich smell of a newly started fire drifts into the bedroom. The house will warm quickly, but Celia wonders if even then she'll want to get up.

She pushed Arthur away last night, gently, but firmly, and this morning, she pretended sleep. She should tell him but won't because it'll only make things worse. She can't tell him how Ray looked at her out there on the porch the other night, how she can see what Ray is thinking and that it makes her ashamed. Or maybe Arthur would think her silly, or worse yet, selfish for thinking of herself instead of Ruth. Maybe she is silly and even selfish, too. Whatever this feeling is, shame or guilt, it'll pass. No, she can't tell Arthur, because if she really made him understand, if she made him appreciate that in the privacy of a single glance, a man can tell a woman that he is coming for her, he'd kill Ray. Just like that. He'd kill him.

"Morning, sir," Daniel says.

Uncle Ray looks at Mr. Bucher with his good brown

eye, while the bad eye seems stuck on Daniel. He laughs and says, "Would you look at the manners on my nephew?" Then he stands and gives Daniel a solid pat on the back. "Thank you for the hot wake-me-up, Ida. Real kind of you." Nodding to Mr. Bucher, he says, "Monday morning, then?"

Mr. Bucher stands and shakes the hand Uncle Ray has held out to him.

"Are you off so soon, Ray?" Mrs. Bucher says, poking her bacon with one hand and balancing her new baby on her hip with the other. "Bacon's almost done."

Uncle Ray holds up a hand and shakes his head. "No, thank you all the same. I'll leave you to your family, Ida."

"Will we be seeing you at church this morning?" Bouncing the baby so she won't fuss, Mrs. Bucher spears the fatty end of one piece of bacon with her fork, flips it and lays it back in the grease.

"Well, how about that. Today is Sunday, after all." Uncle Ray says it as if Sunday snuck up on him. "I guess I'll get along and put on something decent."

"We'll all be glad to have you back," Mrs. Bucher says.

Uncle Ray gives Daniel another pat on the shoulder. On the last pat, he holds on. "Nice manners. Real nice."

Mr. Bucher walks Uncle Ray outside and waits there until a truck engine fires up before walking back into the kitchen. Mrs. Bucher gives him a nod, or maybe she is taking a deep breath and they both turn to Daniel.

"Ray's going to be working with your father and me," Mr. Bucher says.

The clatter of silverware stops and chewing mouths go quiet. The brothers sitting around the table and the one scooping potato peels and the one poking through the cabinets and Ian pause to listen.

"Down at the county. Driving a grader, I suppose. Your pa called last night. Asked me this favor. Said he'd be sending Ray over this morning."

Mr. Bucher glances over at Mrs. Bucher again.

"Your pa's a smart man, Dan. Keeping that snake where he can see him." Mr. Bucher takes another sip of coffee. "Got a warmer-upper for me?" he says, holding his cup out for Mrs. Bucher to fill. "You understand that, Dan?"

"Yes, sir. A snake. I understand, sir."

After eating two biscuits dipped in maple syrup, something Mama would never let him do, Daniel follows Ian and four of his brothers outside. His gut hurts, maybe because Mrs. Bucher's biscuits were soggy in the middle, or maybe because he can still feel Uncle Ray's hand squeezing his arm, or maybe because he isn't as good a shot as Ian says he is. Before they left the kitchen, Mrs. Bucher said they had only a half hour because everyone needed to wash up before church. She said the whole mess of them was a sorry sight, so a half hour and no more. Daniel pulls his coat closed and, slapping his leather gloves together, thinks that if the older boys go first there won't be time for him. Mrs. Bucher will call them inside and Daniel will shrug and say, "Maybe next time." Walking toward the barn, four Bucher brothers leading the way, Daniel wishes he had never seen Uncle Ray and that Ian hadn't told his brothers that

Daniel is such a great shot—a good shot maybe, good for a city kid, but great means better than everyone else, better than every other brother.

"Who goes first?" Daniel whispers to Ian.

One of the brothers, the smallest, walks ahead of the group and lines up three cans on the top rung of the wooden fence that runs between the house and the barn. The wind blows down one of the cans. He kicks it aside, slaps his bare hands on his thighs and shouts, "All ready. Fire it up."

Ian nudges Daniel forward.

"Me?" Daniel says. "You want me to go first?"

"Sure," one of the brothers says.

The two oldest brothers didn't bother following everyone outside. Instead, they are watching from the porch. "Hurry up with it, already," one of them shouts.

"Here," says the brother who's two years ahead of Daniel in school. He hands Daniel a rifle. "You use a .22, right? This is a good one. Got a nice straight sight."

"Yeah, Daniel," Ian says. "Show them. Show them what a great shot you are."

Pulling off his gloves and tossing them on the ground, Daniel takes the rifle. The morning air is cold and wet, making his neck and arms stiff. He squints into the sun rising above the bank of trees on the east side of the house, shakes out his hands and bends and straightens his fingers. "Sure, I'll go first," he says. "Those cans over there?"

"Yeah," says Ian. "Get them both."

Daniel brings the rifle up to his shoulder, rests his cheek against the cold wood, and with one eye closed, his breath held tight in his lungs, his feet square under his shoulders, he fires, flips the bolt action and fires again. Both cans fly off the railing.

"Got them," Ian shouts.

"Na," says the youngest brother and the one with the loudest mouth. "The wind knocked them off."

"That wasn't the wind," Ian says. "Daniel got them both. Clean shots."

"Na, just the wind," another brother says.

"Doesn't matter," Daniel says, flips on the safety and hands the rifle back to the brother who gave it to him.

"It was the wind," a brother shouts from the porch.

"I'll show you," Ian says, limping toward the spot where the two cans landed.

A few of the brothers laugh and mimic Ian's awkward gait, while the brother holding the rifle takes aim like he's going to shoot Ian.

"Told you," Ian shouts, holding up the cans. "Clean shots both."

The brother holding the rifle lowers it. "Okay," he says. "So maybe you are a good shot."

Ian limps back to Daniel's side. "Told you so."

The same brother says, "Maybe good enough to go hunting with us."

All of the brothers nod, including Ian.

"Pheasant. They're open season right now," the brother says. "So are quail. Or you might get yourself a prairie chicken."

"Sure," Daniel says, remembering the prairie dog's head that he blew off and the body he left behind. "I mean, not today, because it's church."

"Na, next time you come over. In a few weeks maybe," the same brother says. "What do you think, Ian? Maybe when we get a warm snap, so you're not so stiff."

"I'm not stiff. I'll go anytime."

The brother laughs. "Yeah, well, in a few weeks. Next time you're over. We'll all go hunting. Then we'll see what a great shot you are."

"Yeah, a few weeks," Daniel says. He looks at Ian and tries to remember if he is more crooked since it got so cold. "Anytime."

Chapter 15

Before sliding into the pew, Ruth genuflects, pulls off her stocking cap and smoothes her skirt. She winks at Evie as she does the same, and together, the Scott family sits. Celia and Elaine slide forward onto the kneeling bench and bow their heads in private prayer, and from their pew at the back of the church, Ruth scans the crowd. No sign of Ray's brown hat or his dark hair. No sign. He is home now and eventually he'll be back to church. But not yet. Not this morning. Ruth exhales, and feeling Mother's vibration through the wooden floor as she walks down the aisle, Ruth signals the family by waving one hand. Everyone scoots down one spot to make room.

"What a shame," Mother says, holding on to the back of the pew in front of them and groaning as she lowers herself. "What a darn shame."

"Mother, shhhh." Wondering if Arthur heard, Ruth looks down the line of Scotts.

Mother spreads out as she settles in, anchoring one side of the family, while Arthur anchors the other. She is angry because, once again, the Scotts are sitting in the last pew. One Sunday of every month, Father Flannery publishes a list that shows every family's contribution to the church, and Arthur's family remains at the bottom of that list, which means Arthur's family sits in the last pew. Arthur says the good Lord understands about a man starting his life over and tending to his family first. Mother says the Lord is good but that He's losing His patience.

"I thought I raised that boy to have some pride," Mother says, making the sign of the cross. Unable to kneel, she remains sitting, her hands in her lap as she bows her head.

Ruth shifts in her seat enough to shield Evie from the conversation. "Arthur has pride enough for ten men," she whispers, saying nothing more as Daniel peels away from the Bucher family, dips to one knee, makes the sign of the cross on his chest and slides past Mother and Ruth to take his place between Celia and Arthur.

Mother grunts, which means the conversation is over, so Ruth settles back into her seat. She turns and catches Elaine's eye. Elaine winks and gives a small nod of approval to the shiny pink lipstick she painted on Ruth's lips before church. Ruth, returning the smile, touches the corner of her mouth. When she looks back, Mother is frowning. Ruth lowers her eyes, slides forward onto the kneeling bench and with her forearms resting on the pew in front of them, she bows her head.

From this perspective, where she feels safe, she can see the two seats where Ray and she used to sit every Sunday morning. Ray always donated enough, barely enough, to keep their place in the third pew. Now, because Julianne is gone, the pew is empty except for Mary and Orville. Mary is thin, her shoulders frail and rounded, and Orville's hair has gone white.

Ruth has known Mary all of her life, but she didn't meet Orville until her thirteenth birthday. That was the day Orville stepped off a westbound train and walked into the Stockland Café. The café was crowded because dark clouds were rolling in from the south, the kind of dark clouds that meant rain. Every other dark cloud, for years it seemed, had been dust rolling in from Nebraska or maybe Oklahoma. Folks were tired of shoveling it from their homes and draping their babies with damp dish towels. The day Orville Robison arrived, folks were set to celebrate because those dark clouds meant rain. Finally, rain.

Wearing a tattered, old straw cowboy hat with a small red feather stuck in the black band, Orville walked into the café, carrying with him two leather suitcases. He had dark hair, almost black, and skin that made folks think he probably had some Indian blood in him. Sitting together at the booth nearest the front door, Eve, Ruth and Mary were sipping unsweetened tea, and the moment Orville Robison set down his suitcases, Mary smoothed her hair, bit into a lemon and said she liked that red feather. She said it meant good luck, said that feather was what brought the rain clouds. She said she'd marry any man with a feather like that tucked in his hat.

By the time Orville finished his first cup of coffee, he had noticed the three girls, just like they had noticed him. Leaning on the café counter with one elbow while a young Isabelle Burris dropped two cubes of sugar in his coffee, Orville Robison tipped the brim of his hat toward the girls' table. Even at thirteen, Ruth could see that he noticed Eve most of all. She had the kind of beauty that made people stop to stare at her as if they might never see such a thing again. Orville was no different from most folks who saw Eve for the first time. He looked at her once, at all of them sitting around the table, glanced away, and as if surprised, as if unable to trust his own eyes, he looked again. The second time, he looked only at Eve. But Eve was barely fifteen, so within the amount of time it took Orville Robison to finish that cup of coffee, he settled on Mary, the oldest of the three—nearly nineteen. Six months later, Mary Purcell became Mary Robison. Together, the three girls hand-stitched Mary's wedding gown and she wore a red feather tucked in her garter.

Lowering her eyes and pressing her hands together, Ruth prays that Julianne will come home to Mary and Orville soon. So many years, the two of them went without a child, but then, like the rain that came after so many years of dust, Julianne was finally born. Even after Mary's hair had started to gray and her friends were counting grandchildren, Julianne was born. Ruth finishes her prayer for Julianne with a silent "Amen," makes the sign of the cross to bless the Robison family in God's name, opens her eyes and there is Ray, sitting in the third pew.

Celia reaches across Elaine and Evie and touches Ruth's forearm. Her face is pale again, like that first day she slid out of Ray's truck, a strawberry pie cradled in her hands. Ray nods in their direction. His eyes, even the bad one, rest on Ruth. With the tiniest motion, no more than raising one eyelid, he calls Ruth to him. Placing a hand on the back of the pew in front of them, Ruth turns toward Celia again. Celia squeezes Ruth's arm until she can feel the small, tender bone through her wool overcoat. Ruth lowers her head and scoots forward on the wooden bench.

"I can't believe he would sit right there next to Mary and Orville," Celia whispers and shakes her head. "You stay put, Ruth." And then to Arthur, she says, "Tell Ruth to stay put."

It seems that all through the church, in the pews in front of Ray and behind, people begin to scoot in whichever direction will take them farther away from the man they all think took Julianne Robison. Ever since the men from the state came to help Floyd search for Julianne, people have become more convinced than ever that Ray took the child and that he killed Eve all those years ago. Getting their first glimpse of him since he came back home, they raise their hands to their mouths so they can whisper unseen. They take sideways glances. They turn away if Ray catches their eye. Some of them even give Ruth a fleeting look, just long enough to pucker their lips at the sour taste of it all and shake their heads, but Mary and Orville Robison seem to take no notice. Instead, they stare at the empty spot where Father Flannery will soon stand, without even a glance toward Ray.

"Arthur," Celia whispers again. "Tell Ruth to stay put."

Arthur tips his head in greeting to Ray, and with the smallest nod, he motions Ruth to go.

Celia sucks in a mouthful of air, and with Daniel caught between them, she hisses at Arthur. "What? What are you doing?"

Arthur, his eyes forward, says, "The man needs his pride."

Celia reaches across her girls, grabs Ruth's coat sleeve before she can stand, and says, "I do not care about his pride. How can you do this?"

Still staring straight ahead, as if he's not really talking to his wife, Arthur says, "He can't do her any harm here. It's only for the service."

Ruth places her hand over Celia's. "It's okay," she whispers, then smiles at Evie, kisses her on the cheek, and says, "See you after."

Evie reaches out to hug Ruth. "We'll make brownies still?"

"Yes, sweet pea."

Celia, now gripping only the very edge of Ruth's sleeve between two fingers, says, "Arthur, please."

Arthur says nothing else, and without even having to look at Ruth, he motions again for her to go.

Sitting with a rigid back, Celia turns away from Arthur. Ruth gives her a wink, stands and slips past Reesa. Once outside the pew, she wraps her frail arms around her waist, cinching her long coat closed, hiding her belly. All through the sanctuary, heads perk up. People shift in their seats, look from Ray to Ruth and back again as Ruth shuffles down the center aisle, her head lowered, her shoulders slouched forward. At the third pew from the front, she makes the sign of the cross and slips past Ray into her seat. As if she had been waiting for Ruth to be seated, the organist begins the hymn, calling them all to prayer. Ray drapes his right arm over the back of the pew and around Ruth's tiny shoulders.

After the organ plays its final note and the congregation closes and puts away their hymnals, Father Flannery steps to the pulpit. "The Lord be with you," he says.

"And also with you," the congregation responds in unison.

Several rows up, Ray is speaking the words along with the rest of the congregation, loudly, probably so that everyone can hear.

"My brothers and sisters," Father Flannery says. "To prepare ourselves to celebrate the sacred mysteries, let us call to mind our sins."

Celia doesn't look at Arthur, but listens for his voice. She hears every breath he takes, but he doesn't respond along with the others. "Lord have mercy," they all say.

Arthur is silent.

"Christ have mercy."

He says nothing. Even Daniel knows the words. He speaks them quietly.

"Let us pray," Father Flannery says, and Celia bows her head as he delivers the opening prayer.

"Amen," trickles across the church.

Arthur is silent.

Through the first and second reading, Celia watches Ruth and Ray, waiting for Ray to move or stand or take Ruth away. He doesn't. He sits motionless, his arm draped around Ruth, and as Father Flannery begins his homily, Ray slouches in the pew, pulling Ruth closer. A few seats down from Celia, Evie squirms, and Reesa quiets her by placing a hand in her lap. Next to Celia, Daniel slides down in his seat, settling in, probably tired from his sleepover at Ian's. Arthur sits straight, his feet planted squarely on the ground, his hands buckled into fists that rest on his thighs.

Finally, signaling that the end of mass is near, Father Flannery raises the host and breaks it. Several rows ahead, Ruth and Ray stand in tandem with Mary and Orville Robison, file out of the pew and walk to the front of the church. The other parishioners fall back and away from the awkward foursome, leaving a gaping hole in the procession. Orville holds Mary by the arm, helping her to walk, steadying her.

One by one, the parishioners step forward to receive the Eucharist, all the while keeping their distance. Celia stands to follow Reesa and Elaine. She pauses, waiting her turn, watching as Ruth steps up to Father Flannery, her head lowered, her hands cupped to receive communion. Though she can't hear them from the back of the church, Celia knows what they are saying.

"The body of Christ," Father Flannery will say, and Ruth will respond, "Amen."

Father Flannery lays the host in Ruth's hands. She places it on her tongue, bows to him and, with her head still lowered, she begins to follow the procession back to her seat. But before she can take a step, Father Flannery raises a hand, stopping her. He cups her chin in his palm, raises her face toward his, and smiles down at her. Ruth lifts her eyes to Father Flannery. Slowly, gazing down on her kindly, Father Flannery turns Ruth's head to show her profile to the congregation. Then he presses a thumb to her mouth and wipes away her pink lipstick.

Celia grabs onto the back of the nearest pew. Elaine stops.

"Mother," Elaine whispers, reaching for Celia's hand. "Did you see that?"

Celia takes Elaine's hand and looks back for Arthur, but he

isn't behind her. He has returned to his seat and is staring straight ahead. A few of those having already received communion and returned to their seats close their eyes and shake their head, as if sorry to have seen such a thing but certain that it needed to be done. As Ruth passes by, closer now because Celia has made her way to the front of the church, a pink stain smears her lips and left cheek. She slips back into the third pew, kneels and, with her head lowered in prayer, takes a tissue from her coat pocket and wipes the lipstick from her face.

Chapter 16

Daniel grabs the back of Aunt Ruth's seat as Dad takes a sharp turn into Grandma Reesa's drive. He falls to the left, squishing Evie, and when the car straightens, they both sit up and Evie punches him in the arm.

"Get off me," she says.

In the front seat, Mama grabs the dashboard. "Are we in such a hurry?"

Dad doesn't answer until he has stopped near the garage and thrown the car into park.

"This family," he says, staring straight ahead, "will never go to St. Anthony's again."

The car is silent for a moment. Daniel watches for what Grandma Reesa might do because she is the one who cares the most about church. Instead, Aunt Ruth, whose lips are smeared with a pink shadow, speaks.

"That's not the answer, Arthur. Not on my account."

Dad slams his hands on the steering wheel. Mama, who is sitting in the front seat, and Elaine, who is wedged between Aunt Ruth and Grandma Reesa, both jump. Aunt Ruth presses her hands over her mouth, Grandma Reesa lets out one of her groans and Evie's chin puckers. Then the car is quiet. Daniel closes his eyes so his chin won't pucker like Evie's.

"I think you should all hustle inside," Mama says quietly. "Evie, you and Elaine help Grandma set the table. Daniel, maybe you can start a fire. A fire would be nice."

Daniel nods. Aunt Ruth opens one door, Grandma Reesa the other. A blast of cold air shoots through the car as Evie and Daniel crawl out from the last seat in the station wagon. Before Daniel steps out of the car, he turns back. He wants to tell Dad that he saw Uncle Ray at the Buchers' and that he is going to drive a grader. He wants to ask him about hunting for quail and pheasant and if it's as easy to shoot a bird as it is to shoot a prairie dog. He wants to ask Dad to help him practice before the Bucher brothers take him hunting. But when Dad glares at him, Daniel knows not to speak. Instead, he climbs out of the car and closes the door behind him.

Waiting until the others have gone inside, Celia inhales, filling her lungs with crisp, dry air, and lays her hands in her lap.

"You shouldn't have sent Ruth to sit with Ray," she says.

Arthur crosses his arms on the steering wheel and rests his chin there. "One good snow will bring down that roof," he says.

A few yards in front of the car, overgrown cordgrass, brown and brittle, has nearly swallowed up Reesa's small shed.

"Lot of good snows over the years, I suppose," Celia says. "And it's still standing. Help me understand, Arthur. Why do that to Ruth?"

Arthur is quiet for a moment, staring straight ahead. "Are you sorry I brought you here?" he says, still looking at the shed and not at Celia.

His dark hair has grown past his collar, making him look younger and somehow stronger. Celia stretches her arm across the back of the seat and weaves her fingers into the dark waves.

"No. Well, sometimes." She smiles but Arthur doesn't see. "I'm glad we're here for Ruth. And for our family. Elaine is certainly happy."

"Yeah, Elaine's happy." He nods but doesn't smile. "What about Evie and Daniel?"

Celia crosses her hands in her lap. "Happy enough. They'll make more friends along the way."

"That's where we found her," Arthur says, nodding toward the small shed.

"Who?" Celia says, sitting forward on her seat. "Do you mean Eve? You found Eve there?"

"Don't know why Mother keeps it around."

Celia falls back in her seat. "Right here. So close to home?"

Arthur nods and hangs his head between his arms. "The best I can do is to keep track of Ray," he says. "It's the best I can do. For now." He lifts his head and kneads his brow with the palm of his hand. "I'll take care of her."

Celia nods.

"I'll take care of Ruth," he says again, this time speaking more to himself than to Celia.

"Yes, Arthur, you will. I know you will." Wishing she meant what she said, Celia brushes her hand against his cheek. He leans into her touch. "People were different today. Did you notice? In church, they were different."

Arthur glances at her but doesn't answer.

"They think Ray did it." Celia pauses but no response. She looks back at the shed that seems larger now. "They really think he took Julianne, don't they?"

Still no answer.

"Because of what happened to Eve. Because Julianne was so like her."

"Small town. Nothing much else for folks to talk about."

"But what if he did? What if . . ."

"Ray didn't have anything to do with what happened to Eve."

"How do you know that, Arthur? How do you really, really know for sure?" Celia touches his hand. "You've always said how much Evie resembles your sister. Like Julianne did. If people really think . . . we have to consider it. For Evie's sake. My God, Arthur. You found Eve dead right here," she says, pointing across the drive toward the shed. "Right outside your mother's house. How can you be so sure? You promised Ruth, remember? You promised her you wouldn't be too sure of yourself."

Arthur nods and lays a hand over Celia's. "We'll go to Hays from now on. For mass, we'll go to Hays."

Celia needs to trust him. Now, more than any other time, she needs to trust Arthur. And maybe she could have until she saw the looks on people's faces today. Most of them have probably known Ray all their lives. And all of them believe.

"I think it would be a nice drive for all of us," Celia says, trying to swallow the lump that has formed in her throat. "It's a lovely church."

Arthur nods. "Hays'll be fine."

E vie listens for Daniel in the hallway outside Aunt Eve's room. He is supposed to start a fire and that always takes him a good, long time. Grandma Reesa says the trees of Rooks County are plenty safe if the matches are in Daniel's hands. Hearing nothing, she opens her small plastic tote and lays it on the bed. She blows the dust out of the corners and looks around the room. The Virgin Mary won't fit inside the small case, and even if she did, Grandma Reesa would notice if Mary went missing. She is still mad at Daddy for gluing the hands back on, even though she said he could do it. Grandma says it's shameful to use plain old glue on the Virgin Mary and to leave clumps of it stuck to her wrists. Evie walks to the table where the statue sits and touches the seam where Daddy glued her left hand onto her left wrist. She lifts Mary, tilts her back and forth, feels the weight of her before gently placing her back on the table.

Pausing to listen for footsteps again, but hearing nothing except the faraway clatter of Grandma Reesa's pots and pans, she walks to the dresser next to the Virgin Mary's table, opens the small, center drawer and peeks inside.

"Are these your pictures?" she says.

She giggles, feels that she's done something naughty by talking to Aunt Eve like she's right here in the same room. Glancing around, she muffles another giggle with one hand and, with the other, lifts out a small silver frame with a picture of Grandma Reesa when she wasn't so big and a man, who must have been Grandpa. Evie holds the picture close to her face.

"He doesn't look so nice. Was he a nice dad?"

No one answers. After propping the picture up on the cabinet, she takes out another.

"Just look at you," she says, smiling down on a picture of Aunt Eve and Daddy. "Your hair is like mine. Look," she says, holding up one of her own thin braids. "Just like mine."

Evie sets the picture next to the first one and pulls the drawer open a little farther.

"Who is this?" she asks, and then nods. "It's you, isn't it? You seem so happy. Look at how you're smiling."

Pulling one sleeve down over her hand, Evie wipes the glass in the last frame and holds up the picture. A young man, much younger than Daddy, is lifting Aunt Eve off the ground. His arms are wrapped around her waist and Aunt Eve is smiling and holding a wide straw hat on her head with one hand so it won't fall off. She is a girl, almost as old as Elaine, but not quite. The man is wearing a brown cowboy hat pushed high on his forehead. He has dark hair and is staring at Evie through the camera lens. Evie tilts her head left and right.

"He looks like Uncle Ray," she says, smiling. "He's so young and his eye is not so bad."

Then she remembers the Uncle Ray who came to the house wanting a piece of Aunt Ruth's pie and frowns. She looks around the room, at the closet full of dresses, at the Virgin Mary, at the window over the bed, wishing Aunt Eve would tell her the man isn't Uncle Ray, but she doesn't. Still hearing the clatter of Grandma Reesa's pots and pans, Evie puts the first two pictures back in the center drawer, closes it and lays the third picture, the one of Aunt Eve and the happy man, in her small bag.

Chapter 17

Sitting at the kitchen table while waiting for the potatoes to boil, Celia fans the book for a fifth time, stirring up a small breeze that fluffs Evie's bangs. On the count of three, Evie pokes a finger between the pages to mark the stopping point. The book, an early Christmas present from Ruth to Evie, falls open on the table. Celia takes a sip of spiced cider and stands to turn down the burner, leaving Ruth to study the book with Evie.

The family hasn't returned to St. Anthony's for a month of Sundays, and it is clear that mass in Hays doesn't suit the rest of the town, almost as if mass in a different church, even if it is catholic, isn't really mass at all. Even before the family had attended a single service at St. Bart's, the other ladies in town stared and whispered when they saw Celia and Ruth in the grocery store. Good Christians attended St. Anthony's every Sunday and good Christians didn't leave their husbands, for any reason. Arthur had promised Reesa that the family would go back to St. Anthony's for midnight mass on Christmas. Perhaps that would do a little something to make the town happy.

Though the rest of the town shakes their heads at the Scotts attending mass in Hays, it has kept Ruth out of Ray's sight and he seems content to see Arthur at work every day, at least the days that Ray makes it to work. Arthur says Ray is probably drinking again so he doesn't have time to worry about bringing Ruth home.

In the front room, Arthur struggles to force a crooked trunk into a straight tree stand, and out on the back porch, Daniel sifts through the boxes they moved from Detroit in search of the ones labeled CHRISTMAS DECORATIONS. The air smells of evergreen needles, sap and Ruth's homemade spiced cider, making the house warm and cozy even as the wind whips though the attic and the sky darkens with signs of snow.

Studying page 275 of Evie's book, Ruth wraps both hands around her mug, lifts it to her lips but doesn't drink, and makes a *tsk, tsk, tsk* sound as she shakes her head.

"Is that not a good one?" Evie asks.

"Very poisonous," Ruth says, glancing up at Celia and tapping the page that lays open on the table.

Celia leans over the book and reads the caption beneath the picture—narrow-leaved poison wedge root. Ruth stops tapping and lays one hand flat over the picture, spreading her fingers so she hides the plant. She leans back in her chair, as if checking on Arthur and Daniel.

"It's good for her to learn about the poisonous ones, too, Ruth. To be on the safe side."

Ruth lifts Evie's chin so she'll look Ruth in the eye. "This is definitely a bad one. Very bad. One of the worst."

"Would it make me sick?"

"If you ate it, it would," Ruth says, swallowing and clearing her throat. "But you'd never, ever eat something you found growing outside."

"Except if it was in your garden."

"Yes, that's true." Ruth points to the white leaves that look like tiny tubes with pointed ends. "Cows eat them sometimes. Not often. They don't like the taste. But if they do, it makes them stagger and bump into things. The blind staggers. Very bad. You leave this one alone."

Evie nods and before Celia can sit again, the back door swings open followed by a gust of cold, dry air. Elaine and Jonathon stumble into the room, their cheeks and noses red, both of them breathing heavily.

"What's all the commotion?" Arthur says, pounding his leather gloves together as he steps into the kitchen.

Evie giggles at the pine needles stuck in his hair. Celia quiets her with a finger to her lips.

Elaine, still wearing her coat and mittens, sticks out her hand. "We're engaged," she says, gazing down at her brown mitten. "Oops." She pulls it off to show the new ring on her finger. "We're getting married."

With a sideways glance toward Arthur, Celia stretches her arms to Elaine. "Oh, sweetheart," she says, holding the tips of Elaine's fingers as she admires the new ring. "It's lovely." Then Celia lifts up onto her tiptoes and gives Jonathon a hug.

Celia had known this was coming. Not because of any secret Elaine had shared, but because of the speed at which Jonathon was building his scrap house. Every night at dinner, he came with news of his latest find—a load of two-by-fours, a few solid windows, a cast-iron tub. He was especially proud the day he finished the roof because he beat the first snow.

"Married?" Arthur says, holding his gloves in one hand, both arms hanging stiff.

Ruth slides out of her chair, steps up to Arthur and, as she plucks the needles from his hair, she says, "Yes, Arthur. Married. Isn't it nice?"

Arthur makes a grunting noise but doesn't answer.

"Arthur," Jonathon says, sticking out his hand. "I intended to ask your permission. Planned to wait until Christmas day, but it snuck up on us this morning. I meant to ask you first."

Arthur brushes Ruth away and shakes Jonathon's hand.

"Have you talked about when?" Celia asks, wiping her hands on her apron. With her eyes, she motions to Arthur that he needs to hug his daughter. He doesn't seem to understand. "A date, I mean. Have you set a date?"

"Spring, I think. Before the baby," Elaine says, resting her hand on the small bulge in Ruth's stomach as the two share a hug.

"What do you mean, before the baby?" Arthur straightens to his full height. His shirt is lopsided because he has threaded his buttons in the wrong holes, his hair is spiked like a rooster's crown where Ruth pulled out the needles and his face is pale.

"I mean Aunt Ruth's baby," Elaine says, her cheeks flushing red. "Before Aunt Ruth's baby comes along."

"Isn't that thoughtful, Arthur?" Celia says, also embarrassed at what Arthur was thinking, and also relieved. "But not until you've graduated." She turns toward Jonathon. "You understand, don't you?"

"I told her the very same."

"That doesn't leave us much of a window," Elaine says. "Aunt Ruth, your little sweet pea will be along in late June or early July, don't you think?"

Ruth smiles down at her stomach. "That's my best guess. But rest assured, she'll be along no matter when you plan this wedding, so you choose whatever date you like."

Evie leaps toward Elaine, grabbing for both of her hands. "I have a wonderful idea," she says. "The dresses. Aunt Eve's dresses. You can use them in your wedding. That's why she has so many. She made them all for her own wedding. Sewed them all by herself. With Mrs. Robison. Isn't that right, Aunt Ruth?"

Ruth looks between Celia and Arthur. "Yes, Evie, but . . ."

"She won't mind. She won't mind if Elaine uses them. Aunt Eve made them for her very own wedding. They're the most beautiful dresses ever. We'll go to Grandma Reesa's. We'll go there and I'll show you. Can we go, Mama?" Evie stops jumping for only a moment. "And now that Elaine is getting married, Aunt Eve will come home again. She'll come to see Elaine get married. She'll come and see how much we look alike. She'll see that I'm little like her and I have braids like her. Won't she be surprised? Won't she?"

"Evie," Celia says, gripping Evie on both arms to stop her from bouncing. "There's plenty of time for wedding talk later. Let's not give Elaine too much to think about."

"I told her about Eve's dresses," Ruth says, stepping back to the table and lowering herself into her seat. "Told her what a wonderful seamstress Eve always was. She saw them in the upstairs bedroom and asked about them." She turns toward Arthur. "I hope you don't mind."

"Mama," Elaine says, nodding toward Evie. "Go ahead."

"Not today," Celia says. "It's your day."

Arthur lays his gloves on the table and runs both hands over his hair, smoothing it. "It's probably best," he says.

Taking a few deep breaths, Celia squats so she is Evie's size. "Evie, dear," she says. "I know Aunt Eve is very special to you."

Evie puckers her lips and nods. The very roundest part of her cheeks and the tip of her nose are red, chapped from the cold dry winter air even though it's barely December. A lot of cold weather to go. The ends of her white, silky bangs catch in her eyelashes when she blinks. She tilts her head.

"She was very special to all of us," Celia says, inhaling and holding the air in her lungs to steady her voice.

"Aunt Ruth showed me her picture. So now I know what she looks like."

Celia takes Evie's hands. They are warm and soft and still smell like the pink lotion she rubbed on her arms and hands after her bath the night before. "We know how you love Aunt Eve's room and her dresses."

Evie nods and starts to smile, but then stops and nods again.

"Honey, Aunt Eve won't be coming to Elaine's wedding." Celia clears her throat. "Aunt Eve has passed on, Evie."

Evie crosses her arms and bites her lower lip.

"You know what that means, right?" Elaine asks, reaching a hand toward Evie.

Evie ducks away from Elaine, plants her feet shoulder width apart and rests both fists on her waist. "I'm not stupid. I know what it means."

"When she was quite young, Evie. She died when she was quite young."

Celia glances at Arthur. He is leaning against the doorframe with his head lowered and his arms crossed. Less than five months in Kansas, and it must seem to Evie that everyone disappears or dies. First Julianne Robison and now Aunt Eve. In Detroit, Celia knew how to care for her children. She shut off the news when they came down for breakfast, locked the front gate, walked them to school. But here in Kansas, she doesn't know what to lock. Now her fears walk through her very own kitchen, stand on her back steps, sneak up on her at church. In Kansas, she doesn't know how to care for her children.

Celia stands from her squatting position and takes a few steps toward Evie. "We all miss Aunt Eve very much. We should have told you sooner, but we didn't know when it would be right."

"Why?" Evie asks.

"What, honey? What do you mean, why?"

"Why did she die?"

"No good reason why," Arthur says. "Never a good reason."

"Daddy's right," Celia says, tilting her head and smiling. "And we don't need to talk about what happened right now. That'll be for another day, but you should know that she would have loved you very much."

"Is that why Aunt Eve didn't get married and wear the dresses?" Evie asks. "Because she was dead?"

Ruth presses a hand over her mouth.

"Evie, let's not talk about that," Celia says. "Let's just remember how much we loved Aunt Eve."

"That's why he hates Aunt Ruth," Evie says, pointing at Ruth. "Uncle Ray wanted to marry Aunt Eve, but she died. She died and he had to marry you."

Celia sucks in a quick breath, and Ruth closes her eyes.

"Evie Scott, that is a terrible thing to say," Celia says.

"I saw a picture. I saw Aunt Eve and Uncle Ray. Uncle Ray is happy. He is smiling in the picture and his eyes are almost normal. Aunt Eve is wearing a straw hat. I saw it."

Arthur steps into the kitchen and tosses his leather gloves on the table. "You will not say another word, young lady."

"Aunt Eve died and Uncle Ray had to marry Aunt Ruth. That's why he hates you."

"Stop it now," Arthur shouts, silencing the kitchen.

Evie pushes Celia's hands away and takes a step backward.

"Please, Evie," Ruth says. "I loved your Aunt Eve. I loved her so."

"You could have told me. I'm not a baby."

"No, honey," Celia says, reaching for Evie with one hand and for Ruth with the other. "We never thought you were a baby."

"Everyone thinks I'm too little."

"No, Evie," Elaine says, one arm still wrapped around Jonathon.

"No one thinks that, squirt," Jonathon says.

"I'm not a squirt either." Evie takes two more steps away. She is almost out of the kitchen. "I'm not too little. You could have told me she was dead. Dead, dead, dead. Dead like Julianne Robison." Two more steps and Evie stands where the living room meets the kitchen. "I don't even care. I don't even care about either one of them," and she runs across the wooden floors, into her bedroom, and slams the door.

Standing just inside the back porch and holding a box of Christmas ornaments, Daniel sees his reflection in the gun cabinet. Behind the glass, his .22-caliber rifle hangs next to Dad's shotgun. After Evie's door slams shut, he sets the box on the ground and bends to pull off his boots. Mama bought them at the St. Anthony's yard sale two weeks after they moved to Kansas. She said they were a good deal and would be plenty big enough to last a good long time. Now, a short five months later, Daniel's feet ache because the boots are too small. Small boots make crooked toes, God damned crooked toes that don't have room enough to grow. He sighs, thinking crooked toes are one more terrible thing about Kansas.

Dad and Mama never told Daniel that Aunt Eve was dead, just like they never told Evie. He never thought much about her, but if someone had asked, he would have said Aunt Eve moved away and was living somewhere else, probably with a husband and children of her own. Two probably, or maybe three. Had someone asked, he would have said Aunt Eve was like Mama. He would have said she wore aprons trimmed in white lace and had long blond hair. She probably smelled like Mama, too, and had soft, warm hands. But Aunt Eve is dead, and it makes Daniel feel the littlest bit like Mama is dead. Maybe that's why Mama and Dad never told Daniel and Evie.

Ian and some of the kids at school said Aunt Eve was dead. They said Uncle Ray killed her twenty-five years ago and now he's killed Julianne Robison—either he or Jack Mayer did it. One of them's guilty for sure, that's what the kids at school said. Daniel never believed them about Aunt Eve. Even though he never knew her, he didn't like to think about someone killing her, but now he knows it's true. Now he knows that his parents didn't tell him about Aunt Eve because they think he's a baby like Evie.

Still staring at the gun cabinet, Daniel wonders about the shotgun, wonders if it will be heavier than his .22. Maybe too heavy. Maybe too heavy for someone who doesn't have many friends and everyone thinks is a baby. But Ian says he needs it for pheasant hunting. A rifle won't work. Not even Daniel is a good enough shot to use a rifle. Ian has enough ammunition, but Daniel has to bring his own gun. The Bucher brothers say that if Daniel is really a good shot, he'll handle a shotgun just fine. He will use the key on top of the cabinet, take the gun before Mr. Bucher picks him up next Saturday afternoon, and hide it in his sleeping bag. Dad always takes a nap on

Saturday afternoons. Mama says the week wears him out and that Dad needs a little peace and quiet. He'll take the gun while Dad is sleeping. Ian says the plan will work, that the sleeping bag will hide the shotgun. But Ian, who walked too slowly before he got his black boots, has never been pheasant hunting either and he's never stolen a shotgun, so how does Ian know what will work and what won't?

"Daniel," Mama calls out from the kitchen. "Is that you?"

"Yes, ma'am."

"Come in here, sweetheart. We have something to tell you."

Daniel hangs his coat on the hook closest to the gun cabinet. If he drapes it carefully, it almost covers enough of the cabinet to hide Dad's shotgun. It'll hide an empty spot, too. He will remember this for next weekend.

"Coming, Mama," he says and picks up the box of ornaments.

Chapter 18

Celia frowns across the table at Arthur as he drops a second sugar cube in his coffee. He is about to drop in a third but stops when Celia raises her chin and shakes her head. From the front of the café, the bell over the door rings, a blast of cold air floods their table, and Sheriff Bigler walks in. He pulls off his heavy blue jacket, which makes him shrink to half the size he was when he walked in, drapes it over a stool at the counter and sits. Arthur lifts a hand to greet him. Floyd nods in return.

"Wonder what brings Floyd out?" Arthur says.

"Having a little dessert like everyone else," Celia says, pulling off her coat and laying it over the seat back. "And I called him. Just in case."

Ever since the holidays ended, Father Flannery has been calling the house, saying he hoped the Scotts were a good Christian family who hadn't forgotten about forgiveness since they started attending St. Bart's. Tired of the phone calls and thinking that maybe they could get that annulment after all, Arthur finally agreed to meet with

Ray. Ruth shook her head at the idea and Celia said an annulment would never happen once Father Flannery found out about the baby. Still, Arthur wanted to try. Celia said she would approve only if they met Ray in the café because he certainly wasn't setting foot inside her kitchen.

"Shouldn't have done that," Arthur says, taking a sip of coffee and making a sour face as if it isn't sweet enough. He taps his teaspoon on the white tablecloth, leaving a small, coffee-colored stain.

"Why on earth not?"

"Just gonna get Ray riled up."

"He won't know Floyd is here for us."

"Man's not a fool, Celia."

Celia brushes him away with a wave of her hand. "Are you doing all right?" she asks, turning to face Ruth, who is sitting next to her in the small booth. She takes Ruth's hand with both of hers. "Are you feeling okay?"

"I'm fine," Ruth says. "Please don't fuss."

At the front of the café, the door chime rings again. Orville and Mary Robison walk in, stamping their feet and pulling off their coats. Arthur tips his head toward them as if he's wearing his hat and slouches back down into the wooden bench.

"What do you suppose brings them out?" Celia asks.

"They come every night," Ruth says, picking at the frayed end of her jacket sleeve. "Have ever since they first got married. Dessert and coffee usually."

The dinner crowd has cleared out and only the folks who, like the Robisons, have come for cherry pie and coffee are left. Half a dozen at most. At a table near the front counter, Orville Robison waits while Mary takes his coat and hangs it on the rack inside the door. She leaves on her own coat and as they sit, Floyd Bigler swivels around on his stool and walks over to them. He shakes Orville's hand and takes the seat that Mary offers him.

The two men begin to talk while Mary tips the white creamer, pouring milk into her coffee. The sleeves of her gray flannel jacket hide her hands, making it seem that she has shrunk in the months since Julianne disappeared, and the hair peeking out from under her tan hat is gray, almost white. How can she go on—standing, walking, sipping her coffee—now that no one is searching for Julianne anymore? There hasn't even been an article in the paper about the disappearance since before the holidays, and Father Flannery said a special prayer for Julianne at midnight mass on Christmas Eve, a prayer that sounded like good-bye. Maybe that's why folks stopped talking about it and writing about and searching for poor Julianne. They all thought good-bye meant Julianne would never come home.

The chime rings a third time, and Ray walks into the café. He takes off his hat, nods toward Isabelle Burris, who is folding napkins behind the counter, and lifts a finger in her direction.

"Cup of black coffee, Izzy," he says and, as he winks at her, he notices the Robisons and Floyd Bigler. He pauses for a moment, looks at them and at all the others in the café. Folks have laid down their forks, pushed aside their coffee and are watching. "Get back to it," Ray says to the room, glaring at them with his good eye while the cloudy eye goes off on its own, and without even a polite nod toward the Robisons, he walks past.

Isabelle follows Ray to the table with a pot of coffee and a white cup and saucer. She stays several feet behind him and only approaches the table after he has pulled a chair up to the booth and sat.

"I'll leave the pot for you folks," she says.

"How about a piece of your cherry pie, Izzy?" Ray says, scooting up to the table. "What about you all? Anyone else for pie?"

All around the café, folks pick up their silverware and go back to sipping their coffee.

"Nothing for us, Ray," Arthur says, sliding the creamer and sugar bowl to Ray's end of the table.

Ray takes off his hat and coat, fanning the table with a gust of the cold air he brought in from outside. It smells like campfire smoke and oil, but mostly whiskey. After draping his coat over the back of his chair and tossing his hat on the next table, he reaches for the coffeepot and, as he pours himself a cup, his hand shakes, causing a few drops to spill over the side and onto the white tablecloth. He fills the cup only halfway and glances at Ruth. Tiny red veins etch the yellow skin around his nose and mouth and his dark hair is matted against his forehead and temples. He is nearly the man he was twenty years ago—the strong square jaw, the heavy brow, the dark brown eyes. He still has these features, but they have wilted. He begins to drum one set of fingers and, under the table, where he occasionally brushes against Celia, his knees bob up and down.

"Arthur says things are going well for you at the county," Celia says, although this is not true. Ray has been showing up hours late and looking as if he hasn't slept. First, he said it was the flu, then trouble with the truck and finally food poisoning by that damned Izzy at the café.

"Things are good enough," Ray says, taking a sip of his coffee and wincing because his shaking hand spills too much into his mouth. He clears his throat and leans back when Isabelle sets his pie in front of him.

"Anything else, folks?" she asks.

"No," Ray says. "That's it." And he pushes the pie into the center of the table.

"Well," Arthur says, after Isabelle has walked away. "I guess you've been back about a month now." He pauses, taking a drink of coffee. "And things are working out. Working out fine the way they are."

"I think it's long about time Ruth comes home," Ray says, setting down his coffee and staring at Arthur, but not even his good eye can hold the gaze. "Time she gets back to church, too. Once on Christmas just isn't right."

"Ruth's been to church every Sunday. Hasn't missed a one." Arthur shakes his head. "Nope, can't have her living with you."

"I'm sober, Arthur. Have been since the day I left."

"Fist hurts all the same," Arthur says, glancing at Ruth.

With her eyes lowered, Ruth touches the edge of her jaw.

"You want to come home, Ruth?" Ray's knees stop shaking for a moment, but they begin to quiver again before Ruth can answer.

Arthur holds up a finger to silence her. "Let's keep on like this for a short time more," he says. "Maybe consider whether staying married is the right thing for you two. Maybe you come for a few Sunday suppers so we can talk about it." Arthur nods at his own idea. "Yeah, maybe a dinner or two."

Ray presses both hands on the tabletop, steadying himself. He shifts in his seat, the cups and saucers rattling when his knees bump the table. "That's a damn fool thing to consider." His good eye lifts to look at Ruth.

She shifts in her seat, pressing back into the corner where the wooden bench meets the wall.

"You considering not staying married?" he says. "This how you start thinking when you quit the church?"

Celia ignores Arthur's signal to keep quiet. "She has every right to think as she pleases, Ray. You hurt her very badly."

Ray looks at Celia as if noticing her at the table for the first time. He never quite meets her eyes but instead looks at the individual parts of her. Tonight he studies her neck, the dimple where the two halves of her collarbone meet. After a long silence, Ray pushes back from the table. He stands and stumbles a few steps, knocking over his chair. The loud clatter silences the café again.

"Ruth is coming home tonight," he says, dropping two dollars on the table. "I've been patient enough." He leans forward, resting his palms on the table. "We'll fetch your things tomorrow, Ruth. Come along now."

Arthur tries to stand, but Ray, who is already on his feet, shoves him back down, reaches across the table and grabs Ruth's forearm. He tries to yank her from the booth as if she's no more than one of

Evie's ragdolls. She cries out. Celia presses her body against Ruth's, pinning her in the corner. With both hands wrapped around one of Ruth's small wrists, Ray pulls. Across the table, Arthur struggles to his feet, tipping over the coffee and creamer. He grabs Ray's collar and drags him up and away. The weight pressing down on Celia is suddenly lifted. As quickly as Ray attacked, he is gone. Celia takes in a deep breath. With her body still pressed against Ruth's, she turns. Both men have stumbled over Ray's fallen chair. Arthur is first to scramble to his feet. He dives at Ray again but finds Floyd Bigler instead.

Even though Floyd is a much smaller man than either Ray or Arthur, he grabs Ray by his upper arm, shakes him and pushes him from the table. With the other hand, he stiff-arms Arthur.

"What's going on here, gentlemen?"

"Taking my wife." Ray wipes his forearm across his nose. "High time she comes home." He rocks from one foot to the other and shifts his eyes from side to side. "Ain't got nothing to do with you, Floyd."

Floyd tugs at his belt. "I guess if Ruth wants to go with you, she'll go on and do it." He looks at Ruth.

She wraps one arm around her midsection and shakes her head.

"All right then, I guess you're leaving alone."

Celia slides away from Ruth, pushes aside the table that has wedged them both in the corner and begins mopping up the coffee and cream that has spilled. The men in the café, the ones who had been eating dessert, including Orville Robison, are standing. Ray waves them off, grabs his hat from the nearby table and stumbles toward the door.

"It's wrong, what you're doing, Arthur Scott," he says, once he has reached the front of the café.

Standing with one hand on the doorknob, he sways a bit and seems to notice Orville Robison standing nearby. Orville crosses his arms over his chest. Still sitting, Mary stares down at her hands folded on the table. Ray leans forward to get a good look at her.

"Don't know a man who doesn't have a say when it comes to his own wife." Then he pulls open the door, letting in another blast of cold air. "It sure enough is wrong. Sure enough."

Once Ray is gone, Floyd motions for all of the men to sit.

"Everyone all right?" he asks, picking up Ray's chair and sliding it back to its original spot at a nearby table.

"Ruth, honey," Celia says, laying a hand on Ruth's stomach. "Is everything okay?" Ruth sits with one hand clutching her stomach and the other lying motionless in her lap. Her face has gone white and when Celia touches Ruth's hand, it is cold.

"You folks are in a tough spot, I'd say," Floyd says, nodding at Ruth. "You should probably shoot on over to the hospital. Let the doctor have a look."

Celia and Arthur exchange a glance, but neither one speaks.

"He doesn't know, does he?" Floyd asks.

Arthur shakes his head.

"Yep, that's a good enough mess, all right."

"Floyd's right," Celia says. Obviously, Floyd has figured out that Ruth is pregnant, and if he figured it out, so will others. "We need to get Ruth to the hospital. I think he hurt her arm."

Ruth slides across the seat. Arthur helps her to stand while Celia helps her on with her coat, pulls it closed and buttons it. With Arthur on one side, Celia on the other and Floyd following behind, telling folks to get back to Izzy's pies, Ruth shuffles toward the front of the café. Near the door, she stops and turns, her one bad arm dangling at her side.

"He wasn't home that night, Floyd," she says.

Celia starts to speak but Floyd holds up a finger to silence her.

"Ray, he wasn't home like I said." And then facing Mary Robison, she says, "I don't know that he did anything, Mary. I don't know. But he wasn't home like he told Floyd. He wasn't home like I said."

Floyd nods as if he's always known.

"I'm so sorry, Mary," Ruth says. "I'm just so sorry."

Evie slowly opens her closet door so that it doesn't make any sound. Then she squats and crawls under the coats and dresses that Aunt Ruth brought when she first moved into Evie's room. The clothes smell like Aunt Ruth and, for a moment, Evie thinks Mama and Daddy and Aunt Ruth are home. She wiggles backward out of the closet and listens. They don't usually go out on a school night. Mama said they wouldn't be late and that Evie should mind Daniel and Elaine. Evie frowns to think she has to mind Daniel. Waiting until she is sure the house is quiet, she crawls back under the low-hanging hemlines, coughs as she reaches for the extra blankets that

Mama stores in the closet, and so that they don't come unfolded, she pulls them out slowly, one hand on the bottom, the other on top. Next she drags out the box of photo albums that can't be stored in the basement because they might mildew and there, behind it all, she finds her hatbox. She pulls it from the dark corner, sits crisscross in front of it and, after checking the door one last time, she lifts off the lid.

"This is my favorite," Evie whispers, taking the perfume bottle from the box with two fingers.

The creamy white bottle has a short belly and a tall, thin stopper decorated with tiny red roses. Evie pulls out the stopper, and even though the bottle is empty, she smells Aunt Eve.

"I'm always afraid I'll break it," she says, and setting the stopper back in the bottle, she places it on top of the stack of blankets.

Dragging the box farther out of the corner and wrapping her legs around it, Evie takes out the picture of Aunt Eve and Uncle Ray and props it up on the closet floor. Next, she pulls out a compact, a brush and a hand mirror—all decorated with the same red roses—and lays them on top of the blankets. She took all four from Aunt Eve's room on the same day, but the pink heart-shaped brooch and purple scarf with gold stitching that she removes next, she took one at a time on separate days. Last, she slips one hand into the box and slides it under a carefully folded blue dress. She wiggles her fingers in the soft ruffles and rests her other hand on top of the dress, the silk sash feeling cool and smooth. Lifting the dress from the box, she takes it by each shoulder, holds it to her neck and lets it drape down her front as she stands.

"It's too long," Evie whispers, slipping the dress over her head and threading her arms through each sleeve.

The blue silky skirt flutters against her bare toes and the waist falls past her hips. At the neckline, six inches of blue piping left unstitched hang from the dress and the shoulder seam is torn because she tripped over the dress when Daddy and Uncle Ray were fighting. Evie gathers up the low hanging waist and ties it off in the proper place with the silk sash. The feathery sleeves tickle her elbows. Looking down, she thinks the dress is short enough, but without Mama's help, Evie can't do anything about the wide, torn neckline that slips off her shoulders or the dangling trim. Mama would pin it all up with safety pins, like she does the Halloween costumes that are too big, but Evie can't ask Mama for help.

"It'll be fine," she says. "Just fine."

Sitting in the backseat of Arthur's car, Ruth recognizes the throb in her shoulder and the lopsided way her coat hangs. It's probably dislocated, has happened before. She lets her bad arm lie at her side and, sliding down in the backseat of the station wagon, she slips her good hand inside her jacket so she can feel her little girl. She hasn't told anyone that she can feel Elisabeth kicking or that she has named her baby. She deserved a name. From the moment Ruth felt she was a girl, Elisabeth deserved a name. A name would give the tiny new baby something to hold on to, a little more courage, or maybe it was Ruth who needed the courage. She smiles at the tiny flutter that stirs her insides and, laying back her head, she closes her eyes as the car rambles over the gravel road.

Up in the front seat, Celia and Arthur are silent. No one has spoken since Ruth told Floyd the truth about Ray. Not a word since they walked out of the café into a strong north wind, not as Arthur pulled away, the café's lights dwindling behind them, not now as they drive down Bent Road on their way to the hospital. Celia is no more than a shadow, occasionally checking on Ruth, reaching over the seat to pat her knee. Next to her, Arthur sits tall, stiffening and bracing his arms each time a truck passes and he has to ease the car toward the ditch. Celia is the first to speak.

"Will Floyd arrest him now?" she asks, her shadow turning toward Arthur.

"Don't suppose he has reason to."

"But he'll look into it, right?"

"Don't really know." Arthur rubs his palm against his forehead. Father used to do the same thing. "I suppose he'll ask Ruth some more questions, pay Ray another visit."

Celia reaches back and pats Ruth's knee again and probably smiles though Ruth can't see.

"Well, he's not coming to dinner. I can't imagine why you invited him."

"I didn't invite him, not for certain. Just suggested. Tried to ease my way in. Maybe buy a little time."

"Well, I don't want him around the kids. He did something to that girl. I just know it."

"I'm handling him the best I can for now," Arthur says.

Ruth closes her eyes again when another truck, driving in the opposite direction, flies past. The friction between the two automobiles and the heavy north wind rock Ruth from side to side. She closes her eyes and tries to hold her arm still.

"He's waiting him out," Ruth says into the dark car.

Celia's shadow turns, stretching one arm across the back of her seat. "Waiting him out? What do you mean?"

"He thinks Ray will die soon. That he's drunk himself nearly dead."

A set of oncoming headlights outlines Celia with a yellow frame. "Is that true?"

Once the other truck has passed and its headlights have faded, Arthur shrugs. "Can't help what a man does to himself."

"I don't even know what to say about that," Celia says. "Besides being a horrible thought, what are the chances?"

"Pretty good from the looks of him." Fending off the wind and the rough gravel roads, Arthur's hands and arms shake on the steering wheel.

"I'm sorry, Ruth. I can't imagine what he's thinking."

"He's thinking he's seen a man nearly dead from drinking before and that Ray looks about the same."

Celia glances between the two of them.

"Papa," Ruth says. "Papa drank himself dead. But Ray's not that close yet, Arthur. Not like Papa. Not as bad as Papa was in the end."

Another car approaches. Ruth sits up. The more she talks, the more numb she feels inside. She didn't realize it in the café, or the night Ray came back from Damar, or the day Arthur asked Gene Bucher to give Ray a job, but sitting in the car, blinking against another set of approaching headlights, she knows that Arthur is counting on time because he doesn't know any other way.

"Arthur," Celia shouts. "Look out."

Arthur jerks the steering wheel, his shadow falling to the right. The car slides across the gravel road, throwing Ruth against the doorframe. Her head bounces off the window. Something jabs her side. Pressing her one good arm straight out, she braces herself against the front seat. The car grinds to a stop. Heavy tires spinning on the hard dry gravel fade in the distance. Outside the front window, a dust cloud settles like dwindling smoke in the headlights and a long winding tail and arched back appear—tumbleweeds caught up along the fence line on Bent Road. Someone had better clear them away soon, Ruth thinks, or they'll pull down the fence, and she closes her eyes.

Daniel lies in bed. Through his wall, he hears Evie fumbling about in her closet when she should be sleeping. Elaine told them lights out so she and Jonathon could sit on the couch and talk about flower arrangements, cummerbunds and the house that Jonathon will finish before they marry. Already, the wedding is the only thing Elaine talks about and already Jonathon is around even more, being Dad's extra set of hands. Daniel pulls his pillow over his head and rolls toward the window. He stares at the white sheers lit up by the porch lights so that they shine with an orange glow and wonders if Jack Mayer really stole Nelly Simpson's 1963 midnight blue Ford Fairlane.

Ian brought the newspaper clipping to school last Monday. He said that Nelly Simpson was married to the richest man in Hays and there wasn't a man, woman, or child in Rooks County who would dare leave a fingerprint on Nelly Simpson's Ford Fairlane. Never mind, steal it. No man except Jack Mayer. Ian said Jack Mayer wouldn't give two God damned cents about Nelly Simpson or any other Simpson.

"We got trouble now," Ian had said, sitting across from Daniel at the cafeteria table and propping up his short leg on the cross bar. He didn't need to do this with his new boot because both feet could touch the floor at the same time, but he did it anyway. "He's got himself a car now. He can get to anyone he damn well pleases."

"I thought he was living in your barn."

"Sure he was, but now he's got a car. It's trouble. Real big damn trouble." Ian glanced around as if Jack Mayer might be standing right behind him. "My brothers say maybe we can hunt him down." He lowers his voice. "After we go to shooting pheasant, maybe we'll go to shooting Jack Mayer. It'll be practice. Real good practice. We'll track him down."

"How we going to track a Ford Fairlane?" Daniel asked.

Ian opened his brown bag lunch, looked inside. "Dogs," he had said, pulling out a sandwich wrapped in waxed paper. "We'll use dogs."

When Daniel opens his eyes again, the white sheers still shine with an orange glow, his pillow is lying on the floor, Evie's room is quiet and the telephone is ringing. Outside his door, footsteps cross the living room floor and move into the kitchen. The phone stops ringing and Jonathon's muffled voice drifts into Daniel's room. He closes his eyes and opens them again when there is a tap on his door.

"Daniel," Elaine says. She knocks again, louder. "Daniel, wake up."

She cracks the door and the light from the living room makes him blink. He lifts up on one elbow. "Yeah, I'm up. I'm awake."

"Get yourself dressed. That was Daddy. There's been an accident."

Daniel sits up, resting his hands on his knees.

"Get yourself going," Jonathon says, taking Elaine's place. Daniel wants to tell Jonathon to get his own damned self going, but instead he swings his legs over the side of the bed and puts both feet on the cold floor. In the next room, Elaine taps on Evie's door.

"No time for questions," Jonathon says. "Get a move on."

Chapter 19

Sitting in Elaine's lap, Evie wraps herself in a blanket and buries her nose in it. Elaine tightens her hug, kisses the top of top of Evie's head and says, "You try to sleep, pumpkin. Daddy will tell us when there's something to know."

Though she closes her eyes, Evie can't sleep because everyone's shoes make an awful noise on the tile floors and the hospital smells make her want to pinch her nose closed. She presses her hands over her ears as more people walk down the hall, their footsteps ringing off the gray block walls and shiny tile floors.

"Mama, you're here," Elaine says, lifting Evie and setting her on the ground. "You're okay."

Daddy wraps one arm around Mama while reaching out to Evie with the other. They both are as gray as the walls and Daddy looks smaller in the hospital than he does at home. Evie drops her blanket, letting it fall to the ground, and hugs Daddy's leg.

"I'm just fine," Mama says, kissing Elaine and Daniel's cheeks and hugging Evie as she drifts from Daddy's leg to Mama's. "Everyone is fine."

Mama's eyes are red, like she's been crying, and her hair is mussed on top. In Detroit, Mama's hair was never mussed. Every morning before they moved to Kansas, Mama backcombed her hair with a pink long-handled comb and sprayed it twice with hairspray. She always wore a dress and usually her tan shoes with the two-inch heel that she said were good for walking. She trimmed and buffed her nails every Saturday morning, rubbed petroleum jelly on her elbows every night and plucked the stray hairs that grew between her brows. Seeing Mama now, standing in the gray hallway, Evie thinks she doesn't do any of those things anymore. She looks sleepy and sad like maybe she's tired of being a mom in Kansas.

"Was it that curve at the top of Bent Road?" Jonathon asks, stepping up to Daddy and shaking his hand.

Daddy nods. It must have been the same monster that scared Mama off the road on the night they first drove to Grandma Reesa's house.

"Tricky spot," Jonathon says. "A little ice, a little wind and those trucks drive awful fast for that narrow road. Sure is a tricky spot."

"Threw us on the shoulder," Daddy says, turning again when the double doors at the end of the hallway open. "Shook Ruth up a good bit, but she's all right."

The overhead lights make Mama squint. "Doctor says Aunt Ruth bruised a rib or two and her shoulder was pulled out of place."

Mama lifts Evie's chin. "But the doctor fixed her up. Aunt Ruth and her sweet baby are just fine."

Mama's hands are rough and cold. Not liking the feel of it, Evie pulls away. At the same time, Daddy lets go of Mama and marches down the hallway where two men are walking through the double doors. One man, wearing a long, dark coat, walks a few steps behind the other. The other man looks like Uncle Ray, except smaller. Daddy begins to walk faster, his footsteps tap, tap, tapping across the tile floor. The man without the coat stops in the middle of the hallway. He looks up at Daddy and then back at the dark coat man. Daddy walks faster.

"Oh, dear," Mama says.

Jonathon follows Daddy, and Daniel starts to tag along, but Mama grabs his arm and shakes her head at him. The dark coat man nods at Daddy. They are closer now and Evie knows the other man is Uncle Ray, even if he is smaller, even though he's shriveled up like someone left him in the drier too long and forgot to press out the wrinkles. Uncle Ray steps away from the dark coat man who Mama calls Father. Yes, it's Father Flannery all bundled up for the cold. Uncle Ray stumbles. He braces himself against one of the gray walls and points at Daddy. Uncle Ray may have shriveled up, but his voice hasn't.

"That woman," Uncle Ray says, pointing at Aunt Ruth's door. "That woman is none of your business now, Arthur. None of your concern. That's what you said. Now I'm saying it."

Daddy holds up two hands and, when Uncle Ray stumbles again, Daddy uses them to catch him.

"There's a God damned baby in there," Uncle Ray says, pushing off Daddy and falling on Father Flannery.

Father Flannery shoves Uncle Ray toward the wall and steps back.

"You told him about the baby?" Daddy asks and Father Flannery nods yes as Daddy dances this way and that so Uncle Ray can't stumble into Aunt Ruth's room.

Jonathon slips behind Daddy, pulls Aunt Ruth's door closed and stands in front of it, his arms crossed over his chest and his feet spread wide as if he's bracing for a big gust of wind.

"I assure you that a man should know about his own child," Father Flannery says, backing away from Uncle Ray. "I assure you that is true."

"This was not your business," Daddy shouts at Father Flannery.

Mama scoots Evie off to stand with Elaine and walks down the hall but Jonathon waves her away. She stops when Daniel walks up to her side. He pats Mama on the shoulder, probably because he saw Jonathon do that and he wants to be grown up like Jonathon, and then he walks toward Daddy and Uncle Ray.

Nobody answers Daddy when he shouts out again wondering who told Father Flannery about Aunt Ruth's baby. Daddy stops searching for someone to be angry at and turns back to Uncle Ray.

"Go on home," he says, taking Uncle Ray by the shoulders and pointing him toward the double doors at the end of the hallway. "You go home. Sleep it off. Jonathon'll drive you."

"No damn thing to sleep off," Uncle Ray says, pushing Daddy

away. His cloudy eye is white under the bright lights. "I've been patient enough with you, Arthur Scott." He points at Daddy first, swings his arm around, stumbles and points next at Aunt Ruth's room. "That woman didn't get nothing wasn't coming to her. Feeding those Robisons after they aimed their God damned finger at me."

Uncle Ray sways a few steps and shoves Daddy with both hands. Daddy stumbles backward, trips over Daniel who didn't listen to Mama when she said to stay put, and falls on his hind end. Daniel falls, too, knocking his head against the gray wall. The crack his head makes when it bounces off the concrete is loud enough that Evie hears it. Mama hears it, too, and she jumps forward. This time Jonathon can't stop her even though he holds up the same hand that turned her around before. She rushes down the hall to Daniel as Jonathon shoves Uncle Ray away from Aunt Ruth's door. Daddy stands and tries to catch Uncle Ray as he staggers backward, but he misses and Uncle Ray trips over Mama and Daniel, who is trying to stand. All three fall to the shiny tile floor.

Elaine shouts out but it isn't loud because she has one hand pressed over her mouth. With the other hand, she tries to cover Evie's eyes, but Evie can still see. Daniel's legs are tangled up with Mama and Uncle Ray's legs. Mama lies flat on her back and Uncle Ray is spread out on top of her, his arms and legs straddling her, his chest pressing down on hers. Their noses would touch if Mama lifted her head an inch. Uncle Ray seems bigger again, lying face to face with Mama. She pulls her chin in tight and rolls her head away. Uncle Ray smiles down at Mama. Evie wishes he would go away.

She wishes he were the happy man in her picture. She starts to cry as Daddy reaches into the pile and yanks out Uncle Ray.

"It's moving day," Uncle Ray says as Daddy shoves him. "You got no business doing what you're doing, Arthur Scott."

Evie chokes on her tears but she can still hear Uncle Ray shout. He doesn't stop, not even when Father Flannery walks back through the double doors with two more men. Daddy holds up one hand so the three of them stand back and watch.

"You go on home, Ray. Your time with this family is done."

The two men who came with Father Flannery push open the doors and Uncle Ray walks through, still mumbling. All four disappear.

Celia arches her back so Daniel can slip his arm out from under her but she doesn't stand. Focusing on a blank spot on the wall, she draws in full, deep breaths until the feel of Ray on top of her, the pressure that he laid down on her, is gone. It must have been her imagination, his hips grinding into her. He didn't have the time, couldn't have had the presence of mind, to take the opportunity. But she did feel him, pressed against her upper thigh and into her hipbone. She closes her eyes and hopes she doesn't cry. Next to her, Daniel sits up. She inhales, two deep breaths, pushes up on her elbows and reaches out to touch the spot where his head hit the wall. He pulls away and stands. At the end of the hallway, the double doors fall shut, swing back and forth and finally hang motionless. Above her, Daniel reaches down, offering a hand. Celia clears her throat, smooths her hair and the gathered pleats on the front of her skirt and takes Daniel's help.

Once standing, Celia tugs at her waistline, straightens her collar, and when she looks at Daniel, she realizes she is looking up at him. Surely she has been for quite some time, but suddenly it strikes her how much he's grown, how close he is to becoming a man, and how, like a man, his ego is bruised. She smiles and reaches for him but he pulls away again and walks down the hall toward Elaine and Evie, where he sits in one of the chairs lined along the hallway and rests his head in his hands.

"My good Lord in heaven," Reesa says, her voice shattering the silence. Wearing her blue flannel housecoat, a pair of galoshes and the brown hat that she normally saves for Sundays, she shuffles through the doors. "What is going on here?"

"Everyone is fine, Reesa," Celia says, rubbing her tailbone. "We had a little car accident but everyone is fine."

"Well, from the sounds of Ray," Reesa says, motioning toward the closed doors, "things are not fine."

"Nobody's worried about Ray right now," Arthur says, shaking Jonathon's hand and slapping him on the back. "Ruth is in there." He nods toward her room. "Doctor checked her out. The baby's fine. She can come home in the morning."

"Seems that Ray plans on being the one to take her home. He knows, doesn't he?" Reesa scans the room before finally resting her eyes on Celia as if she wears the most blame. "He knows about the baby?"

"He does," Arthur says, pulling a speck of fuzz from Celia's hair. "You okay?" he asks.

Celia swallows and nods.

Reesa snorts, shaking her head at Celia and scoots Jonathon away from Ruth's room, sending him back down the hall to stand with Elaine. "Well, I've said it before, and I'll say it again," Reesa says, taking Jonathon's position as guard. "I think Ruth should move in with me."

Arthur wraps one arm around Celia and rubs his forehead with his other hand. "No need for Ruth to move anywhere. She's fine where she is."

"Ray is going to come knocking now that he knows about the baby. She needs to live farther away. She needs to move home."

"Ruth is not living in that house." Arthur's voice is calm but his body is rigid, and the arm around Celia's shoulder is like a clamp.

"Maybe it's not such a bad idea," Celia says. "Only because you seem to upset Ray. Maybe he'd be less upset by Ruth living with your mother."

"And you think we should care about making Ray happy?" Arthur says.

Down the hall, Daniel sits alone, his shoulders slumped, his head in his hands.

Shaking his head at Daniel, Arthur continues. "You think I give two God damned cents about making Ray happy?"

"I think nothing of the sort. But I do know we're trapped in a terrible place. All of us, but mostly Ruth and her sweet baby. You were the one who said you wanted to keep the peace. I want whatever will keep Ray away from them."

Celia doesn't want to say it, or even admit it to herself, but mostly she wants Ruth to move so Ray will never come near her house again. She doesn't want him near Evie. Doesn't want him to start thinking that Evie is close enough to Eve, something that he might have thought about Julianne Robison.

"I will keep Ruth and this family safe," Arthur says to Reesa. "And keeping the peace ended the second he found out about the baby."

Reesa takes a breath to say something back to Arthur but stops when the door opens behind her. Ruth peeks through the small opening, hiding her body with the door, and motions for Arthur to come inside.

Jonathon stands next to Elaine, one arm wrapped around her waist, the other cocked on his hip as if he is wearing a holster and gun and is ready to draw if Uncle Ray returns. When Dad disappears into Aunt Ruth's room, Jonathon turns to Daniel.

"You okay, sport?" he says.

Elaine looks at Daniel, too, as if she were Mama and he were Evie.

"I'm fine," Daniel says and shoves away the hand that Jonathon holds out to him. "I can stand by myself."

Jonathon steps back. "Suit yourself."

Daniel stands from his chair and, crossing his arms over his chest, he leans against the wall. Ian says that the morgue is in the basement floor of the hospital and that's where the police will take Jack Mayer when he and Daniel shoot him dead. He says they'll take Julianne there, too, if they ever find her. He says that maybe he and Daniel will sneak into the basement morgue to see them both. Next time, Daniel will be ready for Uncle Ray. He is a good shot, a damn good shot, probably even better than Jonathon. Just like he told Mama and Aunt Ruth the night Uncle Ray showed up at the house asking for dessert and a jump start. He could make a real mess of Uncle Ray with Dad's shotgun. Next time, he'll damn sure be ready.

Ruth shuffles across the cold tile floor in her paper slippers and crawls into bed, using her good arm to hoist herself. Behind her, Arthur walks into the room and the door falls closed. With her head, she motions toward a wooden chair sitting in the corner of the room. Arthur moves it next to her bed and sits in it backward, straddling it with his legs—the way he sat as a boy. The moonlit room eases the creases around his eyes and because his hair has grown longer, like it was when he was a teenager, he looks younger. Tired, perhaps a little scared, but young again.

"We haven't talked much since you moved back, just you and me," Ruth says, wanting to touch Arthur's hand. "But I'm always around, aren't I?"

"Glad to have you. You know that."

"I do." Ruth rests both hands on Elisabeth and smiles when she feels a familiar flutter. "Do you remember how Eve used to tease you for having so little to say?"

Arthur nods.

"But when you did decide to talk, she always listened. She said you were worth listening to because you made darn sure you had something worth saying before you said it."

"Be nice if that were true."

"It is true, Arthur." Ruth reaches out and rests one hand on his. "I know you'll take care of us. If you say it, I know it's worth listening to."

Arthur drops his head into his folded arms.

"I know it's true. And I know if you could have saved Eve, you would have."

For a moment they are silent.

"What happened to Eve was not your fault," she says. "I know you think it was. I know Father made you think it was. But it wasn't. You were a boy, Arthur. No more a man than Daniel is now." Ruth touches Arthur's cheek and lifts his face. "I listened to you, Arthur. So now you listen to me. There was nothing you could have heard. Nothing you could have seen. It was a terrible thing, but you can't save her by saving me."

"I should have moved back home earlier. Shouldn't have left you alone for so long."

"All these years, I was afraid that you thought like the others. So many in town believing that Ray hurt Eve all those years ago. Like Floyd. All of them believing I married the man who killed my own sister. But he didn't, Arthur. I know he didn't. I promise that I'm certain of that. I hope you never believed like the others." Ruth lowers her eyes. "I hope that isn't what kept you away for so long."

Arthur drops his head, shakes it from side to side and exhales. "You're too forgiving of me. Far too quick to forgive."

"We all did the best we could," Ruth says, lifting Arthur's chin and smiling down on him. "I'll tell Floyd everything. I don't know what Ray was up to that night, I really don't. But I'll tell Floyd everything." She squeezes his hand. "I'd like to stay with your family, if you'll still have me, if you think it's best."

"Good enough," Arthur says.

She smiles and lays both hands over her stomach. "Her name is Elisabeth."

Arthur stands and nodding his head, he says, "Elisabeth, it is."

Chapter 20

Celia leans against the kitchen sink and rubs her tailbone. Two days since she fell in the hospital and it's still sore. The aches and pains won't last much longer but every time she kneads a sore spot, she feels Ray on top of her again, pressing into her thigh, smiling down on her. Wishing she had never suggested they meet Ray at the café, she swallows and tightens the belt on her robe. When Ruth asks if Celia is feeling all right, she smiles, embarrassed that Ruth would be worried about her, and turns to face her family. Arthur, wearing his denim coat and work boots, reaches up and catches the kiss that Evie throws from across the kitchen.

"You sure enough about me leaving today?" Arthur says, tucking the kiss in his pocket. Evie giggles.

"We'll be fine," Celia says and follows him to the back door. "Not much choice really." Standing together at the top of the basement stairs, she kisses him and, as he climbs into his truck, she calls out, "We'll lock up tight."

Before walking back inside, Celia looks toward Ray and Ruth's house. Ruth says he'll drink for a good long time once he gets started but eventually he'll remember there's a baby to contend with, and he'll come again.

Back in the kitchen, sitting at the table, Evie breaks off a piece of biscuit and shoves it in her mouth. "When will the poppy mallows bloom again, Aunt Ruth?" she says before her mouth is empty.

Celia frowns and shakes her head at the bad manners.

The poppy mallows were the first flower Ruth taught Evie about because a thick patch grew every year in the ditches alongside their new house.

"We'll start to see them as early as April," Ruth says, snapping the lid back on the box of oatmeal with her good hand while keeping the sore arm tucked closely to her body. "But sometimes not until May. Depends on the rain. And how early spring comes."

Celia shouts for Daniel to hurry along or he'll miss the bus, and then she gently touches Ruth's hand. Ruth nods that she is doing fine.

"They're Aunt Eve's favorite, right?" Evie says, stirring her oatmeal and testing the temperature by touching a small spoonful to her upper lip.

"They *were* her favorite," Celia says. "A long time ago. Remember?"

Evie closes her eyes and takes a deep breath as if smelling a bouquet of flowers.

"You do remember, Evie. Don't you? You remember about Aunt Eve being gone?"

Evie smiles. "Sure," she says. "May I be excused?"

"You may. But hustle along or you'll miss the bus."

"Thanks," Evie calls out as she skates across the wooden floor and slides into her room.

Daniel pulls out his lunch and lays it on the cafeteria table. Ian does the same. Both boys have similar lunches except that since Aunt Ruth came along, Daniel has better desserts. He slides an extra oatmeal raisin cookie to Ian's side of the table even though he knows Ian won't eat it.

"Did you hear?" Ian asks, pulling the waxed paper off his sandwich and holding one half to his mouth. "About Nelly Simpson's car?"

Daniel shakes his head.

"Police found it near Nicodemus. It's all over the newspapers." Ian glances around the crowded cafeteria and whispers, "You know about Nicodemus, don't you?"

His mouth full of ham and cheese, Daniel shakes his head again.

"It's where all the coloreds live. Every one of them in the county. Proof positive Jack Mayer took that car. Took it and drove to Nicodemus where he must know pretty much everyone."

Daniel takes another bite.

"Folks there will help hide him."

"My mom says I can still come tomorrow," Daniel says because he doesn't know anything about Nicodemus and doesn't know what else to say.

Ian takes a bite of his sandwich and sets it aside. "You going to bring your dad's shotgun?"

Daniel nods.

"Your .22 won't do you any good. Not for pheasant hunting. My brothers say if you have a shotgun, we can be the pushers." Ian pokes his elbow into the center of an unpeeled banana. Its guts squirt out both ends. He does the same thing every day and throws it away so his mom will think he ate it. "You know about pushers and blockers, don't you?"

Daniel shakes his head.

"Blockers stand along the road, blocking the pheasant, and the pushers walk across the field, pushing the birds so they get squeezed between. Being a blocker is no good. Blockers get hit by buckshot if they're not careful. Pushing is best. Pushers flush out the pheasant, take an easy shot. We want to be pushers."

Daniel holds up a hand and shakes his head when Ian slides his uneaten sandwich across the table. A few months back, when Ian first started giving Daniel his leftovers, he took them. Ida Bucher made her sandwiches with double mayonnaise and extra thick slices of cheese, but when Daniel began noticing that he could see Ian's backbone through his shirt and that he wasn't growing like everyone else in the grade, he stopped taking Ian's sandwiches, no matter how much mayonnaise Mrs. Bucher used.

Ian wads up the sandwich in its waxed paper wrapper and drops it into his lunch bag. "My brothers say we'll be hunting late-season pheasant. They're the hardest to shoot. Early-season pheasant are stupid. They get shot straight away. But late-season pheasants, they're the smart ones. You got to be tricky to get the late-season birds. My brothers say that if we're smart enough to get us some late-season pheasants, we'll go hunting for Jack Mayer."

Daniel starts to ask why early-season pheasant are stupid but stops because a group of kids breaks out laughing. At first, he thinks they're laughing at Ian, but the kids are sitting two tables over and couldn't hear Ian talking about Jack Mayer and Nelly Simpson and late-season pheasant.

"What are they all laughing at?" Ian asks, putting the rest of his lunch back in the brown bag his mom packed it in and squishing it down with both hands.

"Don't know," Daniel says, thinking Ian looks a little blue. Or maybe it's the gray light from an overcast sky. He turns toward the laughter as a couple of kids at the next table stand. He leans to the left and sees her.

Two tables down, sitting by herself as she always does at lunch, Evie is wearing one of Aunt Eve's dresses—the blue one, the one with ruffles and a satin bow, the one she said was her favorite. The dress is too big and falls off her small, white shoulders. She tugs at it, gathering up the collar where it has torn away at the seam. She smiles as if she doesn't hear the kids laughing. She smiles as if Aunt Eve is sitting across the table from her. Daniel throws down his sandwich, jumps up and runs two tables over.

"Hi, Daniel," Evie says.

Turning to the kids sitting at the other end of Evie's table, Daniel says, "Shut up. All of you, shut up." Then he looks back at Evie. "What are you doing?"

"Eating lunch," she says, laying out two napkins—setting a place for two people.

"Why are you wearing that dress?"

Evie smiles and shoves a piece of peanut-butter-and-jelly sandwich in her mouth. "It's my favorite. Aunt Eve's favorite, too."

"You shouldn't be wearing that, Evie. It's all torn and it's not yours."

Two tables away, Ian is watching them. He still looks blue.

"You're going to get in trouble."

Evie takes another bite and dabs one corner of her mouth with her napkin. "No, I won't. Don't be silly." She stands to show Daniel how she rolled up the middle of the dress and tied it off with the sash. "See, I made it fit. I fixed it myself."

Daniel stands and holds out his arms, blocking the view of Evie modeling her dress. "Sit down already. Does Mama know you're wearing that?"

"Aunt Eve said I could."

"Aunt Eve said?"

Evie nods. "Yes, Aunt Eve said."

Chapter 21

The school bus hisses and slows near Daniel's house. Holding onto the back of the seat in front of him, he gathers his books and lunchbox, stands and waits until the bus has stopped before stepping into the aisle.

"Now, you're sure Evie wasn't meant to take the bus home today?" Mr. Slear, the bus driver, asks.

"No, sir. Guess my mama picked her up early."

The bus door slides open and Mr. Slear says, "She not feeling well?"

"Yes, sir. Not feeling well at all."

Daniel waits at the end of the gravel drive until Mr. Slear pops the bus into gear and drives away. Once it has disappeared over the hill, leaving behind a trail of gray exhaust, he walks up the drive. The tailgate of Dad's truck peeks out from behind the house. He has come home early. The only other time Dad came home early from work was when the first black boy in Detroit called Elaine. Now he's home because Evie wore Aunt Eve's dress to school.

After a few more steps, Daniel sees all of Dad's truck. It's parked in its normal spot. Mama's car is parked next to the truck and the spot where Jonathon normally parks is empty. Daniel smiles at the empty spot until he hears a low rumble. He takes a few more slow steps. There it is again. Almost a groan. Rounding the back of the house and seeing nothing, he stops and stomps his feet, trying to warm his toes. The cold air burns his lungs and the inside of his throat. Inching closer to the back of the house, he hears it again. He takes a few more steps. Aunt Ruth stands at the far end of the screened-in porch. She must hear it, too.

"What should I do, Arthur?" Aunt Ruth says. "What do you need?"

Aunt Ruth's voice is quiet as if she's trying not to scare something. Daniel shifts direction and walks toward the gap between the garage and the far side of the house. As he nears Aunt Ruth, she begins to sidestep toward the back door. She looks at Daniel. Her eyes are wide and she is shaking her head. She looks small, as small as Evie, as small as the day Uncle Ray came asking for pie and a jump for his truck. On his tiptoes now, so his feet don't crunch on the gravel drive, Daniel takes a few more steps.

Dad and Olivia are standing in the small alleyway between the house and garage, the space that Daniel always forgets to mow. But the grass has died off with winter and the ground is hard and bare. With one hand, Dad pats Olivia on the hind end. With the other, he waves Aunt Ruth away. Olivia is too large to turn around in the narrow space and she can't walk through and around the house because old Mr. Murray's rusted car blocks the far end. The only way out is for Dad to coax her to back up.

"There you go, girl," Dad says to Olivia in a quiet voice. He sounds like he's talking to Evie. "Get on back now, girl."

Step by step, Olivia backs out of the narrow passageway.

"Dan," Dad says, seeing Daniel standing in the driveway. "Get Evie inside. Get her inside now and get me my gun."

Blood is splattered across Dad's white work shirt, the one with the Rooks County patch that Mama sewed on the left pocket before his first day of work. Both sleeves are rolled up to his elbows, and his hands are shiny red like he dipped them in red paint. Olivia turns, leading with the top of her head, followed by her round, brown eyes.

Aunt Ruth said Olivia was a good mother to many calves, but she's too old now and she's apple-assed. No one wants her apple-assed calves anymore. Daniel gags into a closed fist and stumbles backward.

A gash runs the length of Olivia's neck and down into her dewlap and her jowls hang like parted curtains. Most of her blood is gone, drained out on the ground, soaked up by the dirt. What is left is thick and dark, almost black. A shadow grows out of the wound and spreads up and across her neck, staining her chestnut coat. She staggers, moans, barely more than a whisper. Dad pats her right haunch. Coughing and choking, Daniel thinks of Evie. Dad thinks Evie came home on the bus. No, she's with Mama. Mama came to school for her, picked her up early. The nurse was going to call Mama because Evie wore Aunt Eve's dress. The nurse was supposed to call.

"Get my gun," Dad says, starting to back up again and coaxing Olivia with his quiet voice. "Get on back, girl. Get on back now."

Daniel's legs won't move. He sees the steps leading to the back porch. He'll go up them, two at time, unlock the cabinet, grab the gun. Evie's already inside, hiding her face in Mama's apron, probably crying because Olivia is going to die. The gun is inside, too. But Daniel's legs won't move.

"My gun, Dan," Dad says, wiping his forehead with his shirt-sleeve and leaving a red smudge. "I need a gun."

Daniel takes a step toward the porch. Only one. Another low rumble drifts up from Olivia. Dad yells again for him to get moving. He takes the stairs two at a time. Inside the back door, Mama and Aunt Ruth already have the gun cabinet open. They stand back as Daniel reaches in and grabs the shotgun. Dad said it once belonged to Grandpa Robert, but he's dead so now it's Dad's gun. It's heavier than his rifle, the weight of it pulling him forward. With one hand on the stock and the other on the double barrel, he swings around, careful to not hit Mama or Aunt Ruth, and runs back outside.

"Careful, Dan," Mama calls out.

Olivia and Dad stand in the driveway now, clear of the small space that had trapped Olivia. Dad has one hand on a leather lead that dangles from Olivia's neck strap. Evie left it on. Damn it all, she's always leaving on that lead. Olivia stomps her front feet, staggering from side to side as if she's frightened now that she is in the open. She starts to swing around, throwing her head to the left. Dad looks behind, measuring the distance between him and the garage because Olivia might crush him against it.

"There's a girl," he says, dropping the leather lead and coming at her from the front end where she can't hurt him. "There's a good girl."

Olivia staggers a few steps to the side and back toward Dad. Waiting until she staggers away again, he grabs at the strap and walks her in a half circle, coaxing her quietly until she is facing the opposite direction. Still talking to her, telling her she's a good girl, he backs toward the fence, and without taking his eyes off of hers, he wraps her lead around the nearest wooden post and ties it off. Olivia's blood is smeared across his face and his neck. Giving the lead a tug to test that it is good and tight, Dad sidesteps away from her.

"Go ahead on, son." He nods, and as he steps away, he pulls a handkerchief from his pocket and wipes the blood from his hands.

Waiting until Dad is clear, Daniel lifts the heavy gun and walks toward Olivia. With the wooden stock pressed to his cheek, he wraps his finger around the stiff trigger and stares down the wide barrel until Olivia is lined up in the sight. She is a Brown Swiss with long thin legs and dark lashes that trim her brown eyes. Akin to a deer, Dad had said. She'll be a jumper, quick and light on her feet. She'll be a good girl, a good cow. But a quick one. You'll have to take good care. She throws her head again, stumbling left and right, the lead pulling tight against her weight. Daniel's finger is numb on the trigger.

"Go on with it, son," Dad says. He stands with his back to Daniel and Olivia. "No need letting her suffer."

Daniel stares down the barrel at Olivia. She flicks one round ear and swats her long black tail.

Dad turns back to face Daniel. He exhales loud enough for Daniel to hear and reaches out as if wanting Daniel to hand off the gun. Instead, Daniel lines it up again and begins to pull the heavy trigger.

"Hold on there, Dan," Dad says. "Wait. Dan, no."

Daniel pulls. He thinks he pulls. And jumps when a shot fires.

It catches Olivia square between the ears, and the sound of her exploding skull seems to surprise her. She tosses her head, shaking away the echo, but the lead holds firm. Another shot. She drops her snout, nuzzles the ground, stumbles, her front feet crossing one over the other. Her back feet are rooted. The lead holds firm. A third shot. She falls. Daniel lowers the shotgun and turns. There, standing in front of his truck, ready to take another shot, Jonathon holds his position, but Olivia is already down. He had perfect aim with all three. He lowers his gun and leans against the hood of his truck. He's parked in his usual spot.

"Got herself caught up back there," Dad says. "Tangled up in her lead." He takes another deep breath and shakes his head. "Couldn't find her way out. Threw her head through the garage window."

Jonathon nods and wipes his brow with the palm of his hand like Dad always does. In the passenger side of his truck, Elaine sits, her face hidden in her hands.

Daniel looks down at his gun and back at Dad.

"Wouldn't want a shotgun for a job like this, son," Dad says.

Jonathon lays his rifle in the back of his truck. "Shotgun'll do the trick if something's coming at you," he says. "Good for protection and hunting. But if you have time to take aim, you want a rifle."

"Should have told you to get your rifle," Dad says. "Man'll always do right with his own gun."

Jonathon nods and Daniel wants to lunge at him and beat him in the face for always being Dad's extra set of hands. Instead, he nods like he understands about shotguns and rifles.

"Hustle on in and get me some clean clothes," Dad says, noticing the blood smeared across his shirt and arms.

Unable to say anything, Daniel nods again, lays down Grandpa's shotgun and steps around it. At the top of the porch stairs, he turns. Dad has picked up the gun and he and Jonathon are looking at it, studying it. They stare at each other for a good long moment, like they are saying something without having to speak, and then propping the gun over one shoulder, Dad walks into the garage.

"Damn shame," Jonathon says, walking toward Olivia.

Daniel says nothing while he waits for Dad to come back out of the garage. When he does, he is empty-handed.

"Dad," Daniel says before opening the screened door. "Evie's home, right? Evie's already here."

Finding Mrs. Robison's house was easy. From school, Evie had only to follow the church steeple, and even though it wasn't a long walk, Evie's toes are cold and the tops of her ears burn. She knocks again, this time with the palm of her hand because knocking with her knuckles makes them sting. Mama will be angry if she knows Evie left the house without gloves and a hat. She forgot them because she was so worried about the hem of Aunt Eve's dress sticking out from under her winter coat where Mama might see it.

Standing at the front door, Evie pulls her coat closed so Mrs. Robison won't see the torn part of the dress before Evie can explain. It's Daddy's fault it tore some more. He hit Uncle Ray, and Evie tripped over the dress and the collar ripped. Maybe that's why Uncle Ray's red truck is parked down at the church. Maybe he is talking to Father Flannery about how Daddy hit him and how Aunt Ruth has his baby inside of her. That's Uncle Ray's truck for sure. It's parked in the same spot he and Aunt Ruth parked in every Sunday before Aunt Ruth came to live with Evie. As soon as Mrs. Robison answers the door, Evie will show her that Uncle Ray is at church because Daddy and he had a fight and made Evie tear her dress. Surely Mrs. Robison will fix it. She'll have the needles and thread and she'll sew it up tight, and maybe she'll fix the trim, too. Mrs. Robison might even be able to make the dress a little smaller so it will fit Evie better next time.

Knocking on Mrs. Robison's door again and hearing nothing, Evie walks to the picture window, cups her hands around her eyes, and tries to see inside, but the curtains are closed and the house is dark. She taps on the glass and presses her ear to it. Still nothing. Back at the door, she knocks again. The sun is starting to fall lower in the sky. The air is colder now than when Evie first left school, and soon, Mama will be thinking about supper. Mrs. Robison doesn't live far from school but Evie does. Her house is a long way away. Her house is so far from school that Mr. Slear drives them in the bus every day.

Not knowing why, except that the cold air and the gray sky make her think that she might never find home again, Evie starts to cry. She tries to stop by holding her breath and knocking with her knuckles so the sting will make her forget about how far away her house is, but the harder she knocks, the harder she cries. Mrs. Robison isn't home and she can't fix Aunt Eve's dress. Evie will have to go home with the torn collar and Mama will scold her for wearing Aunt Eve's dress and for ruining it. Laying one hand flat on Mrs. Robison's door, Evie drops her head, pulls her collar up and over her mouth and nose and walks away from the house.

At the end of the Robisons' sidewalk, with her face buried in her coat, Evie turns toward St. Anthony's. She knows to take Bent Road straight out of town. It will change from concrete to gravel, twist and bend, exactly like the name says, and after a good long way, it will break in two. One branch will lead to Grandma Reesa's house and the other will switch its name to Back Route 1 and lead toward home.

Crossing the street to the church, Evie sees that Uncle Ray isn't visiting Father Flannery. He is standing inside the white wooden fence that wraps around the graveyard, staring down on one of the graves. The new graves, like the one dug for Mrs. Minken who died because she was 102, are way in the back of the cemetery, so Uncle Ray must be visiting an older grave, one for someone who died a long time ago. Three large pine trees stand over the grave Uncle Ray is looking at as if they are guarding it. He stands with those trees, his arms crossed, his feet spread wide like he's standing guard, too. In one hand, he holds his hat and his dark hair blows off his forehead. Evie calls out, good and loud so Uncle Ray will hear her over the wind.

"Hello," she says, and then is sorry for it. People are supposed to whisper in cemeteries.

Uncle Ray turns toward Evie. He watches her for a good long time, then pulls on his hat and looks back down on the grave.

The wind is colder once Evie steps onto the sidewalk and walks toward home. She pulls her sleeves over her hands, dips her head and tries to take long steps that will get her home quicker. Beyond the shelter of the church, the wind kicks up and dies down again when she passes Mr. Brewster's house. A light switches on. Mr. Brewster, carrying a plate, walks past the window. Mama says he's a widower because his wife died and that he doesn't get out much. Even Mr. Brewster, who is all by himself, is sitting down to supper. That's what Mama and the others are doing by now. Mama likes an early supper because going to bed on a full stomach never does anyone any good. Evie closes her eyes as she passes Mr. Brewster's house. He must be lonely in there all by himself and that makes Evie feel like she may never see home again.

At the last stop sign before the road changes to dirt, a car pulls up next to Evie. It rattles to a stop and exhaust swirls up, clouding the gray air around her. She unwraps her hands, lowers her collar and looks into the side of a big, red truck.

*   *   *

Celia clears her throat, and taking a deep breath to calm herself, she pulls a fresh shirt from the top drawer and a clean pair of pants from the closet. Out in the kitchen, Ruth is busying herself by setting the table and skinning the chicken for dinner. She's seen things like this before, probably much worse. If Arthur hadn't been able to come home in the middle of the day when Celia called to tell him that Olivia was out again and was apparently stuck between the house and garage, even with one bad arm, Ruth probably would have coaxed the cow out herself. Right this moment, she is probably planning how to best slaughter Olivia and where they will freeze so much meat. No, that's not true. Ruth wouldn't think those things. Reesa would, but not Ruth. Ruth will be thinking how to help the children understand that this is part of life on the farm. She would never tell them that Olivia will soon be wrapped in white butcher paper and stacked in the freezer.

Folding the blue and gray plaid flannel shirt for no reason other than to stall, Celia wonders if Arthur knew things would be this way when they moved from Detroit. Did he know that sometimes the eggs wouldn't be eggs when Celia cracked them into her skillet but that sometimes they would be the beginnings of a tiny, bloody chick? Did he know Daniel wouldn't have many friends and that Evie still wouldn't grow? Did he know Ray was beating Ruth all those years, beating the life out of her, and did he still stay away? Not wanting the answer to the last thought, Celia clears her throat again and walks from the bedroom with the clothes stacked neatly in both hands.

Standing at the kitchen table, one hand holding the back of a chair, Ruth doesn't look the way Celia thought she would. Her face is pale, her neck flushed. For a moment, Celia is relieved because Ruth is as upset as she by what has happened to Olivia. For a moment, Celia doesn't feel alone. Thank goodness for Ruth. Celia holds the clothes out to Daniel, who stands in the hallway leading to the back porch, but he doesn't reach for them.

"For your dad," Celia says, taking another step forward.

Daniel's arms hang limp and he steps aside when Arthur walks up from behind. Celia takes two quick steps backward and pulls the clothes to her chest, hugging them.

"Arthur, take this outside," she says, shoving his clothes at him. "You're an awful mess."

Reddish brown smudges that end with feathered edges travel from Arthur's right hip up to his left shoulder, as if Olivia threw her head against him, and dried blood is caked on his hands and forearms.

"Your shoes," Celia says. "Take those off. Outside."

Muddy tracks have followed Arthur into the house, bloody mud. Celia looks at Daniel's feet instead. He keeps telling her he needs new boots, that his toes are going to end up crooked if he doesn't get some bigger shoes.

"Please, take those off outside."

"Is Evie here with you?" Arthur says.

At this, Celia lifts her eyes.

"She's not outside," Jonathon says, walking up behind Arthur. Elaine stands next to him. She nods. "We checked the barn, the road. Elaine looked downstairs."

"She came on the bus," Celia says, looking Daniel in the eye. "With you. She came home on the bus. Like always."

"The nurse said she was going to call," Daniel says. "Because Evie wore the dress. I thought you came for her."

Ruth steps forward and takes the stack of clothes from Celia.

"The dress?" Celia says. "What dress? No one called."

"The school nurse." Daniel clears his throat the same way Celia does when she's trying not to cry. "She was going to call. She said maybe Evie should go home for the day."

Daniel looks up at Arthur. There's not so much difference anymore. They're almost the same height.

"Evie wore one of those dresses to school. One of Aunt Eve's dresses. From Grandma's house. I thought you picked her up." Daniel takes a deep breath. His chest lifts and lowers. "She didn't come home on the bus, Mama."

"Well, then she's still at school," Celia says, nodding. "Right. She's still at school."

"We'll go, Mama," Elaine says, pulling Jonathon toward the back door. "We'll check the school."

"I'll give them a call," Ruth says, setting the clothes on the table and taking care that they don't spill over and come unfolded. "I'm sure she's fine. Probably got caught up after class. Nothing to worry about."

"I thought you came, Mama," Daniel says. "I wouldn't leave her. I wouldn't."

Staring again at Daniel's boots, Celia thinks how much he's grown in the short time they've been in Kansas. And other things have changed, as well. His brow is starting to push out, the bridge of his nose is taking the same curve as Arthur's, his neck has thickened ever so slightly where it drapes into his shoulders. Celia cocks her head to the left and says, "Today at work, Arthur. Was Ray with you today at work?"

"Hasn't been in all week. Not since we saw him at the café. Not since Tuesday."

Chapter 22

The truck smells like a coyote wagon. That's what Mama would have said. Whenever Mama rode in Daddy's truck, she said it was becoming nothing more than a coyote wagon. After that, Daddy would take a leftover grocery bag and clean out the wadded-up newspapers, the half-eaten apples, which were half-eaten because Daddy only likes the bites that have red skin with them, and the cigarette butts that make Mama especially mad because she hates that he sometimes smokes in Kansas. Uncle Ray is a smoker, too, but he doesn't have anyone to tell him to clean out his butts so they spill over the small tray and some of them lie on the floor. Uncle Ray is an apple eater, too, but he eats his down to the core.

Wrinkling her nose and clearing her throat, Evie steps off the sidewalk and reaches for the inside door handle. It's cold in her bare hand. An old red and blue flannel sheet is draped over the spot where Evie is supposed to sit, probably because Aunt Ruth used to sit there and without the thin cover, the seats would be cold and hard. The sheet is tucked in tight where the back and the bottom of the seat meet. Aunt Ruth did that. She is always tucking and straightening. This makes Evie feel better, makes her feel that it is okay to get into Uncle Ray's truck. Bracing one hand against the doorframe and pulling on the inside handle with the other, Evie steps up into the truck, careful not to look at Uncle Ray's face because she can't help but stare straight into the bad eye and Mama says that's not polite. So instead, she keeps her head lowered, drops down on the flannel cover and swings her legs into the truck. Propping both feet on the toolbox that sits on the floorboard, she pulls the truck door closed.

"You call the school?" Arthur says, walking out of the bedroom and grabbing his keys from the table on his way outside. He has washed up and is wearing clean clothes. "She there?"

Ruth shakes her head and starts to speak, but Celia cuts her off. "No, she's not there. No one's there. No one to even answer the phone."

Standing face to face with Arthur, her hands on her hips, Celia suddenly hates him. She hates the way his hair curls when it is damp. She hates that he doesn't shave every day like he did in Detroit and that he can't be bothered with a tie on Sundays. She hates that he stretches and groans when he eats Reesa's fried chicken and doesn't use a napkin until he's eaten his fill. And most of all, she hates him for yelling at Daniel because he's not enough of a man yet. Arthur is the one who isn't man enough, and now, because of that, because he did nothing, because he isn't the man he is supposed to be, Evie is gone. Gone like Mother and Father. Gone like Julianne Robison. Gone.

"What about Jonathon and Elaine?" Arthur hops on one foot, pulling on a boot that has Olivia's blood caked in the tread. "They back yet?"

"No," Celia says, taking her own boots from the closet and reaching past Arthur for her coat. "Why would they be back?" She pushes him in the chest so he'll look her in the face. "It's a full thirty minutes there and home again. Thirty minutes at best. That's how far it is."

Cupping Celia's arms with both of his hands, Arthur says, "Take it easy. I'm sure she's fine. We'll find her. You stay here. You and Ruth. In case she comes home, you should . . ."

Celia shoves his hand away and yanks on her jacket. "This is your fault," she says, quietly at first, but then it feels so good, like beating on something with both fists, that she says it louder and louder until she is shouting. "I've been telling you, begging you to do something. I knew it. I knew it. He's angry. Angry that we kept the baby from him. First Julianne and now." But she can't say it. She can't say he has taken her Evie. "You brought us here. To this godforsaken place. This is your fault. All your fault."

It must be Ruth, laying a warm hand on Celia's back, and that must be Arthur, wrapping both arms around her, holding her to his chest. Someone is saying, don't panic. No need to panic. Won't do us any good. All these months that Julianne has been gone, Celia has thought of her every day, made herself think of the little girl she never met. If ever she found her day slipping away without a thought of Julianne, she stopped her scrubbing or ironing or weeding and looked up. If inside, she looked out a window. If outside, she looked to the horizon, always remembering, always searching, always hoping. Out of respect for the fear of losing her own children, she did these things every day, without fail. But no one ever found Julianne, and now Evie is gone and Celia is facing the same life Mary Robison must live.

The road under Uncle Ray's tires changes from asphalt to gravel. Evie feels the change in her stomach, the same tickle she gets when she rides with Daddy in his truck. Getting to Evie's house from church is easy. Now that the road has turned rocky, they will keep driving on Bent Road for a good long while, and when it breaks off to go to Grandma Reesa's house, they'll keep driving straight and the road will turn into Back Route 1. This is where Evie lives. Once Bent Road becomes Back Route 1, they're almost home. Except Uncle Ray turns before the twist in Bent Road that leads to Grandma Reesa's house. He turns on a road Evie's been on before but she can't remember when.

Daniel stands in the middle of the gravel drive, looking first toward the barn and next the garage, but he knows Evie isn't either place. He could check inside Mr. Murray's rusted old car, but she isn't in there either. Besides, he'd have to walk past Olivia to get to that old car, and he can't do that. Steam isn't rising from Olivia anymore. This must mean she's turning cold. Jonathon patted Daniel on the back before rushing off with Elaine to go to the school. He said he'd take care of the old gal when he got back. He said she'd keep just fine in the cold. Daniel doesn't want to think about what this means. There's a smell, too. Maybe it's Olivia's insides starting to rot out, or maybe it's mud and her wet, bloody hide.

Something is different now. It's the color of things. The sun is hanging on the horizon and its light is gray instead of clear. Everything is gray. It's almost night. It happens so quickly this time of year. Night didn't seem to settle in so fast in Detroit where there were streetlights and neighbors' lights and headlights. The gray air makes Daniel's stomach tighten and his chest begins to pound as each breath comes faster than the last. He backs away from Olivia. Evie isn't in the barn or the basement or Mr. Murray's old car. She's not anywhere. He takes another backward step and then another. Eventually, he'll run all the way to school. He'll find Evie there and bring her home. A few more steps, but he can't turn away from Olivia yet. She lies on her side, one rounded ear sticking up, one bright eye staring at him. He realizes he is waiting for that eye to blink, but it doesn't. It never will.

I t's not quite dark yet. As soon as Uncle Ray turns off Bent Road, Evie sees a small group of men standing in the ditch. Uncle Ray must have seen them, too. They must be the reason Uncle Ray turned because he stops the truck in the middle of the road and shines his headlights on them. A few of the men hold a hand up to shield their eyes and they look at Uncle Ray's truck. Evie scoots to the edge of her seat.

"Those two men have dogs," she says.

Uncle Ray doesn't answer, but instead pulls down hard on the gearshift, backs up, rolling the steering wheel so the truck's tailgate swings around toward the ditch and throws the gearshift forward again.

"Do you know those men, Uncle Ray?"

Again, Uncle Ray doesn't answer. His hat sits high on his forehead, and even though his eyes have plenty of room to see, he doesn't look at Evie. Turning the steering wheel the other way, passing one hand over the other the same way Daddy does, Uncle Ray presses on the gas and the men and the two dogs disappear when Uncle Ray drives back onto Bent Road.

The sky is almost all the way dark now, but even so, Evie remembers the place were they saw the men and dogs. She went there a time or two with Daddy when Uncle Ray was away with his other family in Damar. It's Mrs. Hathaway's farm, except Uncle Ray uses it because Mr. Hathaway died a long time ago. Evie slides back in her seat and grabs onto the blanket that Aunt Ruth left behind. For one quick second, something smells sweet and light like Aunt Ruth. Evie feels like she wants to cry again, though she doesn't know why. She grabs two handfuls of the rough quilt, wadding it up in both fists and watches for home.

Daniel is standing in the center of the gravel drive, staring down at Olivia, when Dad starts to beat on his steering wheel. Only then, does Daniel notice the empty sound of the truck's engine. It is rattling and choking but it won't turn over. Dad throws open the driver's side door.

"Go get your mother's keys," he shouts at Daniel.

Daniel doesn't move.

"Hurry up about it," Dad says, reaching behind his seat and pulling out a set of jumper cables. Next, the hood pops open. "The keys, Dan. Get your mother's keys."

Daniel backs away a few more steps. Dad is going to search for Evie but his truck won't start. How will they find Evie if Dad's truck won't start? One more time, Dad shouts. Daniel jumps, spins around, takes two running steps and stumbles.

"Olivia," Evie says. "Is that Olivia?"

Daniel straightens and grabs Evie by the shoulders. Her cheeks and nose are red, her eyes watery. She steps to the side so she can see Olivia.

"What's wrong with her?" Evie says. "Her neck is bad. Her head isn't the right shape."

From a few yards away, Olivia's one eye is staring at them. It's big and black, and like a piece of polished glass, it shines where it catches the porch light. Daniel turns back to Evie and checks her over top to bottom, searching for missing parts. Two eyes, two ears, a whole head.

"Come inside," he says, stepping in front of her so she can't see Olivia. "Dad," he shouts, pulling Evie toward the house. "She's home. She's home." Stumbling up the stairs, across the porch and pushing open the back door, he shouts, "Mama."

Warm air meets them inside. It burns Daniel's cheeks and lips. He inhales, drops down to one knee and holds Evie's hands.

"Evie's here. Evie's home."

Mama rushes in like the hot air, sweeping Evie up. She checks for missing parts, too. When she gets to Evie's hands, Mama presses them to her cheeks and rubs them between her own hands, warming them, softening them up.

From behind Daniel, Dad says, "Where have you been, child?"

But Mama quiets Evie, tells her that it doesn't matter. "You're home, sweet pea. You're so cold. So cold." And then to Daniel. "Where?" is all she says.

"I turned around and there she was." Daniel stands and whispers. "She saw Olivia. She saw what happened."

"I left her lead on," Evie says. "I did it. I left it on." She cries into Mama's shoulder. "I did it."

Mama looks over Daniel's head at Dad. Aunt Ruth wraps a blanket around Evie's small body. The old quilt smells sour and moldy like the basement. Mama hates drying clothes in the basement.

"No, Evie," Mama says. "It was an accident. No one's fault." Mama stretches out her arms, holding Evie where they can look into each other's eyes. "Where were you, Evie? How did you get home?"

"Uncle Ray brought me," she says. "We went to Mrs. Hathaway's farm, but there were men there so Uncle Ray brought me home."

Chapter 23

Celia cracks a third egg, cracks it so hard that the shell collapses in her hand leaving the yolk and white to slide through her fingers and into the dumpling dough. Dropping the shell into the sink and wiping her hands on the dishtowel tucked in her apron, she picks up a wooden spoon and stirs the thick dough. After a few minutes, she shifts the spoon to her other hand and continues to dig and grind until she's breathing heavily. Pausing once to roll her head from side to side, she shifts hands again, wraps her forearm around the bowl, drops the spoon and kneads the dough by hand. On the front burner, the chicken stock grows from a simmer to a rolling boil.

"Take it easy," Arthur says, leaning back in his chair and stretching.

Celia glances up at Arthur, but says nothing, and instead reaches for another egg. Reesa shakes her head. Celia grabs the egg anyway, cracks it as hard as the last and throws the empty shell toward the sink. She misses, and as it falls on the floor, she wipes her hands across the front of her white blouse.

Her right arm still in a sling, Ruth leaps from her seat to scoop up the shell. "A nice warm meal always makes things better," she says. "Always makes the house smell so wonderful." She talks as she picks up every piece of the slippery shell as if no one will notice the mess if she keeps talking.

"Making this house smell pretty good, that's for sure," Arthur says, leaning forward and resting his elbows on the table.

Celia takes a teaspoon from the drawer and begins to dip up the dough and drop it into the boiling broth, ignoring the fact that it's too runny because she's added one too many eggs. She clears her throat and chokes back a sob when Ruth, after cleaning the egg shell from her fingers, steps forward and whispers, "The kids are fine, Celia. Evie is fine. Safe and sound."

Pausing mid scoop, while Ruth kneads another cup of flour into the dough, Celia says to Reesa, "I've asked that Evie return all of Eve's things to you, along with an apology. I don't know what she was thinking. And getting in that truck with Ray." She stops, swallows. "We need to call Floyd and report this."

"Report what?" Arthur says. "He gave the girl a ride home. Damn fool that he is, he just gave her a ride home."

"They are searching his farm," Celia says, stirring her broth. "Searching it with dogs. And he took Evie there. You know what that means."

Arthur brushes his hair back from his face and takes a deep

breath before speaking. "For twenty-five years, Floyd has been thinking Ray had something to do with what happened to Eve." His eyes are swollen from his having rubbed them and from being tired. "That's the only reason he's keeping such an eye on Ray. Listen, I'll keep him clear of this family, that's for sure. And I know the man is up to plenty of no good, but I don't believe for a minute that he hurt Julianne Robison."

Celia throws her teaspoon into the broth, jumping back when it splashes up. "What about the night Julianne disappeared? He wasn't home. Ruth said so." Celia stands, hand on hips. "He could have done it. How can you know?"

"Evie doesn't have any friends."

Everyone turns. Daniel stands outside his bedroom, his hair tousled and his eyes red as if he woke up from having cried himself to sleep.

"At school. She doesn't have any friends at school. Neither do I, except for Ian. It's not like in Detroit. Nobody likes us here."

Celia, pulling off her apron, walks toward Daniel. He takes a few steps backward. "What do you mean, Daniel?"

"Just that. No friends. Except for Aunt Eve."

"Of course she has friends," Celia says.

Daniel shakes his head. "She did back home. Had plenty back then. But not here. They call her nigger lover. Have ever since we started school. Because we lived in Detroit. Called me one, too, until Ian started being my friend. The kids, they all tell Evie she's here because Jack Mayer stole Julianne Robison. Or maybe Uncle Ray took her. They say one of them's bound to steal Evie next."

"They say that to Evie?" Celia drops back against the kitchen counter.

Arthur shakes his head. Reesa makes a clucking sound.

"She sits by herself every day. At recess. Lunch. Everywhere. She's so small. They call her names. Tell her she's too small for Kansas. Sometimes Miss Olson sits with her at lunch. But Evie just pretends Miss Olson is Aunt Eve. Miss Olson isn't so small, though."

Ruth steps up to Celia's side. Her body is warm and she smells like Elaine's lavender lotion.

"How did I not know this?" she says to Ruth. "How could she be so unhappy and I not know?"

"She wasn't unhappy," Daniel says. "As long as she had Aunt Eve. That's why she took all that stuff. I guess that's why she wore the dress. But now she doesn't even have Aunt Eve. I think she's kind of scared about getting taken like Julianne. And she feels pretty bad about Olivia, too." He takes a few more steps away when Celia pushes off the counter. He shakes his head. "I understand though, about it being the kindest thing. To kill her, I mean. Just wish I hadn't left that gate open."

Arthur glances up at Celia before lowering his head to talk into the tabletop. "Cows like that get out all the time," he says. "They're jumpers. Could have jumped out."

Daniel stares at Arthur, not like a boy looks at his father, but like one man looks at another. Arthur tries to hold the stare long enough and hard enough that Daniel will believe Olivia was a jumper, but he can't manage it. He drops his eyes.

"I don't want to go to Ian's tomorrow," Daniel says, still staring at the top of Arthur's head.

Celia nods. "Certainly, Daniel. Whatever you want. Get some rest now. I'll call you when dinner's ready."

When Mama calls him to dinner, Daniel says he's too tired. Even when Mama opens the door a sliver and offers him a plate of Aunt Ruth's stewed chicken, Daniel rolls away and says no. Now, he can hear them, all of them, in the kitchen, their silverware clattering on the table, pots and pans being passed from place to place. They are probably talking about poor Evie and Daniel who have no friends. They probably think Evie is sick because she wore Aunt Eve's dress to school and that Daniel will never grow to be a man. He should have pulled the trigger and shot Olivia. No matter how stiff and heavy, no matter what kind of mess he would have made, he should have pulled it. That's what a man would have done. He would have carried the weight of that shotgun on his shoulder and pulled the God damn trigger.

Rolling over again and staring at the light shining under his door, Daniel hopes Ian will go pheasant hunting without him. He hopes Ian can be a pusher and that his black boots will help him keep up with his brothers. Maybe they'll do well, shoot a dozen birds or so, and then Jacob, the oldest Bucher brother, who only comes home on occasional weekends, will toss them all in his truck and drive to Nicodemus so they can flush out Jack Mayer. Maybe Ian will even get a shot at old Jack Mayer. Through the sight on his dad's shotgun, Ian will spot the man who's big as a mountain and black as midnight, and he'll take a shot. Even if he misses, even if Jack Mayer slips away because he's dark as night, Ian will have gotten off a shot and he'll never be quite as crooked again. And Daniel is Ian's friend, his best friend. Daniel will never be a city kid again if Ian gets off a good shot.

Chapter 24

Celia props the last dish in the drying rack, hangs her dish towel on the hook over the sink, and taking one last look around the kitchen to make sure everything is in its place, she flips off the light. Daniel and Evie's rooms are quiet, have been since dinner. Daniel didn't eat a bite. Celia will make pancakes for breakfast—his favorite. A light still shines in Elaine's room where she and Ruth are quietly talking, probably planning the bodice for Elaine's wedding dress or picking the flowers for her bouquet. Elaine thinks lilies but Ruth likes carnations. Checking that someone locked the back door and giving the deadbolt an extra tug, even though Arthur has twice done the same thing, Celia walks toward her bedroom and meets Arthur as he comes out of the bathroom, a towel wrapped around his waist, the steam from a hot shower following him.

His skin is thicker since they moved to Kansas, like a hide. His face and neck are dark, his hands rough, his back and chest broad. Celia touches his collarbone as she slips past him into their bedroom. He smells of soap. He takes her hand, stops her, makes her look up at him. She knows what he wants. He wants Celia to believe in him, to trust him. Laying her hand flat on his chest, she closes her eyes, breathes in the warm air about his body and prepares to tell him the truth. While he was in the shower, she called Floyd, even after Arthur said it would do no good, that it would only stir up Ray, stir up more trouble. She called Floyd and told him that Ray tried to take her little girl. She lied to Arthur and she was hateful to him, if only in her thoughts. Not once, not ever, in all their years together, has she been so hateful. Not even when Arthur brought home the new truck and lashed her Detroit life to it, did she have a hateful thought. She made herself trust him then and she wants the same now. More than anything, she wants to trust him.

Pulling their door closed, Arthur backs Celia toward the bed. As she lowers herself, Arthur standing before her, she lifts her hands and lays them on his stomach, bending her fingers, gently denting his dark skin with her nails. If he is more of a man now, then she is more of a woman. When they lived in Detroit, Arthur wore a starched shirt to church, shined his shoes once a week and sat for a haircut every fourth Tuesday. Celia wore pearls on Sundays and set her table with pressed linens. But here in Kansas, Arthur's shirts are fraying at the collars and cuffs and Celia's pearls are packed away in a box in her top dresser drawer. They are different, both of them.

Letting her hands slide down Arthur's flat stomach, Celia pulls apart the towel at his waist. She needs him to make her feel clean again because the showers and shampoo and soap did not. She needs Arthur to make her forget the way Ray looked at her or the feel of him grinding himself into her thigh, to make her forget the thought of Ray with her little girl, his dirty hands touching Evie's yellow hair. Clawing Arthur's back, she draws him down on top of her and buries her face in his shoulder where the muscle dips into his neck. He pulls her skirt up, presses aside the crotch of her cotton panties, and forces himself inside of her with one quick motion. The pain lasts only an instant. His movements are quick, fierce, almost angry. Pressing his face into the mattress, he muffles a groan. And then his breathing quiets. He shudders and is still. Celia needs something more, wants something more. But it's over.

Waiting until Arthur has rolled off her, Celia inhales a full breath, sits up, unbuttons her blouse and skirt and pushes them to the floor. The night air chills her damp skin where it was pressed against Arthur. Kansas has made her body harder, like it was when she was younger. Her stomach is flat again though marred by silvery white lines where it stretched for her babies. Her hips are soft and white, but narrow, slimmer than they were in Detroit. She reaches for Arthur's hand and places it on her left breast, holding it there until he begins to roll her nipple between two fingers. He breathes faster again, slips the same hand between her legs and presses apart her knees. Celia lies back, exhaling and not hearing the dry grass that crackles outside her window.

Evie rolls on one side, afraid to close her eyes because every time she does, she remembers the red silky inside of Olivia's neck and the black blood that she lay in. Daniel tried to cover her eyes before she saw but he was too slow. Evie always thought blood was red. Now she wonders why babies are blue and cows bleed black blood. She should have asked Uncle Ray. He is more of a cowboy than Daddy. Uncle Ray would know about blue babies and black blood, but he didn't want to talk much on the ride home. He didn't even ask about Aunt Eve's dress even though it stuck out from under the bottom of Evie's coat. She saw him looking at the blue ruffles. Mostly, Uncle Ray looked like he hadn't slept a single night in his whole life.

"Girl ought to wear trousers when it's so cold" is the only thing he said.

Thinking that next time she sees Uncle Ray she'll ask him about black blood, Evie rolls over and looks at the drawer where she hid the picture of Aunt Eve and Uncle Ray. Mama made her return the rest of Aunt Eve's things to Grandma Reesa and she has to write an apology letter on Mama's best stationery so they can send it through the mail. Mama doesn't know Evie kept the picture.

Across the kitchen, Mama's bed creaks. Sometimes, when the house is dark, Evie hears it. Mama always says they are making up the bed with clean sheets. Tucking in hospital corners, straightening the quilt, fluffing the pillows. Soon enough, Mama is done tucking her sheets and the house is quiet again. Maybe Evie can sleep without closing her eyes. Cows do that sometimes, or is it horses? Another question for Uncle Ray. But Evie isn't a cow or a horse. She tries closing her eyes. First one, then the other. Everything is black for a moment and then she hears a knock. Maybe Mama is making the bed again. Evie opens her eyes and sits up. She hears another quiet knock. Tapping on glass. *Tap, tap, tap.* Someone is at the back door.

*　　*　　*

Daniel wants to bang on his wall. He wants to punch a hole all the way through to Elaine's room and into her fat mouth. She and Aunt Ruth are still whispering about the wedding. All night long, probably all through dinner, and even now when they should be sleeping. Elaine doesn't care one damn bit that Olivia died. She doesn't care that Evie wore Aunt Eve's dress to school or that everyone calls Evie a nigger lover. She doesn't even care that Evie almost got swiped like Julianne Robison. All she cares about is studying and finishing high school so she can have the wedding that she spends all night, every night, planning with Aunt Ruth. Daniel sits up, lunges toward the wall he shares with Elaine, pulls back his fist, ready to punch a hole all the way into her room, when he hears a knock. The last time Mama checked on him, he pretended he was asleep so she left his door ajar. Unwrapping his fist and dropping his hand to his side, Daniel walks to his open door and listens. Yes, someone is knocking.

Ruth keeps talking, thinking that Elaine won't notice the quiet creaks coming from Celia and Arthur's end of the house. She gathers the fabric at Elaine's waist with the fingers that stick out of her sling and weaves a straight pen into the satin sash. "That should do it," she says as Elaine muffles a laugh. "Now, be still." Ruth ignores the giggle. With so much to be sad about that day, the laughter is sweet. "I can't keep taking this in. You need to eat better. You'll waste away to nothing by the wedding if you're not careful." She folds over another patch of loose fabric farther down Elaine's hip and this time when she smiles at the quiet creaks, it's because they make her feel that maybe things will be fine again. In these quiet moments, the house binds together.

"Will that do?" Ruth says, patting Elaine's hip and looking past her into the mirror on the back of the door.

Elaine so resembles Celia, though her features are dark like Arthur's. Still, she has her mother's long, soft waves, and even late at night, her eyes and cheeks shine the same way Celia's did when she smiled at Arthur through a cascading white veil.

"Perfect," Elaine says. "Just perfect."

The creaking stops and the house is quiet.

"Let me help you," Ruth says as Elaine wiggles out of her wedding dress.

"I need to use the restroom first," Elaine says, stepping off her stool and reaching for the doorknob as she hops from side to side.

She must have been holding it, waiting for the creaking to stop. They both begin with a smile before breaking into giggles.

"I can't wait anymore." Trying to muffle her laughter, Elaine opens the door a crack. "Did you hear that?" she says, turning toward Ruth.

"Sounds like someone is on the porch."

"Who would come so late?" Elaine says, and stepping out of her dress, she slips on a robe.

Ruth waves Elaine aside. With one hand pressed to her full, round belly, she says, "I'll have a look."

Celia opens her eyes. She rolls her head toward the dark window. No moonlight. No sparkling Battenburg lace curtains.

Next to her, Arthur's eyes are closed. Covering her bare chest with one arm, Celia sits up and feels for the quilt. She finds it at the end of the bed and tugs but it is tangled in Arthur's feet. She tugs again, causing his eyes to open, and she hears it. A knock at the back door. She drops the quilt.

"Arthur," Celia whispers, poking his shoulder. Yes, she hears a knock. Louder now. "Arthur, did you hear that?"

Arthur rolls on his back to see Celia leaning over him, bare-chested. He lets out a quiet moan and reaches for both breasts.

She pushes his hands away. "Shhhh," she says. "Listen. I think someone's at the back door. Do you hear it?"

Reaching with one hand for the spot between Celia's legs, Arthur mumbles something about the wind. Celia slides off the end of the bed, yanks the quilt from under Arthur's feet, causing him to startle, and after wrapping it around herself and securing it by tucking in one end, she stands and looks straight into the eyes of a black silhouette standing in the window.

"Arthur," she says through clenched teeth.

Backing away from the window, she trips over the quilt and, as she stumbles, each step yanks down the blanket until she is naked again. The black silhouette still stands in the window.

"Arthur, someone is there," Celia says, squatting behind the bed and gathering up the quilt.

Arthur sits up, swings his legs around so that he is staring directly into the window. He is close enough to touch the glass. It's black. Empty.

"No one there, Celia," he says.

"Well, I saw someone. And I heard knocking."

Arthur exhales, loudly enough that Celia can hear, stands, pulls on the jeans draped over the end of the bed and walks past her, giving a playful tug on her quilt. She slaps his hand and gathers the cover under her chin with two fists.

"It's probably Jonathon. That kid might as well put his name on the mailbox."

As Arthur opens the bedroom door and steps into the kitchen, Celia whispers, "Jonathon wouldn't peek in our window."

"Suppose not," he says. "I'll give a look."

Evie pulls her robe closed and presses her face to the glass in the back door that leads onto the porch. With each breath, a frosty patch balloons on the window. Soon, she can't see outside. Rolling her head to the left, she presses her ear against the cold, wet glass. Quiet. She looks again and, seeing nothing and hearing nothing, she takes a step back, pulls the sleeve of her flannel nightgown down over her hand like a mitten and rubs a circle in the icy patch of glass.

"Evie," Daddy says.

A light switches on in the kitchen.

"Evie," he says again, taking a step toward her.

He fills up the small hallway that leads from the kitchen, past the basement stairs, to the back door.

"Step away, Evie."

Evie smiles at Daddy, turns back to the window and looks up to see Uncle Ray's face where it was dark before. She knows it's him because he wears his hat high off his forehead, but something about Uncle Ray isn't quite right. As Evie steps away, he steps forward. His head sways, like it's not screwed on tight enough, and one shoulder hangs lower than the other. Pressing both hands against the glass, he says something and smiles a crooked smile.

"What?" Evie says, stepping forward again and putting one hand on the door handle. It's cold but she squeezes it anyway. "Uncle Ray's out there," she says, looking back at Daddy.

Uncle Ray doesn't scare her like he used to, like he did on the night he asked for pie, because Aunt Eve loved Uncle Ray even if one of his eyes wanders off where it doesn't belong. She loved him so much she wanted to marry him but then she died and he had to marry Aunt Ruth. He wouldn't even be mean at all if Aunt Ruth had died instead.

"Don't open that, Evie," Daddy says, taking another step toward her. "Come away from there."

Uncle Ray looks over Evie's head. He sees Daddy standing behind her. Daddy isn't wearing a shirt and his feet must be cold, too. The handle is warm in Evie's hand now. Uncle Ray isn't smiling anymore, and in the dark, his cloudy eye is a black hole. With one hand, he knocks on the glass. With the other, he rattles the door.

"You tell Ruth to come out here," Uncle Ray shouts through the glass. "I should have left your girl to freeze."

Now Mama and Aunt Ruth are standing behind Daddy. All

three of them creep closer, looking like Daddy and Daniel when they found a rattlesnake in the barn. Daddy snuck up on the snake with a long-handled spade. He hacked it in two and said to Daniel, "Careful, son. Rattlers never travel alone." They found another snake coiled up in the back corner of Olivia's stall, its tail shaking like a tin of dried beans. Daddy hacked it up, too.

"Evie, honey. Come on back to bed," Mama says, peeking around Daddy. "You must be so cold."

Aunt Ruth, standing at Daddy's other side, nods.

"You know they think I was taking their girl, Ruth? That what you think, too? That why Floyd's got his God damn dogs over at our house?"

Evie presses against the door, the knob still in her hand. She can feel Uncle Ray on the other side, jiggling the handle, wanting to come in. He shakes it harder. It sounds like the second snake when Daddy crept toward it, the dry hay snapping under his black boots. Evie frowns, imagining that Daddy is carrying a long handled spade.

"Go on home, Ray," Daddy shouts, taking another step toward Evie. "It's too late for this now."

Daddy must make Uncle Ray mad because he starts banging on the door. Just over Evie's head, his fist pounds into the glass. The door rattles in its frame. Evie knows what Uncle Ray is doing is bad. She can see it in Mama and Aunt Ruth's faces. Their eyes are wide and they are both leaning around Daddy like they want to scoop up Evie and wrap her in her favorite patchwork quilt. Evie presses against the door. The glass shakes overhead. Uncle Ray is pounding with both fists now, probably because he sees Aunt Ruth. He wants to talk to her and to see his baby. That's what he said in the hospital. That's all he wants. And now the men with dogs are at his house and he's mad about it. Daddy reaches to grab Evie's arm.

"Go on, Ray," Daddy shouts.

"What'd you tell them?" Uncle Ray keeps beating on the glass.

Evie pulls away from Daddy and wraps both hands around the knob. It's so warm now, almost hot. Daddy grabs both of Evie's shoulders. His fingers dig into her arms, like a snakebite, like a rattler bite. She cries out. Her breath fogs the glass. Uncle Ray looks fuzzy. Maybe he smiles, but Evie isn't sure because the glass is cloudy. He pulls back both fists in one motion and brings them down as Daddy lifts Evie up and away.

"What'd you tell them?" Uncle Ray shouts.

The glass shatters into tiny pieces and rains down like the fuzzy-tipped seedlings Evie and Daniel blew off the tops of dandelions when they first moved to Kansas. Dangling from Daddy's arms, Evie watches the feathery glass sprinkle down around her. Daddy holds her, crouched over, shielding her so she can't see Uncle Ray or the door or Mama. Only the feathery glass. The house falls silent.

Because she can't breathe very well, Evie twists and squirms until Daddy stands. He turns away from the window, and after taking a few steps toward Mama and Aunt Ruth, his body tensing each time he steps on a piece of glass, he hands Evie to Mama like a cup of hot soup, carefully so none of her spills over. Laying her head on Mama's shoulder, Evie can see Daddy. He is staring at the broken window. Uncle Ray is there, his fists frozen where they hit the glass.

He looks at Evie, or maybe he's looking at Mama. Mama sets Evie down, gathers the top of her robe under her chin with one hand and waves at Evie to go back into the kitchen. Yes, he's looking at Mama. He smiles.

Daddy stands still for a moment, watching Uncle Ray smile at Mama and then he lunges, leaping over the scattered glass. He grabs at Uncle Ray through the broken window, but Uncle Ray is gone, across the porch and down the steps. Daddy throws open the door.

"Arthur, no," Mama shouts. "Leave it be."

But Daddy doesn't listen, and he runs after Uncle Ray.

Hearing the glass break, Daniel slips by Elaine, who has just hung up with Jonathon. She grabs for Daniel's sleeve, but he is too quick. A few short steps and he is across the kitchen and standing at the top of the stairs that lead to the basement. He reaches for the gun cabinet but it's locked, and the spot where Dad's shotgun usually hangs is empty. But Daniel's rifle is there, right where it should be. Aunt Ruth hears him, grabs his hand and shakes her head. He pulls away from her. This time, he'll take a shot. He'll have his own gun and the trigger won't be too heavy. He could shoot Uncle Ray, kill him dead just fine with his .22. And he'd do it, too, in three perfect shots, if the cabinet weren't locked. No time to fish for the key. He pushes between Aunt Ruth and Mama and follows Dad out the door.

Before Daniel crosses the porch, a light flips on. In the center of the gravel drive, near the garage, Dad catches up to Uncle Ray, whose legs can't keep up with his top half. He is stumbling and falling from side to side until Dad grabs his collar. For a moment, Uncle Ray is steady on his feet until Dad yanks him backward, causing Uncle Ray's boots to fly out from under him. Landing flat on his back, he lets out a groan. As Dad kicks Uncle Ray in the side, wincing and bouncing on one leg after he does it because he is barefooted, snowflakes begin to fall, sparkling in the porch light.

Making no noise, Dad drops down and drives one knee into Uncle Ray's ribs. Something cracks. Sitting on Uncle Ray's chest, Dad holds him square with his left hand and beats him in the face with his right. Uncle Ray's shoulders bounce off the ground with each punch. He lets out muffled grunts, like Dad is beating all the air out of his lungs. The black tangled hairs on Dad's chest sparkle with wet snowflakes. He pounds Uncle Ray's face again and again until a set of oncoming headlights flash around the corner of the house. With one fist caught in midair, Dad stops. His sparkling chest lifts and lowers, and thick frost floats from his mouth, up and around his head and neck. Daniel turns and squints into the bright light. Stepping out of the truck and seeing Dad and Uncle Ray, Jonathon reaches back inside and flips off the headlights. He pulls on his hat and tugs the brim low over his forehead.

"How about I take it from here, Arthur?" Jonathon says.

Dad stands, his bare feet straddling Uncle Ray. He nods and says, "Good enough."

Jonathon walks a few yards across the gravel drive, his footsteps the only sound, bends down and slips his hands under Uncle

Ray's shoulders. Without saying anything to Elaine or Mama or Aunt Ruth, who are all standing at the top of the stairs, Jonathon drags Uncle Ray's limp body to his truck, his boots leaving two thin trails in the dusting of snow that has started to cover the gravel drive. Daniel runs to the passenger side of the truck and opens the door. He blinks away the snowflakes that catch in his eyelashes and watches Jonathon try to lift Uncle Ray, but when he can't quite get him into the truck, Jonathon looks to Dad for help. Dad, having not moved, stares at Jonathon for a moment before walking inside. First, the screened door slams shut, next the door off the kitchen. Mama and Elaine follow him but Aunt Ruth doesn't move. She stands, watching Jonathon try to lift Uncle Ray into the truck.

"Dan," Jonathon says. He breathes heavily and jostles Uncle Ray to get a better hold on him. "Can you give me a hand?"

Daniel glances back at Aunt Ruth, the only one left standing on the porch. She gives a nod, so Daniel steps up to Jonathon's truck and grabs one of Uncle Ray's arms.

"Should have left that girl to freeze," Uncle Ray mumbles. Both Daniel and Jonathon turn away from his breath. "God damn dogs. Even dug up my yard."

Clearing his throat and trying to suck in fresh air, Daniel slips under Uncle Ray's left arm and pulls it around his own shoulders so he can use his legs to lift. Together, he and Jonathon toss Uncle Ray into the truck.

"Tell your folks I'm taking him to the hospital," Jonathon says. Once Uncle Ray is inside the truck, Jonathon walks around to the driver's side. "From the looks and smell of it, he's mostly drunk. Nothing a few stitches won't take care of."

Daniel nods and steps back as Jonathon slides into the truck. Not certain why he does it, Daniel lifts a hand to wave good-bye. Starting the engine, Jonathon gives Uncle Ray a shove, causing his head to bounce off the passenger side door. He smiles and waves back.

Ruth counts out three tablespoons of coffee, plugs in the pot and watches, waiting for hot water to bubble up in the small glass lid. She startles, her shoulders and neck tensing, when Arthur begins to pound again. Each blow of the hammer vibrates through the floorboards. Soon, he'll have the broken window covered over with plywood and they can all go back to bed. Daniel is with him, fetching nails and scraps of wood, just like he did when the two worked together to repair the broken window in the garage. Elaine has gone to her room and Celia is taking a shower. Ruth didn't ask why she would shower so late at night when she's sure to catch a chill and maybe a nasty cold. She knew enough, had seen enough, to know the answer.

Soon, steam begins to leak from the coffeepot and it gives its first gurgle. Outside the dark kitchen window is the beginning of a good snowstorm. Making herself smile first, Ruth turns to face Evie, who sits at the kitchen table, swinging her legs because her feet don't reach the floor yet. With a creased brow, Evie watches Ruth. In the back of the house, Arthur begins to pound again.

"Your daddy and Daniel must be nearly finished," Ruth says, taking a loaf of sourdough bread from the top of the refrigerator and readjusting her sling. Her arm isn't so sore anymore. Tomorrow she'll take it off. "Do you feel it? The draft—it's almost gone. The house will warm up again soon. They'll be hungry, don't you think?"

Evie nods.

"And then it's off to bed with you."

Evie, still swinging her legs, leans forward and rests her chin in her hands. "Why does Uncle Ray hit you?"

Ruth stops in the middle of cutting a slice of sourdough and with her eyes lowered, she says, "I don't know, Evie. Except that life is harder on some people."

"Is it harder on Uncle Ray?"

"Yes," Ruth says, finishing one slice and starting another. "I'd say it has been."

"Because he wanted to marry Aunt Eve but she died and he had to marry you instead."

Ruth nods. "Yes. Yes, that's hard on a person."

"But he wouldn't hit you now. Since you have a baby in there." She points at Ruth's stomach. "He wouldn't hurt the baby."

Ruth lays down her knife and brushes a handful of crumbs off the counter into her palm, which she dumps into the sink. "No, Evie. He wouldn't hurt the baby." Ruth says it even though she's not sure it's the truth.

Evie stops swinging her legs and lifts her chin. She doesn't look like a little girl when she raises her eyes to Ruth. Her skin is pale and gray, her eyes old and tired and the fringe of white bangs that usually hangs softly across her forehead has been pushed back, sharpening her jawline and cheekbones.

Tilting her head, Evie says, "Then maybe it's time you go back home with him."

Ruth smiles with closed lips. Her chin quivers. "Yes," she says. "I think it's time."

Chapter 25

When day breaks on Saturday morning, the snow continues, but because the wind that blew all through the night has stopped, it falls straight down, in thick, heavy clumps. Outside the kitchen window, where the maple tree sparkles with an icy skin, two sets of tire tracks cut through four inches of snow that blanket the drive—one set going, partially filled in now with fresh snow, and one set coming, deep ruts that still show the indentation of the chains on Jonathon's truck. Knowing the back door will swing open at any moment, followed by a blast of cold air, Celia slides her eggs off the hot burner and makes herself touch Ruth's sleeve. Something to comfort her. The only thing Celia can manage. Ruth sets aside the potato she is grating for hash browns and wipes her hands on her apron.

Arthur walks into the kitchen first. Jonathon follows, shaking out his blue stocking cap and brushing the snow from his coat. Arthur takes off his hat and sets it on top of the refrigerator. His dark hair is wet and matted on the ends, his nose and cheeks are red and his shoulders are dusted with snow.

"Smoke coming from his chimney." Jonathon slaps his hat against his thigh. "Someone must have driven him home from the hospital."

"I spoke to Floyd," Arthur says to Ruth. "He says they're done over at your place. Done all they could. Didn't find anything."

"Been so long," Jonathon says. "Since it happened, I mean. They didn't really expect to."

Ruth nods, and turning her back on them, she continues shredding her potato into a hot skillet, the paper-thin slivers sizzling and popping in melted butter.

After everyone has finished breakfast, Arthur asks Jonathon and Elaine to drive over to Reesa's and bring her back to the house before the storm strands her alone and he tells Daniel to get busy shoveling the snow off the roof.

"The flat roof over the porch," Arthur says. "That'll be the trouble spot. The rest should be fine. Just fine."

Daniel nods. "Yes, sir," he says, holding his fork in his left hand and his knife in his right. Like Arthur, like a Midwesterner. All night, Daniel stayed awake with Jonathon and Arthur, boarding up the broken window, listening for Ray, and from the three cups that Celia found on the kitchen table this morning, he even drank coffee with them.

Once Jonathon and Elaine have left for Reesa's, Arthur heads outside to bring more firewood up to the house and Ruth excuses herself to do some sewing, all of them leaving Celia alone in the kitchen. Even Evie shuffles back to her room, her head and shoulders slumped as if she's thinking about Olivia. Outside, there is a thud as Daniel drops the ladder against the house. His footsteps cross overhead. Warming her coffee with a refill, Celia pulls out a chair, sits and cradles her mug. After a few deep breaths, she stares across the room at Elaine's closed bedroom door, the one where Ruth and the baby were supposed to stay once the little one came along, except now Celia doesn't want them here anymore. After the snow stops and the storm has passed, Ruth can go home with Reesa. She can live there, anywhere, as long as it's away from Celia's family. She doesn't want Ruth and her baby in her home for one more day.

In Elaine's room, Ruth pulls her suitcase from under the bed. The last time she touched it, she had just moved in with Arthur and Celia. She had been remembering the devil's claw growing outside Mother's house, the smell of it, the feel of the sharp pods. She had known she was pregnant, known it for sure, but didn't know how to be happy about it. Now, even though Ruth has lived in Arthur's house for nearly five months, even though she thought she had found a way to be happy, the moment she lays back the top of the blue suitcase, she smells home. She smells Ray. There was always something musty about him and that house. No matter that she scrubbed with bleach and washed with lye soap. No matter that she always hung out the clothes and towels to dry so they wouldn't mold. The house still smelled old and damp. Now she breathes in the smell, soaks it up, so she'll be ready.

Daniel pushes his shovel across the flat roof, clearing the last patch of snow. Standing straight, he plants his shovel like a pitchfork in a drift that has collected where the angled roof meets the flat. Up the road, Jonathon's truck creeps into sight. As he starts down the hill, his back end fishtails, leaving crooked tracks in the fresh snow, but then it falls back into a straight line. Watching the truck, Daniel arches his back and groans the way Dad would have. He thinks about Ian and all of his aches and pains. Mrs. Bucher says they're worse in this cold weather. Ian won't be hunting pheasant today. He won't be a pusher or a blocker, and he damn sure won't be hunting Jack Mayer.

As Jonathon's truck slows at the bottom of the hill and turns into the drive, Daniel looks back toward Uncle Ray's house. White smoke drifts up through the falling snow. Yep, Uncle Ray made it home, made it home in good enough shape to keep a fire going all morning long. Daniel stretches again, pulling his wool cap down over his ears, and leans on the shovel. The snow is falling straight down, harder since Daniel climbed onto the roof. A new layer of white has filled in where he already shoveled.

Walking to the edge of the roof, Daniel stands over the header board where he is sure not to fall through and squats to wait for Jonathon's truck to pull up. The chains on his tires make a crunching noise as he drives around the house. The truck stops and both doors fly open. Elaine steps out of the passenger's side, and Jonathon, the driver's side. Both hold out a hand, but Grandma Reesa takes Elaine's. Jonathon doesn't move, instead standing near the truck until Grandma Reesa has started up the stairs, leaning on Elaine with one hand and the handrail with the other. When she is at the last step, Jonathon slams his door, walks around the truck and, when he passes under the spot where Daniel squats, he calls up to him.

"I'll be needing a hand later today if you got one."

"Sure," Daniel calls down. He coughs and spits in a pile of snow on the ground below. "What do you need?"

"Ran into Norbert Brewster this morning," Jonathon says, removing his hat and shaking off the snow. "Said I'd better get what I want out of their old place quick. Said the roof is caving in on a good day. Won't hold up to this snow. Thought about driving out there. It's a decent road on toward Clark City. Things'll ice over tonight and we won't be going anywhere for a day or two." Jonathon glances back at his truck. "Says he's got some good hardware out there. And some cabinets might be worth saving. Could use an extra set of hands ripping it all out. Won't be any good if the weather gets to it."

"Sure, I'll go." Daniel drops the shovel into a mound of snow below. No sense staying at home. Once he goes back inside, even before he can hang up his gloves and hat to dry, Mama will be asking him how he's feeling. She'll press her hand to his forehead like his not having any friends is a sign of the flu and then she'll cock her head and say once again how lucky they are that Uncle Ray didn't get his hands on Evie. She'll whisper that part so Evie doesn't hear.

"Hustle on in and put on dry clothes," Jonathon says, offering Daniel a hand as he steps off the ladder. "We'll head out when you're done."

Chapter 26

Route 60, leading Daniel and Jonathon fifteen miles southwest, was plowed sometime during the night, but as the snow continues to fall, a fresh layer, blowing like thick fog, covers the narrow road. Still, the chains on Jonathon's tires rattle over the hard, frozen ground. Outside, snowflakes fall in a heavy white curtain, larger and fluffier then they were at home. Squinting into the white haze, Daniel tries to follow one flake all the way to the ground.

"Here we go," Jonathon says, slowly rolling the steering wheel, his leather gloves stiff as he passes one hand over the other.

He pulls off the main road where a rusted mailbox hangs from a wooden post. The fresh, unplowed snow quiets the chains.

"Haven't seen this old place in years."

Daniel leans forward, both hands resting on the dashboard. The small two-story farmhouse has a flat roof and a wrap-around porch. Other than a single barren tree standing in front and to the side of the house, the landscape is empty. Flat, snow-covered fields stretch as far as the horizon in every direction. The snow makes everything crisp and new, tidy. It's as if Norbert Brewster and his wife never left the house, or perhaps it's as if they never lived there at all.

"Doesn't anyone live here?" Daniel asks.

"Not since Norbert lost his wife and moved to town. Couple years back, at least." Jonathon throws the car into park and leans over the steering wheel. "Let's have a quick look around. Doesn't seem to be much worth saving," he says and looks up at the thick white layer of snow on the flat roof. Grabbing his toolbox from the center seat, he climbs out of the truck.

The icy stairs creak when they walk up them to the porch. Standing at the front door, Daniel shoves his hands in his coat pockets while Jonathon fumbles with the key that Norbert Brewster gave him. The emptiness of the snow-covered fields surrounding the house makes Daniel think of Clark City. Jack Mayer would have come across this house first when he escaped, even before the Scott house, but if he did stop here, looking for food or anything else, he wouldn't have found it.

"Got it," Jonathon says. He steps inside, stomping his boots on the threshold even though no one lives here anymore, and Daniel follows closely behind, stomping his boots, too. Their heavy footsteps echo in the empty house and something scurries.

Jonathon winks at Daniel. "Rats, I suppose." He takes a few steps into the entryway, and stops. "Well, that's a shame," he says.

Daniel looks off to the right where Jonathon is looking. A snowdrift, littered with leaves and dirt, has spilled through a broken picture window into what was once the dining room.

"Might have pulled up those oak floors," Jonathon says, setting his toolbox on the third step of the stairway leading to the second floor. He opens it and hands Daniel a screwdriver. "Take a look around up there," he says, nodding up the stairs. "If you find a decent door, take it down. Give a shout if you need a hand. I'm going to see about the kitchen cabinets."

Daniel steps into the wide entry that leads into the dining room. A gust of wind catches him in the face. He shivers. Most of the glass in the picture window is gone. Only a few pieces hang from the top of the frame. They are called shards. Daniel knows because that's what Dad called them after Uncle Ray broke their window. Dad knocked those shards loose with a hammer and boarded up the window with scraps of plywood from the basement.

"Looks to have been broken a long time," Daniel says, watching Jonathon rummage for another screwdriver. Maybe he isn't so bad. It's not his fault he's always the extra set of hands.

"No telling," Jonathon says and walks toward the back of the house. "Holler if you find anything worth keeping."

Evie sits on the edge of Aunt Ruth's bed, swinging her feet so the bedsprings creak and watching Aunt Ruth try to thread a needle. She is still sleeping in Evie's room, but once Elaine gets married to Jonathon, Aunt Ruth and her baby will live in Elaine's old room.

"You know your mother doesn't like you doing that," Aunt Ruth says.

Evie glances at Aunt Ruth, offers no response and the bed continues to squeak.

Aunt Ruth misses the needle's eye with her thread for a second time and smiles. "Light's not so good today," she says. "Would you like to try?"

"Daddy says Olivia won't die all the way until spring."

Aunt Ruth lowers the needle and thread. "What do you suppose he means by that?"

"He said things don't all the way die when it's so cold outside. He said she'll finishing dying in spring. He said she'll sink into the ground and come back as a tree or something."

Aunt Ruth rests both hands in her lap. "I guess I understand that."

Evie nods. "Yeah, me, too." She stops swinging her feet. "Was it cold outside when Aunt Eve died?"

Aunt Ruth wraps her thread around the small bolt and lays it and the needle on her bedside table. "It was warm," she says. "A beautiful time of year."

"Is she all the way dead now?"

"Yes, she is."

Evie leans back on both arms and begins to swing her legs again so that her feet bounce off the box frame. "I saw Uncle Ray at church," she says. "He was visiting a grave." She stops swinging. "Is Aunt Eve's grave there? Was he visiting Aunt Eve?"

Aunt Ruth flips on the lamp near her bed, opens the small drawer in her nightstand and lifts out two round stones.

"Perhaps," she says, holding the stones in the palm of her hand. "I suspect he was."

*   *   *

Daniel stops at the top of the stairs where a long hallway leads to the far end of the house. While the downstairs felt like a barn because of the wind blowing through the broken window and the leaves and dirt scattered about the wooden floors, the upstairs feels like a home, like he might find Mrs. Brewster living right behind one of the five doors that line the hallway. He takes a step toward the first room, slowly, carefully, leading with his toe and only rolling back onto his heel when the wooden floor doesn't bow underfoot.

Grabbing the knob on the first door with two fingers, he gently pushes and pulls, testing the hinges. They creak but swing freely. He takes one step closer, testing the floors again with his toe, and inspects each hinge. They are tarnished and black but Jonathon will want them. He'll scrub them with acid and a toothbrush and by the time he hangs them in Elaine's and his house, they'll be like new. Before continuing, he knocks on each of the door's six panels, happy to be doing something that doesn't involve Mama's rubber gloves and a bucket of soapy water. Solid. Yep, Jonathon'll want this one.

Pushing open the second door, Daniel coughs at the dust kicked up and squints into the light that spills across the hallway. A bathroom. Better paint job on this door. Frame is in good shape. Hinges look the same. The third and fourth are keepers, too, making Daniel wonder how many doors Jonathon needs for his new house. The biggest bedroom, which was behind the first door, was empty, but the smaller two still have furniture in them—dressers, a rocking chair, two single beds—all covered with white sheets.

Daniel steps into the second small bedroom and carefully pulls the sheet from a rocking chair. He coughs and waves away the rising dust. Evie would like the red-checkered seat cushion, even if the rocking chair might be too big for her. Maybe, if Norbert Brewster doesn't want it anymore, Dad will come back with his truck after the snow melts and take the chair home for Evie. It might make her forget about Olivia rotting away in the back pasture and Aunt Eve being dead and Julianne Robison still missing. Before draping the sheet back over the chair, Daniel looks at the ceiling and hopes it won't cave in on Evie's chair before they can come back for it. Black mold seeps out from each corner and a single crack runs the length of the room. He backs away from the rocker, watching the snowfall through a dirty window.

Once outside the room, Daniel looks down the hallway to the last door. All of them are fine, and after Jonathon gets through with them, the hinges will be fine, too. Taking a few steps toward the staircase, Daniel calls down to Jonathon.

"Got five good ones up here," he shouts. "Hardware looks good, too."

"Did you say five?" Jonathon calls up. "Five? All in good shape?"

Daniel looks at the last door. "Yeah, five." He coughs.

"All have good hinges?" Jonathon calls back as he appears at the bottom of the stairs.

Daniel motions for Jonathon to come up and see for himself.

Celia takes two mugs from the cabinet overhead and fills them both with coffee. Reesa, sitting at the head of the kitchen table, stitches the belt back onto the body of a lavender and green plaid apron. The fabric is faded and frayed at the seams.

"I've never seen that one before," Celia says, setting one of the mugs in front of Reesa.

"Haven't worn it." Reesa drapes the apron across her lap, demonstrating how little of her it protects. "Covered more of me when I was younger." She smiles, which makes Celia smile and realize that Reesa, after all these months, is making a joke. "Made from a feed sack," she says, holding the apron up again.

"From a feed sack?" Celia asks. "But it's such lovely fabric."

"Mother always picked the nicest ones for aprons. Different sack, different fabric."

"Do you have others?" Celia asks, looking at the bag sitting near Reesa's feet.

"Mmmm," Reesa says, meaning yes, and she lifts the bag into her lap. "Here's another." She holds up a blue calico bib apron with a solid blue ruffle sewn at the waistline. "Mother always liked ruffles. Here," Reesa says, handing the apron across the table to Celia. "This'll fit you still."

Celia frowns at the comment, thinking Reesa means that someday Celia will outgrow it, too.

"I couldn't, Reesa," Celia says. "Those are antiques. They're too special."

"Mmmm," Reesa says, again meaning yes.

While Reesa inspects the blue calico apron for torn seams, Celia takes a deep breath, and says, "Will you tell me about Eve?"

Reesa continues to run her fingers over the worn cotton, pulling the thin belt through two fingers and tugging when she gets to the end. "What's there to know?"

"Well, I'm not sure."

Behind Celia, her bedroom door is closed. Having been up late fixing the back window and watching for Ray, Arthur is taking a nap.

"Arthur is getting more . . . well, more angry. Don't you think? I'm worried about him. And about Ruth. It seems that . . . there is something else. Something I don't know."

"The child is gone. Dead and buried. Not much more matters, does it?"

"No, definitely not. But something is eating away at him. You see that. I know you do. He stayed away from here for so long."

Celia waits, but Reesa doesn't respond.

"He thinks he should have saved her, doesn't he? His father thought that, too. He blamed Arthur. Blamed Arthur for Eve's death."

Reesa pulls a spool of blue thread from her sewing case, wets one end by dabbing it on her tongue and, lifting her hands to catch the light coming through the kitchen window, she pokes it through the eye of her needle.

"Reesa," Celia says, leaning forward. "Please tell me what happened. I'm worried about what Arthur might do."

"What happened twenty-five years ago won't change what's happening today."

"Maybe it won't," Celia says. "Or maybe it will." She stops talking when Arthur walks out of the bedroom, running a hand through his dark hair.

"The boys back yet?" he says, buttoning his flannel shirt and walking past them toward the bathroom.

Celia looks at Reesa as she answers. "No, but soon I hope."

Reesa pulls off a yard of thread and ties one end in a knot. The bathroom door closes.

"I just can't help but worry," Celia says.

Daniel steps back as Jonathon walks up the stairs, carrying with him a small paper bag filled with hardware from the cabinets. "Here," he says, handing the bag to Daniel. "Cabinets are no good, but I got all of the handles and knobs."

Daniel takes the bag, cradles it in one arm and points at the first door with his screwdriver. "Looks good to me," he says. "Scrape them and paint them. They'll be okay."

Jonathon nudges Daniel as he passes by. "You're finally learning something worth learning, aren't you, city boy?"

They start with the closest door. Daniels holds it while Jonathon unscrews it from its hinges. The job is easy until only the bottom hinge is left attached and Daniel has to hold the door square so it doesn't bend the hinge and ruin it. He uses his legs for leverage and tries not to grunt so Jonathon won't know how heavy it is for Daniel.

Once they have removed the door from its frame, the two of them carry it down the stairs and prop it up in the foyer where the wind and snow can't get to it. Then they go back upstairs and do the same thing three more times. At the second small bedroom, Daniel asks Jonathon if he thinks Mr. Brewster would let them have the rocking chair for Evie. Jonathon says that he thinks a bottle of bourbon for Mr. Brewster would be a fair trade.

By the time there is only one door left, both Jonathon and Daniel have pulled off their coats and hats. "Just one more," Jonathon says. "We'll get it downstairs, wrap them up in a tarp or two and head on home."

At the end of the hallway, Daniel opens the last door enough to grab onto the edge with one hand while holding the knob in the other. He waits while Jonathon unscrews the top hinge and braces himself as he pulls off the middle one. The door is instantly heavier. Daniel uses his legs to stabilize himself, and this time, he can't help the grunt that escapes him.

"Here," Jonathon says, taking part of the weight once he has removed the last screw. "Let's lay it down for a minute."

Daniel rests the bottom of the door on the floor and, following Jonathon's lead, he slowly lowers it, walking backward so it can lie down in the hallway.

"Good Lord," Jonathon says, dropping the door the last few inches.

The sudden movement makes Daniel stumble backward. When he catches his balance, Jonathon has already stepped over the door and taken two steps into the bedroom, blocking the entry. Daniel follows, slipping around Jonathon, stumbling again as he steps into the room.

"Jonathon," he says. "What is that? Is that . . ."

Sheets cover none of the furniture in this room. A dresser and chest of drawers stand on opposite walls and a lace curtain hangs in the room's only window. Bright white light spills inside, making the pale yellow walls shine. The snow is still falling. And there, its wrought-iron headboard centered on the largest wall, is a single bed made up with a white quilt that someone has carefully tucked around the remains of a very small person.

"Julianne Robison," Jonathon whispers. "After all these months. It's Julianne Robison."

Chapter 27

Celia steps back, giving Ruth more room to roll out the noodle dough. Soon the white floury clump is nearly paper-thin and Ruth is dabbing her neck with a dish towel. She smiles at Celia, only half a smile really, and after pulling a tea towel from the top drawer, she drapes it over the noodles.

"They have to dry a bit now," she whispers.

Celia nods, and she and Ruth sit at the kitchen table with the others.

"Part of the roof had collapsed by the time we got back with the sheriff," Jonathon says. "Fellows from Clark City came out, too."

Arthur stretches and rests one arm on the back of Celia's chair. Ruth sits next to Reesa; Daniel, across the table from them.

Jonathon continues. "They had a hard time of it, getting up the stairs to find her."

Reesa shakes her head and makes a *tsk tsk* sound. Daniel props his elbows on the table and rests his chin in his hands. His nose and cheeks are red and probably chapped, too. And Elaine, who was checking on Evie and making certain her door was shut tight, walks back to the table and stands behind Jonathon.

"Floyd brought her down. Couldn't do much looking around, though. Wrapped her up tight as he could in that quilt of hers and brought her on down. Nothing left. Not a damn thing of her left."

Celia presses her hand over her mouth. "Are they sure it's her?"

"Sure as they can be. She had blond hair. Looked more like dried straw, what was left of it. But Floyd, he said that means blond. And she was no more than a bit of a thing."

Ruth stands. Everyone stops talking.

"Just checking my noodles," she says, slipping behind Celia.

"So, what's next?" Arthur says. "Has anyone told Mary and Orville?"

"Floyd was going there straightaway from the house. Roads weren't so bad yet near town, so I'm sure he got there. Didn't want to bring them out to the house." Jonathon takes a sip of coffee that must have gone cold. "Funeral's next, I suppose."

Everyone around the table nods and Reesa makes her *tsk tsk* sound again. "How are those noodles coming along?" she asks Ruth, who is still staring at the counter.

"You know the strangest thing about it all?" Jonathon says, not really asking anyone in particular. "She's been there all along. The mattress, well . . ." He pauses, scans the table and whispers, "Floyd said it was stained, badly. From all the decomposition."

"Good Lord in heaven," Reesa says.

"But the quilt that was laid over her," Jonathon says, "it was clean. White as brand new. And the room. Spotless. Furniture dusted. Windows clean. But that quilt. That's the strangest of all. Clean as brand new."

Celia pushes back from the table and goes to stand with Ruth at the counter. "You all right?" she asks, touching Ruth's shirtsleeve.

Ruth nods that she is fine, and says, "Who would do such a thing? Who would do such a terrible, terrible thing?"

"Jack Mayer," Daniel says. "That's who."

A few days later, when the snowstorm has passed and the trucks have cleared all the roads into town, Evie has to go back to school. Miss Olson called Mama on Sunday night to say all the teachers decided it best not to disrupt the children's lives anymore than they already had been. Julianne had been missing for such a long time, after all. Mama shook her head after she hung up with Miss Olson and told Evie and Daniel to rustle up some clean, warm clothes because Monday was a school day.

On Evie's very first day of school in Kansas, everyone had known that she had to sit where Julianne Robison would have sat if she hadn't disappeared, because everyone had to sit in alphabetical order. Scott sat where Robison couldn't, but this morning, as Evie walks into class, pulling off her coat and mittens, Miss Olson has mixed up all the desks. Some point forward, some sideways, some toward the back of the room. Most are still empty.

"Today is crazy mixed-up day," Miss Olson says. "Pick a seat, Evie. Pick any seat you like."

Evie hangs her coat on one of the hooks inside the door and

walks past Irene Bloomer and John Atwell, toward the back of the room, wondering why Miss Olson mixed up all the desks, but she doesn't wonder for long. Miss Olson doesn't want anyone to know which desk would have been Julianne's if she wasn't dead. But Evie knows. She knows because she sat in it for the whole first part of the year. The pencil holder in Julianne's desk is covered with black scribbles and someone carved a five-pointed star in the bottom right corner. At the very back of the room, in one of the desks turned sideways, Evie sits. She lowers her head as the rest of the kids walk into class, everyone giggling at the silly messed-up desks even though they're supposed to be sad about Julianne being dead. Some of them must remember this, because after they giggle a little, they cover their mouths and lower their heads, too.

After the second bell rings, Miss Olson tells everyone to settle down and turn their desks if they can't quite see the blackboard. Squeaks and squeals bounce around the room as everyone scoots until they can see Miss Olson. Once the room quiets again and Miss Olson begins to call attendance, Evie lays her index finger on the tip of the star, slowly traces each of its five points and wishes she could be dead like Julianne Robison. If she were dead, being small wouldn't matter because no one makes fun of a dead person. If she were dead, Julianne Robison could be her friend. If she were dead, she wouldn't have to miss Aunt Eve and Olivia.

Feeling tired, like he might never feel good again, Daniel walks into his classroom, hangs his coat and hat in the closet at the back of the room and sits. Ian is there, teetering on the edge of his seat, waving at Daniel from four rows over. He wants to tell Daniel something but since Mrs. Ellenton separated them on the third week of school, he'll have to wait until lunch. Daniel waves back and presses a finger to his lips when Mrs. Ellenton walks into the room, her high heels clicking across the tile floor. From the front of the classroom, she smiles at Daniel and tilts her head like people do when they feel sorry for someone.

At noon, Mrs. Ellenton dismisses the class for lunch. Daniel doesn't wait for Ian like he normally would. Instead, he takes his bag-lunch from the shelf near the door and races through the halls with his head down because every kid in school is staring at him—the kid who saw Julianne Robison dead. He hears Ian calling out but his crooked legs can't keep up. The cold weather seems to have made Ian stiffer, like every step he takes is painful. If it were possible, Daniel would say Ian looked even smaller, like he shrunk during the snowstorm. Everything except his head. It seems to have grown, and Daniel rubs his own neck thinking how heavy Ian's head must be to carry around all day. Once inside the cafeteria, Daniel sits at his usual table, which seems to be more crowded today, and opens his lunch. When Ian finally sits, he is panting for air. His eyelids are gray and sunken into his head and a bluish tint surrounds his mouth.

"Hey," he says, tossing his lunch on the table. "What are you doing?"

All around the cafeteria, kids watch Daniel. Not one of them has been his friend all year, but now they all want to hear about Julianne Robison.

"Doing nothing," Daniel says. "Eating."

"So you found her. You really found her." Ian smiles at the full table and leans forward. "What'd she look like?"

Daniel shrugs. He sees Julianne every time he closes his eyes, but he thinks he's really seeing only what he imagines. Once Jonathon realized what they were looking at up there on the second story of Norbert Brewster's house, he grabbed Daniel's arm and shoved him back into the hallway, telling him to stay put, stay damned well put, until he could figure things out.

"Come on," Ian says, cupping his mouth with both hands so no one can hear what he's saying. "You got to tell me."

"She didn't look like anything," Daniel says, taking a bite from his sandwich but thinking if he chews or swallows, he'll vomit.

"Did it smell bad?" Ian asks, but then answers his own question. "I guess not, because of the cold. Frozen, huh?"

Daniel lifts his eyes, looking out from under his brow without moving his head. "Yeah."

"You know, most folks say your Uncle Ray did it." He leans forward and whispers, "But I still say it was Jack Mayer. Swiped her up the second he broke out. Swiped her up and killed her there in Brewster's old house."

Ian leans back and studies his lunch like he's thinking about eating it, but he pushes it farther away instead and closes his eyes. He sits that way, taking in deep breaths for a good long minute before opening his eyes, ready to go again.

"She's the first person murdered around here in twenty-five years," Ian says. "The first in twenty-five years." He waves at two of his brothers sitting at the other end of the table. They both jump up and sit back down next to Ian. Once they are settled, Ian starts talking again. "'Course you know who the last person murdered was."

Daniel shakes his head and keeps eating even though he feels sicker with every bite.

"'Course you know."

Both of Ian's brothers nod but neither says anything.

"It was your own Aunt Eve. Your dad's sister. You know that? Murdered right there in your Grandma's shed. Everyone says your Uncle Ray did it but they couldn't ever prove it."

Daniel stops chewing.

"Say he killed her same as Julianne. You know, blond like Julianne. A girl. Older, of course. But blond just the same. Say he couldn't help himself." Ian looks at his brothers again, like he's making sure he's telling everything right. Both brothers nod. "But I say it was Jack Mayer killed them both. Killed your aunt before they locked him up. And now Julianne, just the same, twenty-five years later."

"Shut up," Daniel says, holding half of his sandwich with both hands. "You don't know anything about my aunt. You shut up."

"Jacob remembers," Ian says, talking about his oldest brother who is grown with his own two kids and lives in Colorado. "He remembers when it happened. Told us all everything. Ma told him to hush up about it, but he told us anyway. Says it was exactly like Julianne. Except they found Eve Scott before she rotted all away. All bloodied up between the legs. Just like Julianne Robison. Right?"

Daniel didn't see much of Julianne, but he saw enough and

heard enough from Jonathon to know Julianne didn't have any legs left to be bloodied up—nothing but bones.

"You knew about her, right?" Ian says. "You knew about Eve Scott?"

Daniel doesn't answer.

"Everyone else says it was your uncle. But I know it was Jack Mayer. I know it was. He bloodied them both up. Right there between the legs."

Daniel drops his peanut-butter-and-jelly sandwich, squishing it with his knee as he lunges across the table. He grabs Ian's collar and punches him square in the nose.

Chapter 28

Celia feels Arthur behind her, his body so much broader and taller, shielding her from the northern wind. No snow has fallen in four days, so while Arthur and the other county workers have cleared the roads and driving is easy enough, the temperature has continued to fall and not a flake has melted. Fourteen inches of snow covered the ground by the end of the day that they found Julianne, and the wind has stirred up the landscape, driving the snow into five-foot drifts in some spots and leaving frozen barren ground in others. Inside the cemetery, snow disguises the graves that lie in St. Anthony's shadow, making them almost beautiful. Someone, probably the two black men standing near the fence line, waiting and smoking, shoveled a path from the gate to Julianne's gravesite and the area around. Still, Celia's feet are cold and damp and beside her, tucked under one arm, Evie shivers. Celia pulls her closer, letting Arthur shield them both.

Beside Evie, Daniel stands with his hands folded and his head lowered. The entire town is here, a sea of dark coats and hats that surround a tiny grave, lying in the shade thrown by three large pine trees. The pines' branches are thick and white and clumps of snow drip when the wind blows. Celia tries to think it is a lovely spot for Julianne, so much nicer with the trees and the view of the church than the newer section of the cemetery where Mrs. Minken was recently buried. Here, Julianne lies near the grandparents she never met. Here, she lies in a grave that was probably meant for her mother.

From their spot near the back of the crowd, Father Flannery's voice, fighting with the heavy wind, is no more than a broken few words. "Tender young life . . . accept God's will . . . forbidden . . . we powerless sinners . . ."

Arthur touches Celia's arm and points to a closer spot, but Celia shakes her head and squeezes Evie. She is afraid to go closer, afraid that whatever took Julianne might find its way to her family. After a brief silence, the mourners around Julianne's grave say "Amen" in tandem and, following their lead, though she can't hear Father Flannery, Celia makes the sign of the cross, nudging Evie to do the same.

Behind her, Celia feels Arthur make the sign across his chest and his deep voice echoes "Amen." She leans into him, letting the sound of him comfort her. As everyone parts, filtering down the narrow shoveled path toward the gate, Evie tugs on Celia's sleeve. In a whisper, she asks to go to Elaine, who is standing a few rows up with Jonathon, Ruth and Reesa. Celia nods, and watching until Elaine has wrapped both arms around Evie, she turns toward Arthur. He is gone.

*   *   *

Daniel offers his arm to Mama because when Dad slipped behind him and started to walk away, he whispered for Daniel to take care of her. Mama takes Daniel's arm and smiles up at him. She does that now, smiles every time she has to crane her neck to see into his eyes, as if she's proud that he's finally become a man. Except maybe taller doesn't really mean he's a man yet. He hasn't fired a shotgun. He's still afraid of Jack Mayer and Uncle Ray, and he cries when he has to be alone at night and remember Julianne Robison lying under that white quilt. Being taller isn't all it takes to be a man. A man doesn't hit a crippled kid square in the nose. Only a boy does that, no matter how tall he is.

Watching the others leave, Daniel wonders if Ian told yet and if his pa will see Daniel standing there by Julianne's grave and come punch Daniel in the face for doing the same to Ian. Ian's brothers had picked him up from the ground after Daniel punched him, and one of them shoved a napkin under Ian's nose. Then they both looked at Daniel like they had never seen him before and dragged Ian, only his one good leg able to keep up, to the bathroom, where they cleaned him up so not even Mrs. Ellenton knew anything happened. Daniel doesn't see either of those brothers walking away from Julianne's grave. In fact, he doesn't see any Bucher brother, or Mr. or Mrs. Bucher or Ian. Maybe he should tell first. Maybe he won't get in as much trouble if he tells what Ian said about Aunt Eve getting bloodied between her legs and murdered in Grandma Reesa's shed. Watching Dad walk away from Julianne's grave, Daniel decides to tell because that's probably what a man would do.

* * *

Ruth reaches for Evie, but she slips into Elaine's arms instead and buries her face in Elaine's wool coat. Jonathon begins to say something, probably words of comfort. Ruth pats his hand, silencing him, and nods as if she understands why Evie can't love her right now. Then she steps away from the crowd, not liking the feeling that everyone is leaving Julianne cold and alone, not liking the feeling that everyone is leaving her. Many of these mourners for Julianne have come from the country—farmers who have probably checked every abandoned barn and deserted tractor, fearing that another tiny body will turn up. Some of them stare at Ruth, at the swell she can't hide beneath her coat anymore, because they haven't seen her, only heard. They look at her as if they think Ruth should be with a husband. They stare as if she is sinning against poor little Julianne and her parents. Orville and Mary wouldn't squabble. Mary wouldn't keep her baby from Orville. Orville and Mary have to witness their baby in a casket, withered away to nothing but bones. Orville and Mary, standing at their daughter's graveside, withered away themselves, the life gone out of them, two people as dead as the daughter they're burying. They wouldn't waste time thinking a beating was so bad. Ruth closes her eyes and lifts her face into the icy wind, hoping it will be easier to breathe, and when she opens her eyes, she sees Arthur wading through the deep snow, away from Julianne's grave. She holds one hand over her baby girl and follows.

Ruth has come here every week for twenty-five years, and she's watched the pines grow, first standing with them to her back on the day they buried Eve. They were green then, not snow-covered, and thin and widely spaced. Now they've filled in and grown tall, their branches tangling together. The pines have always marked the way—two headstones to the north of the biggest pine, which was bigger than the rest even twenty-five years ago, and three headstones east. She doesn't have to count anymore, never really had to. Arthur must remember, too, or maybe he's been here to visit Eve since he came home. Maybe every week like Ruth. He seems to know the way as he steps through the smooth, clean snow and stops directly in front of Eve's grave. He looks back when he hears Ruth behind him and takes her hand. On the ground, a few feet ahead, stands a gray stone. EVE SCOTT. OUR DAUGHTER. OUR SISTER. OUR LOVED ONE. Ruth pulls off one of her brown gloves and reaches into her coat pocket. Pulling out two smooth rocks, she sidesteps along Eve's grave, through the snow, and lays them on top of the headstone.

"I always leave two," she says, stepping back to Arthur's side. "One for both of us, since you weren't always here. But you are now."

Arthur nods. "I couldn't come before," he says. "Before now."

"My stones were always missing," Ruth says. She feels Arthur watching her, but she keeps her eyes on Eve's headstone. "My two stones, every time I came to visit, they were gone. Strange. Don't you think?"

Again, Arthur nods.

"Ray was here that night, the night Julianne disappeared. He was here and he took my stones. All these years, I imagine. Why do you suppose he would do such a thing?"

"I hope to never know the answer to that," Arthur says and slips around Ruth to block the wind, taking her arm so that she won't fall.

But Ruth doesn't move to leave.

"He loved her," she says. "He would have been such a different man with her."

Arthur wraps an arm around Ruth. "Doesn't much matter what might have been."

"While she was here, while Eve was with us, she was happy because Ray loved her." Ruth takes Arthur's other hand, presses it between both of hers. "He would have been a different man."

"But he's not, Ruth." In the dry, cold air, Arthur's voice is as deep and raspy as Father's ever was. "He's not a different man. I'm sorry for it, but he's not."

Ruth lifts her chin, turns her face into the wind and nods that she is ready to go. Together, she and Arthur step out of the snow onto the cleared space around Julianne's small grave. With all the other mourners gone, the tiny casket sits alone, waiting to be covered over by cold, frozen dirt. Two Negro men stand nearby, one of them stubbing out a cigarette in the snow, the other leaning on a shovel. Beside them lays a mound of dirt covered by a blue tarp. Ruth hadn't seen the open grave before because of the crowd of people, and seeing it now brings tears to the corners of her eyes.

"Come, Ruth," Celia says, stepping forward. "Let's get you home."

Standing near the gate, Jonathon holds Evie, who seems to be crying into his chest, and Daniel and Elaine stand next to him. At the head of the small grave, Reesa talks quietly with Father Flannery. As Arthur, Celia and Ruth walk past on their way toward the gate, Father Flannery steps forward.

"Ruth. Celia. Arthur," he says, bowing his head to greet them. "I was just mentioning to Reesa that we miss you fine folks at church."

"Been to church every Sunday, Father," Arthur says. "Haven't missed a one."

"I told Father Flannery that maybe we're getting tired of that drive to Hays. Don't you think, Arthur? Maybe we'll see him at St. Anthony's this Sunday."

Arthur continues on, holding Ruth's hand and reaching for Celia's. "St. Bart's is suiting me just fine. Nice to see you, Father. If you'll excuse us."

Reesa shakes her head.

"The gates to hell are wide," Father Flannery says. "Much wider than those to heaven."

Arthur stops.

Father Flannery looks back toward Eve's grave. The wind has started to fill in the footsteps Ruth and Arthur left in the snow.

Arthur drops Ruth's hand, steps up to Father Flannery, and in an instant, Ruth knows. She realizes that all along, all these many years, Arthur has known the truth. He's known the truth about what killed Eve.

"Is there something you want to say to this family?" Arthur says to Father Flannery.

"My concern is for the child, Arthur. For the child and Ruth. I don't want to see things come to the same end."

"Arthur, he doesn't understand," Celia says, reaching for his arm. "Let's go."

"I understand that he's telling me Eve is in hell."

"Arthur Scott," Reesa says. "He's saying no such thing."

But he is. Ruth knows he is. Father Flannery thinks Eve is in hell because of what Ruth always feared Eve did to herself. Ruth presses both hands over her belly, protecting her sweet baby girl, sweet baby Elisabeth.

"That child died with a mortal sin on her soul. Would you have that for Ruth?"

Feeling as if Father Flannery can see inside her, Ruth takes two steps away. There was a moment, no longer than a blink, when she wondered if not having a baby would be best. This is what Father Flannery sees. Even now, all these months later, he can see inside and know that she once had the thought. She had considered it, for only a moment, in the very beginning, as it must have been for Eve.

"Eve died because of you and my father," Arthur says, jarring Ruth back to the present. "She died for fear of you and that church. For fear of her own father."

Celia is looking between Ruth and Arthur. As certain as Ruth is that Arthur knows, she is equally certain that Celia does not.

Father Flannery takes a step toward Arthur. "The gate is wide," he says, and after tipping his head at Reesa, he walks away.

Father Flannery walks down the narrow path, through the small gate and out onto the street in front of the church. When he has disappeared into his car, Celia turns to Arthur. He stands with his head down, shaking it back and forth, back and forth.

"I don't understand," Celia says. "Arthur. Ruth. I don't understand."

Ruth steps up to Arthur and takes his hand in both of hers. "You've always known?"

Arthur nods.

"Did she tell you who it was?"

This time, Arthur shakes his head no.

"I hoped she wouldn't do it," Ruth says. "I begged her not to. She was so young. So young and afraid."

"Ruth, what are you saying?" Celia says, trying to see Arthur's face because then maybe she'll understand.

Still holding Arthur's hand and ignoring Celia's question, Ruth says, "I'm so sorry, Arthur. It was my books. She must have read them. I think she used wedge root. I begged her. Really I did. I told her to tell Mother and Father. To tell them the truth. I told her we would all love her baby, no matter what."

Celia reaches for Arthur but he pulls away.

"She was pregnant," Celia whispers.

Beyond Julianne's grave, Elaine and Jonathon walk toward the car parked in front of St. Anthony's, Evie wrapped in Jonathon's arms. Daniel stands alone near the gate.

"And she tried not to be," Celia says. "But she was so young. Who? Was it Ray's?"

Ruth shakes her head. "No. She swore it wasn't. Ray loved her. Loved her so much. He wanted to marry her." She crosses her hands and lowers her head like she has done so many times before. "We never knew who. She'd never tell. Never really admitted to being pregnant. But I knew she was. I just knew it. Someone hurt her very badly. She was different after it happened. Never the same." Ruth is quiet for a moment and, as if she realizes something, she lifts her eyes. "Did Father know the truth?" she asks Reesa.

Reesa does not answer. Instead, she raises her chin ever so slightly, just enough that the wind catches the wisps of silver hair sticking out from under her hat.

Ruth leans forward. "Did he know?" she shouts.

Arthur, still facing Eve's grave, says loud enough for everyone to hear, "He's the one who told her to do it."

Ruth's shoulders collapse.

"And you, too," Arthur says, turning to face Reesa. "You told her, too, didn't you?"

Reesa stands motionless, her chin in the air, gray wisps of hair blowing across her forehead.

"She was too afraid to do it alone," Arthur says. "So I helped her. I gathered up the wedge root. I boiled it in one of Mother's pans. I did it."

Daniel stumbles backward when Aunt Ruth screams at Grandma Reesa. Up until that moment, he had been planning what to tell Dad, how to tell him about Ian's nose and how Daniel almost broke it. But now, something else seems more important, and Aunt Ruth is shouting about Aunt Eve and how it wasn't Dad's fault that she died. She wasn't murdered and bloodied up by Jack Mayer.

Something else killed her. Something that Daniel thinks a man should know, but he isn't a man yet. He takes a few steps backward until he feels snow underfoot, turns to follow Elaine and Jonathon, and there, in the shadow of a large pine tree growing near the fence line, stands Uncle Ray.

He must have been there all along, standing behind everyone who came to say good-bye to Julianne Robinson, because his collar is up and his hands are buried in his pockets making him look like he's been cold for a very long time. He probably hid back there because more than ever folks are talking about him being one of the rabble-rousers in town and how they think he must have taken Julianne Robison for sure. But he isn't causing any trouble now, only watching Mama and Dad and Aunt Ruth talk, but also he looks like he's not really seeing them. A blue bruise lies over one of his eyes and his bottom lip is still swollen from the beating Dad gave him. As Daniel takes a step to follow Jonathon and Elaine, his boot snaps the icy crust on the cleared path and Uncle Ray turns. Seeing Daniel seems to wake him. Daniel stops. He should call out, warn them, because none of them notices that Uncle Ray is coming at them from behind the pine.

Standing by the mound of dirt that will bury Julianne, the two Negro men see Uncle Ray. One of them is leaning on a shovel and he pulls it out of the snow like he's ready to hit Uncle Ray with it if he needs to. The other man throws back his shoulders but doesn't have anything to hit with. Dad sees the men bracing themselves. He sees Uncle Ray.

"Ray," Dad says, which stops Uncle Ray. "Not today, Ray. This isn't the place."

"You knew all this, Ruth?" Uncle Ray says, ignoring Dad and looking straight at Aunt Ruth across Julianne's grave. "My Eve was pregnant?"

Aunt Ruth doesn't answer but instead wraps her arms around her baby.

"She did it to herself?" Uncle Ray asks.

"I said, not now, Ray," Dad says, louder still.

Again, Uncle Ray ignores Dad.

"That was a child bled out on the floor of that shed?"

No one answers. Mama turns away. Aunt Ruth looks down at her stomach. Grandma Reesa tips her face to the sky like heaven is up there and she can almost see it.

This time, Uncle Ray shouts as loudly as he can.

"That was a child?" His voice booms across Julianne's grave.

Mama presses a hand over her mouth, which means she is about to cry. Grandma Reesa turns to leave, and Dad starts toward Uncle Ray but Aunt Ruth grabs his coat sleeve, stopping him.

"Yes, Ray," Aunt Ruth says quietly, but the wind is to her back and it carries her voice for her. "That was a child, he or she—a baby."

Uncle Ray steps back when Aunt Ruth says it, almost like she slapped him, slapped him hard right across the face. Then he looks up at Dad. He looks directly at Dad and points at him. "And you did it," he says. "You killed my Eve."

The two of them stare at each other, waiting for something.

"Yes," Dad says. "I did it."

Uncle Ray's hat is cocked high on his forehead, showing off his tired eyes and gray skin. His face is thin and his cheekbones, like his hat, are cocked a little too high. His coat hangs on his shoulders and his pants bag around his boots as if he must have shrunk since he bought them. Dad once said too much drinking will wear heavy on a man. It looks like it has weighed Uncle Ray down about as far as he can go. After staring at Dad for a few more minutes, long enough that the Negro man with the shovel takes a few steps toward him, Uncle Ray walks away, down the cleared path, toward the station wagon where Elaine sits inside with Evie and Jonathon. He walks past the car without saying anything to Jonathon, who has stepped out probably because he heard all the shouting. He walks away, until he disappears down Bent Road without ever looking back.

Chapter 29

Celia takes Reesa's coat from the hook near the back door, hands it to Jonathon and steps aside as Reesa walks by. She fills the small hallway leading from the kitchen to the back porch, fills it with her size and with a sweet yeasty smell from the cinnamon rolls she mixed up that morning, intending to take them to the Robisons after the funeral. Now someone else will have to bake and deliver them to Mary Robison. Reesa says nothing as she sets her suitcase at Jonathon's feet and extends one arm so he can help her on with her coat.

"I'm sure the road home will be fine, Mrs. Scott," Jonathon says to Reesa. "Plows have had plenty of time to do their work."

Reesa makes a grunting sound and, after buttoning her top two buttons, she walks out onto the porch, leaving her suitcase for Jonathon to carry.

"She made her bed," Celia says to Jonathon. "Now she's got to sleep in it and try to make it again in the morning."

Jonathon shakes his head, signaling that he doesn't understand.

"Just a saying my mother liked to use." Celia swallows, something she does when she feels guilt. "And we have to think of them now, Ruth and the baby. They're most important."

Jonathon nods.

"You'll see to it that the house is warm before you leave her?"

He nods again. "Sure thing."

"Thank you, Jonathon," Celia says, reaching up to hug him. "And I know Arthur thanks you, too."

Overhead, footsteps pound across the roof. Arthur and Daniel climbed up there almost the instant they got home from the funeral to shovel more snow.

"He always goes to work when he's feeling bad. We'll have the cleanest roof in the county before this all settles." Celia hands Jonathon his coat. "You drive careful and come back for dinner."

"Yes, ma'am. I'll see Mrs. Scott home safe. Safe and sound."

Hearing the screened door open, Daniel stops shoveling and looks over the edge of the house. Behind him, Dad continues to scrape his shovel across the black roof.

"Grandma's leaving," Daniel says, slapping his leather gloves together. He looks over the edge again, the wind sweeping up and catching him in the face. He squints into the white sunlight bouncing off the snow below. "Jonathon's taking her."

Dad nods, lifts his shovel and begins to chip away at a patch of ice.

"Jonathon's carrying a suitcase," Daniel says.

Specks of ice sparkle as they fly off the end of Dad's shovel.

"Grandma's going home."

Jonathon's truck chokes a few times, rumbles, and then slowly starts down the driveway. Daniel watches, waiting for the truck to disappear, because once it's gone, he has to tell Dad. He has to tell because the weight of it is too much. Maybe a man could carry it around, but not Daniel. At the top of the hill leading toward Grandma's house, the truck fishtails.

"Dad," Daniel says. "I hit Ian Bucher. I hit him in the nose."

Dad stops hammering the ice.

"At school. In the cafeteria. I hit him."

Dad leans on his shovel. "You have good reason?"

Just like that. The weight of it is gone.

"Yes, sir. He said Aunt Eve was murdered. He said she was bloodied up between the legs and killed like Julianne Robison."

Dad nods, and lining up his shovel to take another whack at the ice, he says, "Bloody nose between friends never hurt anyone. But you be mindful of Ian's size. The boy can't help his size."

Daniel nods. "Sir," he says, and Dad stops again but doesn't meet Daniel's eyes. "I'm sorry Aunt Eve died. I'm sorry that happened."

Dad nods. "Yep," he says. "Me too, son."

Ruth sits on the edge of her bed, tulle draped across her lap and a small box of pearl beads on the nightstand to her left. She glances up when Elaine and Celia walk into the room, then continues trying to thread her needle.

"There's no hurry with that," Elaine says, sitting opposite Ruth on the other bed.

Ruth pulls the white thread through the eye of the needle. "The light's good today," she says. "Especially in here. We don't always have such good light."

Celia sits next to Ruth, lowering herself slowly and scooting close enough to drape part of the tulle over her own lap. "It is good," she says of the sunlight shining through the window. "This is beautiful work, Ruth. Did you see, Elaine? She's started to bead the pearl flowers." Celia lifts one edge of the veil so Elaine can see it, then lets it fall across her lap again. "Elaine, would you excuse us?"

"Certainly," Elaine says, standing. "It's beautiful work, Aunt Ruth. Beautiful." And she walks out of the room, leaving Celia and Ruth alone.

"Reesa is gone," Celia says, running her fingers along the veil's scalloped edge.

Ruth nods.

"She took her things. Jonathon is seeing her home." Celia pauses. "She'll be fine. Hardheaded as she is, she'll be fine."

"Why do you suppose we did this? Why so much hiding?"

"People get used to things," Celia says. "Without even realizing. We get used to the way things are." She reaches for the box of beads, plucks out one of the smooth, oval pearls between two fingers and passes it to Ruth. "Too afraid of the truth, I guess."

Ruth lays her hands in her lap and closes her eyes. Deep inside, Elisabeth shifts and flutters.

The elderberry was in full bloom by early June 1942. Ruth's father, Robert Scott, was due to plant his soybean, and Ruth woke, thinking it would be a fine morning to make elderberry jam. Before the day turned hot, she decided to wake Eve so they could walk a quarter mile down the road to the ditch where the plants grew best. The exercise would do Eve good, maybe chase away the blue mood she had been carrying around for a few months. Whether it was a touch of dropsy or a lingering flu, the elderberries would clear it right up. Mother always cooked with too much salt, and the summer heat could make a person swell and feel out of sorts. That's all that troubled her—too much salt and humidity. That's all it was. After a day of fresh air, Eve would get her color back and feel like finishing the blue satin trim on her latest dress. Mary Robison said she could sell it if Eve would finish it, said she could sell all the dresses she and Eve had made together, but Eve never wanted to part with them. Until now. Now she said that once she felt well enough to stitch on the blue satin trim, she'd sell it and the rest, too.

Ruth stood at Eve's door and tapped on it, leaning forward to listen. "You up?" she whispered, even though the rest of the house was already awake.

Eve was always the last to get out of bed on the weekends, leading Mother to lecture her about laziness being an engraved invitation from the devil. Ruth tapped again, this time hard enough to push open the door that was not latched. She peeked through the crack, and seeing Eve's bed made, she walked downstairs.

At the bottom step, Ruth remembers that the air chilled, but it couldn't have. It had been June. Still, a shiver had slipped up her spine to the base of her neck. A pot boiled over in the kitchen, a heavy, rolling boil. Water hissed on a hot burner. Placing one foot flat on the wooden floor, holding tight to the banister, Ruth listened. Boiled eggs, probably, for Father to take along to the fields. He was quite precise—half a dozen eggs, fourteen minutes at a heavy boil, and Mother poked small holes in the large end of each one so they wouldn't crack. Father wouldn't eat a cracked egg.

Ruth walked across the living room, taking long slow steps because she knew something was wrong, and stopped inside the kitchen. She stood looking at the white, foamy water spill over the sides of Mother's cast-iron pot, and without turning down the flame or sliding the pot to a cool burner, she walked on toward the back porch.

At the top of the stairs leading down to the gravel drive, Ruth looked east, toward the patch where yesterday she had spotted the finest elderberries. She couldn't see them from the house, but Eve would know the spot. It was the same every year. The berries had a special liking for the odd stretch of ditch where Bent Road took a hard curve. Passing cars kicked up dust there. Maybe that's what the plants liked so well. It was the same stretch of road where the wind swept over the rolling hills, down into the valley, and where the barbed-wire fence scooped up all the tumbleweeds. She and Eve would have a nice bunch in no time at all, and they could pick some of the flowers, too, and dry them on the back porch for tea. If the jam wasn't enough, a nice tea with honey and sugar would definitely fight off whatever bug had slowed Eve down over the past several weeks. Ruth walked down the stairs one at a time and across the drive toward Bent Road.

"Ruth," Arthur said.

Only yesterday, it seemed, he had had a smooth, fresh voice that sometimes he sang with in the bath. Now, suddenly his words came from deep inside his chest and rattled like Father's.

"Ruth," he said again.

Ruth stopped in the middle of the gravel drive. Knowing they were there, she had been trying not to look. It was where Eve always went for privacy. She said a young woman needed quiet, even if it was in an old shed. Ruth turned. Arthur stood outside the small building. His arms hung at his sides, the Virgin Mary dangling from his left hand. Next to him, Mother kneeled inside the doorway. She shook her head as she fumbled with her apron strings, untying them and pulling off her apron. She passed it inside the shed. A hand reached for it, Father's hand, bloodied. Mother began to rock on her haunches. Back and forth. Back and forth. She breathed out a low, rumbling moan.

"She's gone, Ruthie," Arthur said, dropping the Virgin Mary.

Mother fell backward and scrambled for the two hands that broke off the statue and settled in the soft, dry dirt. She picked up each tiny hand and the rest of the Virgin Mary and started to slide them all into her apron pocket, but it was with Father now.

"She's gone," Arthur said.

The ditch was only a ten-minute walk. The elderberries were in full bloom. They'd have plenty for a dozen or more jars, and Eve would feel fit again, fit and fine.

*   *   *

Ruth squints into the fading light, picks up a pearl bead but doesn't thread it onto her needle.

"Arthur thinks he did it," she says. "All this time, did you know?"

Sitting next to Ruth on the bed, Celia shakes her head but doesn't answer.

"He was about Daniel's age. When Eve died. Just Daniel's age."

Celia nods this time and holds a handkerchief to her nose.

"Everyone thought a crazy man killed her," Ruth says. "Everyone in town. That's what Father told them. I always assumed Arthur believed the same, but he never did. Even standing there in that shed, wiping up all her blood, he knew the truth. Mother knew, too. After Eve died, after we found her, I told Mother that I thought Eve had done it to herself, trying not to be pregnant. I told her about wedge root and blind staggers, told her that I was sure someone had hurt Eve, hurt her badly, but she'd never tell who. Mother said the truth didn't matter once a person was dead."

Ruth lifts her face into the sunlight spilling through the window. "Worst of all, we never told Ray. He was a good man back then. Really, he was. Why did we do that to him? We were so cruel."

"It wouldn't have brought her back," Celia says, her voice cracking at the end. "You were young, all of you. So young." Clearing her throat and taking out another bead, she says, "Let's get to work. We're going to lose this nice light soon."

"We wasted so many years," Ruth says, hooking the bead on the tip of her needle.

"It'll be better now," Celia says. "Now that everyone knows."

Ruth takes a stitch, securing the bead. "Yes," she says. "Better."

Chapter 30

Letting the powdered sugar frosting drip from the tip of the fork, Evie is sure Julianne would have liked these cinnamon rolls. When she was alive, she must have liked extra icing, too. But she's been buried underground for a whole day now, and she won't be eating these rolls or anything else.

Evie should be in school instead of sitting on the counter and stirring the icing for Mrs. Robison's rolls, but after Julianne's funeral and all the trouble with Uncle Ray, Mama said Evie and Daniel would stay home until Monday. Mama is afraid to let Evie out of the house ever since Uncle Ray brought her home. She's been to school only once since Jonathon and Daniel found Julianne dead in Mr. Brewster's house, and when Evie told Mama that she still got to sit in Julianne's desk, Mama cleared her throat and said that was enough of school for a while.

The only bad thing about missing school, Evie thinks as she stirs the powdered sugar and milk with a fork, is that the kids in her class will think she's scared to sit in Julianne's desk now that Julianne is rotted away and buried underground. But Evie isn't scared. She picked that desk, even after Miss Olson mixed them all up, because she wanted it especially for her own, and she told every kid at recess that she wasn't afraid one bit. They told Evie that she'd be next, that whoever killed Julianne, and everyone knew it was either Jack Mayer or her own Uncle Ray, would kill Evie, too. Evie put her hands on her hips and told every kid that she didn't care at all if she was next. That shut them up. That shut them up good and tight.

"Icing's done," Evie calls out, thinking that Aunt Eve would have liked the icing, too, but, like Julianne, she's dead. All the way dead. "I made extra."

Behind her, Aunt Ruth opens the oven a crack. "Rolls are too," she says.

She smiles at Evie, but Evie doesn't smile back. Grandma Reesa made those rolls. Yesterday, she mixed up the dough and punched it down twice when it rose up too high. Then Grandma had to go away because she made Aunt Ruth cry, and now Aunt Ruth is baking the rolls that chilled overnight in the refrigerator and she's acting like she made them all the way from scratch. Aunt Eve is gone, too, and Uncle Ray thinks it was Aunt Ruth's fault. Now only Aunt Ruth is left, even though she packed up two suitcases.

"They smell good, don't they?" Aunt Ruth says, slipping on two oven mitts and pulling the pan out of the oven as Mama walks into the kitchen. "Would you like to come with me and your dad to take them to the Robisons?"

Mama takes a few steps toward the oven. "It's so cold outside, Ruth. And icy. You let Arthur and me take the rolls over."

"Grandma made those," Evie says, folding tinfoil around the edges of the bowl filled with white icing.

Mama and Aunt Ruth look at each other the way they did when Evie wore Aunt Eve's dress to school.

"Yes," Aunt Ruth says. "Grandma makes the best cinnamon rolls. I can never get the dough so nice." Aunt Ruth sets the hot pan on the table in front of Evie's spot on the counter. Thick sugary steam rises up. "We'll tell Mrs. Robison that Grandma made these."

"Please, Ruth. Let us take the rolls. You need your rest. You and Elisabeth."

"I should go," Ruth says, wrapping her belly with both hands. "I really need to pay my respects."

"Cinnamon rolls won't make them feel better," Evie says.

"Yes, Evie," Mama says, pressing her lips together in a way that means Evie should stop talking. "You're probably right about that."

Evie hops off the counter. "I want to come, too," she says.

Someone definitely needs to tell Julianne's mom that Grandma Reesa made these rolls, not Aunt Ruth.

The pan of rolls is still warm on Ruth's lap when Arthur parks in front of the Robisons' house. Everyone else in town would have paid their respects yesterday after the funeral, but the Scott family didn't make it because they had a run-in with Ray. Ruth pulls on her mittens, cradles the pan with one hand and takes the frosting from Evie. Both Ruth and Arthur had decided that Mary Robison's house wasn't the place for Evie. She would be too much of a reminder. No sense stirring up more tears with Evie's blond braids and blue eyes. Before crawling out of the truck, Ruth looks back at Arthur, thinking she should say something, but not certain what that should be. He is staring straight ahead, lost in some thought. He turns. His eyelids are heavy, as if he can't quite hold them up. He looks tired, and suddenly so much older. He looks like Father.

"We'll probably visit a bit," Ruth says, sliding across the bench seat toward the door. "You two will be warm enough out here?"

He nods. "Go on and take your time. And watch the ice. Sidewalk'll be slippery."

Ruth holds tight to the truck's doorframe, steps onto the newly shoveled sidewalks, and walks toward the Robisons' house.

Celia hangs up the telephone, sits at the kitchen table and lays both hands flat on the vinyl tablecloth. She presses each finger into the table, holding on for a moment. After one final deep breath, she calls out.

"Daniel."

The house is silent.

"Daniel, come on out."

Daniel's bedroom door swings open and he steps into his threshold. His hair is matted on one side and his shirt is misbuttoned.

"Sorry if I woke you," Celia says.

Daniel glances at the telephone and at Celia.

"Come have a seat. I have some news, Danny. Some sad news."

Ruth's shoulder isn't so sore anymore but still she favors it by balancing the dish on one hip. Someone has shoveled the sidewalk for the Robisons this morning, probably one of the men from church. Surely they didn't do it themselves. Even so, it's icy in spots. Ruth shuffles her feet, taking small steps and, at the bottom of the stairs leading to the Robisons' porch, she stares up at the black door. For a moment, she remembers being on the other side. A different house, a different day, a different death, but otherwise the same. Church ladies brought casseroles in porcelain dishes and biscuits wrapped in tinfoil. They tried to gather around Mother, to comfort her with hugs and gentle words, but Mother wouldn't have it. She sat them all down, served them coffee and crumb cake. The shirts that Father and Arthur wore that day smelled of starch and the cigars that the men brought and smoked on the back porch. Orville Robison is a smoker. The sweet smell meets Ruth at the top of the stairs. She breathes it in, raises her hand and knocks.

Celia pulls her hands off the vinyl tablecloth and lays them in her lap when Daniel walks from his bedroom into the kitchen. He has to duck now when he walks under the heavy beam that runs through the house.

"Have a seat," she says, gesturing toward the chair opposite her.

As Daniel sits, quickly at first and more slowly when he looks into Celia's face, the back door opens and Jonathon walks in. The sound of him coming home brings Elaine out of her room. They both walk into the kitchen and, like Daniel, they seem to feel that something is wrong. Celia motions to them and they both sit. She doesn't look at Jonathon or Elaine, just at Daniel. She reaches across the table and takes his hands.

Ruth knocks, lightly because she doesn't really want them to hear her. On the other side of the closed door, a set of footsteps approaches. The doorknob rattles. The door opens.

"Ruth," Mary Robison says. "Lord in heaven. What brings you out in this cold?"

Ruth lifts her pan. "Mother made them. For you."

"Her rolls?"

"Yes. She let them rise twice. Evie made extra icing. We're all so sorry for your loss."

"You're cold out there?"

Ruth shakes her head because the cold doesn't matter. "We're all so very sorry," Ruth says, raising the pan again so Mary Robison can see it. "They're still warm," she says, though the pan has gone cold. "Would you like them in the kitchen?"

"Yes," Mary says. "Thank you." Then she steps back, ushering Ruth inside.

Mama's fingers are cold. Usually they're warm. Every other time, they've been warm. Daniel lets her hold his hands, but he doesn't hold back, and he wonders how he knows. Even before she tells him. By the look in her eye, or the sound of the phone ringing late in the day, or the smell in the air. He knows. He looks at Jonathon and Elaine. They don't understand. They don't see it or hear it or smell it. But Daniel does.

"That was Gene Bucher on the phone," Mama says.

Daniel nods. Yes, he already knew that.

"Ian has been ill, Daniel. Did you know? He's always been, well, fragile."

Mama thinks Daniel knows about Ian being sickly, but now she isn't sure. Yes, he already knew that.

"Daniel," Mama says, exchanging a glance with Jonathon and Elaine. "Ian didn't wake up yesterday morning. They expected it would happen. Eventually. Maybe it was this cold. Maybe it was too much for him. But he didn't wake up."

Daniel nods. Ian was more blue. Almost by the day. And shrinking away. He never got to be a pusher or shoot pheasant. He never found Jack Mayer's tracks or stared into the whites of his eyes. He said Aunt Eve died in the shed, bloody and murdered, and then he fell backward, off the cafeteria table, blood spilling down his chin and into the creases in his neck. Yes, Daniel already knew that.

"I thought they'd find her sooner," Mary Robison says.

After first laying a dish towel across the kitchen counter, Ruth sets down the rolls and puts the icing in the refrigerator. She is surprised to find it empty. When Eve died, Mother defrosted casseroles for weeks. She said not a single dish would go to waste. Waste was another invitation from the devil. Closing the refrigerator, Ruth steps to the sink, pushes open the curtains and raises the shade. She blinks at the late day light that spills into the room. Maybe folks weren't bringing food because Julianne first disappeared so long ago. Maybe they thought Mary Robison had had time enough for grieving.

Walking into the living room, Ruth tries to smile for Mary and says, "Pardon? What have you lost?"

"I didn't think . . ." Mary says. She sits in the center of her gold couch, facing an empty wall. ". . . it would take so long."

Ruth stands in the threshold between the kitchen and living room, her hands clasped under her belly. The chill she caught outside has stayed with her and she realizes the house is cold, too cold, as if the windows are open and the heat has shut down. She scans the room for rustling curtains and wonders what she should say to Mary. What did they all say to her when Eve died? They touched her, probably because, like Ruth, they didn't know what to say, and they brought chicken casseroles and apple cobbler. She should sit with Mary, touch her sleeve, pat her hand.

"We're all so sorry."

"Your baby is well?"

Ruth nods, pulling her coat closed and lowering her head.

"You should take care of yourself," Mary says, tilting her head as if looking at something on the empty wall. "I took care." Every few feet, at about eye level, nails stick out from the wall. "I took the best care I could. Waiting." Mary nods toward the corner where her sewing machine sets on a bare card table. When they were young, and Ruth and Eve came for sewing lessons, fabric and piping and measuring tapes had covered the table, leaving barely enough room for the three of them to huddle around the machine. Now it is bare, and the table droops in the middle.

"I even made new curtains while I waited. But it took so long."

Ruth steps closer, looking where Mary is looking.

"Can I do anything for you? Do you or Orville need anything? Anything at all?"

"I kept things nice, as nice as I could."

"Things are lovely, Mary." Ruth takes another step, watching the front door. She shouldn't be in a hurry to leave. Were they in a hurry to leave her and Mother and Arthur? "But you shouldn't work yourself like this. Where is Orville? Arthur is here. Outside. Do you need help with anything?"

"I did it myself, you know." Mary doesn't seem to see Ruth standing near the sofa, her coat wrapped tightly, hat and mittens still on. "All the cleaning. So much to take care of for one person."

"Too much really. You should rest now."

Mary tilts her head again, still staring at the empty wall. Ruth takes another step. They are hooks to hang pictures. She remembers. Family pictures. A whole wall of them. Even a picture of Mary, Eve and Ruth when they were girls. They are gone now. The wall is empty.

"He wrapped her in feed sacks, you know."

Ruth turns on one heel to face Mary, stumbling and bracing herself against the bare wall.

"Before he buried her, I mean, so she was still beautiful when I got her back." Mary brushes gray wisps of hair from her eyes and smoothes them in place. "She was too beautiful to bury. Still so beautiful. I took care the best I could."

Evie curls up next to Daddy, laying her head against him. His hands are crossed on the steering wheel and he is resting his head. His breathing is quiet, not deep and loud like when he's sleeping. Evie scoots closer, snuggling up as best she can. His arm tightens around her shoulders. Still, Daddy doesn't look up. She wants him to lift his head to smile at her, and then maybe he'll notice. She could say something right out loud. She could pull on his shirt and point out the windshield so he would see, but Evie does nothing and Daddy doesn't move, not even to squeeze any tighter. She remembers the picture—Uncle Ray happy and lifting Aunt Eve high off the ground. Aunt Eve laughing under her straw hat, smiling and not dead.

Without moving in her seat this time, Evie glances at Daddy, quickly so he won't notice. Straight ahead, at the intersection of Main Street and Bent Road, sits a red truck. It is parked right in the middle where another car might crash into it. A white frosty cloud drifts up from the truck's tailpipe. Uncle Ray pushes his hat high off his forehead and the red truck rolls slowly through the intersection and disappears.

"After I took Mother's quilt to Julianne, I didn't go again." Mary Robison lays back her head and closes her eyes. "What with the weather blowing in. I worried about how long I'd be gone. Things get dusty so quickly."

Ruth swallows. The floor is uneven underfoot, and the front door seems to slip away. She coughs into a closed fist and walks across the room, sidestepping the coffee table.

"I'll call Arthur in," she says. "Maybe he can get the heat going."

"Orville, he never went. Couldn't bring himself to it."

"Arthur," Ruth says. "I'll get Arthur. He's right outside."

Mary lifts her head. "I threw away those nasty feed sacks. Orville left her and only I took care."

The front door opens slowly and Aunt Ruth slips outside. She stops at the top of the stairs, grabs onto her big stomach with both hands and hurries toward the car. Daddy doesn't look up until he hears her footsteps on the sidewalk. Then he throws open the door and jumps out. Aunt Ruth meets Daddy at the front of the truck, grabbing his arms, leaning on him. Daddy turns toward the house and, holding Aunt Ruth by the arm, he walks her to the truck and helps her inside.

"You two sit tight," Daddy says as Aunt Ruth crawls into the truck. "I'll go see about Mary."

Cold air sticks to Aunt Ruth and she smells like ice and snow.

"We'll be fine," she says, scooting closer to Evie, her knees bobbing up and down. "Just fine. Your daddy will be right back."

Evie scoots away, toward the spot behind the steering wheel, while Aunt Ruth watches Daddy walk up the stairs and onto Mrs. Robison's porch.

Hoping the red truck will drive past again, Evie says, "Did Aunt Eve die because her baby came out too early?"

"Where did you hear that, sweet pea?"

The sunlight bouncing off the white snow makes Evie squint. "I heard you all at Julianne's funeral. Will yours come out too early?"

Evie used to worry that Aunt Ruth would have a baby who was blue like Ian's baby sister and that they'd have to put her in the oven. Maybe the baby would wake up and cry. Maybe not. Maybe she'd die. Maybe Aunt Ruth will die, too.

"No, Evie," Aunt Ruth says. Her knees stop bobbing and she crosses her mittens on her lap. "I hope not."

Up on the Robisons' front porch, Daddy knocks on the door and pushes it open. Straight ahead, at the end of the street, the red truck is there again, rolling across the intersection. And then it is gone.

Chapter 31

Celia stands at her kitchen sink, her back to the conversation going on at the table, and dries the last dish from an early supper. Outside the window, as dusk falls, the light bouncing off the snow is gray. On the back porch, Jonathon is prying the wood from the window that Ray broke so he can lay in the new glass. Elaine is in her room, waiting for him to finish. Celia startles each time his hammer slams down. If only he would stop, for a moment at least, she could catch her breath. A piece of wood falls and clatters across the porch. Celia leans against the sink, and Arthur talks on, over the noise.

He called Floyd Bigler from Mary Robison's living room, relit her heater, and while they waited for the sheriff, Mary told Arthur that she had visited the house to tidy up for Julianne who lay dead there since summer. Mary had shined the windows with vinegar-water and swept the corners. Before the weather turned, she laid a new white quilt over Julianne because the house carried a terrible chill. It didn't seem right to bury the girl. That's what Orville did at first. He wrapped her in feed sacks and buried her on Norbert

Brewster's land. But Julianne was too lovely, too tender, and when she was dead, first dead, still too beautiful to be buried. So Mary dug her up, carried her inside the old house, and tucked her in tight. When the sheriff arrived, she retold the same story.

"Yes," Mary Robison said. "Orville killed her." She nodded toward the garage behind the house. "Done the same to himself."

Arthur and Floyd found Orville Robison on the garage floor, frozen solid, a hole blown out of the back of his head. Mary told Arthur and the sheriff that she thought to clean up after her husband, but then decided it wasn't her business to tidy up another one of his messes. She didn't know for sure how he killed Julianne, only that he said it was an accident, same as snagging a fish instead of catching it proper with bait and a hook. Didn't much matter how it got done—there's a fish on the end of the line either way.

"Some men don't know the difference between a daughter and a wife," she said. "Don't let Ruth go back to that husband of hers. Don't let him have that sweet tiny baby like Orville had mine."

Arthur turns away from Ruth and chokes as he repeats Mary Robison's words.

"Don't let Ray have that sweet tiny baby like Orville had mine."

Celia slips behind Arthur's chair and kneels next to Ruth. "You're safe here. You and Elisabeth are safe." Holding Ruth's narrow shoulders, she raises her eyes to Arthur. "Is she not well? Has the sheriff taken her for help?"

"She didn't seem altogether aware. That's the only way I can put it. Not at all aware."

"That poor family," Ruth says. "That poor little girl."

Celia presses her palm to Ruth's cheek. "You should rest. This can't be good for you."

Celia says this because she has to. If she is to be a good person, she has to say it, and if she weren't so scared, she'd mean it. She reaches to touch Ruth's hand, but stops when Daniel's bedroom door opens. She doesn't want him hearing any of this conversation, doesn't even want him close to it. It's not fitting for a child to hear, but when he walks out of his room, he has become a man. Just like that. He is a man.

"You hungry?" Celia asks.

"Na," Daniel says. His voice, like Arthur's, is a low croak. When did his voice change? She thought she would hear it coming in cracks and squeaks along the way. His neck is thicker, too, and triangular muscles fix it to his shoulders, which are suddenly wide. Even his hands, they're larger. Just like that, when she was wasn't looking, he became a man.

"You should eat," Celia says, but he shakes his head and walks across the kitchen toward the back porch where Jonathon is still pounding. As she watches him walk away, tears well in the corners of her eyes.

He is gone.

"I won't have the children hearing any of this." Celia spits the words at Arthur as if it's his fault this has happened, his fault that the town will bury Julianne Robison and Ian in the same week and that Daniel grew up when her back was turned. Another funeral before Julianne's grave is even settled. Another small coffin, too small. Another child grown. What if it were one of her children instead of Julianne or Ian? How does a father kill his own child? How does a mother turn her back and find a man has taken over where once she had a boy?

She says it again. "None of it. Not a word."

Because Arthur is a good man, he nods and lowers his head, gladly taking the fault. Now the tears spill onto Celia's cheeks. She lays aside her dish towel and goes to him. He is stiff at first, not letting her feel him, but then his body warms, his muscles soften, and his shoulders fall. He leans into her for this moment.

Before he walks onto the back porch where Jonathon is pulling the last board off the broken window, Daniel stops in front of the gun cabinet. He takes his winter coat from the hook and sees the small gold lock hanging in place, snapped tight. Glancing back to make sure no one can see him from the kitchen and waiting until he hears Jonathon working at the back door, he stretches up and reaches for the key on top of the cabinet. He's never been tall enough before but Mama says he's growing like a weed. Dad says like a stinkweed. Lifting onto his toes, he reaches over the ledge. He stumbles, reaches again, his side starting to ache. He feels it.

Checking again and waiting until he hears Jonathon fumbling in his tool chest, he slips the key into the lock, turns it, thinking the click will echo through the house. No one hears. The lock falls open. But then he considers Jonathon working there on the back porch. There is no other way out. He won't let Daniel walk by with a rifle in hand. He'll tell him to put the damn fool thing away and then he'll tell Dad and Dad will hide the key somewhere higher. So Daniel snaps the lock closed and reaches overhead to replace the key. He stumbles again, not very steady in his leather boots because they cramp his toes. Bracing himself against the wall, he tries again and, as he slides the key back over the ledge, he knocks several coats off the crowded hooks. Pausing to make sure no one heard, he bends down to pick them up. Jonathon's, Dad's, Elaine's, another of Dad's. Then he stands and, as he begins to hang them up again, he sees the empty spot where Dad's shotgun usually rests.

Evie sits on the edge of her bed where she can see out her bedroom window. It is nearly dark, but through all the trees that have dropped their leaves, she can still see the road. A truck drives over the top of the hill. So many cars since everyone started to die. And phone calls. First Olivia the cow died. Evie doesn't like her anymore. She brought death to them and now it has settled in for a good long stay. She's probably not even all the way dead yet because of the cold. It will keep her for a while, that's what Ian said before he was dead. But not Julianne. She died all alone, all the way dead, in a little bed in a strange house, and now she's buried, still all alone. How did they dig it up, the frozen ground? Will the same two Negro men dig Ian's grave? They are small graves. Not so much digging. What if Aunt Ruth's baby comes too early and it's blue and it doesn't wake up in the oven? That will be a very small grave, but Aunt Ruth's will be regular sized, almost regular.

The truck is still driving down the hill toward their house. Daddy says there's black ice. It's the most dangerous. The truck knows it, too. It drives slowly, and at the bottom of the hill, it stops, white smoke spilling out of its tail end. Then the truck, the red truck, drives slowly past.

Chapter 32

Standing on the back porch, Daniel watches Jonathon, who is squatting near the door, a pane of glass balanced on his two palms. At first, Jonathon doesn't notice Daniel standing there. Daniel could push him down with one kick in the butt and he'd topple over and the glass would shatter all over him. It might even kill him, and he'd never find cabinets for his new house. Then there would be room for Daniel to be a man. Jonathon is a pocket clogger. That's what Dad called the men who worked in the car factories and made sure not to work too fast or too slow. Lots of the men complained about the Negroes taking jobs. Dad only complained about the men who did just enough to keep on working. Dad said they took a job from another man, a better man, who would take pride in his work. They were the pocket cloggers. Jonathon is a pocket clogger—clogging up the spot that Daniel should have.

"Hey," Jonathon says. Balancing the glass on his two flat palms, he begins to stand. "You going out?"

Daniel nods but doesn't answer.

"Getting dark," Jonathon says, glancing outside. "Want some company?"

Across the porch and beyond the screened door, the gravel drive isn't white anymore. All the cars coming and going have ground it down to dirt again. One thing is for damn sure. This roof won't collapse because he cleaned off every speck of snow himself.

"Na," Daniel says to Jonathon because he most definitely does not want his company.

"Cold out there." Jonathon slides the glass into place. "Would you look there in that toolbox?" he says, motioning toward a silver box on the floor. "You see a small can in there?"

Daniel flips open the lid with his foot. He shakes his head.

"Well, damn it all. Forgot the glaze." Jonathon lifts the glass out again and lays it back on the cardboard box it came in. "A lot of banging around for nothing. You want to help me put this wood back up?"

Daniel shakes his head as he buttons his coat. Then he takes a hat from one of the pockets and pulls it down low on his forehead. Inside, a kitchen chair scoots across the wooden floor and someone walks through the house.

"I'm real sorry about Ian," Jonathon says, closing the cardboard flaps over the glass and looking at the ground instead of Daniel. It seems everyone is afraid to look at him. "Real sorry that had to sneak up on you."

"Didn't sneak up on anybody. I knew he'd die soon enough."

Jonathon lifts his eyes, one hand still on the pane of glass. "Well, so it wasn't such a surprise. Still sorry, though."

When Jonathon looks away again, Daniel wants to kick him hard, so hard that he flies through the door and lands in the kitchen at Elaine's feet. Instead, he says, "See ya," and starts to walk outside.

"Hey, Dan," Jonathon says. "Listen, I'll be taking off when I get this wood back up. But you ever need anything, just call. You know where to find me."

Daniel nods and walks across the porch.

By the time he reaches the last stair but before he steps onto the gravel drive, a thought starts to gnaw at him. He stops on the bottom stair and lets it gnaw all the way through. When it does, he looks toward the garage and smiles because now he knows where he'll find Dad's shotgun.

Celia offers Ruth a third cup of coffee when she excuses herself to go lie down, but she shakes her head and pats her stomach to signal a tired baby and Mama. At this, Celia smiles, but Arthur still can't look at Ruth. Celia nudges him for being impolite even though she knows it's not bad manners; it's fear. Mary Robison showed them all the truth about the very worst that a man can do to his own daughter. She made them all think, believe even, that Ray might do the same to little Elisabeth. She made them believe it so strongly that it still seems Ray is the one who hurt Julianne. It still feels like he is the one who wrapped that poor child in feed bags and dropped her in a hole.

"Rest well, Ruth," Celia says. "Things will be better tomorrow."

Daniel waits in the garage until Jonathon and Elaine leave, and then, thinking someone will put out the porch lights, he waits even longer. No one ever does, so taking a deep breath, he slips behind the oil drum, pushes aside an old woolen blanket and lifts the shotgun. He cracks it open and sees the brass end of two shells. Loaded. It's heavier than he remembered, and the barrel is cold, even through his leather gloves. He slaps his palm against the wooden stock, getting a good feel, a good God damned feel, and then props it on his shoulder, barrel pointing up like Dad taught him. After looking through two loose slats in the door and seeing no one on the porch, he slips outside and runs across the hard gravel drive, through the gate that used to hold Olivia before Jonathon shot her dead. High stepping it through the snow, he runs toward the spot where the prairie dogs once lived.

Evie crawls into her closet but scurries out when someone walks across the living room floor, footsteps rattling the floorboards all the way in Evie's room. Through her terry-cloth robe, the floor is hard and cold on her legs. She sits back, pulling her knees to her chest, and listens. The footsteps pass by and Elaine's door opens. Aunt Ruth has moved into Elaine's room where she and the baby will live after the baby is born, so long as the baby isn't blue and dies in the oven. She switched rooms because Evie doesn't like her anymore. Aunt Ruth said it was because Elaine needed so much help with the wedding. Evie told her it didn't matter one bit and to go ahead and change rooms. After Aunt Ruth closes her door, Evie falls onto her hands and knees, pushes through the hems of Mama's skirts and dresses, the ones she only wears in the spring, and drags out a wadded-up blanket.

Waiting and listening and hearing nothing more, Evie slowly untangles the blanket and pulls out the Virgin Mary. She holds her up, looking first into her ivory face and her tiny blue eyes and then at the seams where her wrists meet her hands. She thinks she'd like to talk to the Virgin Mary, but someone might hear. So instead, cradling the statue like a baby, she hops back onto her bed, scoots until she can see out the window, and together they watch the red truck, driving down the road from the other direction, drift over toward the ditch and stop.

Soon it will be all the way dark. Setting the statue on the bed next to her, Evie stands and presses her nose to the cold glass. Out on the road, beyond the bare trees where the red truck is parked, the driver's side door opens and a man steps out. He stands still, his hands on his hips, and looks up at the house for a good long minute. He wavers, like the tall wheat stalks on a windy day. He must be cold, even with his jacket. The brim of his hat rides high on his forehead. Tugging it down, Uncle Ray reaches inside the truck and pulls out a long, thin gun.

Chapter 33

Celia shuts off the hot water when the bubbles reach the top of the sink. Gathering her cardigan sweater closed and wrapping her arms around her waist, she stares out the dark window. The tree is there, holding out its bare branches, reminding her of the cold, harsh winter. In the dim light, its icy coating doesn't sparkle. The tree looks nearly dead, standing in the dark, making Celia doubt it will come to life again in spring, making her wonder if spring will ever come.

"It's been such a long few days," she says to Arthur, who is sitting at the table. "You should have something more to eat."

Arthur holds his head in his hands and nods, though to what, Celia isn't sure.

"I could make you a sandwich for now. Then you could sleep."

"I found her in the shed, you know," Arthur says, his head lowered as if talking to the table. "I did. I found her."

Celia slides into a chair without pulling it back or making any noise.

"I knew she was in there, even before I opened the door." Arthur presses both hands around his coffee mug. "How does a person know something like that? Even before I opened the door. I could feel it, feel something on the other side."

He looks up at Celia.

"How does a person know?"

Pressing a dish towel over her mouth, Celia shakes her head.

"She had Mother's statue with her, holding it in one hand. Must have thought it would help her." Arthur exhales, almost a laugh. "She was so tiny, lying there. More like she was sleeping, except for the blood."

"It's so long past, Arthur. It wasn't your fault. Wasn't anyone's fault."

"I dropped her, the statue. Broke both hands off. Mother lost them in the laundry. For days, Ruth searched for them. Long past the funeral. Through every sheet and sock and basket. Looked until she found them both."

From behind the cover of her dish towel, Celia nods because that is so like Ruth, hunting and searching—probably the only helpful thing she could find to do. Because there is nothing she can say, Celia reaches for Arthur's hand instead. He lets her touch his fingers. They sit this way, their fingertips intertwined, not speaking, until their coffee has gone cold. Celia wants to remind Arthur that he was a boy when Eve died. He did what his sister asked, thought he was helping. She wants to soothe him, but before she finds the proper words, a familiar sound outside the kitchen window distracts her. Olivia has gotten out again. Arthur will be so angry with Daniel. No, it's not Olivia. Olivia is dead. Celia slowly pulls her hands away and turns toward the dark window.

Arthur hears it, too, because he lifts up a hand to silence her when she begins to speak. A rustling. A snapping. The wind. Or a coyote. It's always a coyote. Whenever Celia is lying in bed late at night and hears something outside, Arthur wraps an arm around her, pulls her close and whispers that it is a coyote. Celia waits for him to say the same now, but instead, he holds up a hand to keep the silence and slides his chair away from the table. Celia mirrors his movement, pushing back her own chair, silently, slowly. Arthur steps up to the kitchen window, leans so he can see around the side of the house and exhales.

"Looks to be Mary Robison," he says, walking toward the back of the house. "Awful cold night to be out and about."

Celia stands and presses out her skirt. "Well, heaven's sake, invite her in. I'll start some fresh coffee."

Dumping the stale grounds into a tin can near the sink, Celia shivers at the rush of cold air that spills into the kitchen when Arthur opens the back door. She spoons fresh coffee into the percolator and takes three mugs from the cabinet as Arthur and Mary walk into the kitchen, Arthur helping Mary out of her coat. Neither of them speaks. Mary is smaller here in Celia's kitchen then in St. Anthony's or the café or her own living room when Celia delivered Ruth's food. Her face is small enough to cup in one hand and, standing next to Arthur, she seems she might disappear in his shadow. Once Mary is seated, Arthur kneels in front of her, takes both of her hands and rolls them front to back. Then, he unlaces one of her boots and slips it from her foot. Celia steps forward. He sets the boot aside and begins to rub Mary's foot.

"Arthur," Celia whispers.

Shaking his head to quiet Celia, Arthur removes the other boot. Mary's small shoulders fall forward as he rubs her second foot. Celia sets down the coffee mugs, goes to the linen closet outside the bathroom and pulls out her heaviest quilt. As gently as she can, she wraps it around Mary, pulls it closed under her chin and tucks it around her narrow hips. Rubbing both feet at once now, Arthur glances up at Celia.

"She must have walked," he whispers. Then, leaning forward and inspecting Mary's eyes, he says, "Did you walk, Mary?"

Mary smiles down into Arthur's face but doesn't answer.

"Best you go wake Ruth," he says to Celia. "Think Mary'll be needing her about now."

Within five minutes, the glow of the porch lights has faded and Daniel is breathing hard, fogging the air around him though he can hardly see it. His thighs ache from running through the snow, throwing his knees waist high for every step, and his left side throbs. Deep in his chest, the icy air burns his lungs. His own breathing is the only sound he hears. When he reaches a low spot in the snow at the bottom of a drift, he stops, the shotgun still propped over his shoulder, leans forward, and rests with one hand braced against his knee. He is nowhere near the prairie dog mound, or where the prairie dog mound used to be. Ian went back there, flung that dead prairie dog for his brothers to see. The brothers said prairie dogs wouldn't live there anymore, not since Daniel killed one. Ian said, "Who the hell cares? It was a good shot, a damn good shot, so who the hell cares about some God damned old prairie dogs?"

Standing straight, Daniel lifts the gun. He braces the butt against his right shoulder and brings the stock to his cheek, keeping his head high. Ian showed him how with a sawed-off broomstick.

"Don't let your head sag," he had said. "Keep it straight. Point; don't aim. That's the big difference. Aim a rifle. Point a shotgun."

Problem is Daniel doesn't have anything to point it at. Staring down the barrel, he sees nothing but dark rolling fields. He listens hard, thinking that maybe he'll hear chains. Chains dangling from Jack Mayer's wrists. He'll see Jack Mayer, his black skin, his white eyes glowing bright as the snow in the dim light. He'll see those thick heavy arms again, pumping hard with every stride. He'll shoot Jack Mayer. He'll shoot him because Ian said Jack Mayer killed Julianne Robison. Except he didn't. Mr. Robison did, and he's dead already. So Daniel will point, not aim, because Ian is dead and Daniel doesn't have any friends left. He'll lead the target that will be running through the snow, high stepping under the weight of shackles and chains, and he'll spatter buckshot across Jack Mayer's back. Daniel will shoot him dead and then he'll be a man.

But, in the fading light, on the distant horizon where the last of day is sinking, Daniel sees nothing. There is no Jack Mayer. He's dead somewhere, lying in a ravine or buried under a snowdrift, or maybe he escaped across state lines. For months, he's been gone, been gone all along. He didn't do any of those things that Ian read in the newspaper. Didn't live in Ian's garage or steal Nelly Simpson's Ford Fairlane. He's gone. Daniel lowers the gun and walks toward home, still a boy.

*   *   *

Ruth slips on her robe, pulls the belt tight and opens her bed-room door a crack so no one will see her packed suitcases at the foot of her bed. Celia peeks inside.

"So sorry to disturb you, Ruth," she whispers. "But Mary Robison is here and she isn't well. Arthur thinks maybe you could be of help."

"Goodness, it's awfully cold for her to be out."

Stepping aside so Ruth can pass, Celia whispers, "And it appears that she walked. She's frozen. Frozen solid."

Ruth shuffles into the kitchen, her slippers sliding across the cold floor, and sits next to Mary. Until Ruth touches Mary's sleeve, she doesn't seem to notice Ruth. When she does, Mary lifts her head and smiles.

"So good to see you, Ruth."

Ruth takes both of Mary's hands and rubs them gently between her own. "You're like ice. Some coffee?"

"Milk, please, and one sugar."

Kneeling in front of Mary, Arthur wraps one end of the quilt around her feet. "That better?" he asks.

Celia pushes two mugs across the table and sits in a chair opposite Ruth and Mary. Arthur sits next to her.

"Nice of you to visit, Mary," Ruth says. "I hope you'll let Arthur drive you next time."

She holds up a finger to quiet Arthur when he starts to talk. After so many years, at least twenty, she feels like the big sister again.

"Did you mean to come here?" Ruth asks even though she knows the answer.

"We used to be such friends, didn't we?" Mary says, watching Ruth rub her hands over Mary's. "The three of us. When we were girls."

"We're still friends," Ruth says, beginning to knead each of Mary's fingers. Slowly, they are warming.

"Only two of us. And not like we were."

"Girls grow up, I guess," Ruth says. "Responsibilities and such. Not so much time for friends."

Making a humming noise, Mary presses her face toward her coffee cup as if letting the steam warm her cheeks and nose. "I remember when we stopped being such friends. The three of us. Do you remember?" Mary pauses and says, "The day Orville Robison got off that train."

Ruth lifts her eyes toward Celia and Arthur. "Yes, that was a long time ago."

She swallows. Her heart begins to beat against her chest. She tries to slow it by taking one deep breath after another. Massaging Mary's littlest finger, Ruth concentrates on the tiny veins that spread like frail blue vines across the back of Mary's hand.

"Do you remember?" Mary says. "It rained the day he came. First good rain in so many years. All the dust put to rest that day. Do you remember? Everyone in town thought Orville Robison brought us a miracle."

Ruth tries to lift her eyes to Mary but she can't. Instead, she lays Mary's hands in her lap and covers them with her own.

"I thought I was marrying a miracle worker. So carried away with him. Big and broad as a barn. And so handsome. Wasn't he handsome?" Mary lifts Ruth's chin with one finger. "He did it, Ruthie. He hurt your Eve. When she was so young. He hurt your Eve, did things to her no man should be doing to a child. And then your family came home again. After all these years, they haunted him like a ghost. Hurt him especially to see the little one." She cups Ruth's face with one hand. "I didn't know how to stop him."

Wondering if Arthur hears the rustling outside the kitchen window, Celia nudges him, but he is listening to Ruth and Mary Robison and he brushes her away. She has been trying to follow the conversation, but isn't able to because she can't shake the feeling that something is watching her. Outside the window over the sink, the maple tree's bare branches tap on the side of the house and the porch light throws long, thin shadows that skip into the corners of her eyes, startling her. She's a little jumpy, that's all. So much has happened. Celia takes a deep breath and exhales as she moves her chair closer to Arthur's.

"What is it you're saying, Mary?" Arthur asks, scooting to the edge of his seat.

Ignoring for a moment that it seems someone is lurking outside the kitchen window, Celia realizes that she missed something very important. She reaches for Arthur's arm, but he pulls away.

"Arthur," she whispers. "Let's not lose our tempers."

Again, Arthur ignores Celia. "Tell me, Mary," he says.

Keeping one hand on Arthur's forearm, Celia shifts in her seat to face Ruth. "I don't understand, Ruth," she says. "What's going on?"

Ruth doesn't answer. Instead, with her hands covering Mary's, she stares over Celia's shoulder. Celia slowly turns. There, in the dark window with the maple's bare branches bouncing in the north wind, a large shadow slips by. Celia jumps up, the back of her chair bouncing off the kitchen cabinets and catching her left ankle. She stumbles and cries out, but before she can steady herself, Arthur grabs her arm and yanks her backward.

"Go," he says, stepping in front of her and waving them all toward the front bedroom. "Get all the girls. Shut the door. Lock it."

Celia limps around the table, keeping her eyes on the window even though the shadow is gone now and hurries Ruth and Mary toward the farthest bedroom—Ruth's room now that she stays with Elaine.

"What is it, Mama?" Evie calls out from her room.

"Here, Evie. Come here." Celia grabs Evie's arm like Arthur grabbed hers, hustles Ruth and Mary into the room, and pulling Evie in after them, she slams the door behind her.

"Mama," Evie says, jumping into the middle of Ruth's bed and tucking her knees up under her. "What is it?"

Celia presses her ear to the closed door as she waves at Ruth to back away. "Sit down," she says. "It's nothing. Nothing."

"Celia, did you see?" Ruth says, helping Mary to sit on the bed.

Celia glances around the room, which is brightly lit with two lamps and the overhead light. At the end of Ruth's bed sit two suitcases. "The lights," she says, though she doesn't know why. "Put out the lights."

"Why?" Evie says. "What is it?"

"Please, shut them off."

Ruth turns off the two lamps near the bed as Celia flips the switch on the wall. The room falls dark. The house is quiet. Celia stands at the door, listening but hearing nothing.

"I know what it is, Mama," Evie says, her voice floating up out of the darkness.

Three silhouettes sit on the bed, smallest to tallest. The smallest sits up and lifts her head.

"It's Uncle Ray."

Chapter 34

Daniel stops in the shadow of the barn, his shotgun propped over one shoulder. His crooked toes are numb and his fingers have gone stiff. The cold, dry air burns his mouth and throat each time he inhales. The day was only warm enough to melt the very top layer of snow. Now, with nightfall, the slippery coating has frozen to an icy shell. With every movement, every step, the snow crackles underfoot. Trying to stand still, he breathes into a cupped fist to warm the air before taking it in again. He leans forward, out of the shadow. Straight ahead, between the house and the barn, the porch light glows in a perfect circle, and in its center, stands Uncle Ray.

Evie says Uncle Ray has shrunk since they moved to Kansas, that little by little, he has started to dry up. She showed Daniel the picture of Aunt Eve and Uncle Ray when they were young, not so long before Aunt Eve died. Back then, Uncle Ray was tall and straight and strong. Like Dad. Looking at Uncle Ray now, his legs spread wide, a rifle braced against his chest and pointed straight at Dad, who is walking out of the house, his hands calming Uncle Ray the same way he calmed Olivia when she slit open her neck, Daniel thinks Uncle Ray looks plenty big.

Pressing back against the barn, Daniel feels suddenly hot. His jacket is heavy, so heavy that it's suffocating him. He rips off his stocking cap, takes a deep breath in through his nose and blows it out slowly through his mouth. He lets the cold burn his insides so it will wake him up, help him to think. Calm now. Calm. Breathe. In and out. Slowly. In and out. Watching the ground at his feet so that he steps only where he's already broken through the snow, he leans out again.

"I've had about enough," Uncle Ray says, his cheek lying on the stock of the gun. His head is hanging. Bad form, Ian would have said. "I've God damned had enough."

Uncle Ray shifts his weight, putting his left foot slightly forward and then his right as if he can't remember how to get off a good shot.

"Sure, Ray," Dad says, still trying to soothe Uncle Ray, and when Uncle Ray stumbles because he's still shifting his feet, Dad takes one quick glance at the house. "We've all had enough. Damn right about that."

"Ruth is coming home today. Ruth and that child of mine. And that'll be the end of it."

The porch light glows on the two men. Flakes of snow blowing off the roof sparkle in the air around them.

"Let's talk a bit," Dad says and begins to sidestep across the drive toward the garage a few yards away.

"No more damned talking." Uncle Ray stumbles again.

Dad stops, stands still.

"You call Ruth." Uncle Ray rams the gun toward Dad. "Call her now."

Continuing to sidestep away from the house toward the garage, Dad says, "She's not here. Left with Jonathon. Taking rolls on over to the Buchers."

Another step, farther away from the house. Closer to the garage.

"You heard about Ian, yes?" Dad says.

The closer Dad gets to the garage, the easier it is for Daniel to see him, but he can't see Uncle Ray unless he steps out of the shadow and around the side of the barn.

"You know how Ruth is. Always trying to help out. She'll be back later. Soon enough, I'd guess."

Holding his breath and leaning as far as he can without stumbling outside of the shadow, Daniel listens for Uncle Ray's voice. He leans too far, and when startled by a loud bang, he falls forward through the icy crust on a patch of fresh snow. There is another bang. Metal against metal. Olivia's gate. He ran through it on the way to the prairie dog mound, and like he did when Olivia was alive, he left it open. Now it's banging in the wind that has stirred up since the sun set. Daniel jumps up, scrambles to his feet and falls back against the barn.

"What the hell?" Uncle Ray shouts.

He must be looking straight at the barn now, probably with his gun pointed at the dent Daniel made in the snow, except Daniel is standing in the shadows, not breathing, not moving, and Uncle Ray doesn't see him.

"Just that old gate," Dad says.

From the sound of his voice, Dad is almost to the garage. Daniel leans against the barn, breathing so fast and deep that he doesn't have time to think. He swallows and leans forward. Dad has taken a few more steps toward the garage, and Uncle Ray is following Dad with the tip of his rifle again, slowly turning his back on the house. Pressing against the barn, Daniel remembers the shotgun propped over his shoulder. Grandpa's old shotgun. Dad thinks he'll find it in the garage, behind the door, behind the oil barrel, under the blanket. He knew Uncle Ray would come one day. He knew it and was ready. Except he isn't ready because Daniel has the gun.

"Where you going, Ray?" Dad says. "I told you she's not here. Gone off with Jonathon."

Uncle Ray is backing toward the house, his rifle still pointed at Dad.

"I'm no damn fool, Arthur. You stay put. Stay right there."

Near the bottom stair leading up to the porch, Uncle Ray slips. He drops the tip of the rifle for a moment and grabs the railing to right himself before aiming the gun back at Dad. If he would turn slightly to his left, he might see Daniel, leaning out of the shadows, watching.

"Ruth," Uncle Ray shouts up the set of stairs. "Get your damn self out here."

"She won't hear you, Ray. She's gone off."

Uncle Ray backs up the stairs, stumbling but holding onto the railing with one hand and balancing the gun with the other. At the top of the stairs, he pushes the latch on the screened door with his elbow, kicks it open and disappears onto the porch. Before the door has slammed shut, Dad slips into the garage.

The path from the side of the barn through Olivia's gate is waist deep with snow. Daniel runs toward the garage, throwing his knees high, but before he reaches the gate where he can step onto the cleared gravel, the porch door swings open again and Uncle Ray walks out, dragging Aunt Ruth behind him. She carries two suitcases with her, causing her to stumble and trip.

"Ray," Mama shouts from inside the house. "The baby. Be careful of the baby."

By the time Uncle Ray and Aunt Ruth reach the bottom step, Dad is back outside the garage, looking left and right as if he might find his shotgun wedged there in a snowdrift. Daniel, having squatted behind a fence post outside the glow of the porch light, squints toward the house. Mama is there, standing inside the screened door. Ahead of him, Olivia's gate bounces in the wind, the slide bolt rattling and the strap hinges creaking.

"Ray, stop," Mama shouts. "Leave her be."

Really, it's more of a scream, something Daniel has never heard before. The sound makes his stomach tighten as if he might vomit right here in the snow. Mama's scream seems to surprise Uncle Ray, too, because he shoves Aunt Ruth away from the house and aims his gun at Mama. Dad takes two quick steps but then stops.

"Take it easy, Ray," he says.

"I'll go, Ray," Aunt Ruth says. "See. I'm packed. Already packed to come home." She is standing on the hard, cold gravel in only her slippers and she is wearing Elaine's beige housecoat. Her hair hangs loose and blows into her eyes. "Please. Let's go. Leave Celia be."

Uncle Ray jabs his gun at Aunt Ruth, but she doesn't flinch the way Mama did. She's seen a gun up close before, Daniel thinks. She's had one pointed right in her face.

"You think I should leave here, Ruth?" Uncle Ray says.

"Yes. Yes. I'm coming with you. Coming home with you now. I'm ready. See?" she says, lifting one suitcase. "I was waiting on the weather. Just waiting for it to clear."

Dad takes two more steps toward Uncle Ray.

"Come down here, Celia," Uncle Ray says, aiming his gun at Mama again.

At this, Dad backs up.

Mama stands at the top of the stairs, her eyes locked on Dad. She starts to cry.

"Get down here, now."

Mama presses both hands over her mouth and doesn't even bother to brush away the hair that blows across her forehead and eyes. She shakes her head and takes the stairs one at time.

"You've been drinking, Ray." Dad is trying to calm him and, at the same time, looking all around at the ground and in the air for anything that might help.

When Mama reaches the bottom step, Dad presses one hand

in the air to make her stop right there. Behind her, the porch door opens again. Mary Robison and Evie step outside. Standing side by side on the top stair, Mrs. Robison holds Evie's hand.

"Did you tell him, Ruth?" Mrs. Robison shouts across the drive.

Aunt Ruth shakes her head. "Not now, Mary." She chokes before the words come all the way out. "Go back inside, Evie."

Mrs. Robison smiles down at Evie, nods and Evie runs down the stairs and grabs onto Mama's legs.

"I owe it to you, too, Ray," Mrs. Robison says, walking down the stairs.

Mama is trying to push Evie away, trying to make her go back inside but Evie won't let go.

"Shut up, the all of you," Uncle Ray shouts, and waving the rifle tip at Mama, he says, "Get on over with Ruth."

Mrs. Robison walks past Mama and when Dad steps forward to stop her, Uncle Ray jabs at him with the gun and Dad stops.

"Don't involve yourself," Dad says to Mrs. Robison.

Ignoring Dad like she doesn't know he's there, Mrs. Robison keeps walking, slowly because she doesn't have anything on her feet. "I owe it to you most of all," she shouts over the wind.

Uncle Ray backs away as Mrs. Robison walks toward him. He staggers closer to Daniel. The weight of the gun seems to throw him off balance. He takes aim at Mrs. Robison, too, but she doesn't stop like Dad. With the rifle poised on his shoulder, Uncle Ray dips his head, presses his cheek to the stock and fires.

*   *   *

C elia must have screamed, maybe she is still screaming. Some-one shouts at her. It's Ray.

"I said get your damned self over there." He waves his gun at her.

Celia starts to walk toward Ruth, but Evie has latched onto her legs, stopping her. She rips open Evie's arms and pushes her toward the stairs.

"Go. Go now," she screams.

Evie falls against the stairs and crawls on hand and foot toward the porch. Arthur is yelling, too, telling Celia to stay put, stay God damned well put.

"Don't you move, Celia," he tries to shout over Ray. "Don't you take one God damned step."

Behind Ray, Ruth stands in her robe and slippers. The hem of her robe slaps her legs. She shakes her head and presses both hands in the air as if she doesn't want Celia to come any closer.

With his rifle pointed at Arthur now, Ray walks forward, steps around Mary Robison's lifeless body, grabs Celia's arm and flings her toward Ruth. Stumbling backward and falling on her hind end, pieces of ice and gravel bite into her palms. Ray roots himself and points the gun at Arthur's head. Celia shuffles backward like a crab on her hands and feet until Ruth grabs her from behind and helps her to stand.

"Please, Ray," Celia says, wiping Mary Robison's blood from her cheek and drying her hand on her blue-checkered apron. "Enough. Please stop."

"Don't know who the hell you think you are," Ray shouts, aiming at Arthur. "Coming around after twenty years. God damned coward. How you like me taking your wife?"

Arthur lifts both hands, surrendering himself. Blood shines on his cheek and neck and stains one side of his shirt.

"Take it easy now, Ray," he says. "I should have told you. Should have told you about Eve. Christ, Ray, I was a kid."

Ray backs away, stumbling as he tries to step around Mary Robison's feet, and takes aim at Arthur again.

Celia grabs Ruth and guides her down the driveway. "We're going, Ray," she calls out. "Do you see? We're going. Wherever you want." She pulls Ruth backward, leaving the two suitcases. "Come on now," she calls out again. "Like you said." Ruth is stiff, but Celia knows they have to get clear. She needs Ray to back away a little more. "Come on, now."

They need to get clear. She sees Daniel there behind the fence post. He has a shotgun. They need to get clear.

D aniel drops his chin to his chest and rests his forehead against the wooden fence post. Without looking up, because he isn't ready for the sight of Mrs. Robison again, he sticks the index finger of his right glove between his teeth, bites down and pulls his hand away. Letting that glove drop into the snow, he does the same with his left. Maybe he only thought he saw blood splatter across Dad's chest and into Mama's face. Maybe blood didn't spray onto the snowdrift that runs along the back of the house. With the shotgun balanced on his lap, Daniel presses his bare hands between his knees and raises his chin.

"Don't do anything foolish now, Ray," Dad says. His hands are still in the air and Mrs. Robison's blood is a black stain across his shirt.

"I ain't no damn fool," Uncle Ray says, beginning to back down the driveway toward Aunt Ruth and Mama. "You're the fool. All of you." He staggers a few steps and his head wobbles. "You killed her," he says to Dad. "Same as if you put a gun to her head."

"Please, Ray. We're leaving," Mama says.

For an instant, she seems to look right at Daniel.

"Come on now." Yes, Mama sees him. "Ruth and I, we're leaving."

Uncle Ray backs away until he can see Mama and Aunt Ruth and Dad all at once. He seems to settle on Aunt Ruth. He points the gun at her and waves it like he wants her to come closer. "You tell me. You tell me that you knew what he did."

"Please, Ray. Don't do this," Mama says, pulling Aunt Ruth away, farther down the driveway.

"Tell me now," he shouts.

Aunt Ruth lowers her head. She must be crying because her shoulders are shaking but she isn't making any noise. Uncle Ray swings around, presses the stock to his cheek and aims at Dad.

"You God damned well better tell me."

Uncle Ray pulls back the bolt action, presses his cheek to the barrel. He is steady now, lined up, ready for a solid shot.

Daniel slowly stands, his leg unfolding beneath him. Feet shoulder width, Ian had said with a sawed-off broomstick in hand. Left foot forward. Toes pointed straight ahead. Knees slightly bent.

Uncle Ray tilts his head an inch to the right the way a man does when he closes one eye and looks down the barrel of his rifle.

"No," Mama shouts. "Ray, stop."

Daniel lifts the shotgun. Brings the stock to his cheek. Back straight.

"Ray, please." Aunt Ruth is crying. She sounds far away, like she's inside a dream.

Daniel lines up the bead sight with the notch at the tip of the gun. Something snaps. A gun is cocked. Inhale. Exhale halfway. Just halfway, Ian had said. Hold steady. Be careful of the blockers. Give them twenty feet or so. Buckshot will scatter. The target will rise up between the pushers and the blockers.

"Now, Daniel," Mama shouts. "Now."

Uncle Ray squares his stance. Dad lunges. Daniel fires.

There is a crack in the air. A loud pop. Celia grabs for Ruth, pulling her so closely that together they nearly fall, tumbling and tripping over one another in their matted and muddy slippers. No matter what they see now, what they saw Ray do, he was Ruth's husband, a good man long ago. So many things led him to this moment, things set in motion twenty-five years earlier. What man would have taken a different path? Not even Arthur. Wouldn't he have started to drink? Wouldn't he have eventually hated the woman who could never be Celia? Wouldn't he have tried to kill the man who took her away? No, Ruth won't be able to live with the sight of what's happening to Ray.

She needs to remember him through pictures. A younger man, smiling, in love with Eve. She needs to remember that he would have been a good father had life turned a different direction. She'll love him because he loved Eve and she'll pass on these memories, but none of that will be possible if she sees Ray now, his shirt tearing open, his blood spraying up toward the porch light, his lower skull ripped open. She could live with the knowledge, but not the sight. Holding Ruth's face against her side, Celia pulls her backward, down the drive as Arthur dives back and away. Daniel's shotgun echoes in the clear night air and ends with a sharp clap. There is silence.

The force throws Ray forward. He lands near Mary Robison's feet. Steam rises up from his torn body and, like Mary Robison's blood, Ray's splatters across the snow that drifts near the back door. It soaks in, leaving holes and dents in the soft white mound. At the top of the stairs leading into the house, Celia checks for Evie and exhales with relief when she isn't there, peeking through the screened door. She'll be in her closet, huddled under the skirts and dresses. Celia screamed at her to make her let go. She screamed at Daniel, too. She told her only son to kill a man. Had there been a kinder thing, she would have done it. Standing with the wind whipping at her skirt and blowing her hair from her face, her body harder and leaner than the day they arrived in Kansas, this is what she knows. Sometimes there is no kinder way.

Daniel is the first to move. He lowers the tip of his grandfather's shotgun and lets it slide off his shoulder. His movement pulls Arthur from the ground, slowly. He doesn't want to startle Daniel. He has that look about him, as if he's not quite inside himself anymore, as if he doesn't know his own father, as if he might fire again. Staring down at Ray, Arthur nods. He is dead. So is Mary Robison. Arthur knows dead. It takes him no time to see that. Then, he walks to his son, lays one hand on Daniel's wrist and the other on the barrel of the gun. Daniel lifts his eyes.

"It's what had to be done," Arthur says in a strong voice.

There was a time when Celia would have quieted him, asked him to lower his voice. Some things are best whispered, for the sake of fine manners. But she knows that Arthur speaks in a full voice so Daniel will never feel shame.

"You did a fine job, young man. Just fine."

Daniel turns to Celia and she nods.

Fine. Just fine.

Chapter 35

Evie closes her eyes, tilts her head toward the sky and inhales. This warm day, after so many cold, has a special smell about it. Aunt Ruth says things are greening up, so this must be what green smells like. With the sun warming her cheeks, Evie leans into Aunt Ruth, who pulls Evie close and kisses the top of her head. Aunt Ruth doesn't have to lean down as far anymore. Lately, most often at night when she lays in bed, Evie's shins and elbows ache. Mama says they are growing pains. Just that morning, she marked Evie's height on her bedroom doorframe with a black pen. Since moving to Kansas, she's grown almost an inch and a half. Mama has always said Evie would grow in her own sweet time.

Laying one hand on Aunt Ruth's hard, round belly, Evie cradles Aunt Eve's Virgin Mary statue in the other. In less than a month, Aunt Ruth will have a baby instead of a big belly. Evie holds her breath, waiting for a gentle nudge from Elisabeth.

"Get ready," Aunt Ruth says, squeezing Evie even tighter.

Evie clutches the statue to her chest, presses one ear against

Aunt Ruth's stomach, and covers the other with her free hand. Near Grandma's barn, Daniel is wadding up old newspaper as kindling for the fire Dad asked him to start in the old trash barrel. Across the driveway, Jonathon sits behind the wheel of Grandpa's tractor, his hat pulled low on his forehead. Standing nearby, Daddy gives a nod and after a few chokes and coughs, the tractor starts up. Daniel leaves the barrel, smoke drifting up into the air and walks a few feet to stand behind Mama, Elaine and Grandma, his arms crossed, his hat pulled low like Jonathon's.

Aunt Ruth touches the Virgin Mary's head. "I'm glad you fixed her up," she says, leaning down and talking into Evie's ear so she can hear over the tractor.

Aunt Ruth wraps both arms around Evie as the tractor rolls across the drive. First, the wheels crush the tall grass that Daddy never lets Daniel mow, and when the tractor crashes into the small shed, Aunt Ruth's chest shudders. Daddy said the wood wasn't worth saving. He'd rather burn it and all the overgrown grass, too. He said what's past is past and it's time the Scott family puts it to rest. Aunt Ruth lowers her head, and when it's over, when Jonathon has backed away and turned off the tractor, she stands straight and takes a deep breath.

"Smells like green, doesn't it?" Evie says.

Daniel tugs on his hat when the dust settles and walks back to the barrel. Using one of the longer branches he gathered from Grandma's front yard, he pokes at his fire. It's going good now, burning strong, so he drops the branch, walks past Dad who is still staring at the empty spot where the shed used to be, and loads himself up with an armful of splintered wood. When he turns, suddenly feeling like he shouldn't toss the wood on the fire, Dad gives him a nod and a pat on the back.

"Thank you, son," he says and, lowering himself to his knees, he fills his own arms, stands and follows Daniel to the barrel. The two men stop a few feet from the fire and toss in the wooden planks. Soon their arms are empty. They stand together watching the ash and sparks float up into the air and disappear. Mama, Grandma Reesa and Aunt Ruth have gone inside to make Grandma's fried chicken. Dad still says it's the best in the Midwest, but mostly he says it when Mama isn't around to hear. Jonathon has gone off with Elaine, probably so Elaine can make him write his share of thank-you notes for their wedding gifts, and Evie is sitting on the top stair with the Virgin Mary at her side. When the sparks have settled and only smoke is drifting up, Dad and Daniel return for another load.

Celia sits across from Ruth, a paper bag placed between them on Reesa's table where she usually keeps the salt and pepper shakers. Grease sizzles and pops in the black skillet on the stove, and the chicken broth begins to boil, drops of it hissing as they splash on the gas burner. With a wooden spoon in one hand, Celia cracks an egg into the dumpling dough and starts to stir again. Reesa looks at Celia as if to tell her no more eggs but clears her throat instead and goes back to poking her chicken. Reaching across the table, Ruth touches the brown paper bag.

"I did think about it," she says. "In the very beginning."

"Anyone would have," Celia says, pausing for a moment before beginning to dig and stir again. "You thought you were alone."

"But I never would have done it. Not to Elisabeth."

Celia pushes aside the bowl, stands and takes the paper bag. "Do you want me to take care of this?"

"I never could have used it," Ruth says, crossing her hands on the table. "Don't even know why I kept so much." She looks up at Celia. "Things never seemed quite so bad when no one was around to see." She tucks her hair behind her ears, a motion that makes her look like a young girl again. "But then you all moved back, and I was so ashamed for you to know. All the drinking and the times he hurt me. You all made it"—she pauses—"more real. That's when I knew I could never let my own child see those things." She shakes her head and pulls two small brown bottles from her apron pocket. "These will need to go, too."

"Celia's right, child," Reesa says. With a teaspoon, she scoops a dumpling and dips it into the simmering broth. "Any sane woman would have done the same. You were taking care."

Celia picks up the bottles, holds them in one hand and raises her eyebrows because a smile doesn't seem appropriate. Ruth gives her a nod, and Celia carries the bottles and the bag from the kitchen.

Walking across the gravel drive toward Arthur and Daniel, Celia wonders when wedge root is in season. Ruth must have gathered it months ago. Surely it didn't grow under the cover of snow. No, she must have thought ahead. In the early weeks, when she considered how she could end her pregnancy, she could have found the plant growing along every ditch in the county, but by the time her plan changed and she needed to gather enough to kill a six-foot-four-inch 220-pound man, the wedge root must have been harder to come by. How much wedge root did it take to boil out enough oil to fill these two small bottles? When Ruth pulled the bag and bottles from her suitcase, Celia never asked her how she would have done it or if it mattered that Ray wasn't the one who killed Julianne Robison. Would she have seeped the wedge root with Ray's morning coffee over weeks and months until it eventually killed him? Would one strong dose of the oil, maybe mixed with the base of a nice chicken stock, have done the trick? No, Celia never asked.

Outside the screened door, Evie sits on the top step, cradling the Virgin Mary to her chest. As Celia passes by, she touches the top of Evie's head. Evie hugs the small statue with both arms and slips inside before the screened door falls closed. Walking toward Arthur and Daniel, she thinks that there was a time when she would have asked Daniel to step away. When he was a boy, just a year ago, afraid of the monster at the top of Bent Road, she would have asked him to leave. But not today, because now he is a man.

It's still there, that lazy bend in the fence line a quarter mile northeast of Reesa's house, except the fields are no longer empty like they were on the night that the Scott family arrived in Kansas. That spring, the short sprouts that had lain dormant all winter began to grow and when the weather warmed and the spring rains came, those sprouts grew and became shiny, green stalks that carpeted the fields. More time passed, and under the summer sun, the green stalks faded to yellow. The bristly heads are heavy and soon the farmers will harvest their golden crops, leaving the fields bare once again. As autumn draws closer, the tumbleweeds will begin to dry out. Their woody stems will turn brittle and break near the ground. They'll tumble and roll and the curve at the top of Bent Road will scoop them up.

Celia knows now to slow near the top of that hill. She edges toward the shoulder in case of oncoming trucks that she might not see in time. She knows where home is and which way to turn should Arthur's truck slip over the top of the next hill unseen.

Sliding in between Arthur and Daniel, Celia rolls down the top of the paper sack until it's closed good and tight. Heat spills out of the barrel, keeping the three of them at a distance. The wood crackles and hisses as it burns and smells of sweet cedar. Arthur slips an arm around Celia's shoulders, and saying a quiet God bless you to the memory of Aunt Eve, she tosses the bag into the fire.

Acknowledgments

I owe tremendous thanks to Dennis Lehane and Sterling Watson. Together, they introduced the Eckerd College Writers in Paradise Conference to St. Petersburg, Florida, and have inspired and educated countless writers, myself among them. For your generosity and boundless commitment, I thank you. My deepest gratitude also to Christine Caya and the rest of the WIP writers group.

Thank you to my wonderful agent, Jenny Bent of The Bent Agency, for your professionalism and belief in this book, and many thanks to Judy Walters for plucking me from the slush pile. To my editor, Denise Roy: Your dedication to the craft of writing and commitment to your profession are an inspiration, and I thank you for your guidance. My appreciation also to the entire team at Dutton for their support of this book.

To my dear friends Karina Berg Johansson and Adam Smith, thank you for setting the high bar and for sharing so many laughs. Thank you to the following people who have inspired and supported me all these many years: to Kim Turner for being my first reader; to Stacy Brandenburg, for sharing stories over coffee; to Lisa Atkinson,

ACKNOWLEDGMENTS

Chris Blair, and Scotti Andrews, for your guidance in the early chapters; and to my parents, Jeanette and Norm Harold, and my in-laws, Evelyn and Orville Roy. Thanks, also, to my reading group of eleven years.

Finally, and most especially, thank you to Andrew and Savanna for understanding why dinner wasn't always on time. And to my dear husband, Bill, thank you for your quiet, unwavering, and steadfast belief over so many years.